IAB Photo Studio

JEYAMOHAN

WHITE ELEPHANT

Translated from the Tamil by Priyamvada Ramkumar

Jeyamohan is a Tamil writer and literary critic based in Nagercoil, India. He is considered one of India's finest authors writing today, and his work examines and reinterprets India's rich literary and classical traditions. His considerable output includes novels, short stories, volumes of literary criticism, and books on philosophy.

Priyamvada Ramkumar translates literary fiction from Tamil into English. She was awarded a 2022 ALTA Emerging Translator Mentorship and a 2023 PEN/Heim Translation Fund grant for her work on *White Elephant*. Her works have been published in various journals, including *Granta* and *Asymptote*. She lives in Chennai, India.

ALSO BY JEYAMOHAN

Stories of the True

WHITE ELEPHANT

WHITE ELEPHANT

A NOVEL

Jeyamohan

Translated from the Tamil
by Priyamvada Ramkumar

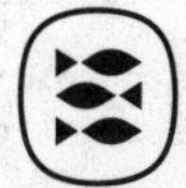

FSG Originals
FARRAR, STRAUS AND GIROUX
NEW YORK

FSG Originals
Farrar, Straus and Giroux
120 Broadway, New York 10271

EU Representative: Macmillan Publishers Ireland Ltd, 1st Floor, The Liffey Trust Centre, 117–126 Sheriff Street Upper, Dublin 1, D01 YC43

Printed in the United States of America
Originally published in Tamil in 2013 by Ezhuthu, India, as *Vellai Yaanai*
English translation published in the United States by
Farrar, Straus and Giroux
First American edition, 2026

Library of Congress Cataloging-in-Publication Data
Names: Jeyamōkaṉ author | Ramkumar, Priyamvada translator
Title: White elephant : a novel / Jeyamohan ; translated from the Tamil by Priyamvada Ramkumar.
Other titles: Veḷḷaiyāṇai. English
Description: First American edition. | New York : FSG Originals / Farrar, Straus and Giroux, 2026.
Identifiers: LCCN 2026015894 | ISBN 9780374619428 paperback
Subjects: LCSH: Famines—India—History—19th century | LCGFT: Historical fiction | Novels
Classification: LCC PL4758.9.J4569 V4513 2026
LC record available at https://lccn.loc.gov/2026015894

10 9 8 7 6 5 4 3 2 1

For P. K. Balakrishnan

Preface: The Footprints of Humanity

In his book *The Great Hedge of India*, my friend the British writer Roy Moxham—a man who researched large-scale famines in India—observes that the great famines of the late nineteenth century were in large measure exacerbated by a massive fence erected by the British. This fence, which was a hedge of thorny vegetation, was intended to curb domestic salt trade and insure British revenues from an unconscionable tax levied on salt. Moxham came to India in search of the hedge, only to meet with astonishment. Not only was there no trace of the physical hedge, but there was no suggestion of it either in the minds of the Indian people. It was back home in British museums that he found documentary evidence of the hedge. No Indian author had written about it. It had been completely wiped out from public memory.

The Indian mind is one that routinely sheds its history. Most things in this country lack formal records. D. D. Kosambi, in the preface to his book *An Introduction to the Study of Indian History*, suggests that Indian history predominantly consists of conjectures. The Indian mind stows away its history in the guise of tradition and mythology. However, the great famines of India did not beget even such fables, either in history or literature. In folk narratives, too, they find scant mention. I doubt if even a few thousand among the hundred million residents of the state of Tamil Nadu today would be aware of the Great Famine of 1876–78, which felled one third of its population and provoked mass migration through enslavement. This is the first novel in Tamil that centres on those famines. In fact, there are only a handful of famine-centric novels to come out of India as a whole. In that sense, this novel is a war against India's historical amnesia. Literature itself is a war against the amnesias that sculpt our everyday lives.

India is a country that is dependent on the monsoons. Consequently, famines have always been a natural phenomenon in this land. But then, measures to alleviate their impact, too, have existed from as far back as the age of the Mahabharata. The migration of population, for instance, was an important measure. Only people who could easily leave their homes lived in famine-prone lands. Even today, in the arid regions of Tamil Nadu, one finds people abandoning their homes during a drought. Another mitigating measure was the reservation of one fourth of tax collections for future famines. India's temples were at the centre of such strategies. However, British rule, by dint of its complete militarisation of India, curbed migration. It also drained every grain of surplus and exported it. In doing so, it made way for devastating famines. Furthermore, the British government covertly encouraged these disasters with an aim to export indentured labour for its plantations all over the world.

Two major famines, one each in the eighteenth and nineteenth centuries, ripped apart the entire fabric of India. The country's ancient social structure disintegrated. Agriculture declined. Temples, which had until then been propped up by the old feudal system, were completely destabilised—as was the culture they nurtured. The famines induced a great stagnancy in India's literature and philosophy. Their profound impact on the Indian psyche is plain to see even today. "Have-you-eaten" is a very Indian way of greeting someone you meet. It is also why the people of this country save up every rupee of income in excess of their basic needs. It was also the famines that made our people ever ready to leave the country in search of a living.

The biggest consequence of the famines, though, was the reduction of the Dalit population by half—either by death or displacement. Since the Dalits back then were bonded labourers tied to the land they worked, they were the first great sacrifice to be made during the famines. How this loss changed Indian culture and politics is an important question, one that the late Dalit scholar Anbu Ponnoviyam raised with me in a private conversation. From his perspective, Dalits had laid the ground for their own freedom by leaving their lands during the famines. They took up many occupations in British India, including the job of butler, as you'll see in this novel. There were also a few who went abroad to make a living and returned with some savings. They partook of the English system of education. All of these, in turn, resulted in the Dalit freedom movement. The Dalit freedom movement was, as a matter of fact, the first political movement to be born in India.

Anbu Ponnoviyam also told me about a protest that took place during the Great Madras Famine at the Ice House, an ice factory in Chennai—a protest by and for Dalit workers. It was a beginning, not just in the history of Madras but in the history of India. It is a story that continues to live among the Dalit people, albeit orally. I wanted to write about that time period, which determined both the course of Indian politics and the mindset of today's India but remains forgotten by the people. When I expressed this to the late V. Alex, a pioneer of the Dalit movement in Tamil Nadu and a good friend, he encouraged me. I would go so far as to say that he was the one who wrote this novel. Aiden Byrne, the protagonist of this novel, was inspired by J. H. A. Tremenheere, a British officer who paved the way for land allocation to Dalits. It was V. Alex who brought Tremenheere to my attention. Alex published two editions of this work in Tamil.

This novel is not just a story of famines, oppression, and exploitation. It is the story of man's undying desire to free himself from their grasp. It is also the story of human conscience that, like the eyes of a tiger in the dark, burns in the gravest of times. Indeed, it is at the intersection of these two forces—the will to freedom and an instinct for justice—that human civilisation has forged itself and defined its humanity.

Jeyamohan
December 2025

WHITE ELEPHANT

1

When a movement in the distance caught Aiden Byrne's eye, he instinctively grew alert. At once, his right hand reached for his sidearm, his left tugged at the reins, and his legs pressed against the sides of the horse. Then, becoming aware of where he was, he eased and broke into a smile. In the year 1878, near Fort St. George in the precincts of White Town in Madraspatnam under the crown of Her Majesty the Queen Victoria, there really was no danger he could expect.

Aiden lifted his hat, ran his fingers through his auburn hair, and placed it back on his head. Even though the morning sun had barely stirred, his hair was soaked with sweat. As the sea breeze grazed the white shirt plastered against his sweaty back, he felt a clammy coldness on his skin. The southerly wind that had blustered all night had swept the beach sand in its wake, and sprayed it generously over the kadappa-stone path. Against the black stonescape, the soft sand caught in a windy swirl hovered like a curtain of steam before being drawn away like delicate muslin.

Starting his horse on a slow trot, Aiden watched the movement he had noticed farther away. Two dark human forms were huddled under the cover of a tree. Indian labourers clothed in dirty white. It was hard to tell what they were up to. A plant that had set down roots where they were seated swayed with the breeze and shielded them from sight. As the horse strained at the reins, Aiden gently patted its neck to quiet it down. It chewed on the bit, tossed its head, hissed, and pawed the stone path with its forelegs. From the sea that lay to Aiden's right, moisture-laden winds swept across in gusty waves and condensed over the city in a heavy downpour.

A crowd of coconut palms and casuarinas combed flat by the wind stood bent over in the distance. Lifting up, they roiled in tandem with the wind currents. But for the odd open horse-carriage or the police officer on horseback who would ride along its length on occasion, the Marina was always deserted at that hour.

Aiden marvelled at his own alertness. It was an instinct he had cultivated when, all of seven, he would set out with his father to hunt in the mountains. Their house was at the foothills of the Toomish Mountains in the Irish county of Kerry. Father had a farm back there, with no fewer than a hundred head of cattle. Wandering the pastures at the foothills of the mountains while taking them out to graze made up his entire existence. There was nothing by way of a pastime in the countryside, except to face out for a hunt. Unless, getting blind drunk in the evenings and scuffling on the floor of barn-like taverns can be called a pastime.

Father was an exemplary huntsman, and like all huntsmen, fiercely solitary. Does hunting foster solitude, or does solitude lead them to hunt? Either way, he hardly ever spoke. Stone, is how Mother referred to him ordinarily. It made no difference to Father even if she did say it within his earshot. He lived amid them in a whole other world partitioned by glass.

Once the grazing that began at the break of dawn and the hunting trips that started at noontime came to a close and dusk began to shroud the evening, Father would lumber into the house, feet shod in mud-scented boots, body steaming with sweat. "Jesus," he would mutter as he took off his hat and hung it in place. With that, his voice would ebb out. Mother was seemingly oblivious to his comings and goings. It was Anya and Aileen who attended to his needs.

Dinner was at the wooden table laid out in a low-ceilinged room by the side of the house, a table his father had carved with his own hands. It was always cabbage soup. When the soup was placed in front of him, Father would close his eyes and observe a moment's silence. Even as the rest of them pretended to pray, they would strain their ears to catch the sounds that emerged from him. The moment he heaved a sigh and uttered "amen," the sound of Liam dropping his spoon into the soup would follow. Sometimes, Father would look up at Liam's loud slurping with narrowed eyes. But he wouldn't say a word. Through the whole of dinnertime, as it happened, he never said a word.

Very rarely did Father stay indoors. More often than not, it was when foul weather prevented him from taking the cows out to graze. Even so, he would keep himself busy all day. He would fashion cattle yokes from wood. He would cut strips of leather and season them. He would tighten the horse saddles. He would nail wooden planks together and build boxes. When night fell, he would nurse a glass of rum in his hand, and sit staring at the cool sky for a time. He knew every soul in town, though there was no one he called a friend. Aiden could scarcely tell if he was happy or sad.

Still, whenever he was with him, Aiden would only feel his heart brim with joy, and so it was that his mind had registered his father as a happy soul. The only time Father spoke was when they went out on a hunt. Then, too, no more than a couple of words. Nonetheless, Aiden liked it when his father's deep voice fell on his ears. He cherished even more the rare occasions when his father's big, rough hands rested firmly on his shoulders. Twenty-five long years later he could still feel his unmistakeable touch when he was all alone. "Catch," "Block": Father would issue one-word orders through clenched teeth in Aiden's dreams.

There were times when Aiden wondered if he had learned anything from Father. He had none of his father's traits. He was drawn to the mountains and meadows, but herding and hunting did not appeal to him beyond a point. The rolling grassy knolls of the flatlands seemed to him like the unread pages of a mysterious book. The undulating shoulders of the mountain peaks seemed like someone seated with their head bowed in silence. He longed to know, to think. When alone, he ventured to transmute those valleys and mountains into words.

The written word magnetised him. His house contained just two books. One was a Bible encased in thin birch bark. A veritable antique. It was the New Testament, printed in large typeface on thick, handmade paper. Owing to its weight, it had to be placed on a table before the pages could be turned. No one other than Aiden bothered with it in his house. Along with the verses, the dates and words his grandfather had scribbled on its pages here and there were so deeply imprinted in Aiden's childhood mind, he had the impression that the Bible belonged only to his family. The second book was a collection of four of Shakespeare's plays. Ever since he learned to read, he had read them. Even when he couldn't make head or tail of them, he had committed *Macbeth*, *King Lear*, *Othello*, and *The Tempest* to memory.

Hearing Aiden reel off the plays from memory, Father

Ian enrolled him in the church school. Aiden's father neither opposed it nor approved of it. One can say only that it was of no consequence to him. For Aiden, learning equalled freedom. It was as if, after days of brooding, when the skies had finally opened up and shone brightly, he had burst out the doors of his house and dashed through the meadows. He would reach the same heightened state one attains while praying in a soaring cathedral in utter solitude.

Aiden wished to attend university. However, he knew that his father did not have the means for it. Those were the times when, all across Ireland, cattle were succumbing to disease. Slowly but surely, a famine began to spread through the villages. Abandoning their farmsteads, people began to leave in great swarms. The dream of immigrating to America took hold of Ireland.

Father grew more and more reclusive. He who used to smoke only the branded cigars procured directly from Dublin now purchased low-grade tobacco leaves from the local markets, toasted and rolled them himself. They were huge cigars that stank of rotting mountain wood. When Father lit them it seemed as if smoke was billowing out of his chest, together with a putrid, burnt odour.

When Aiden conveyed his decision to enlist in the military, Father pulled the cigar out of his mouth and parted his lips as if to say something. But the cigar was between his teeth again just as soon, and he busied himself with securing the horse's saddle.

"I'll be trained in administration," Aiden ventured. "For people like me there is no other path to higher learning."

"Will you have to go to India, then?" Father asked, without looking at him.

"I suppose. When I finish studying I'll be required to serve in one of the colonies. It might be in Africa, too," Aiden replied.

Father said nothing. With one good tug he tested the saddle, and climbed on the horse. The horse trotted down the cobbled path, its hooves clip-clopping rhythmically against the rounded stones. Aiden remained where he was, staring after the mud that splashed in the air as the hooves caught the crevices between the cobbles.

Aiden did not visit Kerry even once until he had finished military school. With his mother alone had he kept up a correspondence. One day, four years later, when he arrived home, his mother, who was in the backyard putting clothes out to dry, straightened out the rolled-up sleeves of her blouse and looked up. Delicate wrinkles crowded the corners of her eyes as she peered at him for a time. When her hand involuntarily brushed her headscarf down towards her brow, a spark of recognition flashed in her: "Aidee!" she cried, and rushed to him, her face wearing an expression Aiden would never forget.

She ran to him, screaming for joy. As though she was frozen in rapture and being carried by the wind. "Aidee, Aidee . . . ," she cried, gasping for breath, all the while holding him in a tight embrace and showering him with kisses. Her clothes wore a bouquet of smells—the harsh odour of washing soda, the raw smell of onions, the bite of kitchen smoke. In a trice, she broke down and began to weep. Aiden wrapped her tight in his strong arms and wiped her tears. "Oh, Aidee. Dear . . . how big you've become, how strong your hands are." She took his hands in hers and looked over them. She guided his palms to her cheeks. All of a sudden, she broke into a laugh. "You've become a big man, Aidee. It's funny to see that bulge in your throat. One look at those sideburns, and the girls about town will up and leave with you."

Aiden ruffled her hair. "I'm hungry. Won't you feed me?" he asked.

"I've saved a nice pig just for you. Come," she said, leading him by the hand. Aileen and Anya poked their heads out from within. Both of them had grown up just like that. The distinctive faces and singular features of their girlhood had morphed into the sameness of ordinary farm women, Aiden observed. In the way they welcomed him and took his hand with laughter, Aiden recognised an all-too-familiar monotony.

Father and Liam returned home in the evening. Liam, too, now resembled any other farm lad from the countryside. That boy who never once stopped jabbering was now as quiet as his father. "Jesus," Liam muttered as he hung his hat up. He removed his coat and gave Aiden a tentative smile. His arms, too, had grown firm as logs. Father entered the house a minute later. "Jesus!" he muttered, taking off his hat and coat just as Liam had done, and gave Aiden a faint smile. It looked as if Liam had grown old in the blink of an eye. The village presses everyone into the same mould, Aiden thought to himself. Although that truth was only now visible to him.

Four days was all it took for him to grow bored of the village. He had planned on spending the month with his parents before leaving for Burma, but it was apparent to him that he was a stranger not only in his village but in all of Ireland. It was not just his manner of speaking and dressing that had changed but the look in his eyes and the movements of his body as well. His family, too, saw him as an outsider, he reckoned. The moment they heard his footsteps, their excited chatter would congeal and dissolve gradually into pallid smiles. Mother alone presented him with a forced informality. As for the rest, their eyes merely offered him the respectful detachment due to an outsider.

When he decided to leave after what was only a week,

only his mother put up a feeble protest. "You lack for nothing here . . . Can't you stay with me for some time?" she asked.

"I need to make arrangements for my journey. I have to meet my travel mates and talk to them," Aiden offered.

Mother didn't argue further. He felt a cutting disappointment when he saw that she wasn't too saddened by his departure. Had he expected her to shed tears? he asked himself. He was about to travel a long way. To far-off lands rife with wars and tropical diseases, insects, and snakes. Lands as distant as death itself. Mother knew all of it. Irish youth were breaking off like ripe apples falling from the trees, and hurtling towards a vast field of death. Every young man who detested the face and physique the pastures had to offer him had no choice but to head there. Like a hostile horse, Ireland was bucking them off its back. He would return many years later, a brand-new person. A man loaded with money and strange diseases. Or else a military notification would arrive in an abundantly stamped yellow envelope. Every time the clattering hooves of a postman's horse fell on his family's ears, they were sure to expect that news, if only for a fleeting second.

When he set off from his home, Liam and his father accompanied him. But not a word was exchanged between them. A travelling coach Aiden had summoned was waiting at the intersection where the horse path met the high road. He watched the cock on the weathervane on top of the coach as it swivelled inexplicably from east to south, then to the east again. He handed the reins to Liam and gestured to the driver positioned on the high seat at the front of the carriage. "Looks like a storm is coming," the driver said. Aiden smiled. He knew not how to take leave of his father. He gently patted Liam on his shoulders. He wished to kiss his father's hands; then again, he reasoned that it might seem like a social pretence.

Father took off his hat and straightened his hair. Contrary to habit, Aiden's eyes remained fixed on him. His father's long auburn hair had all but disappeared. Lines creased his brow like the deep furrows made by a plough. The freckles on his baked red skin seemed as if they had darkened and spread out. Folds, like deep cuts, took up his cheeks and jowls. The loose flesh under his chin hung like a thin leather sac bursting with water. Something caught in Aiden's heart for a second—perhaps he might never see his father again. Yes, this was it. This was their last meeting. He felt an inexplicable urge to touch him. He felt like saying, Forgive me, Father.

But for what? He had done nothing wrong. Still, he felt as if he had meted out some form of injustice to the man who stood before him like a forest boulder, battered and beaten in the rain, in the snow, in the sun. An injustice meted out by being born as his son, by the mere act of choosing a life he could never fathom. No, that wasn't it. He had abandoned his father's lap and raced away far beyond his grasp. He had shed all of his father's customs and beliefs, and turned himself into a complete stranger to the man. With the hundreds of books he contained in himself, he could no longer touch his father's hands.

"Lead the horses back, I'll come," Father said, looking at Liam with ripened eyes. Holding the reins of Aiden's horse, Liam bowed lightly and took his leave. The two horses trotted off, their tails swinging this way and that. The sound of the hooves ebbed. At a loss for words, Aiden stared at the coach's entrance. All of a sudden, the cock whirled to the east. Aiden slipped his hands into his trouser pockets.

Aiden understood that his father wanted to say something but couldn't bring himself to speak. Words always proved complicated to him.

"I'll write to Mam as soon as I arrive," Aiden said. "I should be able to return in five years."

It didn't seem like his father had heard him.

"I've got a job in Burma, as a police officer. I'm told that there's no problem down there, other than the heat and humidity."

Father took off his hat and tidied his hair once again. What was he trying to say? How should he stir up the words that had congealed inside of him?

"Do you know the history behind your name?" Father began. Aiden was taken aback momentarily. He suspected that his father was about to tell him something of far more significance than he had imagined. What he was about to reveal was going to change his life altogether—just as it happens in the stories. Aiden stood there silently. He could not tell what was running through his father's mind.

"Byrne is how the name Ó Broin is pronounced hereabouts. It means 'the dynasty of Bran.' We are descendants of Leinster's King Bran Mac Máelmórda. This, right here, is our country. The nation of Ireland." Aiden began to vaguely grasp what his father was getting at. "You, on the other hand, are going to war on behalf of Britain." The moment he uttered those words, Aiden lowered his eyes.

For a time, the two of them stood in a chasm of silence. *Prrr.* One of the harnessed horses exhaled loudly, flapped its ears, and shifted its weight; Aiden shuddered and came to his senses.

"I'll send money home. Through the bank," he said, visibly discomfited.

"There's no need for that," said Father, in a low but firm voice. Without wasting another moment, he spun his horse around and sped away, the thud of hooves resounding in his wake. Father's heavy frame bobbed up and down in the wind as it disappeared from sight.

It was when a draft of cold air struck him that Aiden realised his body had broken into a sweat. A deep sigh did little to lighten his heart. He boarded the coach and closed the door behind him. He sat on the leather-upholstered seat and stretched his legs. He closed his eyes and received the breeze all over his face. The coachman rang his bell twice and commanded the horses forward. Soon as he flicked the whip in the air the horses set off.

Jolting to a start, the carriage rattled and jounced along the muddy path. The wheels crunched over the pebble-ridden mud and the axle knocked loudly against the hub, as the coach gathered speed. Aiden opened the window of the carriage. It wasn't until a cool breeze laden with the scent of horse dung swept in that Aiden's mind began to quieten. He felt as though his heart had been buried deep beneath a pile of dirty linen, and now, with every gust of wind, the layers were flying away one after the other, causing his heart to lighten and return to normal.

Every day, at seven in the morning, Aiden would set out from his bungalow on the banks of the Adyar River and ride along the horse path that skirted the Marina, through the slums of Ayodhyakuppam, until he reached the police headquarters by the sea. At around nine at night he would head back the same way, all alone. It was the only physical activity he got, for once he entered the office it was well-nigh impossible for him to step out. Sundays, too, afforded him no rest. To Aiden, the daily commute was a deeply private experience. The blue ocean that accompanied him to his right, every step of the way, rendered insignificant all the troubles and irritants of his everyday life. Nothing freed him as much as the thought that he was moving along the verge of the ocean like a tiny bubble of foam.

The stunning sea. It was what Aiden loved the most in all of Madraspatnam. The pristine blue. Like throws of silk being unfurled for display on the long, uninterrupted shoreline, the surf spread over the sands now and again. In the dazzling blue waters, the catamarans of the Sembadava fisherfolk, their puffed white sails aflutter, travelled like one-winged birds. The ships anchored at the port on the horizon seemed like miniature black hillocks. Aiden had made sure that his office overlooked the sea. Whenever he glanced up from the papers that abounded with legal dilemmas, procedural hurdles, protocols, and formalities, the blue expanse abroad his window would whisk him away to the skies, or so he imagined.

What a sea! As if composed of blue light. The waters that he had seen in England were different. That sea had conjured up the vision of a strange, thick, murky liquid that had hardened into a deep blue swathe of marble. It was only when he entered the seas off the coast of Morocco that he first laid eyes on tropical waters. The skies were overcast when Aiden had set sail from the English port of Southampton. The deafening rumble of the ship's machinery as it came to life had resounded like thunder. As the vessel got under way, the passengers lined its decks and gazed at the shore. With its rising chimneys and high, cone-shaped tile roofs, the city of Southampton floated farther and farther away. The vanishing city resembled a great ship submerging in the waters of the firmament. The vessels anchored nearby bobbed restlessly in the sea.

Once the land disappeared from sight, the passengers retired to their respective berths. They pulled the woollen blankets over themselves and tried to catch some sleep. Although each of their faces wore a different expression, it seemed to Aiden that the thoughts running behind them were much the same. *Will I see this land again?* That was the one-line refrain. What else could they be thinking about? Most of them stayed in their beds all through the days and the nights, with visits to the mess hall being the only exception. Despite the many hundreds of passengers on board, the mess functioned peacefully. There arose the clanking of spoons against dishes, the rustle of clothes, the thudding and scraping of shoes on the wooden floor, and, on rare occasions, a hushed exchange of words.

A man from Lancashire was Aiden's roommate. However, he, too, proved to be a recluse who was lost in himself. Aiden scarcely exchanged a word or two with him in the first ten days. Within a fortnight their bodies had acclimated to the lethargy. It became possible to lie in bed for as many as twenty hours a day. The days and nights that wore on in between sleep and wakefulness were strung together by the ship's mechanical drone like a thread that strings a cluster of pearls.

The mess was agog with talk of arriving at Casablanca the following day. Aiden didn't make much of it. As rain rocked the ship and lashed at it, droplets of water seeped in through the gaps around the windowpanes and dripped on the bed, scattering over the woollen blankets like shards of glass. Aiden settled in beneath the covers, closed his eyes, and pictured the green meadows back home. Waking to the ship's horn the following morning, Aiden threw on his overcoat, stooped under the short door frame, and stepped out of his quarters. For a second, he felt as though molten light was pouring into his eyes.

He stood there for a while, shielding his eyes with his hands; after a time, he slowly removed his hands, forcing his eyes to adjust bit by bit, until he could see, stretched out in front of him, a clear blue sky and a great expanse of light that was the effervescent sea. A place that had never known such a thing as darkness, he thought to himself. A flock of white birds went past, as if sliding across the sky. "A blue sea, blue sea," Aiden chanted. "*To mingle with the Universe, and feel what I can ne'er express, yet cannot all conceal.*" A verse rose to his lips. What poem was it?

He repeated those words over and over. In a flash, the next line was upon his tongue. "*Roll on, thou deep and dark-blue ocean, roll! Ten thousand fleets sweep over thee in vain.*" Byron. Aiden marvelled at how his inner self had recalled precisely that verse and no other. "*In vain.*" The phrase crashed into him all day long. Like waves smashing against the hull of the ship. *In vain! In vain! In vain!* He skipped his meal that morning. Instead, he sat gazing at the sea, which shone luminous in the soft sunlight. The ship reached Casablanca that evening. With its dust-cloaked, sand-hued buildings, the ancient port city advanced towards him. Beyond it, as though formed of dust, stretched the sky. A smell very near that of burnt fish oil came from the sea. As did faint human voices. A legion of larynxes rose in a refrain as measured as the humming of bees.

The people on the ship had redeemed themselves from their cocooned state that day, Aiden observed. Ebullient voices rang out from everywhere. Men rushed hither and thither. They were told that the ship would berth at Casablanca for eight whole days. Under the light from the skies, the strange city lay wide open in all its absurdity. The loud and raucous cries of the blacks. The ubiquitous stench of something rotting. Narrow streets with steaming gutters. In its capacity as the first land they had alighted on, the city intoxicated the passengers. And offered them every intoxicant under the sun, too. The strangeness of the place bestowed all it contained with a dreamlike quality.

Aiden, though, was rather immune to its charms. He rented a sea-facing room at an inn on the outskirts of the city, with blankets so filthy dust motes flew out when disturbed. Bedbugs, like shiny copper shavings, scurried out of the cracks in the wall. The rock pigeons settled on the windowsill kept up their throaty coos, evoking the sound of a cow being milked, of bridles being polished, of a carpenter working his handsaw. Down below, the paved stone yard was white with their droppings. Wheels, whips, and hooves resounded in unison from the direction of the road. Aiden sat gazing at the sea all day long. On one of those days, it dawned on him that he would never be free of the sea. That he would never part from that light-filled sea.

Standing by the shore, Aiden was watching the waves. The pattern of the wind was imprinted on the clear sands. The beach lay like a sweeping white fabric that had descended from the skies and settled on the earth. Slowly, Aiden imbibed the wondrous solitude and contentment the sea had to offer him. Just then, the crack of a whip and an incoherent babble of voices jolted him. When he turned around all he could see was a deserted road caught in a sandy haze. Suddenly, a woman's cry pierced the air. Then, again, the sound of whipping.

Aiden swung his horse around and traced his way back a short distance. There was something going on under the tree he had sighted earlier. Two people lay on the ground and a third was bringing the whip down on them. Aiden neared them in a few leaps. As soon as he saw Aiden, the assailant coiled his whip, came up to him, and bowed. A black man. Tall and sturdy of body. He sported a big turban and a khaki-hued coat. The eyes of the Indians never ceased to amaze Aiden. Eyes that were white and protuberant, like oysters. Eyes that threatened to pop out at any second.

"What's this?" Aiden asked, his gaze fixed on the two people on the ground. Only then did he notice that one of them was a woman. Dark, emaciated forms. Their cheek and collar bones were swollen. Their shoulders, thin and skeletal. The man on the ground had hiked his muddied waistcloth up to his knees. The woman's sari, too, had taken on the colour of mud. She was holding the throw of her sari firmly against her meagre breasts. Blood had begun to pool in the cut on her shoulder, where the whip had caught skin. Blood oozed from the man's neck and shoulders, too. The man with the whip bowed once again, and said something. It was English. Even so, Aiden could not comprehend a word.

"Slow down, slow down," he urged.

"Yes, sir," acknowledged the man with the whip. "These are workers from the Ice House. They did not come to work. They were in hiding."

A sharp cry of words emerged from the man on the ground even as he made to grab hold of Aiden's feet. The assailant let loose a mighty crack of his whip; its tongue licked and coiled against the man's dark back. Writhing and screaming, he collapsed to the ground. The woman shrieked as she caught hold of him.

"Don't," came Aiden's voice, stopping the assailant.

The man bowed another time. "They are criminals," he declared.

"What's your name?" Aiden demanded.

"Neelamegam. I am a foreman at the Ice House," he replied, pointing in the direction of the edifice visible in the distance.

"Neelamegam, you have no authority to punish them. All right?"

The man seemed lost. Aiden repeated himself haltingly, one word at a time.

Neelamegam brought his palms together in fear. The whip was between his folded hands. "They are criminals. Criminals," he repeated.

"Maybe so. Take them away and hand them over to their custodian. Let him decide what punishment is due to them as per the law."

Neelamegam bowed deferentially.

"These people are workers. Not slaves. The Crown's laws make no allowance for Her Majesty's subjects to flog their workers. Understand?"

His eyes, like two white eggs, were agape.

"You've committed an offence by lashing them. I will have to take this up with your supervisor. I'll order him to hand you the rightful penalty."

The man stared wide-eyed, as before.

"Lend them a hand," Aiden commanded.

Neelamegam shouted something in the local tongue, at which the workers joined their palms and strained to get to their feet. When he tried to push himself up, the man lost his balance and fell down again. "Hold him," Aiden ordered, throwing his arm out in his direction. Neelamegam stood there, unmoving. The woman pointed at the man's leg and said something. Once more, the man tried to hoist himself up. It was evident that his right leg was unresponsive. At first, Aiden assumed that it was a wooden leg, not unlike the blackened, ossified branch of some native tree. The man had to lift and move his leg with his hand in order to move forward.

"What's wrong with him?" Aiden asked, turning to the woman.

She pointed at his leg and repeated herself.

"Neelamegam, what's she saying?" Aiden demanded.

"He is putting on an act, sir."

Aiden felt a sudden rush of blood to his head. A man of the kind he was running into everywhere and all the time. A kind as bloodthirsty as vampires. A garrison that hung upside down from the tower of imperial authority. They roamed all over the city at night, sucking blood.

"I didn't ask for your opinion. I asked to translate what she said."

"She says the ice block has numbed his leg."

"Oh," said Aiden. "All right, I'll have a word with your manager. Pick him up now, and take him to your company. Make sure he gets the medical attention he needs." With that, Aiden leaned in the direction of the black man and said, "Company. Go. Medicine—marndhu. Marndhu. There."

Whatever went through the man's head, tears glistened in his eyes as he brought his palms together. The woman held him by the shoulder as he tried to rise again, only to collapse with a painful groan.

"Give him a hand," Aiden cried to Neelamegam.

"He will walk on his own, sir," came the response.

It was only then that Aiden was struck by Neelamegam's obstinacy. The firm resistance displayed by black servitors from within their cloak of unwavering servility whenever something threatened their self-interest. A resistance that poked at the throat like a fishbone nestled in fat. "Do as I say. Hold him up," Aiden said in a stern voice. Neelamegam tightened his body wordlessly and looked at the ground.

Aiden understood what was going on. Many of the natives avoided touching one another. They believed that to touch a person from a lower caste would pollute them. Sometimes even a bath would not suffice to cleanse them of it. They had to ingest cow dung mixed in water. They had to visit their temples and perform expiation. Some castes even believed that to be purged of the sin of pollution they had to suffer the punishment of thrusting their hand into fire.

"Idiot," spat Aiden, bristling with irritation. "Lift him up. That's an order." His face flushed and his breath quickened.

"Forgive me. I cannot," said Neelamegam.

"Will you do it or not?" Aiden's voice cracked as he drew his strap out.

"Forgive me," Neelamegam repeated. It didn't seem like he was speaking at all. His eyes were as lifeless as two balls of metal.

"Idiot," Aiden shrieked as he raised the buffalo-skin strap in the air. The strap's tongue grazed past his face.

Neelamegam stood rooted to the spot, stock-still. Aiden lowered the strap. "I'll throw you in prison," he said breathlessly. "It'll be six months before you see the light of day." Neelamegam did not budge. His whole body stood like a clenched fist against Aiden.

A few moments passed without event. The two people on the ground looked on with stunned eyes and still bodies. Neelamegam looked cold and frozen, as though he had come to a grinding halt, as though he had been carved out of ice. Aiden imagined that his hand would turn cold and numb if he so much as touched him. A tremor took hold of his body. His legs twitched involuntarily. "Jesus," he said, as he removed his hat and wiped his head. He pressed his handkerchief to his face and rubbed downwards.

"Very well. I'll take care of you." So saying, Aiden dug his spurs into the sides of the horse. With a start the horse leaped forward and broke into a gallop, its hooves clip-clopping against the black stone path.

2

As soon as Aiden rode into the front yard of his office, Duraisamy and Kannan came running. Duraisamy took the reins from Aiden while Kannan removed the saddlebag from the horse's back. Aiden tossed the strap to Duraisamy, strode towards the office, his boots resounding against the stone ground, leaped up the stairs, and seeing Sepoy Samikkanu across from him, said: "Sam, ask Nar to see me at once."

When Aiden entered his room and took the chair, Ammasi, the old untouchable seated on his haunches outside, began to pull the punkah. Even though there was a generous breeze gusting into the room through the windows, the punkah was a symbol of authority. The wicker chair made of densely woven palm-leaf spines creaked under Aiden's weight as he settled in and closed his eyes for a moment.

Hearing the screech of the push door, Aiden opened his eyes. Narayanan came in and offered him a crisp salute. Aiden stared vacantly at him for a second or two. A turban-like blue hat. A leather belt sequinned with a string of bullet pockets ran across a bright-red linen coat. The coat flaps that parted at his midriff revealed a white cotton tunic and a second leather belt secured around his waist. On one side of the belt was a dagger; on the other, a brass-handled pistol. Khaki knee-length trousers. Khaki puttees. Clumsily cobbled tough leather boots of local make.

All the British sepoys across India, Burma, and Malaysia wore the selfsame uniform. However, the persons they clothed in each place were disparate human beings. No identity could unite them. On the contrary, they regarded identity as a means to differentiate themselves. This man had decorated his forehead with a thin red line that ran perpendicular to his brow. Evidently, he wished to show that he was not one of the others.

"Sir," said Narayanan.

Awoken by his call, "What's that?" Aiden asked off-kilter, pointing at Narayanan's forehead.

Baffled for a moment, "It is the mark of my religion, sir," said Narayanan.

These people had imbibed that word with precision. One of the many stringent orders laid down by the British Crown that had taken over the government from the Company after the Sepoy Mutiny was not to interfere with the religious identities of the sepoys. Overnight, the sepoys had deftly transformed all their caste markers into religious symbols. The British could not fathom how they had learned to do it.

"Oh," said Aiden. "Would you touch those outside your religion?"

Narayanan fell silent.

"Speak up," Aiden commanded.

"There are those who cannot be touched, sir," said Narayanan.

Instantly, Aiden decided there was no use sending him alone. Lieutenant Mackenzie had gone to Teynampet. Among the white men present in the office at that time, only he knew enough of the local tongue to hold a conversation. No matter their seniority, no matter their length of service, these black sepoys could not be trusted.

"Come with me," Aiden said, getting to his feet. "Bring twenty of our soldiers with you," he instructed as he walked out of the office.

"With weapons, sir?" Narayanan asked.

"The ordinary ones will do." Aiden hastened down the stairs and was back at the front yard again. The sun, having reached its prime by then, had filled the yard like molten glass. The white walls of the building shone blindingly. A yellow litter of neem leaves overspread the low, red-tiled roofs of the office buildings that choked the neighbourhood. A cuckoo's call rang out, over and over, without alteration. Aiden would often imagine that it was saying hello.

There arose the faint sound of the wind being spliced by the tightly drawn hawsers holding up a tall mast salvaged from some ship and erected at the office entrance. The Union Jack at the top of the mast fluttered in the sea breeze. The entire building, Aiden often fancied, was a ship moored on the shore. Having covered many thousands of miles, it had beached itself there. With time its anchor will become the roots from which a great tree will rise. Someday, it may turn into a boulder, and in due course, into a mountain, even.

The moment Aiden stepped out of the office, Duraisamy hurried up to him with his horse. The horse turned its head and rested its big muzzle on Aiden's shoulder. Thick spittle dribbled over his forearm. He shook his hand dry and mounted the horse even as Duraisamy was tightening the saddle. The horse started and spun around a bit; when Aiden tugged at the reins, it tensed its head and snorted. Narayanan hastened to a small wooden podium on the right-hand side of the building and blew his bugle. Its strident birdlike call rose up with the sea breeze and dissipated in the wind like ink on water. The clatter of soldiers falling into line at the back of the building replaced the sound of the bugle. "Company fall in!" Narayanan's command reverberated after Aiden as he started out.

When his horse hit the road, the sound of the twenty-man platoon following in a double march filled the air. Aiden did not look back. Hearing the din of the marching forces, a few people in the two warehouse-offices along the seashore lifted the vetiver-grass screens covering the windows and poked their heads out. A two-horse phaeton coming from the opposite end hesitated and hung back. The reined-in horses twitched their heads, neighed softly, and lifted their stick-like legs. The left wheel shuddered and the carriage keened to one side before finding its balance again. The driver jumped off the coach with whip in hand and stood holding the horses. A white woman wearing an ornate, red tricorne hat looked out of the carriage. Her pale, powdered face was dense with wrinkles. Blue eyes shorn of all emotion flitted this way and that, taking in the sights.

It was only when he crossed the phaeton that Aiden became aware of the presence of Narayanan's platoon marching ten feet behind him. Like a swaying shadow creeping into view from the corner of his eye, a pitch-dark elephant emerged by the side of the road. Its trunk was curled around a big wooden box. The man seated on its back appeared naked. A mere illusion, for his blackened loincloth had camouflaged him against the elephant's body. At its feet stood a twelve-year-old boy, also clad in no more than a loincloth, with sticks in hand. Somewhat startled by the elephant, Aiden's horse began to back up; he patted its neck and pacified it.

For a split second, Aiden met the elephant's glistening eye—like a speck of water pooled in the deep crevice of a boulder. What lies buried in the soul of a black boulder? With his little stick, this little man trains the elephant to dance to his tunes. Its feet, its tusks, its trunk, its ears have each submitted themselves to him. But those eyes are yet to accept him. Eyes that are beyond man's comprehension. There is something in them, like fire buried in the recesses of darkness.

Aiden paused when he neared the Ice House. There was no one now at the spot where he had seen those workers come under the whip. A little farther away, the curved façade of a red-tinted edifice rose in front of him like a fortress. A cluster of arched windows dotted the façade. Fitted with amber-stained glass panes, every one of those windows was closed shut. Two flags fluttered atop the circular crown of the Ice House. The Union Jack flew high, and beside it, the flag of Frederic Tudor & Co. Red stripes against white. It was indeed the New England flag, save a blue square bearing a circle of white stars in one of its corners.

A fine phaeton coach stood at the entrance by the side of the building. Ostensibly an import from London, it was crafted in mahogany that gleamed as if it were leather or wax, and bronze that glistened like gold. Silver trims adorned its doors. Four beautiful black horses, unharnessed from the coach, were tethered nearby. Hearing the platoon, they lifted their heads out of the bags of horse gram suspended from their muzzles; when they turned their necks, a shiver rippled through their hides. *Prrr*, exhaled one of the horses, at which the others gave a gentle whirl, lowered their heads, shook their necks until the soft hair on their hides stood up tall, and tilted their saggy-jowled jaws upwards.

Aiden instructed Narayanan to hold the platoon back, and rode into the compound. The minute he set eyes on the manager of Tudor & Co., who, dressed in a short coat, loose trousers, and high boots, approached him with fake calm while holding down his American-style top hat against the wind, Aiden knew it. Everything had already been arranged.

The manager came up to him and bowed with utmost propriety. An old geezer. His chin hung in two flabby folds. With his sagging cheeks and a prominent red nose that resembled a big, bursting pustule, he had the mien of a white hog.

Aiden got off the horse, threw the reins to one of the sepoys, and walked up to the manager. "Captain Aiden Byrne," he declared. "I'm here to make a few enquiries apropos your company."

"By all means, officer. The business we run here is strictly legal," said the manager. "My name is Nick Parmer. I see you nearly every day, but haven't had the occasion to be introduced. Please come in." His greeting was theatrical. Aiden met his eyes, which were like tiny, burnished balls of iron.

"I caught your overseer lashing one of your workers this morning. Beating an employee is a crime in British territory. I wish to interrogate your overseer," Aiden said, proceeding up the stairs.

With caution in his eyes, Parmer said, "I'm sorry, but it can't be one of our supervisors. We never resort to beatings. Our business abides by all the laws. You're welcome to inspect all our documents and books of accounts."

Aiden locked eyes with the manager. "I have not come to inspect your documents. I'm here to interrogate the overseer in question."

"Of course," Parmer said deferentially. "I'll line up all my supervisors for you," he said. "Feel free to conduct your enquiry in as much detail as you please. There's no way such an incident could have come to pass. Our own laws don't allow it, either."

Their eyes stood still for a few seconds, testing each other. Then Aiden drew a deep breath and broke the silence. "Can I inspect your warehouse?" he asked.

"Do you have a permit . . . ," Parmer stalled.

"I don't need permission," Aiden retorted, cutting him off mid-sentence. "I'm an officer of the Imperial Police."

"But we're Americans. We've signed a legitimate treaty with the British government."

"Be that as it may, your warehouse is on our land. I cannot tolerate the commission of an unlawful act under the crown of Her Majesty the Queen."

"If I allow you entry, I'll be held responsible."

"Very well. You may tell your bosses I went in of my own accord." Without waiting for a response, Aiden charged up the stairs, the metallic clang of his shod heels resounding against the stone steps. Parmer hastened after him. Signalling to Narayanan to wait at the entrance, Aiden entered the building. A tall, heavy door stood in front of him, half-open. On the other side of the door hung a thick, black curtain. When he parted the curtain and stepped in, Aiden could not see a thing. The near-total darkness of the place had blinded his sun-exposed eyes.

"Open the windows," Aiden commanded.

"We can't. Sunlight isn't allowed in here," said Parmer.

"Why not?"

"Light equals heat. This is a tropical country."

"Oh . . ." Aiden blinked deliberately until his eyes accustomed to the dark. Little by little, the shadowy outlines of the walls and doors came into view. In a few seconds, they bulged into three-dimensional forms. There arose the sounds of workers going about their duties, but they were muffled and faint. Like sounds on the surface heard from underwater. Breathing, moaning, heaving noises.

A semicircular veranda circumscribed a huge, semicircular hall. Every one of its windows were shut and overlaid with thick, black, woollen curtains. Heavy woollen drapes covered the doors to the hall, too. Aiden parted one such curtain and proceeded inside. The scene that presented itself to his now darkness-accustomed eyes would forever put him in mind of a medieval European painting. As though Dante's inferno had been sketched in coal. The icy frigidity of hell surged wave-like, and attacked his fingertips and the rims of his ears.

Staircases descended from the hall in all four directions leading five feet underground to a place where no fewer than fifty human forms were at work. Dim, shadowy forms. One could hear the sounds of hushed speech, of breaths being drawn; still, it was hard to tell what they were doing. They twisted through the darkness like worms squirming in black mud. They were pushing the darkness forward with all their might. No, they were scooping up the darkness with their bare hands. Or were they trying to cling to the darkness and ascend it? A white-turbaned overseer, clad in a woollen coat and khaki trousers, was issuing orders in the local tongue, his hand outstretched.

"What're they doing?" Aiden asked.

"Let me show you," said Parmer. "Light," he commanded. One of the men climbed an iron ladder to reach a small opening at the top of the hall and released its tiny shutter. A pillar of sunlight slanted in through the opening like a glass beam. At the point where the beam hit the surface there lay a massive block of ice. The instant the light touched the ice, its top layer began to bleach. As if the protective skins of white fabric that had covered the ice till then were now peeling off one after the other, causing the even brighter layers beneath to fray, the ice block grew lucid right before their eyes and turned into a light-filled, glass tank.

Absorbing the light from the ice block, the ash-grey walls of the room took shape. Against the backdrop of light,

Aiden could see slim silhouettes of human forms. They were removing slats of wood from around the ice block. Gathering the slats that had been prised off the walls of the ice block—six feet in height, six feet in width, and eight feet in length—with a crowbar, they piled them in a corner. The fully naked ice block absorbed every possible ounce of light, and shone luminous. Bubbles and cracks were visible on its insides.

"Where does it come from?" Aiden asked, unable to avert his gaze from the scene.

"From America. We harvest all our ice from the lakes of New England. You won't find clearer water anywhere in this world. Nor ice as delicious as ours," Parmer responded.

Aiden's gaze was still fixed on the ice block. It had arrived there after a journey of eight thousand miles, over six months.

"How did it reach here without melting?"

"The bigger the ice block, the less it thaws. The coldness the ice generates is, in itself, sufficient to stop it from melting. When the lakes of New England freeze in winter, we saw out the ice in blocks, float it to the shore, and load it into our vehicles. From there, the ice is taken to cargo ships. We pack them in huge boxes lined with slabs of salt and sawdust. The blocks are loaded onto the lower decks, so that the heat from the outside doesn't reach them. Maybe five percent of the blocks melt off in their six-month journey, but that's nothing."

"How much does it weigh?"

"Thirty tons. The weight of ten elephants."

Aiden's gaze was still frozen on the ice block. The edges had thawed and blunted, turning it into a bevelled square. A square elephant. A white elephant. It shone radiant, as though the look in its eyes had become its very form. *Still, snowy, and serene— Its subject mountains their unearthly forms. Pile around it, ice and rock*. Meaningless lines, or else lines with unknown meaning. Must be Shelley's.

Kreeekkk—the sudden noise jolted Aiden. His consciousness, reduced to a mere barrage of random words by Parmer's voice and his own surroundings, recoiled in horror. Set in motion by an unknown force acting on it from one end, the ice block began to slide, grating against the floor. The white elephant rumbled, lowered its crown, and moved forward, baying for blood. The workers shrieked in panic. The overseer ran across the ledge of the block, gesticulating and screaming wildly. He flicked the whip for good measure until the twang of the lashes accompanied his cries.

Another overseer rushed in from the door on the opposite end, hollering. The white elephant set out, determined to butt a few men against the wall and squash them to pulp. Two of them grabbed some wooden planks strewn on the floor and thrust them between the block and the wall. The planks crumbled with deathly moans. In that sliver of time, the workers made their escape. The ice block smashed through the planks, crushing them to pieces, and, unyielding, collided against the wall and came to a stop.

"It's quite heavy," Parmer resumed, "but it slides easily on an even surface. Since the bottom layer chips and thaws under its own weight, the block's always poised precariously. And so, a bit dangerous."

Aiden waited for his body to stop shuddering. "Are lives ever at risk?" he asked after an interval of silence.

"Not often," Parmer replied. "They're used to it."

Aiden observed the workers as they struggled to move the ice block back to the centre. It did look as if they were strapping up a white elephant and moving it into position. It wouldn't rest until it had drawn blood, Aiden thought.

The workers hammered some wedges beneath the ice

block to secure it firmly in place before climbing over it. When they reached the top of the block, Aiden could see their pitch-black bodies tremble and quiver like sailcloth flapping in the sea breeze. They dripped as though they'd just risen out of water. Big white teeth and clam-like white eyes were all that were visible on their dark bodies. The same mute flock of humans he encountered all over Black Town. People whose bodies were forever arched in submission. What was behind those eyes? What meaning lay hidden in their quiet voices?

They were now talking loudly among themselves. Four men climbed up and sat on either side of the ice block. Two long saws were set down on the ice. The men took hold of its ends, two on each side. Aiden watched them as they sawed the ice as though it were wood. *Rrr, rrr,* the block roared in protest. Shards of ice fell to the floor and pooled into white mounds.

"We break the ice into cubes, here. After which, we pack them once again into boxes lined with sawdust, and ship them to wherever there's demand," Parmer went on. "Our ice travels all over, from Secunderabad up north to Tenkasi down south. The Collectors host no banquet in this neck of the woods without our ice. As a matter of fact, our ice is more expensive than even the finest liquor." Parmer pointed ahead. "Those ice shavings are mixed with salt and sawdust and shaped to pad the walls of the boxes, so that the cubes arrive intact."

It was only then that Aiden became conscious of a shivering in his body. He slipped his hands in his coat pockets and walked out slowly. The moment he stepped out, as though touched by the warmth of a stove, his cheeks and ears warmed up. That was when he realised just how cold the room had been. These people toil there, bare bodied, all day long. And to think they were born and raised in the tropics. Would they have seen ice anywhere else?

He was left in no doubt whatsoever that the two workers he had been looking for would not be there. As though roused from a baffling dream, his mind faded in and out in a flurry of inchoate thoughts. "Mr. Parmer, why aren't these workers clothed appropriately for the cold?" he demanded.

A smile crept onto Parmer's face. "Wool will get wet and unbearably heavy in these damp conditions."

In a trice, the fogginess in Aiden's mind cleared; he felt the blood from every part of his body rush to his head. "Mr. Parmer, I suppose you do have waterproof clothing in America."

Parmer nodded and, with the vestige of a smile in his eyes, said, "Sure. But these people don't care to be clothed. You'll see for yourself when you visit Black Town. Most of them go about their lives practically naked."

Aiden suppressed his anger. It was futile to argue with this old fox, he surmised. With a sigh, he said, "All right, Mr. Parmer, be sure to send every one of your overseers to my office."

"Certainly," Parmer said, and made a bow.

When he started out by the seashore, Aiden lowered his head and fixed his gaze on the ground. Blinded by the glare of light, his eyes closed shut, squeezing out droplets of water that rolled down his cheeks. He wiped them with a silk handkerchief.

"Sir?" ventured Narayanan.

"Order the platoon back to the camp," Aiden responded.

The instant Narayanan sounded the bugle and called out the order, the platoon swerved around like a ship's sail changing direction in the wind, and began marching in sequence in the manner of a giant millipede.

As the platoon marched on Beach Road, Aiden counted

time. As soon as they had covered five hundred feet, he plucked the whistle from his waist and blew on it. The platoon stopped in its tracks. "Company! Reverse charge!" he shouted and, swinging his horse around, charged towards the Ice House. Narayanan echoed the command, and the platoon surged behind him like an avalanche of boulders. They swelled forth in the direction of the building, like waves in the sea.

Within a few minutes, Aiden had reached the Ice House. Whipping out his sword, he leaped off the horse and stormed into the building. Parmer came running from the inside. He spread his arms open and tried to say something. For a fraction of a second, Aiden watched Parmer's still face from close quarters as it slowly puckered in the wind towards a pronunciation. Then his foot met Parmer's chest in a mighty kick. With a loud gasp, Parmer landed back-first on the floor.

The platoon entered the building under Narayanan's command, inundating it like a fresh flood. "Round up every last person and stand them in the front yard," Aiden ordered. He kicked Parmer's monocle out of his way, and entered the semidark room of the Ice House. With his boots thudding against the floor, he clasped the drawn-out sword and marched through the veranda that skirted the room. The soldiers caught hold of everyone in the building and pressed them forward. Aiden scoured the rooms one after the other. It was clear that the place was only a warehouse, not an office.

When Aiden returned to the entrance there were more than two hundred pitch-dark, half-naked human figures lined up in the front yard. The whole place seemed to have dimmed in the blackness of their bodies. He climbed down the stairs and walked towards them. Their eyes alone followed his movement, with terror.

Narayanan stiffened into a salute. "Everyone is here, sir," he said.

"Have you checked the whole area?"

"Yes, sir. I ordered our men to search their vaults and drag all of them out."

Aiden came and stood in front of them. The flapping of his shirt's wind-puffed back was all that could be heard. As he neared his horse, it nickered softly, dropped its head, and grazed its jowl against his shoulder. Aiden studied the men in front of him with keen eyes. Twelve overseers. They were dressed similarly, in khaki trousers, and khaki-hued woollen jackets; their legs were wrapped in puttees, and feet immersed in big boots. Clutching their woollen hats in their hands or having tucked them under their arms, they looked on with terror-soaked eyes. Behind the overseers stood an array of men clad in nothing more than filthy, wet loincloths. Bodies whose bones were held together by coiling veins much as a bundle of wood is bound by wild creepers.

Oblivious of the overseers, his entire attention was now directed on the workers. Listening to his heart thump in his ears, he stood there, all eyes and awareness. Ash-like lesions covered the workers' skin, like moss on rock. Reddish white sores speckled their necks and armpits. Some of the sores lay open like the mouths of tiny fish. Others were agape like gouged-out eyes. Skin was peeling off their fingers and toes—like wasting water-snakelings—baring the hardened white flesh underneath.

Then, as though struck on the nape of his neck, Aiden observed something: their legs were all bent and twisted in myriad ways, like a strange thicket of thorns. "Jesus," Aiden uttered under his breath. He wrested his consciousness from the scene and stared at the waves breaking in the far-off sea. All of a sudden it appeared to him as if those men had been ladled out of the ocean and placed on the shore. When he turned back to the crowd, he gazed at their eyes. Overripe, shrivelled, grape-like eyes. The look in them but a hollow stare. Aiden averted his gaze.

He did not know what he ought to do next. Everyone around him waited, watching his lips. Just as he collected himself and began to deliberate his next move, his nose registered the smell of the crowd. The stench of wounds. The stench of rotting flesh. Quelling the wave of nausea that racked his body, he looked over the overseers one by one. Before long, he caught sight of Neelamegam. However, he could not locate the wounded among the crowd of workers. Their faces seemed identical, or so his mind supposed.

Aiden observed that Neelamegam wasn't in the least bit tense or scared. On the contrary, having retracted all his senses, he stood stock-still. His head was unbowed, gaze unlowered. His seashell-like eyes were planted on Aiden.

"Neelamegam, step forward," Aiden called out.

Neelamegam duly marched out to the front.

"Where're those workers you beat up this morning?" Aiden demanded.

"They are not here," said Neelamegam.

"Where've they gone?"

"I do not know who they are, sir."

"You don't know? They work here, don't they?"

"That is what they said. But, as it turns out, they do not work here at all. It is clear from the fact that they did not come back here," said Neelamegam.

Aiden summoned his entire reserve of patience. "Didn't they come back with you?"

"No. I told them to follow me and made my way here. They did not follow me. They are not Ice House workers."

A flash of anger surged in Aiden, and his voice turned shrill. "You told me they're your workers. You said you flogged them because they evaded work."

"Yes, that is what I thought. But they did not come here," Neelamegam repeated.

Aiden stroked the horse that stood close at hand in order to calm himself. Then, with a slow, deliberate breath, he said, "Tell me where they really are."

"They must have returned to their quarters in Black Town."

"Would you know where that would be?"

"I don't. We never go that side."

Aiden did not bat an eyelid. He understood quite well the import of Neelamegam's words. "Produce the two of them in front of me, right away. They are primary evidence for the crime you've committed. Do you hear me?"

Neelamegam said nothing. Aiden raised his voice. "I want them. Right now. All right?"

Pressing his hat down with one hand, Parmer came running out of the building. He slowed down to a hobble as he drew closer, coming to a stop in front of them. "Officer, you're flouting the law," he cried, breathlessly. "You've trespassed on our premises. I'll . . ." As Aiden turned to him, glowering with anger, Parmer caught his eye and faltered. "This is unfair. We run an absolutely lawful business here," he said, piping down.

"Business? You mean letting them die like this?" said Aiden, pointing at the decaying bodies lined up in front of him.

The moment Parmer removed his hand from his hat it lifted off in the sea breeze. He caught hold of it and pressed it down on his head again. "But we tell them everything before they join us. They've taken up the job willingly. No one was coerced. They can quit anytime they please as well. It's a proper business contract, period. If any of them wish to leave, I'll pay them their dues and relieve them of their duties this very moment."

Aiden knew full well that none of them would quit. It was a time when the great Bengal famine had spread its tentacles over the Deccan, and Madras, too. So much so that it had now earned the epithet the Great Deccan Famine. Thousands might elbow one another even for this job. A sigh escaped Aiden. "I don't wish to engage in an argument. Your overseer flogged two of your workers. I saw it with my own eyes. The two workers aren't here now."

"I understand your concern. But I don't know why this man hit those people. We don't employ such methods here. Our company's regulations also prohibit it. What's more, there's really no reason to use the whip. We get as many workers as we need, whenever we need them. To be honest, we're forced to turn away at least a hundred job seekers every day. There's a chance his actions may have been guided by some personal enmity."

"Where are they?" Aiden asked, unfazed.

"You're looking at all our workers. There's no one else in our employ," Parmer said.

"I saw them," Aiden cut in, loudly. "They themselves told me that they work here."

"Is that so? I can't imagine why they'd say that. Maybe just to get away? Plenty of blacks come to White Town just to scrape some food off the garbage dumps hereabouts. I'm told that they tell the police they work at the Ice House. You see, if they were employed in the bungalows, they would have had proper uniforms. We don't provide them any."

Aiden beheld Parmer's little metallic eyes for a time. This isn't a man I can take down so easily, he admitted to himself. "Do you have the names and addresses of your workers? Where are the registers?" he asked.

"Pardon me, but you should understand the state of affairs in this country. We don't go to the trouble of recording the names of the workers, for the reason that most of them are called Karuppan or Sangili. We allot them numbers, which is also their responsibility to remember. So far as addresses go, I'm sure you know, only those who own land hold an address in this country. The rest have never known such a thing. What's more, in these famine-stricken times, people are abandoning their lands and migrating in hordes. No one has anything to show by way of identity."

"Wouldn't your overseers know?" Aiden persisted.

"How would they? These workers are considered untouchable. Our supervisors don't go anywhere near their dwellings. Only when they come here do we associate with them."

Aiden looked at Parmer intently. A man who could not be frightened, he thought to himself. "So what do you propose I do, Mr. Parmer?"

"You've a whole army at your disposal. You rule this gigantic country. Why don't you deploy your men to search the black people's dwellings hut by hut, and find that couple. I do appreciate that working the whip has wounded your sense of justice. My apologies, officer, but I, too, possess that sense of justice. Whenever I visit the hinterlands of this country, I see scores of people begging and scrounging for a lone morsel of food. I've seen their decayed corpses pile up by the roadsides more often than I've wished for. It's because my sense of justice is wounded that I pay half an anna as daily wage to these workers. They haven't so much as known a wage in their previous jobs. Half an anna is a princely sum of money for them. We can safely say they'll be, by far, the richest of their lot."

A sly old fox, Aiden thought, as he ground his teeth. His mind soaked up every poisonous possibility that permeated those words. Inside a century of dominance on Indian soil, the British East India Company had brought upon it man-made famines that had wiped out one fourth of the Indian population by dint of its merciless plundering. When, for that crime, the Company's rule was abolished and replaced by the direct rule of the British queen, even greater famines broke out. The whole of India was being ravaged by starvation.

"You can find those workers quite easily, Mr. Parmer," Aiden countered. "I'm sure you have other workers here from the same locality. If you so instruct, they'll turn up with the people in question. Bring them to me as soon as they come back. Until then, this man will remain in my custody."

Parmer was startled. "How can that be? No definitive charge has been made against him so far," he protested.

"Yes, and I'm taking him away to investigate precisely that. He's not under arrest." With a smile, Aiden tipped his head at Parmer, and signalled to his men. Narayanan grabbed Neelamegam, cuffed his hands, and pushed him forward; Aiden followed behind.

Till he reached the road, Aiden's mind, devoid of all thought, was set like a riverbed of rocks. Stirred into motion the moment he reached the road, the rocks turned into a sea of disquiet. Why am I dragging this overseer away? I can have him flogged for disrespecting my order. But the truth is, I'll get nothing from it save some type of gratification. No, I won't have even that. He will receive the lashings like a cold, frozen corpse. He won't offer me even the feeling of having punished him. If I have him touch a low-caste man I could consider myself victorious. Or if I, at the very least, wear him down and reduce him to tears, I'll be able to feel some semblance of victory. Never will he offer me such an opportunity.

Yes, he is sure to hold his silence. Like a saint who, for the sake of his beliefs, endures torture with fortitude and sacrifices his life with unflappable calm. A saint? Well, what's the difference? It is only a matter of belief. A saint's belief is agreeable to me. Therefore, his sacrifice is instinct with greatness. This man here is giving his life up for something utterly idiotic, for something opposed to the very soul of man. But there's scarcely a difference between his present mindset and that of a saint's. How absurd! Still, that is indeed how the world goes on. That is what the British soldier—who subjugates the people of a nation so far down south, imperils them to abject starvation, and gives up his own life on the warfront in order to enable a handful of companies to make obscene profits—is told: his death is a great sacrifice. It is with the belief that the tremendous act of bravery he's about to perform will bring credit to his ancestors, that he sets out with his guns. Is his psyche unalike those of the mighty warriors in bygone times, who, armed with swords, ventured to protect their land and honour? Not in the slightest. It's laughable. The revolutionary who dies for Ireland, and the British soldier who kills him, fight each other with the selfsame frame of mind. The gun fells without favour. The earth ingests without favour.

How bizarre! After roaming the world for twelve long years the one truth he had come to realise was this: there is no being as bizarre as Man. What reason could there be for this inscrutable mass of life, through which swells both unbelievable greatness and utterly unbelievable baseness, to flourish on this earth? What does God—there ought to be someone like that, for there seems to be no other axis on which one can make sense of all this—intend for this life-form?

As soon as he reached the office, Aiden was freed from his thoughts. For a time, he couldn't quite tell where he had arrived. When Narayanan came up to him, he opened his eyes and looked this way and that. An inexplicable agitation surfaced in him, such as he might feel if he were standing amid a crowd of complete strangers, or if he were all alone in an altogether foreign land. In that moment, the only thing he felt he could do was to hold off everything for later. "Lock him up," Aiden commanded, as he jumped off the horse. He proceeded to his room and sank into his chair. For the first time, the draft of air from the oscillating punkah felt soothing to him. Loosening up little by little, he sat gazing at the fan.

After a time, he brought his hand down on the call bell. An orderly came in and bowed to him. Aiden bade him to bring whisky. He jolted like a man who'd been stabbed in the back with a sharp spear the instant the orderly turned. "Sam!" he cried. In spite of himself, the sound of his voice had arisen like a shriek. "No ice," he said.

"Yes, sir," said Samuel. He bowed again and left the room. Warm whisky for the first time, Aiden mused as he touched the glass to his lips. Vapour permeated every inch of his being; then, just as a boat's sail limpens in a windless sea, his body and mind quietened down.

Suddenly, like the blinding glint of a blade's sweep in the sun, a thought flashed in him. The eyes of his sepoys. Every one of them had held the same emotion. The very same emotion that he'd seen in Neelamegam's eyes. Eyes as white as broken seashells. They all spoke the same language. A cold fear gripped him. It was impossible to serve in the British Army and be deaf to the remembrances of the Sepoy Mutiny of 1857. Of beheaded white men dragged out to the streets. Of slain bodies piled in heaps. Of corpses of women and children bursting the wells.

"Mark my words, Aiden, the most sinister outcome of that catastrophe is the fear it has instilled in all of us. It was through war that we claimed this country. We know very well that enemies are all around us. But the Sepoy Mutiny revealed a different truth. The power we wield in this country has been built on the backs of these black men who are loyal to us. We've cemented our authority with their fear, their self-interest, their depravity. But buried in the foundations of this edifice is something we're oblivious to," the retired Captain J. A. Wright intoned after a few drinks at Calcutta's English Club. "Can you guess what that is?

"Hatred. The intense hatred these black people feel for us. A hatred that resides in the deepest depths, far behind their eyes. It's a potent venom that can wipe us off the face of this earth. That is what we witnessed in the mutiny. Our brethren couldn't believe it, not even when boot-shod feet drove into our faces, or when our women and children lay dying with their throats slit. That those who had wagged their tails and licked our boots, like curs, that those who had wielded swords in our service were capable of such things, our people put down to a bad dream. I walked those streets, taking in the bodies of the dead. It seemed as though the disbelief in their hearts had solidified on their faces as a wide-eyed stare.

"From that day on, something changed within us. It's our good fortune that these blacks are yet to notice it. Whatever we've done since, was born out of that fear. We keep pandering to this black nation. We try to hide their anger from their own selves and direct it elsewhere. The same fear drove Queen Victoria to dissolve the East India Company and take charge of this country. We'll rule these people only for as long as we hide our fear from them. If, one day, even one of them were to apprehend our fear, that will be the beginning of the end of our reign. If there comes a day when this country becomes immune to our pandering, we will be annihilated."

With eyes red from intoxication, the captain went on. "Destruction! A great destruction lies in store for you and me. If not for us, for our children. The elephant never forgets a wrong, they say. We can never know what this black elephant truly has in mind." Time after time, the elephant becomes a metaphor for India. The white man never ceases to be amazed at why this being submits itself to man.

Aiden concluded that he would have to release Neelamegam in the morning; he could do nothing to him. You can beat the elephant, bully it, hurl abuse at it. But the limit to which you can go will always be determined by the elephant.

3

Even as he was riding along Beach Road in the morning, Aiden sensed that the black man in the distance was waiting for him. There was no apparent reason for it, but he felt it in his heart. As he drew closer and closer, Aiden trained his gaze on the man. Prominent cheekbones in a dark, moustache-less face. Big eyes. A length of cloth was wrapped around his head like a turban. The front of his khaki coat was half-open, serving to bare the white shirt underneath. A long vaetti wrapped flat around his waist without flourish stopped just shy of his ankles. Thick slippers of local make. A cloth bag in one hand.

When he drew level with the man, Aiden's horse stayed as though it had read his mind. The man's shirt pocket was unusually big. It bulged with a thick notepad and a stash of papers. A long religious mark adorned his brow. Soon as he saw Aiden, he tilted his head. That infinitesimal movement told Aiden one thing: he was not one to bow in fear, or to curry favour. He was not inclined to offer even an atom of deference beyond the natural regard due to a fellow human. Aiden smiled.

"My name is Kathavarayan," the man spoke. "I am a subject of the British Empire. I was waiting here in the hope of meeting you." His English was flawless, and his pronunciation polished enough to comprehend with ease.

"If it's an official matter, put it down in a petition and see me at the office. I'll be meeting the public for an hour, starting at eleven in the morning."

"Yes, it is official. However, meeting you in your office is no mean feat for me."

"Why?" Aiden asked, his eyes narrowing.

"I belong to an untouchable caste," said Kathavarayan.

"There's no place in my office for such strictures," Aiden snarled. "You've every right to visit. If anyone stops you, meet me at this very spot tomorrow and let me know. I'll take care of them." So saying, he pressed his legs around the horse. As Aiden's heel spike brushed against its coat, the horse stepped forward.

"Pardon me," Kathavarayan called out, hastening after Aiden. "I did not come here to talk about myself. I came to talk about Neelamegam."

Aiden pulled hard on the reins. "Who are you to him?" he asked.

"I do not know him. But I know the workers he attacked. They are my people."

Swerving his horse around, Aiden threw him a piercing look. "Are they your relatives?"

Kathavarayan smiled. "If you put it that way, I have to say yes. Ours is a big clan. Even so, everyone is related by blood. They call us Paraiyars. Or Pariahs, as you say it. The injured man, too, belongs to my caste."

Aiden saw him with new eyes. He was about thirty-five. Or less, perhaps. A thin, scrawny body. How little the Indians eat. They grow up weathering a variety of diseases throughout their childhood. For some bizarre reason, many of them eschew meat as well. And so it happens that an Indian is barely half the size of the average white man. Disregard their faces, and there's every chance one could mistake them for children. "Are you a welfare worker?" asked Aiden. "A Christian?" he added, looking the man straight in the eye.

"No, I am a Vaishnavite," said Kathavarayan. "I have done nothing grand enough to be called welfare work. I am unable to turn away those who come to me for help. That is as much as I do."

"Very well," said Aiden. After a second's deliberation, "Come with me," he said, and patted his horse. Kathavarayan followed him in a slow jog. Before long, Aiden forgot himself; gazing at the sea, he watched the waves ebb and flow. It wasn't until he reached the office gates that he returned to the present. Drenched in sweat, clothes sticking to his body, Kathavarayan was breathing heavily. The guard made Aiden a salute, then turned his eyes to Kathavarayan. "Come," said Aiden, and walked in front. Kathavarayan shadowed him, making sure to stay in step. Aiden could feel the sharp gaze of the soldiers who had risen to their feet in the stable to his right. Despite this man standing far away, despite him being well-clothed, how did they know he was from an untouchable caste, he mused.

"Come in," Aiden announced after he'd turned in to his office and settled down. Kathavarayan entered, but remained standing. "Sit down," said Aiden, gesturing towards the chair. Kathavarayan thanked him and took his seat. Aiden knew that the Indians who were not Brahmins would never sit down as easily. They'd react as though it were a grave sin. They'd squirm in embarrassment. They'd hope for insistence. Then, as though a great honour had been bestowed upon them, they'd offer thanks ingratiatingly. This man in front of him was a rarity, and in some way extraordinary.

One had to admit that he was no more than a young man at present. Someday, in the course of his life, he might well prove himself and become a personage to reckon with.

"Kathavarayan, give me a brief account of yourself before you go on about other things. That'd be a fitting place to start," said Aiden.

"Yes, sir. I, too, know that you will not be able to trust what I say unless you are acquainted with me," Kathavarayan answered.

Aiden smiled. Had he received formal education, this young man could have become a diplomat, he thought to himself. "Go on," he said out loud.

"I was born here, in Chennai. I belong to the Paraiyar caste. My father worked as a butler at the fort. Until the age of eight, I lived in the butlers' quarter in Royapuram. That is where I learned to read English. After that, my father went to work as a butler in the Nilgiris. I grew up there, in the hills, and was educated the Indian way."

"What do you mean, the Indian way?"

"So far as my caste is concerned we have a long-standing tradition of education. We take our elders to be our gurus—our teachers—and learn from them. My father is a scholar. My grandfather, too, is a scholar of traditional texts. Many of the important books the British have taken to press were those preserved by my family for generations."

"Oh," said Aiden. His mind was void of thoughts for a few moments. Then, breaking his silence, he said, "As far as my knowledge serves, your people are among the most depressed classes in this country. People who, having been denied even the right to live as humans, carry on like animals. A human race that is yet to knock at the door of civilisation—that's what's been written about you. And that you're gradually acculturating through British education."

Kathavarayan did not respond immediately. A few seconds passed. He cleared his throat. "If, perchance, the English had defeated the Irish a thousand years back and enslaved them, I would have had to pose the same premise to you, sir," he said.

Aiden felt a sharp sting, as though the tip of a curling whip had licked soft flesh. Instantly, a flash of fury surged through him. Lifting his angry eyes, he beheld the young man seated in front of him whose calm, unflappable gaze suggested that he'd anticipated Aiden's reaction.

"I see," said Aiden, gathering himself.

"Yes. We have been defeated. Enslaved. We formed the intelligentsia of this country at a time when the British land was yet to know civilisation. As a matter of fact, we were the ones who conducted ritual prayers in the temples of this country, a fact that is clearly mentioned in a stone inscription dating back over one thousand five hundred years. We were the ones who learned our texts and taught them to the others. We continue to nurture that literature till today. Somewhere in the sweep of history, we became slaves. Down to the last morsel of rice, everything was snatched from us."

Aiden laughed abruptly. "All right, Mr. Kathavarayan. I believe we haven't met to discuss history today. Tell me, what've you studied? What do you do for a living?"

"A number of texts are studied here as per the prevalent custom. They are mostly devotional works that have gained prominence over the last thousand years. The literature predating these works—ones that dealt with questions of ethics—was written and taught by us. We still learn from it. I have studied every one of those texts without exception. As well as those that form a part of the present convention. In addition, I am formally schooled in Siddha medicine, too. It is what I practise for a living."

"Do you work in the Nilgiris?"

"No. It has been a year since I came to Chennai. I live in the neighbourhood of Thousand Lights. Since I belong to an untouchable caste, I can never grow my practice in the Nilgiris. Only those of my ilk seek me out, but they have no money. Furthermore, my people are leaving the Nilgiris one by one in this famine. I, too, left with them, for Burma. I worked for some time in Rangoon, after which I moved to Chennai and started practicing medicine here. In this city, my people have some change to spare. The Anglo Indians, too, come to me for treatment."

"You said you're Vaishnavite. Isn't Kathavarayan a Shaivite name?"

"Yes. I took to Vaishnavism because of my teacher. He is a staunch Vaishnavite. I learned medicine in the Shuddadvaita ashram he ran, a school that posits the philosophy of pure non-duality. I began treating the poor who visited the ashram. My guru fought determinedly against the proselytization of our people to Christianity. I, too, participated in that movement. I wrote numerous handbills denouncing Christian religious propaganda."

"I see," said Aiden. Just as he had intuited, this young man seemed to have a multifarious life.

"As it happens, I married a woman from the Toda tribe of the Nilgiris. She died. I married again recently. I have two children."

Aiden smiled. "All right, what have you to offer on this matter?"

"The injured man is the reason I got involved in the Ice House issue. He has worked there for four years. The cold damaged his nerves, rendering his leg useless. He had eight children, six of whom died of starvation. He came to me seeking medical attention. I had to treat him at my own expense."

"What's his name?"

"Savarirayan. The Tamil form of the name Xavier. He is Catholic. When he told me he worked at the Ice House, I made a suggestion. Why not ask your employer for some money for your treatment, I said to him. Then I advised him to obtain a letter of recommendation from the pastor at his church. Reverend John Brennen of St. Peter's Church in Royapuram. A good man. He provided the letter, too. I, on my part, gave him a note describing the nature of the illness."

Aiden felt as if the affair was clearing up, little by little.

"Savari and his wife went before the managers of the Ice House, bearing these letters. The managers confiscated the papers, roughed them up, and drove them out. The two of them seem to have somehow limped away and taken cover under a tree. Father Brennen is known to take that route. They had hoped to meet him. But then the supervisor had been set behind them. It was when he was trying to chase them off with his lashes that you saw them. My clans people who work at the Ice House came to me and told me everything—about you arriving on the scene, taking the aggressor to task, and everything else that followed."

"I need the two of them, right away. Where are they?"

"That is indeed what I came to tell you. Neither of them has returned to their hut. Their two children have been left to starve like orphans. They may have been forced to leave town under the duress of threats. Or . . . no . . . there is really no reason to go that far. These poor folk have no wherewithal to create any trouble for anyone."

Aiden shook his head. Perhaps it is I who put them in danger, he ruminated.

"Neelamegam and his men will certainly know their whereabouts. If you question him, we will know. Can you find out if they were killed? That is all I ask of you. If they are alive, there is no occasion for worry, they will come back on their own."

"I will," Aiden promised.

"Thank you, sir," said Kathavarayan and rose to his feet. "We were told that you possess a sense of justice. Just as the enlightened men of medieval times searched for God, we search for those with a sense of justice. Very, very rarely do they meet the eye. When they do they are, more often than not, white-skinned. That is the only modicum of hope left for us in this world today." For the first time, the metallic rigidness that had occupied Kathavarayan's voice until then disappeared and gave way to feeling.

Aiden got up. "I will investigate the matter," he said, extending his hand.

Kathavarayan took it without demur. "I trust you, sir," he said, and began to walk away.

"Mr. Kathavarayan," Aiden called out.

Hearing that, Kathavarayan turned around. "Tell me, sir," he said.

"You spoke of the white-skinned. It's our century-old regime that has produced famines as terrible as this. Today, the whole of India is being ravaged by famines. I hear that hundreds of thousands of people may have died in Madras Presidency alone. This could well be the greatest toll any famine has taken in the history of this world."

"Yes, sir. Bodies have piled up in every corner of this country. People flee in hordes, to Burma, Lanka, and Malaya, only to perish upon reaching those shores. In fact, those who die there far exceed the death toll in this land. I have seen that with my own eyes, too, in Rangoon."

Like a man standing on hot ground, Aiden shifted his weight. Kathavarayan's eyes narrowed a fraction and acquired severity. "Sir, most of those who die in this manner are my people. For generations past, we untouchables formed the majority in this country. The country itself belongs to us. We produced food for this vainglorious society. We nurtured its military. It is with our blood that this society raised its temples and forts. Our blood stains its literature and arts. It is the fruit of our labour that you, too, plunder and pillage today, and cart away in shiploads to erect palaces in London and Yorkshire. We have never lived as human beings in this country. Even so, the entire country belonged to us. After you arrived, there have been more than fifty famines within a span of a century. When the first Deccan famine that struck in 1770 ended, our population had halved. By the time the second Deccan famine, which is upon us now, ends, we will have become a minority in this country.

"But one thing is certain. When we are gone, agriculture will vanish forever in this country. They will try to get by with machines, for some time. But never again will this land feed them as it did before." It was impossible to decipher the emotion on Kathavarayan's face. "Death is a reality, yes. But when did we ever live? How is death any less than such a life? The famine is a good thing, sir. Yes, I mean it. I dare say, even a godsend for our race. Had the land not turned fallow, this society would have never allowed us to leave our villages. If we had not migrated, we would not have so much as dreamed of changing our circumstances. Bound to this land, its orthodoxies and beliefs, we would have crawled along like worms for a thousand years more."

Speechless, Aiden stood staring at him. He recalled what his teacher had once said: there are times when something beyond man speaks through him.

"My people are dropping like flies the world over. They face great ordeals in the jungles of unknown lands, with infants and children in tow. Tormented by hunger and disease, they die a torturous death. Let them die. If the majority of my race succumbing to death offers the remaining few a chance to live a life fit for humans, it is for the better. If the struggle for food should pave the way in the struggle for self-respect, let this go on. Let the precious few who have the chance to live a human life beget a whole new generation. Just as one hacks off the diseased boughs and limbs of a tree, let the famine ravage us. Let it chisel us till blood oozes from our bodies. Let new shoots spring forth from the residues of life. If that be the wish of the all-pervading, we will accept it with bowed heads." Kathavarayan was out of breath.

Aiden parted his lips to speak. It felt as though something were stuck in his throat.

"You are right, sir. You were the ones who brought on the famine. It was not merely a failure of the rains, this time. Or the lands turning fallow. This famine is upon us because you spirit away all the produce due to us from other regions. It is our food that is heaped like mountains in every one of your ports. If we could get what portion of the grains the rats consume, we could stop at least half of our children from dying. That said, what difference is it to us? Until yesterday, some others ate what we cultivated. Now you snatch from them and fill your bellies."

Aiden could scarcely believe the gravity and sharpness his English had acquired.

"Yes, sir. We are grateful for the jobs you have offered us. We are grateful for the opportunity you have provided us to mend your slippers and polish your straps. We are grateful to have been afforded the chance to die for you in battle, to have been made to bear your secret afflictions in our bodies. By the same token, we thank you for bestowing these famines upon us. For, above all, you have bequeathed to us a tiny sliver of your education. By means of your language, you have opened a door and shown us the world outside. You were the first to tell us that we, too, could hope for human justice. Some of you, at least, treated us like human beings. That is why, despite your selfish aspirations, despite your roguery, despite all your scheming, even brutality, you are gods in human form. And for that, we will eternally be grateful to you." Bowing his head, "I will take your leave now, good day," he said, and left.

Out of the blue, a fear for the young man's safety took hold of Aiden. But the very next moment he reckoned that Kathavarayan knew how to protect himself. His strength of mind would cleave a way for him through any scrub. People like him are never defeated. The threads that conduct them are not of this world. They come from the sky that stretches overhead with its unfathomable radiance.

Where words mirror the heart with precision, where emotion and language become one, where blood and tears are unified—was it from there? Aiden remained as he was, meandering through a clutter of disconnected thoughts. After some time, he got up, raised his hands above his head, and gave himself a good stretch. Then he rang the bell. Before Sam could arrive, he heard the sound of Mackenzie's boots at the door. "Come in," said Aiden.

Mackenzie entered. "I was waiting for you to finish your talk with that Indian. Who is he? A newly converted Christian?"

"No. Why do you ask?"

"Well, the white shirt and a clean-shaven face are typical of converts, aren't they?"

"Oh," said Aiden disinterestedly.

"Captain, care to summon a light whisky? It'll be perfect for this time of the day."

"It's bloody hot," said Aiden.

"Sure, but whisky goes well with the heat, too," Mackenzie replied. "Ask me," he added with a wink.

Aiden rang the bell and ordered Sam to bring the liquor.

"It's these gods in whisky form who keep us alive in this city, don't you think?" Mackenzie continued.

"So, what's the matter?" asked Aiden.

"Something sure is the matter. I'll come to it." He picked up the glass that Sam came bearing, and said, "Cheers." A gentle clink, after which Mackenzie downed his whisky in a single gulp, and set his glass down.

"You always drink like this," Aiden remarked, giving his glass a swirl.

"Look, Aiden, I'm a sailor still. A few days on land, and our chaps sprout seven or eight hands, like the gods here. Their umpteen shirt pockets begin to fill. Lo and behold, they fancy themselves to be aristocrats. They read Shakespeare. And sip delicately on their wine."

Aiden couldn't help laughing. "And the two are the same thing?"

"In my eyes, yes. I met the wife of a magistrate in Chingleput. Some lass who'd laboured at a colliery in England. You can still see the coal under her toenails. The day she arrived here, she transformed into a lady. Takes fifteen whole minutes to remove her gloves. Laughs a petite laugh. Struts like a flamingo. The whore."

"So what?" said Aiden, drawing a sip. "She's a good woman, isn't she?"

"Undoubtedly! For soon as I said, 'You look like a real lady,' she came to me," Mackenzie said with a wink. "But I ought to admit, she's a real coal worker in bed. Uttered the choicest words in the finish. Words only a coal worker could've uttered. I'd quite forgotten them myself. Such delightful words. Too bad I couldn't jot them down in the moment."

Aiden smiled. "Tell me. What brings you here?"

At once, Mackenzie's face turned grim. "The lieutenant colonel sent for me last evening." Aiden could feel his heart quicken. With a faint smack of his lips, Mackenzie said, "To discuss your matter, of course. I'm sure you know what that is."

"The Ice House episode?"

The lieutenant colonel of the Madras Staff Corps, Robert Griffith Lewis, was an unerringly stern man. A perfect replica of the British soldier of yore. An administrative machine was how Aiden had often characterised him in his head. Besides, Lewis, too, despised the Irish with all his heart.

"Right. A contingent from the Ice House already met with the colonel last evening, and lodged a complaint. The lieutenant colonel believes we ought to have exercised more caution in dealing with an American enterprise. He wishes to dispose of the matter before it reaches the governor."

"But—" began Aiden.

Mackenzie interjected. "I reckon it's quite pointless to discuss this. The colonel knows the whole story. All the same, we cannot haul up an American venture. We don't have that kind of authority, honestly."

"What do you mean 'we'?" Aiden demanded, fixing his eyes on him.

Mackenzie met his gaze without hesitation. "I mean you and me, and the governor who protects us as well. We're mere gravel on the floor of the British Empire."

Aiden looked down at his glass. He gave the whisky a swirl. Then, swigging it down in one gulp, he said, "Which is to say, the governor, too, is on the payroll of that American venture, and so the colonel daren't breathe a word. Right?"

Mackenzie hardly flinched. Laughing, he said, "Of course. Not to mention the lieutenant colonel, the bishop, and the chief justice, who could well be on it, too. It's hardly possible that the viceroy is not on it. How does one transact business in the holy British Empire minus corruption?" With a gleam in his eyes, he added, "A businessman bribing the government is no different than a customer tipping a prostitute."

Aiden sank back. Looking him in the eye, Mackenzie said, "Lieutenant Colonel Griffith himself has had a word. If we let Neelamegam go and steer clear of the Ice House hereafter, they're willing to let this pass. So I released him first thing this morning."

"What!" exclaimed Aiden, springing to his feet. "Without asking me?"

With a wave of his hand, Mackenzie said, "Had I waited it would've been too late. You waltzed in pretty late today. And then you were chatting with that young chap for ages."

"You should've asked me. He was my prisoner," Aiden shouted.

"What if I had? Are you suggesting you had a choice? It's the colonel's order."

That truth riled Aiden. His fingers trembled. His throat dried up and thirsted for another drink. "Mac, he's a murderer, you know? He may have committed a twin murder. I wanted to interrogate him. We may never be able to catch him again."

"Oh," said Mackenzie perfunctorily. "Unless the people he killed are white, you needn't worry."

"He killed two hapless workers," Aiden spat, vexed.

"Belonging to a dominant caste?"

"No, they were Pariahs."

"That's it? Everyone kills the Pariahs these days. If they aren't killed, they starve to death on their own. And here you are, kicking up a fuss about it. Was it for this that you hauled him here?" Mackenzie's chair creaked as he leaned forward. "Neelamegam belongs to one of the dominant castes. Narayanan is from the same caste, too. They, as a matter of fact, form the main of our troops as well."

"Mac, let me ask you this," said Aiden. "I know the family you come from. We've lived amid such privation in our villages, too. We fled to America in droves to escape the famine, only to die there, wounded and diseased. Shouldn't we see ourselves in these people, if only a little?"

Mackenzie's face flushed; pushing his chair away with a loud scrape, he got up. "There's no need for that. We aren't some uncivilised mob of savages. Exploitation may have subjected us to famines, but we're high-born. Not barbarians, like these people."

"Mac . . ."

"Don't," Mackenzie said firmly, raising his hand. "I've said what I had to say. There's little else for you to do. Should you have a quarrel with it, speak to the colonel yourself."

Aiden watched him helplessly as he walked out. Mackenzie's shirt was fluttering in the sea breeze; after he disappeared from sight, Aiden sank wearily into his chair. Like a windswept sari rag caught in a tree branch, his mind was all aflutter. Before long, his whole body had absorbed that tumult. "Sam," he called out, and struck the bell. He called for whisky and guzzled it like a man desperate to quench his thirst. Unbuttoning his shirt, he drank some more. Sweat trickled down his back. His gullet burned as though his chest were spewing acid. He drank on and on, like a man possessed.

His head grew heavy until his neck could no longer bear its weight. It tipped this way and that like a helmet on a sword's point. The air was frightfully still. "Hey, Ammasi. Pull the punkah, or I'll shoot you. Pull it, I say!" he screamed at the old man outside his room. The din of the pulley rent the air. "Quiet! I'll shoot you. I'll shoot you, I swear. I have a gun. Yes, I do. I'll shoot you," Aiden raged, his voice sounding alien even to himself. He listened to the sound of the punkah. The entire room swayed along with its movement. Later, when his own snores fell on his ears, he awoke with a start. Spittle had dribbled down his shoulders. As he wiped it off, his mind suddenly conjured up the vision of a white elephant. Wading through his consciousness to recollect where he'd seen it, he submerged again.

When he opened his eyes, the afternoon sun had slanted into his office. It had turned the room into a heat trap. He sat staring at the columns of light for some time. His back was sticky with sweat. His whole body was burning up as though it were ready to melt at any moment. Rising from his chair, he filled the tin basin outside with water and immersed his face in it. He wet the rims of his ears and the back of his neck. Without bothering to dry himself, he returned to his chair. Sam peeked into the room and, seeing that Aiden was awake, slipped in and stood silently. Aiden gestured to him to bring his food.

It was the usual fare—bread, meat, and fruit juice. Once he was done with his meal, he turned his attention to the files in the office and began noting his remarks at the bottom of the letters that necessitated a reply. To that end, he perused some old files. By the time he summoned Arunachalam and instructed him to draft the replies, it was five in the evening. He helped himself to the tea Sam served, then threw his coat on and stepped out. Seeing him approach, Duraisamy brought the horse around. Without a word, Aiden mounted the horse and slowly entered Beach Road.

Ordinarily, he would leave the office only after the evening had turned a deep crimson. On most days, darkness would have set in. Aiden could not tell why he had left so early. He could not bear to remain there. His heart longed for the sea. But, when he did set eyes on it, his mind only mirrored the turbulence of the waves. He wished to banish every single thought about that episode from his head. Duraisamy, Kannan, Narayanan . . . faces darted before him one after the other. He discerned a smile in every pair of those eyes. They had dealt him a resounding defeat. They had humiliated him. And it was done with such subtlety that he felt it only as an utterly private pain.

What aspect would Neelamegam's face have borne when he was released from his prison cell that morning? What else, but the same impassive expression. Joining his palms with saintly contentment, he would have bowed and made his way out. Perhaps he'll laugh about it in the company of his people. They'll recount it for years to come, rejoice, and make merry. I erred. I should've chopped his head off the very moment I captured him. A thousand lawful reasons could be ascribed to it. If I ask Mac, he'll take care of it all. Yet, I cannot do it. If I do, I'll lose all respect for myself. At any rate, there's nothing to be gained from it. Should he have died with that saintly expression on his face, he would've handed me an everlasting defeat.

In the bright sun the white attire of the man who stood in the distance blinded Aiden's eyes. As soon as Aiden saw him, the root of his own restlessness became evident to him. He had indeed wished to meet him. Aiden's inner being had well known that he was not one to move on so easily. As he drew closer and closer, as though intuiting his hesitation, his horse eased to a stop.

"Good evening, sir," Kathavarayan greeted him.

"Good evening," Aiden repeated in a subdued voice. Lost for words, he removed his hat and brushed his hair. "Jesus," he intoned under his breath.

“There is no need to feel bad, sir. I came to tell you just that. At your level, you have operated justly. You sympathised with us. For that, I must thank you,” said Kathavarayan.

Startled, Aiden lifted his eyes.

“My clans people are everywhere. I know,” said Kathavarayan.

Aiden sighed. “The British don’t wish to bring justice to this land, as you seem to believe,” he said. “All we want is peace. A trouble-free climate in which we can carry on our business. If exterminating the Pariahs were the only means to it, we wouldn’t hesitate to do so.”

“We know that too, sir,” Kathavarayan said with a bitter laugh. “There are many learned pundits in this holy land to recommend such a course of action to you, too. Even so, the white-skinned are a cut above the rest.”

“Why, is there not one merciful human being among your own kind?”

Stung to the quick, “We are not sinners crawling in hell that we should seek mercy,” Kathavarayan snapped. “Neither are our fellow men gods. We are human beings. What we need is justice. Equality. You shook hands with me and let me sit level with you, did you not? It is that attitude we seek. No matter how your race might have been earlier, you have reached there now. Regardless of how a lone man behaves, your language and law speak of equality and justice. On the other hand, our language is redolent of shit. Our justice is stained with the blood of the innocent.”

This man’s a poet, Aiden said to himself. It is only they who cross the boundaries of their times.

“Thank you again, sir,” said Kathavarayan, and made to leave.

“Wait a minute, Mr. Kathavarayan,” Aiden spoke up, impelled by a sudden thought. Kathavarayan lingered. “Why don't we go to your neighbourhood and enquire about the wounded workers," Aiden proposed. "Should we manage to find them, I'll produce them before the governor. Whatever he might be as an individual, he is British. He won't be able to ignore the evidence staring him in the face."

Kathavarayan looked at Aiden intently. Then, he said, "To be honest, I think nothing will come of it. Even so, I encourage your wanting to visit our quarters. It is a part of town that no ruler—whether from the East or West—has so much as set foot in. There you will see for yourself the wretchedness man is capable of living in."

Aiden turned his horse around. Kathavarayan led the way on foot.

Only a few seconds had passed when Aiden began to feel a strange quivering in his nerves. His body held his mind the way the palm clasps a cloth fluttering in the wind. He had no doubt that he was doing the right thing, and yet it felt as though he were entering a battlefield; as though he were watching something happen to his own self, from afar. There was not a soul to be seen in White Town, for the most part. Small, sparsely populated coconut groves arrayed both sides of the mud road. Within the groves stood diminutive bungalows, with white walls and red-tiled roofs. A lone black nurse, dressed in a white gown and a cap, walked by. When she heard the sound of the horse, she sprang to the side and clung to the fence.

Two sepoys stood guard near a bamboo barrier that had been erected between White Town and Black Town. Catching sight of the horse, one of the sepoys hastened to raise the pole. The other stiffened into a salute. When the horse crossed to the other side, the muted chatter of the sepoys who were lowering the barrier floated through. In the sparse copses on either side of the road thorn shrubs had taken root between the coconut palms. On account of the saline soil, the trees were wizened and gnarled, and their fronds bleached. The mossy smell of stagnant water pierced the air. Glimpses of tiny thatched hutments were visible between the trees. A red dog—a local breed—bolted out from one of them, barking and howling; it stopped at a distance, and jumped up and down.

Within a few minutes of entering Black Town, Aiden felt a peculiar sense of freedom. It was only when he heard himself whistling under his breath that he became aware of it. He could not make sense of the liveliness he felt in him. Was it the sounds about the place that had set him free? he mulled. It was an unruly jumble of noises. The sound of someone hitting something. Of a water pulley creaking over a well. Of someone launching into a volley of abuse. Of utensils being moved. Of dogs barking, children wailing.

Two children who ran out onto the street chasing each other froze in their tracks, then turned on their heels and scurried away. Buck-naked black kids. They'd secured their long hair with a thin strand of plant fibre. Four buffalos wallowed in from the opposite side, the coconut shells dangling from their necks knocking against one another. "Trree trree," the man shepherding them rolled his tongue, and tapped them with his cane to nudge them aside. Frightened, the horse gave a loud snort. A clutch of children were squatting by the roadside, purging their bowels. "Hey, get up. Off with you," Kathavarayan chided. A smile rose to Aiden's lips. The young man had supposed, Aiden could tell, that his mind had flinched in revulsion. However, his mind was only freeing up further and further.

But why? he asked himself. Was it the chaos all around? Unrestraint was the word that came to him. It reminded him of Ireland. Of the villages where the menfolk, having drunk until their eyelids drooped, rode home at first light and, sitting backward on their horses, broke into song. The land where everyone could be howsoever they wished, anywhere they wished. He remembered the bewilderment London had served him the very first time. The city resembled a well-oiled machine, and its every resident, an integral part of the machinery. It felt as though he were the lone misfit there, as though the other parts of the machine were out to crush him underfoot.

From that moment on, for sixteen long years, all he had done was transform himself into a different machine part. He had gradually melted and reshaped himself. He acclimated to the discipline of the military. He learned to speak in a refined tongue. He became versed in social graces and dining etiquette. By dint of keen observation, he discovered the finest in clothes, accessories, and all else, and took them to be his own. He developed an ear for music and learned to dance. He was convinced of having fully metamorphosed. When he later visited Ireland, the land was foreign to him.

But now he realised he was mistaken. Somewhere, deep inside, the memories of his father had remained in him, like yeast lingering on the rim or in the curve of a bastable. It had fermented him in due course, turning him into a version of his father. If not for that, he wouldn't be delighting in this squalor, in this chaos. He could readily smoke a cigar now, if he had one. He could swill some rum. He could whip his horse and tear through the sewer paths, hooting with abandon. Then, piercing through the skin and flesh of a British gentleman, an Irishman would burst forth.

4

The city that Aiden thought of as Madraspatnam was a stretch of land at most twenty furlongs in length and ten furlongs in width, and he knew it, too. The real Madraspatnam lay beyond his line of vision, swelling and advancing in all directions. Like the burgeoning blaze of a fire-licked grassland, Aiden imagined. Flaming on all sides, it spread wider and wider. As was the case with the vast majority of whites, Aiden had never ventured out of White Town, to which his daily life was confined. It was, in fact, the foremost piece of advice his predecessor, Captain Aaron, had offered him.

"Don't try to understand this peculiar country. It's akin to taking a clock apart and examining its insides when all you want is the time. You'll never be able to grasp its complexity. Tell yourself that your job is to reckon with only those problems that are brought to your ken. Simply focus on solving them as quickly you can, from within your limits. Yes, it's not unlike applying a balm on the burns and blisters on our bodies. But, when there's no way to understand this body, what else are we to do? The body may have its own methods, it'll take care of itself. Aiden, we're here to rule this country, not study it," Aaron had said.

Seeing Aiden smile, he ploughed on. "Captain Addison showed me these papers when I arrived here. These are documents from an investigation he'd conducted in a matter concerning land ownership in the Chingleput region. Eight different people had been appointed to study it. Three of them were white. A police officer, a land surveyor, and an administrative officer. All eight reports were markedly different from one another. That's the story, every time. Ergo, just close your eyes, hold the rudder, and sit still. Let the sea and wind determine your journey," Aaron expounded, tossing the file in front of him. At the time, Aiden had not taken his words to heart. But it wasn't long before it became clear to him that he could do nothing else but that.

Besides, there was another delicate truth every British officer was aware of: the absolute power the British wielded over India was a mere act. The British Army, the police force, the courts, the administration, were all products of bargains made with the vast upper class which, in truth, ruled India. Armies and wars were simply threats employed to bring them to the table. Forking into infinite rootlets, it was this class that had been ruling India for centuries now. Sucking every last drop of blood from the ground beneath, they had fattened, branched out, and cast shadows all around. This was their country. Here, too, as with every other country, government was purely a type of drama enacted by the real hegemony.

"British authority is composed of its lords and merchants. Likewise, this country's authority is made up of its upper castes," Aaron said. "When we step on this soil for the first time, it will look as if the Brahmins are at the apex of all authority here. When you begin to rule this country you'll see that they've been allowed to sit there, that is all. Real authority, as it happens everywhere, rests in the hands of those with land, wealth, and weaponry. Brahmins have been afforded their place in order that they may justify and uphold through doctrine the caste system that pervades this country. That's why they're offered the utmost respect and largesse there is. Should they fail to do their duty, the tower they sit on will come crashing down, along with them.

"The warrior castes, the land-owning castes, and the merchant castes have rationed the authority over this nation among themselves. Scattered far and wide, they jostle with each other for power. The one who brokers a compromise between them and regulates the sharing of spoils, thereby establishing some class of order, can claim the highest seat in this country. Until recently, it was the Nayaks, the Marathas, the Sultans, and the Mughals who did so. In that interval of history when they went to war and destroyed each other, we arrived to fill the spot. Even today, a great majority of this land is under the direct control of these ruling castes. By dividing, intimidating, and enticing them, we stay on top, wresting a lion's share for ourselves."

Aaron would always pick the sea-facing balcony of the beach bungalow at the English Club to dispense his theories. A glass of brandy in his hand, with thinning ice cubes floating on top, and fried pork liver. "No aristocrat back in London can dream of the life we lead here. My wife was quite apprehensive when I brought her with me. I said to her that if she only cracks her knuckles, ten maidservants will turn up in India, one for each finger. She refused to believe me. But now she employs four seamstresses just to stitch her clothes. I reckon she won't be able to live in England after this," Aaron scoffed. After a long, pensive sip of his brandy, he said, "This is the price we pay for that. Throwing a fistful of sand over our sense of justice."

There was one thing that always struck Aiden. British

officers do try to comprehend the country they rule over, but nothing they ever read or listen to enters their heads. Instead, they concoct a theory based on their own life experiences, and go on about it for the rest of their lives. They establish their theory by parroting it over and over. They marshal only that evidence which supports their theory. If there were a hundred thousand British officers in East Asia, there's bound to be a hundred thousand theories, too. Felled by smallpox, cholera, malaria, war, or plain old age, the officer goes to his grave along with his pet theory. Then the theory, too, turns to dust. They say this is a land where a legion of enlightened souls and myriad theories—about human existence, about the universe, about god—have lived and died. They have all melded and mingled into this earth as one, it seemed.

Aaron, though, was capable of crossing those bounds, if only a little. He was accustomed to reading not just the journals of British officers but the canonical works of the East, too. He could have, very easily, made an excellent priest or a professor. His erudition was what drew him to Aiden. The son of a factory worker in Yorkshire. The last of seven children, the remainder of whom died in the plague. "Falling to a bullet through your heart is a death more desirable than falling to settling coal dust, my father once told me," Aaron said with bitterness. The next stage of inebriation. The moment when all pretences wither away and you stand as a mere human being, full of self-pity. Liquor is like Jesus Christ; it brings the soul to its knees.

"Listen, Aiden, what we want is to create a place for ourselves here. Of the two powers that can grant us that, the Brahmins are one. The second is the other dominant castes. Dangle carrots in front of the Brahmins and keep them on your side. As for the others, feed them a little fear, too. Do not, under any circumstance, antagonise the Brahmins.

They'll show us how to keep the others under our thumb." That was the advice he had received from all the officers, ad infinitum. "This country is ruled via the Brahmins. By the kings, until yesterday. And us, today," was Colonel Smith's eternal maxim. "Be careful when you deal with the Brahmins. There will come a time when you'll hear the clang of their metal against our crowbar. Stop right there. Go no further."

As he rode through the neighbourhood, Aiden did his utmost to absorb everything around him, but the unrestraint of the place kept scattering his thoughts.

"The butlers' quarter lies beyond this," said Kathavarayan. "They are our people, too. Although they took up residence here as far back as when British rule was still finding its feet."

Aiden looked up. Big-walled, high-roofed houses. "They seem affluent," he remarked.

"They are affluent. Many of them were engaged in trade with the British Company. They continue to transact business with Her Majesty's government now."

"Oh," said Aiden absently.

"The reason they were allowed residence here was to cook beef. A number of them became beef vendors as well. When the Sepoy Mutiny took place, many large army camps were established here. That was when all the butlers became beef suppliers overnight. Today, people engaged in a variety of professions inhabit this locality. If you take the business of supplying hay to the port alone, for instance, there are seven or eight such contractors here. They are among the richest people in this town."

This was news to Aiden. "Are they not in contact with you?"

"For the most part, no," Kathavarayan replied. "It is one of the unwritten rules in this country. When wealth and office come to a low-caste man, he has to extricate himself completely from his own caste. He has to masquerade as a member of the upper castes. He must outdo them in imitating their customs and mentalities. He must renounce his own parents and siblings."

Aiden sighed. "It's no different in my country. The officers who return to England never keep company with their old society. All of them are hell-bent on becoming aristocrats."

"I would not go so far as to say all," said Kathavarayan. "There are a few educated people among us who are different. They give voice to their fellow people. They strive to unite us and fight for our right to live. If not for that, I would not have appeared before you."

"Right, that's a good beginning," said Aiden.

At the end of that neighbourhood, which was crammed with more than two thousand small houses, the wide road came to an abrupt stop. A narrow path began from there, like a sunken creek of running water.

"The locality that lies beyond this is known as Pudhupettai. That is where we have to go," said Kathavarayan.

"Are there butlers there, too?"

"No. Most of them are sanitary workers, or leather workers. Butlers are our upper caste."

Then, too, Aiden did not register the surroundings properly. A mud path forged by footsteps forked away from the gravel-strewn road meant for horse carts and sloped downward. Tiny huts—with coco-grass thatches and coconut-frond barricades for walls—lined the path.

"I hope you can come in?" Kathavarayan enquired.

"Yes, of course," said Aiden.

"This place is actually a big marshland that fills up during the rains. As recent as ten years ago, the entire swamp was covered in a dense growth of coco grass. There were plenty of crocodiles here by reason of which it was completely deserted. Large groups of Muslims who harvested the coco grass for mat-weaving would come here, from Royapuram. They would lay down a bridge of wooden planks across the swamp, and walk over it to reap the coco grass. Out of nowhere, so many people have occupied this place now."

"Because of the famine?"

"Yes. They have been coming here in droves. None of the existing settlements permit them entry. Moreover, they find it convenient to head to White Town from here, for work. A bigger crowd than this has settled down around the port, where, too, only the salt marshes have afforded them space."

They had barely taken a few steps when the mud path narrowed into a slender trail. The ground was damp and muddied with black slush which, when the horse hooves sank in, released a pungent smell. The residents had spread coco grass all over the ground so they could walk without having their legs sink into the marsh. Stirred by the horse's feet, the rotting, decomposing, flattened grass released a vile, vaporous odour. Suddenly, Aiden's mind conjured up a vision of him entering a gigantic midden. Tall coco grass had struck out from between a congested jumble of garbage-mound-like shacks. Many of them seemed to be no more than largish baskets. Aiden could not fathom how it was possible for people to lie down in them and stretch their legs.

Like an infestation of lice in shaggy hair, domesticated black pigs swarmed the coco grass, grunting and bumping into one another. Naked black children, their bodies caked with dirt and sores, were frolicking with the pigs. Startled by the sound of the horse, they froze in their tracks; then, squeaking rat-like, they scurried into hiding and peeked out from their chosen spots. They elbowed each other and whispered, like chirping mice. As if shoved from behind, a little girl turned up in Aiden's path, eliciting a smile from him. Terrified, the child twisted its lips and began to wail. Several heads poked out of the huts only to draw back in. The entire hutment seemed to be crouching like a hunted rabbit, its body atremble, as though a faint touch was all it would take to make it shiver and squeal.

"I trust you are not inconvenienced," said Kathavarayan.

"Extraordinary!" Aiden remarked. "Truly extraordinary. That human beings are able to live in such conditions is, in itself, incredible. Even wild animals live in much cleaner habitats."

Kathavarayan smiled. "Wild animals choose a place most favourable to them. We live wherever we are afforded place."

Aiden exhaled. Hell is a narrow place—that was the phrase that rose to his mind. Yes. Hell's singularity has to be its narrowness. A skyless narrowness with no exits. A narrowness with nowhere to go, with nothing to do. A narrowness in which man is surrounded by all manner of filth ejected from his own being.

If so, darkness. Hell has invariably been dubbed darkness. Is darkness not a kind of narrowness, too? Light is opening. Light is freedom. Light is eternity. Darkness is a prison. Darkness imprisons our eyes. Eyes are the doors to the soul; it is through them that the limitless cosmic expanse catches a glimpse of the soul confined in a knob of flesh. Darkness bolts the eyes shut. The soul bangs against that door in a helpless fit of tears. It slams its head and smashes it into smithereens, spewing fountains of blood. Imprisoned by darkness, imprisoned by air, imprisoned by the ground beneath its feet, by its own words, its own breath.

For a split second, a shiver, as though an ice cube had grazed his spine. My Lord, how could you set the possibilities of humanity so low, then lower them further, lower than the low! He had seen people battered by bullets during the war, writhing in pain. He had seen bloodied soldiers starve for days on end to an agonising death. To be abandoned, to suffer violent torment, to shed despairing tears and die in heart-rending aloneness was an everyday affair in war. But the one who died there was a human being. A man who knew he was a human being. Is such a death, then, superior to a life where man has no inkling of his humanity? Was it true? Could there really be a life lesser than death? Here it was, staring him in the eye. A life in this feculent, noisome quagmire, ridden with disease, hunger, and fear . . .

The words of this black youth: "*When did we live, that we should die?*" My true Saviour, can there be an existence utterly devoid of this thing called life? What is this experiment you conduct on Man? What do you wish to prove? Man's limits? Or yours? If you only deign to look down here, just for a second, would you not feel ashamed? Would you not fall from your heavenly throne into this hell-hole, like a ripe and ready fruit? Come, but not with your eternally merciful Cross again. Come with a bloodthirsty sword. Come with a monstrous mound of explosives to blow this earth away like a bursting pustule.

"This is where they lived," said Kathavarayan.

It was only then that Aiden became conscious of the warm tears rolling down his cheeks. "Why is it so hot in here?" he asked, dabbing his eyes with his handkerchief.

"As I said before, this is a marsh. It will simmer like a steam pot during the summer. Even so, it is only in the summer that this place is somewhat liveable. During the rains, one will have to wade through waist-deep slush to reach here. To sleep inside the huts, one must sit up all night in the dampness. The population here reduces by a third at the end of every rainy season. The empty spots will be taken by new arrivals the following summer." With a wry smile, Kathavarayan said, "Three fourths of the children you see here will die in the next two months."

Stunned by his unfeeling way with words, Aiden turned to look at Kathavarayan.

Kathavarayan carried on with the same smile. "Were God kind enough to tell us which of these children will be left behind, we could feed just them and leave the rest to starve to death. At least the children who remain will turn out strong, would they not?"

For a fraction of a second, Aiden met those eyes. He felt the grazing of an ice cube on his back, yet again. The smile in those eyes had not spilled over to the face. Those eyes were someplace else, somewhere a great distance away from that smile, from those words, from that man. They resembled the eyes of the fiery Kali, the goddess of Calcutta, who wore a bloodied garland of severed heads around her neck and bared weapons in each of her hundred arms.

"Which of these is their hut?" Aiden asked.

"Others have now occupied the hut they were living in. The famine has deepened in the villages and so a formidable stream of people came here every day. In the beginning, the caste groups from the lowest stratum, to which I belong, were the ones who arrived here. Now, though, other agrarian-caste groups have begun to filter in as well. A roof is of unimaginable value in this town. Those who do not find some form of roof over their head within a month have nothing to do but to die."

Aiden breathed out.

"I have left the children of the couple who lived here in the safekeeping of an old woman in a shack nearby," said Kathavarayan.

The door to the shack was made of coco grass. When they

gave it a gentle push, a slew of human faces stared back at them with gleaming eyes, like bandicoots in a dark burrow. Kathavarayan began his enquiries in a low but authoritative tone. One of them, clad in just a loincloth, stepped out, his palms joined in obeisance. An old man. A walking skeleton. Bones held in place by coiling veins shifted underneath ashen, scabrous skin. Eyes like ripened, pus-filled blisters. He bade Kathavarayan to follow, and walked ahead of him. The neighbouring shack, too, had a clutch of people huddled similarly. Infant faces peered through the gaps between their legs.

"Are there really these many people here?" Aiden asked, as he dismounted from the horse.

"Every hut here is already packed. But it is not night yet. When the men return from work after toiling until sundown, you cannot so much as walk around here."

"Jesus," said Aiden, as a sigh escaped him. The old man disappeared into the hut and came out with two children in tow. The older of the two was clad in a loincloth made of some kind of dried leaf. The other child was completely naked. Ridden with sores, their bodies looked ashen. Their noses, fingers, and outer ears were fleshy and inflamed from raw wounds. Eyes screwed shut, and trembling in fear, they were holding the old man tight. The stench of wound-festering human bodies put Aiden in mind of battlefields.

"These are the children," said Kathavarayan. "I had handed some money out to these people to take care of them."

"Couldn't you wipe them down with some sulphur?" Aiden chided.

"We could, but we would need tons of sulphur. For we would have to scrub every soul in town. Although that, too, would be of no use. We need to provide them with dry dwellings. We need to give them food with at least a semblance of nutrition."

Aiden turned to Kathavarayan. For the first time it occurred to him that the man was mocking him. He had scant regard for him. He had brought him here with the sole aim of insulting him. Then again, his eyes, they prove me wrong. Were I to visit this place a few times, a still more pungent bitterness is sure to froth up and fill my heart.

"Ask them. Ask them where their parents are," said Aiden.

Kathavarayan questioned the old man and the children. Not for a second did the old man part his folded hands.

"They did not come back here at all. There has been no news about them ever since they went to the Ice House that day," Kathavarayan relayed.

"What about those who work with them? Are they here?"

"Yes. I had asked them to come." So saying, Kathavarayan pronounced something in a loud voice. The old man backed up in fright, and held the shack's wooden pole as tightly as he could. Kathavarayan flung his arm out in a manner of ordering and shouted again.

"What's he saying?" Aiden asked.

"That the Ice House workers will not come. Apparently, they are scared."

Incensed, "They must turn up here, right this moment. That's an order!" Aiden shouted.

When Kathavarayan repeated the order aloud, the old man answered incomprehensibly in a broken voice that sounded like half a wail. His head quavered and tears rolled down from one eye. The children sank to the ground and glued themselves to the coco-grass walls.

Within a few minutes, ten or fifteen men emerged from a number of shacks here and there. It seemed as though the huts were pushing, squeezing, and birthing them with great pain. One by one, they streamed out with folded hands. Ghostlike humans. Half-rotten bodies, such as those that rise from a tomb.

"Relay my questions to them and tell me what they say," Aiden commanded.

"Yes, sir!" said Kathavarayan.

"Do these people work at the Ice House?"

"Yes," they answered.

"Are they subjected to lashings often?"

Kathavarayan smiled unexpectedly. The smile remained on his face as he asked the question and repeated their answer. "Nearly every day, sir."

"Oh," said Aiden. "Do they know why the two missing workers were beaten?"

The two of them had come to the Ice House at the break of dawn. Staying out of the overseers' sight, they slipped in along with the crowd and hid in the horse stable, inside wooden crates meant for storing hay. As soon as Parmer alighted from his carriage that morning, the two workers scrambled to their feet, rushed up to him with folded hands and moist eyes, and made to fall at his feet only to find a revolted Parmer—his cane stayed in midair, halfway to striking—turn on his heel and get back into the carriage. Savari had held Parmer's shod feet and dissolved into tears. Parmer kicked him away and pulled his feet in.

By then, Neelamegam had come rushing. Just as he was about to bring his whip down on Savari's back, Parmer raised his hand, bidding him to stop. Seeing Savari hold out a sheet of paper, he ordered Neelamegam to collect it from him. Seizing the paper, Neelamegam commanded Savari to stand away, after which he opened the door of the carriage. As Parmer proceeded straight into the building, Neelamegam hurried after him. Parmer showered a volley of abuse on Neelamegam and raised his hand at him. Neelamegam followed him, scraping and grovelling for forgiveness.

The coachman told Savari and his wife, who were still

standing outside, to make off. They tarried. “No, the Father told us we are to bring him a reply,” Savari had said. The staff-bearing coach escort went after him. “You fool! We'll skin you alive, you'll rot to death. Clear out . . . out now, if you love your life.” Savari vacillated. Thinking on her feet, his wife snapped into action; she took Savari by his hand and dragged him along as she scampered out. Savari stumbled a couple of times as his legs gave way; then he picked himself up and followed her out.

Neelamegam reappeared in some time. Beside himself with rage, and breathing heavily, he cracked the whip in the air. “Where are they?” he screamed. When the horseman answered that he had not seen them, he cracked the whip in his direction. The strap came down on the horseman and the harness. Still wielding his whip, Neelamegam rushed out the gate and raced down Beach Road.

“And then?” said Aiden.

Sometime later, Neelamegam alone came back in a huff, the whip coiled up in his hand. The moment he went in, the rest of the overseers surrounded him. They disappeared into Parmer's room and, without wasting a moment, put him away in the cash vault. Aiden had arrived with his platoon soon after.

After giving it some thought, Aiden asked, “Did Parmer send anyone out before I arrived? Did anyone leave the Ice House?”

None of them had noticed such an occurrence. The cash vault at the Ice House was top secret. They had fetched the key, opened the inner chamber of the vault, and locked Neelamegam inside. That was all.

When Neelamegam was arrested and taken away, Parmer had stormed to his coach, ranting and raving, and departed at once. The instant the phaeton left the premises, the overseers flicked their whips and, throwing caution to the winds, tore into the workers ruthlessly. The air rent with abuse as they scoured every inch of the Ice House and flogged the workers. Later, Varadharaju, the oldest among the overseers, upbraided and quietened them, after which all of them huddled into a small passage and fell to discussing. Ethiraju and Varadharaju left the premises. After that, no work was done that day. The rest of the overseers covered the ice blocks as they were, made sure they were well protected, and kept huddling into discussions. In due course, they emptied out one by one.

The workers learned only when they got back to their huts that Savari and his wife had not returned. They waited all night. When there was no sign of them even in the morning, they began to weigh their options. At first, they had considered informing the pastor. He was a white man; concerned that the black pastors would not apprise him as they should, they had gone straight to the doctor.

"Did anyone come here in search of Savari after that?"

They looked at one another, then said no.

"Did anyone ask you anything about Savari, at the Ice House?"

They hesitated.

"Tell me," Aiden demanded.

"Varadharaju threatened us with whip in hand. 'No one by the name Savari works here. We do not know of such a name or such a man. From now on, this is the truth. Anyone who utters a word in excess will not live to see another day. Clear?' he said." It was the youngest of the workers who had spoken. He had opened his mouth for the first time. Evidently, the others were scared of this short man with a pitch-dark, well-built physique. They did not so much as dare to look at him.

"What's your name?" Aiden enquired.

"Karuppan," came the answer, even before Kathavarayan could translate the question.

Surprised, "You understand English?" asked Aiden.

"I can understand a few words," said Karuppan.

"Karuppan, listen to my question carefully. Did they mention anything about killing Savari?"

"Not in my earshot, sir."

"I see. Did they threaten to kill you if you opened your mouth about him?"

"That was what their words meant."

Aiden bored into him. "Karuppan, I want a straight answer. Could they have killed Savari?"

Karuppan fell silent.

"Tell me; don't be afraid."

"What doubt do you have of it, sir? They would have been killed the same day."

Aiden had not expected such a blatant response. "Don't speak without evidence," he snapped, his face reddening.

"They would have been killed without evidence, sir," Karuppan responded.

"Nonsense!" cried Aiden.

"The whole affair is sheer nonsense," Kathavarayan interceded in a stern voice he had made his own. "People are dying here in great numbers. You have lovingly christened it the 'Great Deccan Famine' for your newspapers, too. In your own estimate, more than two and a half million people have died in the last eighteen months. There is every chance that we will lose another five million. What difference does it make, if of the millions who are to succumb to hunger, two fall to a knife?"

Aiden wished to avoid that subject. "Should you receive any information about them, you must inform the doctor, or one of our constables. Understood?" When the order was translated, they nodded their heads as though in a trance.

"Let us head back, sir. It is getting dark. There are no lights in the area."

Without a word, Aiden mounted his horse. When he nudged it with his foot, the horse turned about, and with a short-lived neigh set off at a slow walk. Karuppan and Kathavarayan accompanied him. Gesticulating with her hands, an old woman hurried towards Kathavarayan from the other end, and, huffing and puffing as she neared him, said something to him. She was a dark old crone, with breasts that hung like two black leather pouches and a body as dry as a cigar.

"What's she saying?" Aiden asked.

"She says you have visited her and her clan for the first time. Therefore you must break bread with them before you leave," said Kathavarayan.

For a few seconds, Aiden sat as he was, as if he could not make sense of those words. The old woman went away and returned with a toddy palm fruit. She stood in front of him, holding a knife. Looking up at Aiden, she said something with great deference.

"She had hurried to the seashore, where she managed to find this. She asks for your forgiveness, for there is nothing else fit for you to eat out here. She implores you to find it in your heart to accept it, and honour them."

As a shudder ran through Aiden's body, he thought he might lose his balance. No sound got past the tightness in his throat. He put his hands out.

"You can slice it open with your sword, and drink the liquid. Nothing will happen to you, it is quite clean," said Kathavarayan.

Extending his arms, Aiden asked the old woman to hand

the fruit to him as it was. She cupped her palms under the fruit and held it towards him with devotion. Aiden received it. His hands trembled, and he was unable to grip the fruit firmly.

"Give me your sword, sir," said Karuppan, holding his hand out. Taking Aiden's sword, he shaved the tough exterior of the palm fruit expertly and gave it back to him.

Aiden did not know how to drink from it. "Just put your lips to the fruit and suck the juice. Do not let your hands touch it," Kathavarayan instructed.

Aiden tipped his head back and drank from the fruit. A drizzle of sweet nectar streamed out. He knew not what to do with the nut encasing the fruit. "Give it to me." So saying, Kathavarayan took it from him and extended his hand in the direction of one of the children lurking in a coco-grass bush. The children held each other doubtfully; as their bodies jostled, a girl child leaped out of the bush, grabbed the nut, and scurried away with it. At once, the other children set off after her in a mad scramble.

The old woman pressed her palms together and mouthed something. "A connection from a past life has been reestablished. You have bestowed honour upon her, she says," Kathavarayan translated. Aiden felt as though his breath had turned to ice and was suffocating his heart. The words in his mind had tangled up and lay like an empty heap of metal. "Let's go," he said, and tapped his feet against the horse. When the horse paced forward, he drew the reins in, and swung around. "Thank you," he said. "Thank you very, very much."

When Kathavarayan told her that, the old woman broke into a smile and brought her palms together. Many heads peeped out of the many shacks behind her. The gaze of narrowed eyes surrounded Aiden. After the horse had taken a few more steps forward, he stopped. "Tell her—tell her to bless me. Tell her she is my mother, Cassidy." But he was unable to prise those words out of his throat. His horse kept going.

When it stepped slowly onto the stone road, Aiden heaved a sigh. He felt as though he had awoken from a dark dream. Filled with light, the road lay wide open in front of him. He shook his head, blinked purposefully, and drilled the awareness of where he was into his mind. Pinning down his hat, which flapped as though it were aching to fly, he tipped his head back and gazed at the firmament. A crimson was overtaking the western sky, heralding darkness. The westerly rim of every cloud was lit up like a tongue of flame. Flocks of birds glided in from the east and landed on the shore. As a gust of cold air swelled forth from the far-off sea, and surged like a horizontal cascade sweeping over everything in its path, his clothes billowed and fluttered. Birds drifted aslant in the air current; coconut palms, with their flapping fronds extended westward and their trunks swaying with the wind, seemed as though they were straining to take off.

"Mr. Kathavarayan," Aiden called out. "The lady back there talked about a past life. Is that something they believe in?"

"Could be. I have heard that phrase being used by many different people. There are several such traditional words in use among those of my caste. Often, these words happen to be a culmination of certain established customs or beliefs. They have been handed down generations," said Kathavarayan. With a sudden laugh, he added, "You remember the first word that the frightened worker used when he appeared before you? That, too, can take on a more expansive meaning, in this light. Our meeting is a consequence of the good deeds of a past life—that is the import of that one word."

"Which word was that?"

"Punniyam. Merit. 'Punniyamundu' is what he said. In other words, the merit of a past life has brought about this meeting."

"Oh," Aiden said softly.

Man, who man would be, must rule the empire of himself; in it must be supreme, establishing his throne. His mind summoned those words spontaneously. "What is this, what is this," his mind railed in bewilderment and pored over them again and again. Shelley! Fool. Drunkard. Daydreamer. A tortured soul who could bear not the poverty and baseness of mankind. The man who, with a burning heart, plunged into a sea as stormy as his turbulent words only to drown forever. All Aiden wished for, then, was to return to his bungalow as swiftly as he could and drink himself into oblivion. He took off his hat and straightened his hair. "Jesus. Oh, Jesus," he muttered. *Man, who man would be*—his consciousness boomed like a magnificent church organ. "Oh, Jesus," he repeated, and shook his head.

"I cannot go any farther into White Town, sir," said Kathavarayan.

"Very well. I'll investigate this further. Till we meet again," said Aiden, as he patted his horse and set it off on a fast trot. As the horse galloped away, those words synchronised with the rhythm of its feet. *Man, who man would be!* He whipped the horse and prodded it with his spur to go faster. The horse swirled its tail and, with a boisterous neigh, reared up, pedalled its legs in midair, struck ground again, and raced away. The swamps, the fields, the trees, all fell back and receded from view. The breeze grew stronger, pressed against his face like cool silk, and obstructed him. Piercing through it, over and over, he kept on going.

Only the butler David was at his bungalow. He who hurried out stopped in shock as the horse hurtled into the compound at the same pace. The reined-in horse circled the front yard with vaporous breaths. Aiden jumped off, flung his whip to the ground, kicked his boots loose, and stormed in. Without bothering with orders, he strode straight to the storeroom.

David came running after him. "Good evening, sir," he greeted him. Aiden heaved the door to the room open. Inside, amid a variety of containers, a rust-red bottle of rum lay immersed in a water-filled wooden tub. When he grabbed the bottle and turned on impulse, his eyes fell on an icebox, close at hand. A crate lined with salt and sawdust, in which lay cubes of ice. With a rage that sprung out of nowhere, he drove his foot into it maniacally.

When he looked up breathlessly, he saw David staring at him, his big white eyes agape in bafflement. "Throw this box out, right this moment," Aiden screamed.

"Sir . . . ," said David.

"Do as you're told. Go. Get rid of it. Ice ought not to enter this house, ever again. Understand? You fool! Do you understand?" he thundered, and gave the door a mighty kick. It collided against the wall with a deafening thud.

"Yes, sir."

Armed with the bottle, Aiden stormed into his room and sat down. He drank unrelentingly, like a soldier who'd just disembarked on land. Twice, raked by nausea, he retched a little. Then, resting his head against the top of his chair, he fell asleep.

Aiden awoke to the sound of speech. Marisa was standing in front of him, knocking on the door with a smile on her face. He stared at her vacuously for a few moments.

"May I come in?" asked Marisa.

"Mm," said Aiden, straightening up.

She entered the room, walked up to him, and placed a

gentle hand on his shoulder. "David sent for me. He said you'd want me today," she said in an in-between accent characteristic of Anglo-Indians.

"Get out! There's no need for it. Don't you dare come here anymore," Aiden screamed in a fit of anger.

Marisa absorbed his rage just as a sandbag receives bullets. "Fine, I'll leave," she said. "But how am I to return in this dark? I'll leave tomorrow."

"I don't care, get lost," Aiden flared.

"I'll be in the bedroom next door," Marisa announced, as she walked away. Pausing at the door, she glanced at him for a fleeting second before she left.

Of all the Anglo-Indian women who came for him, it was only for Marisa that Aiden had developed a special affection. Ever since she started visiting regularly, the other women seldom came. The rest of them were all of the same kind. It was not just their laughter, chatter, and amorous prattle but their moaning, too, during intimate moments that was identical. Flesh dolls fashioned exclusively for the purpose. Human bodies the white conqueror of this tropical nation had sculpted for himself by impregnating the flesh of this land with his lust and tyranny. Like white clay moulds that hold firearms in place, they receive the white man impeccably into their keeping. Chiselled cavities that perfectly fit his every protrusion.

Marisa was unlike that. Though that truth had dawned on him a little late. Never had he cared to observe those women. He would not so much as remember their names or speak to them of anything beyond the mundane. She, too, had seemed no different from other Anglo-Indian women. One day, when he got up in the dead of night to write down a line that had come to him in his half-slumberous state, and lit a candle, she woke up. "What is it?" she asked.

"Go back to sleep," he said, as he placed a sheaf of paper on his desk.

"We're out of whisky. I'll ask David for some."

"There's no need for that." Aiden held the dip pen between his fingers, gave it a light tap, and dusted the dried ink off its nib. Her gaze was fixed on him, or so he felt. He slipped a lump of ink into the bottle and lifted the jug of water.

Marisa got out of bed, walked up to him, and took the jug from his hand; with practised ease, she poured just the right amount of water into the bottle and stirred the ink. He watched her with wonder in his eyes. He must have been writing for thirty years by then, but never once had he got the proportion right. Not a drop of water spilled out. She gave the bottle a shake and placed it back on the desk. As she turned away, he held her hand and asked, "Do you write?"

"Mm," she answered.

"What did you study?"

"Nothing to speak of."

He gathered that she did not wish to engage in conversation. Which, too, was surprising. Women like her loved to reel off tales of poverty at the slightest question about their lives.

When he got back to writing, the line had become muddled. He struck out the words and rewrote them a million times. Disheartened, he leaned back and gazed at the neem tree stirring and rustling in the darkness outside his window. Then he attempted to write again. He crumpled the paper, tossed it aside, gave the dip pen a good shake, put it back in its place, and turned in. The breeze from the neem tree circulated about the room. It bore the moisture of the sea. Before long, he began to listen to the sound of the waves. In that final moment of consciousness, when sleep fell on him and smothered him like a heavy, woollen blanket, a line surfaced anew. Like a silver fish breaking out of the water.

He arose from his bed and wrote it down immediately. As soon as he wrote it, he realised it was only a different construction of the sentence that had come to him earlier. But the sentence had duly turned towards the light now. He felt as though his entire being was aglow in its radiance. He lay awake, repeating it to himself unceasingly. It escorted him to the Irish spring. Drifting like a little bird over the green meadows carpeting the mountain slopes and rippling lake waters shimmering with light, he fell asleep.

When he awoke, sunlight was slanting into the room. It was his wont to sleep in the room that received the rays of the morning sun. Somehow, the rapture he had felt the very first time he had awoken in a tropical land in a room like that had lasted in him to this day. As he stretched his arms over his head and rose to his feet, his eyes fell on the paper. He knew, instantly, that she had read it. When he settled in the hall, she emerged in a light-blue gown, her long, black tresses neatly combed and spread over her shoulders. "Good morning," she greeted him, blooming into a smile. A patently Indian smile cast by ice-cube-like teeth.

"Did you read it?"

The change in her eyes the instant the question was posed betrayed her answer.

"Oh, I was at the desk . . ." She dithered for a bit and then said, "I just happened to see it . . ." Colour drained from her face, and her eyes widened in fright.

"How was it?"

"I . . . ," she drawled, without comprehending his question.

"I asked if you liked it," he repeated.

"Hmm," she answered, lowering her head and averting her gaze.

"What did you make of it?"

"You'd described a landscape, but . . ." She paused, once again filled with trepidation.

"Go on."

She looked up and met his eyes. "When you talk of the mountains, you embody them as words, as ideas. You seem like someone who is standing at the feet of those words and ideas, and gazing up at them," she said.

Aiden beheld her for a few moments. Then, walking up to her, he pulled her towards him and held her in a tight embrace. "Thank you. You're the first human soul in this land to have understood that I write poetry," he said, and kissed her.

She laughed. "But they are the lines of a really immature young man."

"Without a doubt. I write to remain in a perpetual state of immature youthfulness," he declared. "Do you read poetry?"

"I do."

"Where do you get your books from?"

"Our church has a small library. It has only classics, mostly. Father is an avid reader."

"Are you Catholic?"

"Yes. As are most of my people."

"Why?"

"The Anglican churches only want the English," she said with a chuckle.

Aiden sighed and got to his feet. He knew, beyond a shadow of doubt, that it would be impossible to pass the night without Marisa. She would not have bolted the door. She would be waiting for him. The moment he reached her door, he knew it. She was standing on the other side. Looking into her eyes, he stood in silence.

"Come," she said, ever so softly, like a mother calling out to her child, like an escaped moan at the height of lovemaking. He ambushed her with urgent embraces, kissed her hard on her neck and shoulders, and buried his face in her soft skin. In that moment, too, the same verse occupied his mind. *Man, who man would be!* Yes, Shelley could not have lived. There is no inch of earth in this world worthy enough to bear his feet.

5

When Aiden opened his eyes in the morning, his mind raced to the memory of having composed something the night before. He stumbled to his desk, only to realise he had written nothing at all; he had merely dreamed about writing. The verse from his dream rose to his mind with great clarity. But it was dreadfully ordinary. In his dream, those lines had invigorated him as though he had penned the beginning of a magnificent poem, a poem that was to become the voice of humanity. They lay in front of him now as drab and direct expression, like a wingless butterfly. Dispirited, he shook his head, and made his way to the hall. Marisa was settled in a chair. Getting to her feet as soon as she saw him, "Coffee?" she asked.

"Stay," said Aiden, and sat down. She smiled, her teeth resembling an array of salt crystals. "David told me you're delayed," she said.

"Yes," said Aiden. "I'm not going into the office today. In Royapuram . . . wait, don't you live there?"

"I do."

"You said you were Catholic, did you not? Do you attend St. Peter's Church in Royapuram?"

Her brows knitted. "Yes. But I won't be able to make an introduction to anyone there."

"Why not?"

"You know the place women like me are given there."

"Oh," said Aiden. After a second's thought, "Is Father John Brennen a part of that church?" he asked.

Her face brightened. "Yes," she replied, "I know him. He's the one who lends me the books."

"He's the man I need to see."

Worry replaced the smile on her face. "Why? Is there a problem?"

"What? What problem can he possibly expect? He's a white man, too, is he not?"

"Of course. But he is not English. He's Austrian."

"I see," said Aiden, a smile playing upon his lips. "You're rather well informed yourself, huh?"

"The English soldiers created trouble for him on a few occasions. They called him a spy, and made a real scene. I was there."

Aiden knew at once that it was Mac. "Come with me today," he said.

Bewildered, "I came in a small cab," Marisa replied. "It'll struggle to keep up with a chariot."

"Leave the cab behind, come with me in the chariot."

Marisa's lips parted slowly, as though she wished to say something. The tender skin sheathing her lips was parched enough for him to hear them separate. A faint movement ran through her honey-hued neck. As her heavy eyelids slanted towards the ground, like the downstroke of a sparrow's wing, her gaze fell sideways.

"Why? What's wrong?"

"Nothing."

"Is it about accompanying me in the chariot?"

She looked up at him with her clear blue eyes and said, "Yes. Nobody does that."

"Well, I will. Why should I care?"

Her lips curved and parted in a tentative smile. "If you don't care, what's it to me?" she said.

Despite her misgivings, he observed her gradually slip into a girlish ebullience as she readied for the trip. Thrilling with every step, she brought her wooden trunk along and handed it to David. "The chariot. Place it in the chariot," she said, only to run after him and load the trunk into the chariot herself. When the horse swirled its tail, "Aw," she exclaimed, and, gurgling with laughter, scampered aside.

Aiden stood holding the whip in hand while Madasamy fitted the boots on his feet and tightened his waistband. The horse stamped the ground impatiently. The coachman fetched a wooden step stool and set it down by the side of the coach. Aiden came around, opened the door for Marisa, and gestured her in with a flourish reserved for a lady.

"Oh dear," she cried, and leaped back. "I don't know how to do this. I've never got on a chariot before. Where do I place my foot?"

"Here." He guided her. Resting her right foot on the wooden step he pointed to, she held the brass handles of the chariot and made to hop on. As she lost her balance and tipped backward, Aiden held her by the waist, and helped her in with a gentle push. Holding her hat with utmost propriety, she sat down on the blood-red Moroccan leather seat. She was as jittery as a sparrow. She laughed a tiny laugh, like a sparrow's twitter. Checking the seat with a gentle tap, she pressed down on it. She caressed the polished mahogany panels on her sides. She felt the brass knobs, and catching a version of herself on them, adjusted her hair.

"To the Royapuram Peter's Church," Aiden instructed the coachman, and got in.

She took his hand in hers. "Aiden, can I tell you something? I have never been in a chariot before this."

"I can see that," he said.

"Is it very expensive?"

"Maybe. It belonged to the captain who was here before me."

"Oh." A momentary change passed over her face, after which she remarked, "A beautiful vehicle."

"Do you know Aaron?"

"Yes," she said, and fell quiet.

"He reads, too."

Pressing her lips, she turned away. "And hits," she said. The coach jounced, and Aiden bumped against her. The cadence of the wheel altered. A succession of tremors shook the carriage as the horses quickened into a fast trot.

Aiden wished to redirect the conversation. "That's a lovely hat," he said.

Thrilled, she felt her hat reflexively, and said, "Really? Really, Aiden?" The next second, her expression changed. "No. This hat doesn't go with my dress one bit. Arumainayagam came for me when I was right in the middle of some chores yesterday. I wore whatever I could lay my hands on and left."

"Things don't fall into your hands so lightly, you know? When a woman with an eye for beauty throws on a dress in haste, it's bound to be the most becoming."

Her face brightened. Still, she struck his hand playfully and said, "You're lying."

"Lying?"

"Yes, lying."

"Look into my eyes, and tell me I'm lying . . ."

She opened her eyes wide and stared into his, in jest. The

next second, she cupped her mouth with her hand and rippled with laughter.

"Why do Indian women cover their mouths when they laugh?" Aiden teased.

"I don't know. I did it out of habit. Would you rather I laugh like a British woman?"

"Not at all. When they throw their heads back in laughter, the blob in their throat looks decidedly ugly."

"Meenvizhungi," she cried, pealing with laughter.

"What?"

"That's how our pelicans eat fish, craning their necks upwards."

When he joined in her mirth, she rested her head on his shoulder tenderly. "Aiden, I want to ask you something. Please tell me the truth."

"Try me," said Aiden.

"You shouldn't get angry," she said, brushing her cheek against his. It felt as though a kitten had brushed against him.

"Hey, out with it," said Aiden, slapping her thigh.

"Do you honestly like brown skin?"

"What sort of question is this?"

"Most white men don't. The moment they're done with sex, they begin to hit and abuse us. I suppose they feel like they're betraying their wives or lovers back home. They hawk and spit on us. Some fling their boots at us. They rarely let us sleep in their bedchambers. They drive us out, and stay up in their rooms alone, drinking through the night. And lament all the time."

"I, too, have hit you," said Aiden.

"Yes, but you haven't insulted me."

A smile rose to his lips.

"What?" she said.

"One cannot serve as an officer in these parts without

treating others with contempt. To feel superior through the act of humiliating those below us is what we are taught formally and systematically."

Marisa laughed it off disbelievingly.

"I'm serious," said Aiden. "Most of the officers who arrive here are the offspring of ordinary labourers. People who scraped by, driving horses, hauling sand, cutting coal. We are imparted this training so that we may fully efface the demeanour and mindset of the ordinary and see ourselves as nobility instead. 'We are white'—that's the very first sentence we are told in our training, a sentence that is repeated tens of thousands of times afterwards. Before long, it blends with our breaths, and runs without end on the inside."

"Why? Of what use is that?"

"Marisa, what authority does man truly have over man? What's the difference between any of these people, and me? Nothing. Authority is something I create. To breathe life into it, I need to teach myself that I'm superior to them. If I'm to make them believe that, I ought to feel it in my bones first. Only when I believe I'm superior can I assume responsibility for them. From that notion a magnanimous image of me being merciful towards them takes shape. The one in whom superiority, responsibility, and mercy have blended together is the true ruler. You should meet our colonel. He's the prototypical British colonist."

He removed his hat and stroked his hair. "For twenty years now, I've observed the alchemic transformation of an ordinary soldier into a British officer. I'd say it's an excellent way to understand how supremacies developed all through history. When a soldier arrives here, he's a simple rural lad, an admixture of inferiority, docility, dread, and honesty. Slowly but surely, you'll see a change in his body language. He will push his shoulders back. Raise his chin. Do you know, that's the first thing they teach us when we enter the military. To roll our shoulders back and raise our chin. That change in the body engenders a change in the mind, too. The very best of clothing, the very best of food, and an army of servants. In under four or five months, their laughter will change unrecognisably. In place of their formerly polite and soundless laugh, they'll now throw their heads back and chortle with laughter. The fear and trepidation they felt in front of an inscrutable people in a new and unknown land would've dissipated without a trace. They'll begin to presume that they can set everything right with ease. It is when the soldier starts expounding his theories about the country with self-assurance that we can tell with certitude that he is fit to be an officer worthy of governing India. He will have an elementary maxim up his sleeve for every situation. Surprisingly, though, these are the officers who turn out to be good administrators. They truly do solve all problems."

"Whose problems?" Marisa asked, with a chuckle.

Laughing aloud, Aiden said, "Ours, of course. Even God cannot fathom the problems of the people in this country."

"Well, most of the British officers abhor Indians."

"You're right. You can't rule a people without hating them from the bottom of your heart."

"Sounds like a new theory."

"Of course, I, too, have my theories," Aiden said, and rubbed his face with his palms. "But, this is a truth. A truth with which we can easily comprehend every class of authority in this world. What does a rule, a government, even mean? No matter how much it may outwardly speak of equality, justice, and compassion, what lies underneath is plain exploitation. Blatant and barefaced exploitation. If I'm to be a good ruler, I ought to exploit without an atom of guilt. I have assumed responsibility for my people, I am protecting them, I am merciful towards them—I must believe so wholeheartedly."

Aiden turned inwards, and his vision grew hazy as he looked in her direction. "The way to build such faith is to think that the people are lowly, witless, uncivilised beasts. When we despise them, no injustice we bring upon them will seem wrong. We begin to believe that we exploit them only to establish a stable administrative system for their benefit. We torture them so they may learn what duty and discipline are, we reason. In return for being merciful towards them, we expect them to be grateful and loyal to us. And when scores of people succumb to our exploitation, we explain it away as a consequence of their own baseness.

"It's the same story the world over. The people we exploit are the ones we despise and humiliate. There's no country where this hasn't happened. One could even argue that without it, nation-states would not have come to be. If the untouchables meet with as much hate in this country it's because they once were the overwhelming majority here. It is to them that this land belongs. This country has grown by oppressing and exploiting them. Therefore, the ruling class must despise them with every fibre of its being. There is no other way."

Marisa gazed into his eyes. Gently placing her hand on the back of his head, she drew him into her arms. When he put up a mild struggle, she tightened her embrace.

Immersed in his thoughts, Aiden fell silent. The grinding crunch of the wheels echoed in the air. Barking its head off, a random dog chased after the carriage and eventually gave up. Aiden exhaled heavily and righted himself. He glanced at the profile of her face. With eyelids downcast, Marisa was lost in some thought. The heavy silence in her face put him in mind of the Mother of Sorrows cradling the Son of God on her lap. Cheeks resplendent with youth, as though sculpted from teak. A neck glazed by a youthful softness. In a rush, he pulled her to him, and flooded her cheeks and neck with kisses. It was only when her body had received a few that her heart grew conscious of it. With a sigh, she returned to the present. Wrapping him in a tight embrace, she planted a deep kiss on his lips.

"Have we reached Royapuram?" Aiden asked.

"Almost," she answered. "You, sir," she said, suddenly dissolving into giggles, "snuffed all the joy out of riding in a chariot for the first time with all that chatter!"

"Did I now?" he asked emptily, and joined in her laughter.

"You know what I was thinking? Women like me, we sport a hat, like a lady. We attire ourselves in gowns, and speak English. But it's only an act we put on for the outside world. Back in our homes, we're just women who stoke a fire with a few dried spathes of palm and stir up some fish curry and rice in bare earthen pots. All white men know that. That is why they hit us."

"I'll visit your home one day. Make me some fish curry and rice," said Aiden.

"Our food is quite hot, I warn you."

"Do you drink?"

"Only when we go out. We consider it a sin for us to drink at home. Though we do have wine during Christmas."

"Do you recognise this chariot?" Aiden asked, wishing to change tack. He feared that she might yield to self-pity.

"You said it was Captain Aaron's."

"Do you know how it came to him?"

She looked at him without answering.

"This chariot belonged to Joseph Collett."

Her face wore a look of incomprehension.

"Joseph Collett served as the governor of Madras Presidency for three years, beginning in 1717. The man had a great penchant for luxury. He had this carriage delivered all the way from London. It's an extraordinary symbol of history."

Marisa's eyes widened in awe.

"This chariot was crafted by William Felton, an eminent coachmaker. Two of the first eight coaches he made were supplied to Buckingham Palace. This piece alone boarded ship. In his later years, Felton even authored a weighty tome called *Treatise on Carriages*. The uniqueness of this vehicle lies in the connection of the driver's seat and yoke to the body of the carriage through a hinged hub. This mechanism allows the coachman to turn the vehicle with freedom. The carriage, too, will turn smoothly. Since the entire body rests on iron leaf springs, you'll hardly feel a jostle. Back in the day, it was entirely gilded in silver."

Marisa was visibly astounded. Her neck and cheeks were covered in gooseflesh.

"The story goes that when this coach arrived at the Chennapatnam port on November 7, 1718, pretty much all the ladies in Madras Presidency lined up to catch a glimpse of it. The panorama of women waving their hand fans resembled a herd of elephants flapping their ears, someone wrote in the *Oxford Gazette* back then. The carriage was given a viceroy's welcome. It was in this very coach that the governor and his lady drove to the fort that year to attend the Christmas celebrations at St. Mary's Church. It is said that nearly a thousand spectators flanked the streets that day as they drove by."

Marisa pressed her hands to her cheeks.

"When he left, Collett passed it down to his successor, Hastings. With the series of changes that followed afterwards, they eventually junked this vehicle. It was wasting away in the garage with a broken hub. It was only when he read Felton's book that Aaron discovered it. He had it restored with the help of local carpenters, and kept the vehicle for himself. The local carpenters came up with new modifications to the coach's hub. It has run for twenty years since then with no trouble at all." He put his arms around her, lightheartedly. "Therefore, Lady Marisa," he said, "you're riding in the coach that Lady Mary Rose Collett herself travelled in."

Marisa teared up all of a sudden, and buried her face in her palms.

"Hey, what's this? Don't be silly. Hush, now," Aiden said, peeling her hands away from her face. Tears trickled into the webs of her fingers. "You silly twit. What's this, stop already," he admonished, at which she wiped her eyes with a silk handkerchief. Her nose was red. Dabbing at the stubborn tears that welled up despite her, she lowered her head and sat quietly for a few moments; then she looked up at him and, with even, white teeth sparkling, gave a wide smile. "What's this? I reckoned you were intelligent," he said.

"Did *I* say so?" she retorted in jest.

"All the more why I assumed so," he said. She laughed.

An interval of silence followed. "Why did you cry?" Aiden ventured, after a time.

"Just that . . . you said it lightly. But . . . but, it's not like that for me. For me, sitting on this leather seat is . . ."

". . . a big gift, isn't it?"

She looked him straight in the eye and said, "That's right, an unimaginable gift. And honour."

"The seat of the white master," he said, knowing full well that it would provoke her.

"Yes. Undoubtedly. The white-skinned masters *are* my gods on earth. The land they tread *is* holy to me. When you said Collett Sahib rode in this coach, I was covered in gooseflesh. Were I to tell my mother, she'd drop everything, kneel down in front of the Cross, and cry her heart out."

"Collett was here for as little as three years. The wealth he amassed in that time far outweighs what many maharajas would've made over ten or fifteen generations. Returning to England with all that fortune, he dabbled in politics. He even contested the parliamentary elections. Today, too, his descendants are filthy rich. All that fortune originated from this land. Every bit of it amassed through crooked and corrupt means," Aiden challenged.

"So be it. Even then, he would've been far more honourable than these black-skinned curs."

"Is that so," said Aiden, reflexively. The moment the words fell on his ear, he realised how hollow they sounded.

"If you are to understand what I'm saying, you need to live as a slave in some hellhole for fifty generations. You should be auctioned off in the markets. You should be born an orphan in some unknown land." Opening her mouth to go on, she controlled herself, and swallowed wittingly. The notch at the base of her throat moved up, then down. "My mother was born in Ceylon. A sailor who bought her there took her with him, and after having his way with her for a few days, sold her off in Sumatra. Afterwards, when she came to Malaya, having changed many hands by then, a Chettiar confiscated her along with other valuables to recover a loan he'd given to somebody; he carted her away to Rangoon and sold her to a brothel. That's where she had me."

He could not make sense of the expression in her eyes. "Mother taught herself a bit of English. My eyes were blue. It was the sole reason I could get an education, and get by without having to endure lashes. My mother lives in a good house now, and eats three times a day without having to beg for food anywhere. In place of protecting her modesty with palm spathes, she goes to church every day, dressed in pristine white. No one yells at her to move aside. Or pelts her with stones. Or spits on her. The Brahmins lower their heads and walk away in silence when they see her. The others call her 'doraisani,' a term reserved for European ladies. Two of my younger brothers have landed respectable jobs as apprentices on a ship. Just a few more years and they'll be fine sailors. The children they beget will grow up free. They'll receive good food, shelter, and education. They could, just as easily, become fine scholars, or poets, one day. Or grow up to be merchants, build a fortune, and live in bungalows. Like other human beings on this earth, we, too, have something we can now call a future."

Becoming mindful of Aiden's steady gaze, she stopped abruptly. After that, she avoided looking in his direction. Aiden, too, having presumably understood her emotions, held his silence. The carriage trundled on. She sighed and, shifting imperceptibly, announced, "We've arrived."

"Come in with me," said Aiden.

"No . . . I . . . ," she dallied.

"You're coming," said Aiden, and picked up his hat.

"The church will be crowded at this hour," Marisa protested.

"Fine, then, let the crowd bear witness to your arrival as Lady Mary Rose."

She met him with a vacant smile.

The coachman came around and held the door open. "St. Peter's Church, Royapuram, sir," he announced, and lowered his head in a customary bow. When the bamboo doors of the church opened, a dark and scrawny sentry came running, a cloth wrapped around his head in a turban, and a dirty length of vaetti draped around his legs in scallops. He doubled over, his black body rippling with sweat, and, lowering himself below the level of the carriage, hunched to the ground. Aiden stepped on his back and got down. "Come," he said, turning to Marisa. Pulling her white silk gloves on, she parted and closed her fingers. As she was about to step out of the carriage, her eyes fell on the man's back underneath her foot; clasping her hands to her bosom, she withdrew in shock.

"What's the matter, get down," said Aiden.

All she could do was open and close her mouth slowly.

"Oh, this . . . it's a military custom. Get down," he repeated.

As her body palpitated, she leaned back unsteadily and held on to the coach's frame. It appeared as though she might collapse any second.

"Po." Aiden switched to the local tongue as he bade the servant to leave, and, wrapping an arm around Marisa's waist, whisked her to the ground. "You're yet to become a lady. Come on," he said, stepping forward.

Marisa clutched his shoulders. The next second, her face was buried in her palms, and she had broken into sobs.

Aiden stopped in annoyance. "What do you expect? That I should comfort you all the time? Stop, now. Everyone's looking at us."

Marisa kept dabbing her face with her handkerchief. Repressed sobs balled up in the veins in her neck. Very soon, though, she composed herself.

"Come quietly," said Aiden, clenching his teeth.

All of a sudden, she stopped. "I'm leaving," she said.

"Why?"

"I'm leaving," she repeated, in a stubborn voice.

"Because of this? It's his job. All our chairs and tables in the army happen to be human bodies. It's a practice that's come from there. No soldier will think twice about it."

With even greater firmness in her voice, she said, "I'm going home. It's near enough, I will walk."

"Look here . . ." he began, only to be cut off by Marisa.

"If you wish to drag me inside, be my guest," she said.

"All right, all right," Aiden conceded. "Hey," he yelled, summoning the servant.

"Sir," said the servant, arriving before him.

"Escort the lady home," Aiden instructed. "Do you have a vehicle?"

"Only an ordinary horse cart, sir," the servant replied.

"Fine, that'll do." He turned to Marisa, gave her hand a squeeze, and said, "Go on. We'll meet later."

"Of course we will," she said in what was nearly a whisper and, lowering her head, parted from him.

Dressed in a humble white cassock, a pastor-in-training hurried towards Aiden. "Welcome. Your arrival brings joy, Captain," he said in a formal greeting.

"Is the pastor in?" Aiden enquired.

"Yes, he is. He is meeting with a few important people, presently. That said, he won't hesitate to call it off on your account. Allow me to announce your arrival to him."

The young priest led him inside. Aiden had not been to the Royapuram church before. Only once had he even visited a Catholic church—it was during the war in Sumatra. The gaping eyes of the church's statues had made him uneasy back then. He had heard about the church in Royapuram. Some hundred years before, a quarrel had erupted among the Komuttis who plied cargo barges via the Adyar River into the sea. The weaker faction of the Komuttis converted to Christianity. The Catholic Church secured the military patronage of the Portuguese sailors for those who had thus converted. When a section of the fisherfolk, too—who, until then, had lived fearfully under the thumb of the hugely successful merchant Komuttis—converted to Christianity, they became a force to reckon with. This was the first church they had built for themselves.

It was a low brick building. Unlike the Catholic Marian shrines, it had no steeple. Instead, a conical roof made of wood rose over two square brick pillars situated at the front. Atop the cone stood a wooden Cross. Buffeted by the wind, the shroud on the Cross had become entangled around the beam. The entrance, made up of big, ungainly doors fashioned from local wood, was wide open. The coconut-frond roof over the entrance sloped down, displaying its bamboo-like nibs at the finish. In the commodious groves flanking the church, poorly tended coconut palms agitated their lifeless leaves in the wind. A flagstaff, transplanted from a small fishing boat, had been erected in the front yard and was held in place by metal cables. But there was no semblance of a flag in sight. Conceivably, the hoisting of a flag was reserved for festivals.

It occurred to Aiden that many of the objects surrounding the church belonged on ships or boats. That seemed to explain why he had felt a type of foreignness there as soon as he had entered. Two rusty anchors, broken oars, corroded boiler parts. An old coach stood by, minus its horses. A clutch of small palm-thatched huts and a long barn were nestled inside the grove. There were a few cows tethered in the barn. Half-submerged in the mud, there was still more wreckage within the grove. A horse tied to an anchor stood chomping on grass.

A cacophony of voices rose up as though a crowd had gathered there. The young priest led him around the side of the building to a small annex with mud walls. The ash-green walls, with something like the upturned scalloped edges of a curtain traced on them, looked rather strange.

"Please have a seat," said the young priest. Aiden removed his shoes and entered the room. Four plush, low chairs had been laid out in the small space inside. They were exquisitely crafted from wood. In the middle was a wooden platform bearing a posy of fresh blossoms. Aiden sat down and took in the space. Above him, a coco-grass screen, glazed with tar, was installed underneath the thatch roof. From the window behind him, a breeze lifted the curtains up in the air and wrapped him in a silken embrace.

"I'm sorry," said Father Brennen, walking into the room. One look at him, and Aiden could see why the English disliked him. A quintessentially German face. A long, ramrod-straight nose. Lips like a knife-carved wound. Tiny green eyes. He had combed his thin white hair to the left. The use of a monocle had produced two half-moon scars around his left eye. He must have been seventy. His cheeks, dappled with moles and florid little pimples, drooped heavily. The flab under his chin dangled in two loose folds, like a bull's dewlap. He wore a white cotton tunic buttoned up to his neck.

"Pleased to meet you. Your friend Mac is known to me," said Father Brennen.

"For which, I beg forgiveness on his behalf," Aiden responded.

Father Brennen laughed heartily. "I like that. I rarely get to enjoy a refined sense of humour in this place. Thank you," he said, and took his seat. "It's an honour to receive you. Can I offer you some wine?"

"No, thank you. I don't drink wine in the mornings."

"I'm afraid we don't have anything other than wine," said Father Brennen.

"That's all right, thank you," said Aiden.

"I'll treat you to some exquisite Chinese tea in some time. My cook should be here shortly."

"Much obliged," said Aiden. "Your place is small, yet neat and charming. Unmistakably the home of an Austrian."

Father Brennen chuckled. "You mean the colours? The black and red? Yes. There's gold, too," he said raising his eyebrows in the direction of his stole, which was hanging from a hook.

"It's much needed in these parts," he went on. "If you happen to set eyes on the golden décor of the Portuguese cathedrals in Goa, your dreams will be filled with treasures for a week or two. Were Christ himself to appear in front of them, these people will accept him only if he were the colour of gold." He stretched his legs all the way. "I pity the poor. For them, God equals gold. The Hindu temples of this land, every last one of them, were once veritable treasure troves. Even after a thousand years of plundering, they're well-guarded vaults of riches, no less. We, on the contrary, receive parts of wrecked ships as offerings. And we duly auction them away to raise funds."

"I visited the Armenian Church once. The pastors there buzz about like golden bees," said Aiden.

Father Brennen cracked up with laughter. "Indeed. Although, I must admit, façades do serve a purpose. The moment we adopt a particular guise, we become that very thing. According to one Hindu belief, God has taken on the guise of the universe. The moment he dons that garb, he becomes the very universe."

"According to which doctrine? Which sect?" Aiden piped up, wonderstruck.

"Vishishtadvaita, as the Vaishnavites call it. It is a part of Hinduism."

"Aren't they the ones who bow to beasts and boulders?"

"That's what we say," Father Brennen chuckled. "They claim that we bow to the fear of death and sin. Religious belief does man a world of good. It prevents us from seeing other religions and secures our faith." He laughed again, only to stop abruptly. "I do laugh more than is necessary. If I didn't, I wouldn't survive in this place," he said.

"The colonel often says that all laws formulated by the British veil a covert laughter directed at the Indians," Aiden offered.

"I agree. Although I'd say that the Indians are but British in somewhat dyed skin. People are the same everywhere." He sighed. "We had a meeting going on back there. The church members were here. A heated debate on the doctrines took place, first thing in the morning. I'm exhausted."

"A caste conflict?" asked Aiden.

"No, not at all. It wasn't an everyday issue like that. This problem has its roots in theology," said Father Brennen.

"Really?" Aiden asked, unable to believe Father Brennen fully even after seeing his expression turn serious.

"So, the matter at hand is the question of whether poverty, disease, and death are God's command or not. The preachers say yes, they are the wages of sin. Our people, too, believe it quite dearly."

"I see," said Aiden. He sensed that Father Brennen was leading up to something.

"Therefore, they argue to the point of tears that to offer any help to those perishing in the famine is antithetical to God's wish. When a police officer takes a criminal to task, should we not help the police? If we were to help the criminal, would it not be against the law, a Chetti asked me with passionate belligerence. I was unable to answer him."

"Is this to do with the ongoing famine?"

"Yes. I had suggested to the Chettis here that we could do something for the suffering. Let's start a famine pot and serve gruel, I proposed. They stopped short of hitting me. None of those vagrants should be allowed to step into the church premises, they exclaimed. And that I shouldn't abandon my churchly duties and venture to help them. If I do, they'll leave the church straight away, it seems."

"The Chettis may say so. What about the fisherfolk?"

"They're the only people unaffected by this famine. For them, famines are seasons for harvest. They mint money by plying men in their boats, to board ship. A rescue ship that throws a line to a sinking vessel will go down, too, they claim."

"That's hardly a surprise," Aiden observed. "I've seen famines across the world. Nowhere has the survivor helped the dying. Watching a man succumb to the famine unnerves everyone else. They begin to hope that they'll be spared such a fate. Before long, any trace of charity they might've possessed will vanish, too. Then man's innate selfishness will rise to the fore. What little food was available till then will be spirited away to the storehouses. The main of the stock will either be consumed by rats or rot to waste. That's how humans have acted, everywhere, every time."

"Yes, I can't refute that. Millions of Hindus are dying in India. Nevertheless, the deities in the Hindu temples are being doused in food. The Brahmins, and the royalty, partake in feast after feast. They drive the poor out, if they so much as dare to near its vicinity. They aren't allowed to feed on the leftovers, even. Our people, too, share the same outlook. Next year, this church will have completed four summers since its construction. The members demand that we throw a grand celebration, and get down to building a new church, too. They're ready to donate money for such a cause. But they refuse to hand me the money in the fear that I may spend it all on these 'rattle-boned refugees.'"

Brennen shook his head. "Utterly coarse human beings. Don't know the language well, either, and they go on repeating the same thing. The debate was never-ending. I sought permission to carry on with my service, but they were taking me around in circles. That's when Arogyam arrived unexpectedly, to announce your arrival. That sparked an idea. A British officer has come to press me into famine relief, I told them, and made my escape. I'll get away with this excuse this time," he said. "The primary issue is one of caste. This crowd believes that the terrible sins committed in a past life are what cause human beings to be born as vile creatures and untouchables. It follows, therefore, that any help extended to them, or even the mere thought of extending help to them, is a grave sin."

"But don't we call them Christians?" Aiden remarked, perplexed.

"How so? You mean to say there are untouchables in the Anglican churches?"

"Not in my church . . . ," Aiden lingered.

"Precisely. Here, too, they have their own designated places of worship. Though they are yet to be built in this town."

Frustrated, "If that's so, why bother with converting them," said Aiden.

"For the faith. We offer them what we believe in. The mercy and compassion of Christ," said Brennen.

"And you suppose they accept these from Christ?"

The look in Brennen's eyes changed in a trice. "Captain, how many people in this world, do you think, have truly accepted Christ?" he asked.

Aiden looked away.

"You know it yourself . . . back in Britain, do the launderers and coal diggers live amid the rest of the people? Will a nobleman sit in a coal miner's church, even if Christ appeared before him and bade him do so? Why, consider the Christian priests who come here, for a moment. How many of them truly know of Christ's compassion? This famine is God's blessing, a pastor told me yesterday. He insisted that a path has opened to draw the people of this land towards Christ, that the famine has thrown open all the doors that were closed here, so far. If this is how God recruits people into his fold, I told him, he's not God, but the devil. Affronted, he left in a huff."

Father Brennen exhaled slowly. "People are like that the world over, with egos like black boulders. For thousands of years, Christ's compassion has been falling on them like rain. Someday, they will thaw, if only a little. Someday, they will break down. We ought not to think beyond that. We have not been conferred such a right."

"The Jesuits' faith never fails to fill me with awe," said Aiden. "Still, I ask you, why don't you issue an order to these Indian Christians in the name of the Cross? Why don't you command them to shed their caste?"

With a laugh, Brennan said, "Captain, a hundred years ago, the man who ruled Madras as governor of the British East India Company was a gentleman named Joseph Collett. You must've heard of him . . ."

"Of course," Aiden piped up, incredulously.

"There was a major caste riot that took place here, during his time. Presumably, it was the first serious caste-related conflict the British encountered in southern India," Brennen continued. "It was not a conflict you could dismiss easily. Collett was so stunned, he was all at sea. You can read his account of it in the personal essays he wrote in later years. Do you know which were the castes involved in the riots back then?"

Aiden shook his head.

"It was a clash between the Chettis."

"What? Why?" Aiden exclaimed with genuine surprise.

"Every caste here is divided into hundreds of subcastes.

The ones we call Chettis are merchants. However, the type of trade they're engaged in determines their station. Those who trade in jewellery and food grains are high-caste Chettis. The ordinary grocers are Komutti Chettis—it was they who ventured in their barges long ago to sell their merchandise to the Portuguese ships. When Madraspatnam was formed, it was the Komutti Chettis who established residence first. But, very soon, the rest of the Chettis arrived here, too. Although they were smaller in number, they had a wealth of capital at their disposal from transacting business with the kings. The East India Company promoted them in order to tease the capital out of their hands.

"It didn't take long for these Chettis to become the master tradesmen of this town," Brennen carried on. "They built numerous temples around here, which the Komuttis, too, began to frequent. That upset the Chettis."

"Did they belong to different faiths?"

"No. Which was precisely the sort of thing that drove Collett mad. Both factions belonged to the same religion. But the Chettis were part of the right-hand castes, and the Komuttis, the left. All the castes here were split into two divisions back then. On what basis, no one knows. It was an arrangement made a thousand years ago, when monarchs ruled this land. The right-hand castes were considered superior. So when the left-hand castes entered their temples, they cried foul and claimed it was 'polluting.' They sent their men to rough up the Komuttis who visited their temples. They had the temples washed with the water from the holy Ganga. The Komuttis were larger in number. Moreover, they were the kind to steer their boat straight. They retaliated, attacking the Chettis. Lootings and killings followed for months on end. The Chettis locked up their homes and warehouses, and returned to the southern Pandya country.

"Till then, Collett had not intervened in the matter in any way. However, when the trade stopped, he was left with no choice. He sent his men and asked the Chettis to come back. They refused. He passed an order and impounded all their properties. He captured twenty, supposedly, Komutti leaders and hanged them from the trees on the banks of the Adyar River. The riots came to an end. The Chettis returned shortly after that. Then Collett promulgated an order, which to this day remains the British policy on caste. According to the proclamation issued in 1719, the various Hindu castes were ordered to follow their own customs. They were to strictly refrain from interfering in the customs of other caste groups. The left-hand castes were to stay away from the temples of the right-hand castes."

"How extraordinary," Aiden murmured. "Though, as you said, that really is the policy we still follow."

"Honestly, it is British rule that has cemented the caste structures in this country to this degree. One could argue that Collett had it in his power to outlaw caste differences altogether, had he so wished. However, he was solely guided by the profit motive of the East India Company, and his own self-interest. He issued an order that no one was to interfere in affairs of caste, and that the caste hierarchies should remain untouched," said Brennen.

"In reality, the caste structures of this country, as if cast in mud, have moulded and shape-shifted all the time," Brennen continued. "If a particular caste group managed to put up a fight, grab some land, and find a foothold, they could readily rise to the station of a high caste inside a few generations. Several caste denominations did make progress in this manner. The Nayakas, too, who ruled all of southern India, were originally pastoral clans that rose upwards through the ages. It's been written about extensively; you must've read of it, too. As it happened, Collett's order solidified the caste hierarchies of 1719 and gave them rock-like permanence.

"Soon there came a stage when it was plain to see that the mighty army of the British East India Company would thwart and crush any budding change in the caste structures. No one enjoyed perpetual ownership of land in this country at that time. Those who had the muscle could usurp it whenever they wished. The British East India Company made land ownership permanent. Think about it; the company offered every scrap of land in this place to those caste groups who already wielded power in the region. In return it exacts tributes and taxes from them. If anyone dares to challenge the authority of the faction in power, the entire might of the company's army will roll in to protect it. As a result, every chieftain and feudal lord who was earlier waging a daily battle to hold on to power has acquired an emperor-like stature now. Regardless of their murdering and marauding, so long as they pay their share of tribute, the British government will uphold their authority. No change is possible now."

It occurred to Aiden that he had turned over everything Brennen had spoken about in his head previously. Still, he could never have articulated it as succinctly as the pastor had. Brennen must have repeated these things to himself several times.

"Do I sound like I'm giving a sermon?" Father Brennen asked with a chuckle.

"No . . . these are things I, too, have contemplated before," said Aiden.

"I have travelled down south," Brennen continued. "Madras Presidency is ruled by hundreds of tyrants. The land is being ravaged by the famine. Still, they fill their palace chambers with women. Decked in gold and pearl, popping pills for digestion, regaling in dance and music, they thrive like pigs in filth. Every day, they throw a feast in the palaces. British officers, magistrates, and clergymen alike go there and while away their time, feasting and drinking, passing lewd remarks, and making merry. They care two hoots about hell. Why, where they live is hell itself." With a face flushed from a rush of blood, and moist eyes, Brennen shook his head. "Jesus, my Redeemer," he moaned under his breath.

"Were you to take part in the governor's banquet just once, you'll realise this is nothing," said Aiden. "Grains meant for the victims of the famine are being shipped away, bag after bag. While frozen water from the West, handled with great care and concern, is transported all the way here. One shipload of ice equals eight shiploads of grain."

A slow breath left Father Brennen. "I figured that's what's brought you here."

"Yes, I visited the slums of those people yesterday. When I saw the life they live there, everything else seemed trivial. All the same, I wish to discuss the issue with the governor."

"Discuss what?" said Father Brennen, dispiritedly. "Do you really think the duke doesn't know what's happening here? Or the reasons behind it? What can you possibly enlighten him about?"

"Father, you're yet to apprehend how British administration functions. We've chosen to administer this country through a policy of nonintervention. The truth is, we don't know this country at all. To be brutally honest with you, even I didn't know it until yesterday. What I have faith in, though, is the duke's conscience. He can do something, and whatever he chooses to do will go a long way. When a tiny morsel from an elephant's feed spills on the ground, it's enough to sustain an army of ants; so goes a Burmese proverb."

"They use that here, too," said Father Brennen. "But what are we going to do with the Ice House issue?"

"I don't know. However, there's a beginning in there somewhere. Frankly, that's where I intend to start. I'm going to tell the duke exactly what I saw. I'll tell him how the workers are harassed there. He has received word of my intervention already. I can use that very reason to meet him. I'll tell him that they released the man whom I'd arrested, without my permission. I'll explain what happened."

"Do you write poetry?" Father Brennen asked, out of the blue. Aiden did not answer. "Dreams imbue your words," he said. Leaning forward a fraction, he said, "Compassion and justice are but dreams in this day and age. Shelley turned a handful of the British into such dreamers before he departed. More often than not, they've drunk themselves to death."

Although that riled up Aiden, he checked himself.

"Do as you deem fit. Informing the duke is a good thing. Whatever he does, even as an eyewash, will be a big feat," said Brennen.

"I trust him," Aiden repeated.

"What do you know about the Duke of Buckingham?" Father Brennen posed.

Aiden fell silent.

"If I'm not wrong, you're Irish. You haven't a clue about British nobility. Will you believe me if I were to tell you that the duke is the biggest debtor in all of England today?"

Aiden was caught off guard. No, he answered with a shake of his head.

"That debt is the capital his father expended towards his parliamentary pursuits. His palace and his estate are sinking. Nonetheless, the duke has remained loyal to the Crown, serving it in a number of places. They've sent him here as reward for the work he's done thus far. He has to discharge all of his father's debts before his five-year tenure in this place comes to a finish. That's easy enough. Every governor comes to India with the sole aim of unearthing a treasure. The trouble is, though, that he's the Duke of Buckingham. He cannot stoop so low as to strike a bargain with the kings and merchants. He cannot threaten the small-time landlords to extract his share. He has to appoint agents to do the dirty work. Only what ice is left over after thawing in their hands reaches him."

Aiden realised, then, how difficult it was to listen to the blatant truth.

"More than a year has passed since his arrival. I hear he hasn't made much yet. There are no fewer than twenty or thirty men raking in the riches in the name of the duke. They're, in effect, paying off the debts their children and grandchildren will contract in the years to come. The duke is anxious about not making enough. Usually, it's the lady who takes charge of such collections. His wife's passing has rendered the duke a loner. The avarice of a noblewoman is yet to be kindled in his daughters. The duke's oldest daughter, Mary, is the only one here. She's interested in nothing other than music. She's a pianist who excels at playing for their guests. That's hardly the job of a lady, now, is it? Shouldn't she be seated atop the money chest!" said Father Brennen.

Enervated, Aiden wearily shifted in his chair. "I feel I ought to start somewhere. Do something," he said.

"That's a noble feeling. There're precious few in this land who feel such a stirring in their hearts. The rest close their windows to shut the stink out and perfume their rooms with incense. What do you propose to do? And how can I be of help?"

Aiden cleared his throat. "I was told that you gave the two workers a letter of recommendation. Can you provide me with a letter stating so?"

"Of course. Certainly. It's my duty, too," said Father Brennen. "They were starving to death. I wished to do whatever was within my powers to help them. The poor souls," he said.

"They haven't returned till now. I'm told they could've been murdered."

Brennen laughed. "All who die in this country right now have indeed been murdered," he said.

"I will apprise the duke of this. I'll explain what happened. The famine is driving millions of people to the city. Like a flooding lake, the city has expanded in all directions, to the point of bursting. Our people, in the meanwhile, exploit the hapless situation of these workers to make a great killing. They work them to death and dispose of them like waste. The Ice House, too, does the same thing. We can start with them for now. The duke can direct them to provide the workers fair wages and ensure their safety. If they do follow it, it might become possible to enforce the same practice in the businesses run by the Chettis, too. Besides, I'll also plead with the duke that the government must do something for these people," said Aiden.

"The most favourable aspect in your plan is that the Ice House is an American venture," Father Brennen said with half a laugh. "The crocodiles, bandicoots, and rhinoceroses in the duke's office will love it. Such a directive will allow them to arm-twist the American company. It may even allow them to spin a history of having upheld justice during the famine. If their greasy minds fail to recognise that this weapon may well turn against them, action is quite certain. You'll be able to modify the order the duke issues in this matter, into a public notice."

Aiden sighed. "Even if only half of what you said were to happen, I'll be happy."

Brennen's cook eased into the room like a shadow.

"Mariyaan, can you make us some tea?" said Brennen.

The cook nodded.

"Did you teach him to make tea?" Aiden asked.

"I taught him everything he knows. He cooks quite well, too. Though he still nurses a discontent about not having had the opportunity to fix a great meal." The clanging of dishes arose from within as Mariyaan set to work.

"I came here with Marisa," Aiden ventured.

"Marisa . . . Oh . . ." said Brennen, "She's a nice girl. Reads a lot."

"Yes, and hence, my friend," said Aiden.

Brennen seemed disinclined to discuss her. "Let me write you the letter. Whom should I address it to?" he asked.

"To me. Two people from your congregation—"

"Wait," Brennen interjected. "They don't belong to my congregation."

"What?" said Aiden, taken aback.

"Yes, we have only Komuttis, Anglo-Indians, and the fisherfolk here. They'll never allow these people entry. There isn't a single untouchable in my parish."

"I had assumed that applied only to this church."

"It applies everywhere. If I allow them entry, I'll be forced to disband the congregation."

"But, Kathavarayan told me . . ." began Aiden.

"Ah, there's a spirited young man," said Brennen. "He dedicates his life to his people. He thinks deeply about why they've come to such a situation. We beget only one or two like him in an entire century. They are never understood in their lifetime, though."

"I was told that those two were Catholics," Aiden pressed.

Brennen smiled. "Like Catholics, you mean. Some foolish priests who set out on spiritual harvests convert these people using one ruse or another, and hang the Cross around their necks. After which, they never look back. So far as these people are concerned, they see no change beyond the change in their names. The same godless life. Occasionally, they'll seek out a pastor on account of some trouble," he said. "Kathavarayan sent those two to me. He had assumed they were Catholics."

After a moment's consideration, Aiden said, "If their names are not on your parish's register, nothing you say about them will carry weight under law, will it?"

"What is it that you're asking me?" said Brennen. "You want some evidence to show that two such people even existed, am I right?"

"To tell you the truth, yes, that's what I'm looking for."

"Then won't it suffice for me to state that I know them?"

"What if the company refutes it?"

"Young man, even if you should dig out the cadavers of the two workers from under the company's nose, they won't bat an eyelid." He dipped his pen in ink and began to write.

Mariyaan brought the tea. "I take my tea with palm sugar, the native sweetener. You can try it, too, if you wish," said Brennen, as he wrote.

"I do not take sugar," said Aiden, slowly lifting the cup to his lips.

6

Aiden returned to his office only after the morning sun had intensified. He proceeded to his desk, post-haste, and began to compose a letter in his own hand. He inserted the letter, which was addressed directly to the governor of Madras Presidency, the Duke of Buckingham, in an envelope, sealed it, and stamped it with lacquer. Then he called for Sam and ordered him to summon the messenger. As soon as the man came in and made a salute, Aiden said, "This letter should reach the hands of the duke himself. Is that clear?"

"Yes, sir," said the messenger.

After a moment's thought, Aiden inscribed "Urgent and Extraordinary" on the envelope, in red ink.

"Bring a note of acknowledgement from whomsoever receives it."

"Yes, sir." The messenger saluted, and left.

Aiden's mind was in disarray. Unable to think coherently, a tumult had beset his stomach. His act was a serious violation of British administrative protocol, and a punishable offence, too. Then again, he could see that it was the whiff of adventure in the act that had impelled him to do it. Seen in plain light, the issue he wanted to raise needn't go so far as the colonel at all. Leave alone the arrest of an Indian overseer, even his killing, was ordinarily a matter that could be laid to rest by a sepoy of the local police. That said, were the duke to take a humanitarian view of what he had to say beyond the immediate issue, he would be pardoned.

Aiden began to doubt if he'd written eloquently enough to convey his intent. He had merely stated that he would explain the background to the Ice House incident in person. Should the duke simply forward the letter to the colonel again, he was sure to summon Aiden forthwith. The colonel would have but one thing to discuss with him—his transgression and the defiance it contained. Irish insolence is what he would put it down to.

Aiden got to his feet restlessly. Should I call the letter back and read it again? he brooded. But the messenger would have covered a fair distance already. What if I send someone at once to intercept him? He rushed out. Narayanan, who was standing outside, came up to him. "Sir?" he said. Nothing, Aiden signalled with a shake of his head, and turned back in.

What do I do? Let whatever happens happen. As he ruminated over it more and more, he could tell that nothing good would come of it. British administration was, in itself, an assemblage of such hurdles. At the very lowest of its reaches, the village guards resolve every problem in sight, seldom letting them travel upwards. Not even murders. It was only in spite of them that a problem reaches the lowest-ranking British sepoy. And, in spite of the sepoys, the officers. At every level, the person in the employ of the British ought to ensure that none of the problems reach his superior. Were they to rise beyond him, it would only mean that he was incompetent, and deserving of punishment.

For an issue to reach the governor, therefore, it must

surmount hundreds of such hurdles. That is when the governor will be in a position to deal with it. Only then will the matter be of such extraordinary importance that it behoves his attention. By the time it reaches him, it would have gathered as many perspectives as would enable him to make a decision. The matter could well be delayed to the point of irrelevance, too. The governor, in British praxis, was someone who ought to do no more than manage high-ranking officers. All he had to do was govern his own administration, not the country or the people who were in turn governed by it. Aiden's breath escaped him without a trace, and his body turned limp. "Sam," he called out, as he sank into his chair.

Drunk to the point where acid seethed in his stomach like fire, drenched in sweat, Aiden unbuttoned his shirt, pulled it up by the collar, and leaned back in his chair. I've been drinking to excess these past few days, he reminded himself. Drinking through the days and the nights. *Almighty Tyrant! And give thanks to Thee! Drink deeply—drain the cup of hate; remit this—I may die!* Yes, undoubtedly Shelley. *Drink deeply—drain the cup of hate!* Here and now, *this* is the hymn of my own destruction. The bird that pecks at me and bores through and through. The droplet of acid that trickles on the terrain of my mind, rousing it to a new dawn. *Drink deeply—drain the cup of hate!* Every drink is drained from the chalice of hate, is it not? I'm dying a certain death! Ye almighty, look down. You tyrant, look down. Here, cradling his heart like a candle flame, a man thaws and melts. Here, like a worm lodged in a fruit's core, a man nurses an idea.

O, drain the cup of hate! I might perish this very moment. A fragile cup filled with the spirit of hate, this. Shelley, you will take my life, too. You, who have felled many thousands of this century's youths. You, who led by example and ventured into the turbulent sea in a ruptured boat. Why did you do that? Did you wish to underscore all your deeds with one symbolic flourish? Did you wish to etch yourself in history as an enduring metaphor? Daring to set out in search of your own tumultuous vistas, you put an end to yourself. You would never have lowered your sails even in that tempest, I know.

But, Shelley, what *is* that depth you went to? When you took wing and plunged down, the sky stretched ahead, dark and murky. Shelley, you fool, you drunkard, you madman. There, in the deepest depths, all that had sunk to the bottom from the very day this world came into being was cushioned on the muddy floor in a motionless wait for your arrival. As you descended, a fleeting welcome, a quiver of shadow and light, rippled through them. You are one among them now, are you not? Stay buried. In the mud. In centuries of mud. In the dredges of history. Even so, you will not decay. Held in a tight embrace by the infinite weight of the ocean, you will lie there, motionless. For eons and eons. Someday, humanity will plumb those depths to reclaim you. Will you, then, shrivelled and hardened like a pearl, be waiting there, radiant?

Drink deeply—drain the cup of hate! Shelley, what you filled and left behind were bitter cups of poison! You Tyrant, Ye Almighty, thanks be to you. You madman, you poet, you drunk, thanks be to you, too. Here, in this moment, I'm dying a silent death. My thoughts are dying. My arms and legs are dying. All around me, this roof and these walls are all dying. My heart blazes as fire, as conflagration. Shelley, here I am, burning from head to toe, turning to ash. For that, too, thanks be to you.

When Aiden opened his eyes, the messenger had returned. He rose to his feet, wiped his mouth, walked straight to the washbowl, filled it with water, and immersed his face in it. Cupping the water in his hands, he splashed it over his head and neck. He delayed having to hear what word the messenger bore as much as he could. Surely, he brings unpleasant news. Yes, of course. What else could it be? Nothing else. Just that. Ill at ease, he pressed his fingers to his temples. After wiping his face, he turned around, and stood silently in place.

The messenger greeted him and held out an envelope. William Russell, private secretary to the duke, had received the letter on his behalf. "It will be reserved for the personal attention of the duke," he had written in a scribble.

Aiden sighed. Every muscle in his body, strained from bearing a load, slackened little by little. He read the note twice over. Letters in black ink slanted in a cursive hand. Letters tossed nonchalantly, and yet with utmost precision. They dripped with assurance, authority, and indifference. Gone are the days when swords and guns ruled the world. What will rule over it, henceforth, are these words.

When the messenger left, Aiden ordered for tea. With his own hands, he threaded the note of acknowledgement into his private file. Afterwards, he stretched his arms above his head, closed his eyes, and, shaking his legs, began to string together the words he ought to employ when meeting the duke. When the tea arrived, he got up and, gently sipping on his brew, gazed at the ocean. Light itself pulsated as sea. Little by little, doubts began to cloud his mind. The letter had not reached the duke yet. The note that Russell would append to his letter would determine the duke's actions. Russell was patently Anglo-Saxon. Whatever the circumstance, Aiden would never be more than an Irishman in his eyes.

By the time Aiden placed the cup on the table, he had made up his mind. The meeting was going to be very adverse. It could thoroughly deflate him. Don't lose your calm, he told himself. Don't give vent to your emotions. For pure-blooded English noblemen such as the duke, emotions are but waste ejected by the body.

For a while, Aiden had not the faintest idea of what to do next. Just like that, every plan he had to present his case turned absurd and lay lifeless in front of him. Still, it was an occasion he had to rise up to. Perhaps the biggest moment of his life.

Suddenly, he was struck by a notion. It was the self-same comment he had made to Father Brennen. This issue was merely a pretext for him. What he really wished to tell the duke about was the type of life these people lived. No, the type of death they had to endure. If that be so, why must he begin with this incident? Why not start directly with what he intended to say? Why not talk about it, plainly and clearly? What would happen if he did bring this up in response to the duke's enquiries about the incident? Russell would address him, with his look of respect seamlessly morphing into censure, "Forgive me, but I doubt you're putting the duke's time to good use," and nip the conversation right that instant. Even so, the satisfaction of having said all that he wished to will prevail in him. Even if he should be punished for it, it will hold some meaning.

But what was it that he had to say? He had visited a small slum in his jurisdiction, and seen how its people live. He could only mouth lines that would make the duke extend his silk-gloved hand, tilt his head, and tell him with a smile on his lips, "The needful will be done." No, I haven't neared the eye of the storm yet. All I have witnessed are the waves at the shore. Aiden shook his head. Yes, that's the only way. He ought to get inside it.

Aiden rose, put on his hat, and stepped out. The handlers had brought his horse around. It welcomed him with a toss of its head. It tapped its forelegs on the ground and snuffled loudly.

"Dorsamy," Aiden called out, his accent lending a strangeness to the name. He instructed Duraisamy to harness the carriage. Boarding the vehicle, he ordered it to be driven to St. Peter's Church in Royapuram once again. He realised that his heart had already settled on a course of action. Sighing, he took off his hat and ran his fingers through his hair. Resting his hat on his knee, he leaned forward anxiously and stared at the marshy cheeks of the backwaters hurtling backward.

The midday sun had spilled the shadows of the coconut palms right at their feet. The birds were all huddled in the scrub. The absence of bird sounds made it seem as if the entire land was aslumber. A dog chased after the carriage and barked, eliciting an echo of barks from here and there. The dogs of this land are unlike their European counterparts. Although they depend on human beings, they live as a distinct social order on par with humans. There are three great societies of creatures in India—humans, dogs, and crows. They feed off each other. The people here worship them as godforms. They won't hesitate to share what last morsel of food there is with this common, ruddy mutt here. There are many who eat only after they've offered the first food of the day to the crow, at the break of dawn. But why am I thinking about all this? What thoughts are these? Aiden smiled to himself.

Brennen was at the church. He betrayed no hint of surprise on seeing Aiden. When Aiden had said his greeting, the pastor crossed himself customarily. "Come in," he said, leading him inside. As soon as Aiden sat down on the low chair in the pastor's hut, there emerged a sort of undefinable intimacy. Brennen removed his cassock and hung it up. "Tell me," he said, as he settled into the chair.

"I'll be meeting the duke tomorrow, most likely. At night," Aiden informed him.

"Oh," said Brennen. "I must admit my calculations were

rather inaccurate. I thought he'd forward your letter to the colonel."

"That's not completely out of the question. However, there's now a greater possibility that the meeting will take place," Aiden responded.

"Has the duke given a time?"

"He doesn't stay up during the day. He rises only in the evening. By the time he concludes the important meetings and gets on to other matters, it will be dawn. Which means I'll only be meeting him in the early hours of the day after tomorrow. I must add more weight to my case by then. I need more information, and firsthand experience."

"Firsthand experience? You need do no more than ride your horse around the city for that."

"I want more facts, more details. I must arm myself with a comprehensive report."

"If you so wish, you can visit the couple of hospitals and orphanages we run, tomorrow morning. Our efforts are small in scale, but they should serve your purpose. If you'd like to, we can visit the Danish mission's hospital, too."

"I want to see the famine with my own eyes."

"That would require you to travel to Chingleput."

"Why? It is to this city that people come to take refuge from the famine, don't they?"

"Those who are too weak to work do not come here."

"Oh? Why?"

Brennen threw him a piercing look, but said nothing.

"It's a genuine question."

"They aren't allowed entry."

"What? By whose order?"

"How would I know? Maybe it's the decree of the queen who rules this world."

Aiden fell silent.

"If I've blasphemed the Crown, you must excuse me."

Aiden smiled weakly.

"You can see the famine in all its glory if you head to Chingleput tomorrow morning. Every road that forks away from this city is the famine's dance floor. It'll be impossible to return by the evening, though."

"I'll leave right away. Even if I were to depart from Chingleput tomorrow afternoon, I'll return by nightfall."

"What do you want from me?"

"Can one of your men accompany me?"

"I don't have a problem sending one of my Indian staff with you. But—"

"Yes?"

"You must assume responsibility for him. That's the only thing I ask. He should return safely."

"Certainly."

Brennen got up and went inside. Immediately, Mariyaan came out, bearing a stick in hand.

"You'll be heading out through the grove. It's full of snakes," Brennen explained. "Mariyaan had set some water on the stove for tea. Can I offer you some, as well?"

"Sure."

While brewing the tea, Brennen carried on from within. "By virtue of its staggering size, this country has evolved a peculiar system of functioning. Only those of us who've come from the outside see it as one huge entity. Those who belong to this place, on the contrary, seldom see it whole. Divided on the basis of their territory, habitat, language, race, and caste, they've splintered into thousands of factions. Factions within factions. And still smaller factions within those factions. The individual knows nothing outside of his or her group. Neither are they interested in knowing. For the reason that they've lived in such ignorance for centuries, they no longer possess the wherewithal to understand the world outside."

"Yes," said Aiden. "I've heard Major Gordon talk about it. If only a hundred of the petty rulers of this land had bothered to look beyond their own fraternity, the Europeans could never have conquered it, he'd say."

"Right. Sometimes it is language that unites us Europeans. Sometimes it's race. There's absolutely nothing that unites these people. Not even caste. Try talking to the untouchables here. There are so many divisions within them, too, it's bewildering." Brennen lifted the boiling water with a pincer-like wooden snatch and set it down. "The Mughals threw all these clans into one basket in order to rule them. And we do so now. Care for some sugar?"

"No, thank you," said Aiden.

"Lord Warren Hastings likened this country to a python that slumbers while its tail's on fire. True enough," said Brennen. Removing a glass jar from the wooden shelf, "Reptiles commonly have very long lifespans," he continued, "for their metabolism is excruciatingly slow. They eat, occasionally. Don't move for months together. This country, too, is a kind of reptile. It has lain here for thousands and thousands of years, without moving an inch."

Bearing cups in both hands, Brennen came back to his seat. "The reptile's ability to feel pain is surprisingly limited. I have observed crocodiles from close quarters—there are plenty of saltwater crocodiles in these parts. When hungry, they don't hesitate to feed on their own offspring. Why, they may devour their own limbs, too, if they were close enough to their mouths. Help yourself," he said.

Aiden intuited what the pastor was getting at. Brennen sat down heavily. "My Redeemer," he muttered.

After a generous sip of tea, Brennen continued. "I've pondered over why the millions of people in this country never spoke a word when a grave humanitarian crisis was going on here. The great famine of the 1700s did not elicit even a single voice of protest. Later, when I spoke with different denominations of the Hindus, I learned why that was so. They knew nothing. A man living in Madras is completely unaware of the Deccan. Why, Madurai itself is a mere word to him. In fact, he would've heard no more than a word or two about Chingleput itself. You'll be astounded if you dig deeper. The people who haven't died in the famine know perfectly nothing about it, other than that the price of rice is escalating. There's not one person in this whole land who thinks beyond the end of his road. Crocodiles. They languish in their stagnant marshes, eyes closed, frozen, forgetting all time. Creatures that know no pain."

"But the Hindus are protesting in Bengal," said Aiden. "Whole swarms of them have looted our warehouses in several places and doled out grains to the poor. There've been more than forty such robberies in the last three months alone. We're told that Hindu renunciate squads are behind these acts."

"There are some of them here, too," Brennen conceded. "But it's our Western education that has given rise to them. It is through our dailies that they get a picture of this country. Today, the biggest challenge the British government faces in the Madras Presidency is the *Madras Mail*. It's their editorials which announce to the world that there's a great famine in this region, and that people are falling by the million."

"Yes, but I barely ever read it," Aiden dismissed.

"Impassioned editorials. They deploy their correspondents to famine-affected areas, and publish detailed accounts of it. However, their voices go unheard in this country. They lack the language required to speak to this nation. The audience they address is in London. All their articles do is plead with the British conscience back home. It's what you and I are doing, too."

"Why haven't they been suppressed?"

"Why have we missionaries not been suppressed? Same reason. Them and us, and everyone else involved in famine relief, we all make up the same side. It's a frightfully small camp. We're like seabirds that attempt to lug a ship forward. The ship knows its power, and its bearing, too."

Brennen collected their cups, left them in the wooden basin, and returned to his chair.

"Do these details about the famine reach London?" Aiden asked.

"They do. The *Mail*'s editorials are published all over the world. The members of the lower house bandy it in Parliament, and kick up a fuss. But to what end?" Seeing Aiden's face, Father Brennen eased into a smile. "I do not wish to discourage you. What you're about to do is very vital. Deeply meaningful. And dear to Christ."

"Thank you," said Aiden.

"When you leave, do pack some dry food for the journey. You must have enough food and water with you to last until your return. Remember one thing—what I'm about to tell you is akin to a commandment for all those who venture to see the famine." Brennen's face was resolute. "Never hand away your own food. Not even when you see a child dying of hunger."

"I don't understand," said Aiden. His heart was beating fast.

"Because it is a stark reality. This famine's like a wildfire. We'll need whole mountains of food to put it out. There's no use throwing what meagre hand of food you have into this fire. At any rate, it won't save the one who receives it. But you, on the other hand, must live. If you live, you can accomplish many things. You can save hundreds of lives."

Aiden exhaled visibly.

"This is truly the greatest challenge one faces in surveying the famine. A Satan of monstrous proportions is what it is. It can penetrate your eyes and talk to your soul. You must have witnessed great fires. Have you noticed how the fire draws you in? 'Come, come,' it beckons. If you gaze at the fire for some time, you'll begin to walk towards it."

"Yes," said Aiden.

"A famine is no different. It deliquesces our thoughts. Decimates our rational mind. Reduces us to tears. Makes us reject all foundations of life. Forces us to believe we'd rather die. Yes, it reduces us to prize idiots who will walk straight into its maws in a dreamy stupor. So far as I know, as many as twenty service workers from the Catholic Church have sacrificed themselves thus to the famine. The famine is Satan's stage. Every thought that advances from it in your direction is sired by Satan. Hold on to Christ with all your might. These good thoughts that Christ kindles in you as you set out are the truth. Hold them close to you, as you would the Cross. If you plant your feet firmly in them, you will be able to return."

Aiden couldn't apprehend the meaning of his words, but he understood that Brennen's soul had known something intensely profound in the famine. The pastor poured another serving of tea; it flowed with a faint gurgle into their white porcelain cups. Steam rose from the tea, diffusing a pleasant aroma. Father Brennen came bearing the porcelain and placed the cups between the two of them. "Your tea," he said.

"Thank you," said Aiden, helping himself to it.

They drank in silence.

Mariyaan showed up at the threshold. "Sami," he said, addressing Father Brennen respectfully. There was another man standing outside. A short black man. With knotty hair like the Africans, a gap between his big, white incisors, strong jaws, and clear, glass-like eyes. He was wearing one of those tunics sewn by the missionaries. With huge arms and a drawstring knot at the base of its collarless, round neck, it was loose-fitting. The fabric, made of unbleached cotton, was straw-coloured.

"Come, Joseph," Brennen greeted. "Joseph has worked extensively in Chingleput. He knows these parts very well. If you can excuse his pronunciation, you'll be able to converse with him in English. He accompanies me in all of my travels."

"Is he from your church?" asked Aiden.

"Impossible, the Komuttis will never let him in. Which is why I instructed that he be brought in through the grove at the back. You can take him along in your carriage, I presume?"

"Certainly."

"I reckon you're armed."

"Should I expect holdups on this route?"

"Everything's to be expected in a famine," said Brennen. "What's your coachman's name?"

"Duraisamy."

"Oh," said Brennen. "In which case, he won't allow Joseph in your carriage."

"I will order him to," Aiden shot off.

"You can't," Brennen said categorically. The pastor's eyes met his, but Aiden could not hold his gaze.

Aiden simmered down. It was the truth, and he knew it, too.

"Joseph drives quite well. Take him with you," said Father Brennen.

As they were about to leave, Father Brennen's servant brought an old document chest and set it down at Aiden's feet. It was a heavy box made of teakwood. Resting on four stubby legs, it had brass-trimmed edges and ornamental handles.

"What's this?" asked Aiden.

"Dried bread and country sugar," came the answer from Mariyaan.

"Why is it in this box?"

"We have to carry food discreetly in these parts. Others cannot know of its presence," Joseph replied. "When my people travel, they store dry bread between the pages of the Bible," he said.

Puzzled, Aiden fell quiet. Mariyaan carted out a leather bag filled with water, secured it to the carriage, and threw a fancy drape over it.

"Shall we leave, sir?" asked Joseph. As soon as Aiden gestured his assent, he clicked his tongue loudly, lowered the reins, and drew them back. With their hooves clattering, the horses bounded onto the cobblestoned road. As the wheels fell into a steady rhythm, Aiden's thoughts, too, began to flow freely.

A series of thatched, low-slung houses passed them by on both sides of the road. Built from a mortar of mud and water, the houses were plastered with lime. Granite stones were arranged step-like. The blackened palm thatch looked like a dry grassy knoll, now a black boulder, now an elephant, now a dungheap.

Another road was arrayed with low, pantile-roof houses. The red roofs resembled the locks of a linen peruke. The space between the roof and the top of the veranda was barely three feet in height. Swabbed with cow dung, the verandas looked like mud beds, dark and damp. Scrawny men with hollow, stubble-overrun cheeks, clothed in nothing more than a half-length vaetti that stopped short of their knees, their hair gathered in a tuft at the back of their heads, were seated on the verandas, deep in conversation. Hearing the clatter of the horses' hooves, they cast a glance in the direction of the sound and quietened down. Their eyes alone followed the visitors. The strange leaf and nut they were in the habit of chewing had rendered their lips wound-like. Teeth, like bones in a pool of blood. Eyes, like those of herbivores. A perpetual lethargy in their movements, like the enfeebled rotation of a windmill in the dying wind.

The very same thought that often arose in Aiden surfaced then, too. Don't they need do such a thing as work? How do they spend the entire day idling? Nor are they perturbed by it. They languish nonchalantly in this immutable state of being as though it were most natural. Like a twig that floats in a lake and hovers over its ripples, they drift in the expanse of time.

Aiden was wont to picture the city as a single, homogenous mass. Like a huge pile of refuse. In time, though, it would differentiate into a variety of shapes. It was when he visited a street of Brahmin households that this difference had struck him for the first time. The ground floors of their houses were made of raised granite. Bands of ochre adorned the walls, as though a series of shoulder cloths or cummerbunds were hung on them. Elaborate patterns of intricate lines were drawn on the thresholds with white flour paste. The residents who were huddled on the verandas in conversation crinkled their eyes to take a good look at the carriage. The religious marks on their brows alone were clearly visible in the dark. It is they that live here, in reality. These bodies are simply vehicles that carry them, vehicles that take birth time and again, only to shoulder those identities.

The next street, manifestly, belonged to the oil merchants. Several of the verandas were occupied by people sitting next to brass oil pots. Oil presses were running alongside the houses. Bells tinkled as a pair of diminutive oxen orbiting the press at a leisurely pace dunked their heads into the bags hanging from their necks, scarfed up a mouthful of tamarind seeds, and reemerged, chomping languidly. A four-year-old boy was seated on the yoke. For a fleeting second, his terrified eyes stayed on the carriage, before looking away hurriedly.

Not a single woman on the streets, Aiden thought to himself. Their women go to bathe in the river, in the pall of daybreak, after which they never emerge during the day. There are narrow pathways at the back of the houses for them to come and go. The same paths through which the sewage courses and flows. The houses withhold the women within them, just as they hold waste. The act of letting them out in the mornings is a type of drainage, too. The womenfolk in these parts are of two kinds—girls with fearful eyes, baby cheeks, and small bodies, and old crones with protruding cheekbones, emaciated shoulders, and sagging breasts.

"Joseph, why aren't there any women on the streets?" Aiden quizzed, opening the small pane of the window in front of him.

"Like us, they, too, are untouchable, sir," Joseph replied loudly, without turning around.

"Really?" Even as the words left his mouth, Aiden realised that Joseph was joking. "I see," he said, his lips settling in a smile.

"Yes. We are made to stand outside. They are locked up indoors. That is the only difference."

This man is extraordinary, Aiden thought to himself. Everyone I meet in this place seems to be a great character right out of a classic play, he mused.

"At least we get some air and sun. They do not get that, either. They are not allowed to step outside. Born in a dark room, they are fated to die there as well. They must eat whatever is left after everyone else has had their fill. They must cook night and day with hunger in their bellies. They must birth children who will go on to enslave them, and feed and nurture them with the blood of their bosom."

When they passed through Sunnambukarar Street, the avenue of lime manufacturers, Aiden brought his handkerchief to his nose. The vaporous smell of roasting seashells had pervaded the entire road. It was an important occupation in the town. "What drivel," Aiden had barked when Mac first told him that the locals popped a large portion of the lime they manufactured in their mouths, only to turn it over for a while before spitting it out. This petty trade, too, was practised by the people who were marked for it by birth. Every job in this place had its own caste group.

"Which caste do those lime makers belong to?" Aiden asked.

"Sir, they are Paravars."

"An upper caste?"

"Sir, everyone here is an 'upper caste' to someone else. And everyone an untouchable, too."

A chuckle escaped Aiden. Talking to this fellow calls for great tact, he observed. "Are the Paravars similar to the Paraiyars?"

"They call themselves Sunnambu-paravars so as to not allow even a similarity in sound. They rank about seven or eight rungs higher than us. Ten or fifteen rungs lower than Brahmins."

"Joseph, how many levels are there in all?"

"Oliver Smitt, who served as collector for Chingleput back in the day, began a census, sir."

"And?"

"They shipped him back to London."

"Why?"

"Within four or five years, he had begun to wear his underwear like a hat. In the end, when he went to work without clothes, covering his waist with a hat, the governor had to take action."

Aiden laughed despite himself.

"There are many levels within each level, sir. Sometimes, when these levels are accounted for, the number exceeds the total population. The English rulers have not been able to crack this mystery till now."

"What job do you hold at the church?" Aiden asked, laughing.

"A Christian's."

"What do you mean?"

"Sir, to be a true Christian is a duty. A big job. I am doing that."

"Christ will like you."

"Of course, sir, he too strove towards it, just as I do. We are colleagues."

Aiden gave up and sat quietly for a time. I should share my poetry with him someday, he said to himself.

The carriage stopped. Aiden looked out. A white-skinned youth was standing in the way. A lick of straw-coloured hair, on the verge of his receding hairline, stirred in the breeze. He was wearing his white shirt over a pair of khaki shorts. Buttoned right up to his collar, the shirt was full-sleeved. He toted a big cloth bag in one hand.

"Excuse me. I need to get to Chingleput urgently. Can you take me along?" he asked, a stuttering lilt in his voice. "I've been waiting here for a long time. The coachman I was counting on duped me."

"I'm on official duty," said Aiden.

"I can see that, but I'm left with no other option. Please take me as far as you can. I'll get off wherever you tell me to. You need not assume any responsibility on my account."

Aiden considered him for a moment or two. Here was a young man, fresh out of college, taking a confused and tentative step into civilisation. Someone whose sole quest in life was to find the chair he was to occupy. "Get in," Aiden addressed him with a nod.

The young man boarded the carriage and sat down beside Aiden. "I must reach Chingleput before nightfall."

"Why?"

"My maternal uncle who's in Chingleput is dying."

"Dying?"

"May even be dead already. It was the first news I received upon landing in Madraspatnam. My mother wished that I pay my uncle a visit, which is why I came directly to Madraspatnam from London, instead of heading to Calcutta." Pausing to smile, he added, "I'm sorry. My name is Adam Andrew. I've come to take up employment in the Department of Accounts."

"Are you an Oxonian?" Aiden asked, with an evident lack of enthusiasm.

"Yes. You too?"

"No," Aiden responded tersely. "When did you come to Chennai?"

"Three days ago. I'm Scottish."

"I see that."

"Thank you. I had no plans to be here, I know nobody in this place. The Free Church of Scotland has established a few places of worship here, you see. There's one in Egmore—St. Andrew's Church . . ."

"I know."

"Our church administrator back home equipped me with a letter addressed to the minister at St. Andrew's. I, too, sent them a letter before departing. I had expected that someone would be at the port to receive me when I arrived by ship. But no one came. When I went to the church, the priest to whom I had written wasn't there. I was told that he had died a whole year earlier, from diarrhoea. So it fell on me to make all the arrangements myself. It took me two full days to find a vehicle."

"You could've written to your uncle."

"He fell out with the family, and left for Burma eight years ago, from where he came to India. He never wrote to us. It was only last year that we received word of him serving as a judge in Chingleput. My mother bade me to visit him. I had no choice but to come. The enquiries I made upon my arrival told me that he'd been suffering from malaria for close to a month, that it'd been a week since he lost consciousness. I want to see him before he dies."

"A good thing, too," Aiden said, removing his hat, and combing his hair with his fingers. "Malaria offers a logical reason to die."

"I should've accepted my position in Calcutta as early as last month," Adam went on. Evidently, he was unaccustomed to wry humour. "My ship was a month late. They will condone that, but my landing in Madraspatnam they'll surely deem delinquent."

Aiden said nothing. His body had effortlessly fallen in perfect harmony with the jolt of the carriage. But Andrew's shoulder kept bumping against him. Somehow, the state of mind he was in made him loathe the presence of a new person in his midst, even though Andrew did seem to him a rather simple and agreeable young man.

"I was told that there's a great famine prevailing in this land. The biggest in the history of the world, they say. There's plenty of news back home in the pro-labour papers."

"That is true."

"Is it also true that more than twenty million people have died?"

"Much more, I'd say."

"That would amount to the death of the entire population of the British Isles."

Aiden felt a lusty blow on his chest. It had never crossed his mind to make such a comparison. He had looked upon the death of the black people of this land as yet another natural catastrophe. One that had kindled his compassion, stung his conscience, and made him argue their case vehemently. But not once had he equated them to himself, or his people. As they succumbed noiselessly, all it seemed to be was a great cosmic drama. Once, on an island back in Indonesia, he had seen whole flocks of seabirds drop dead, swathing the entire marshland. Their bodies had piled on top of one another as though white snow had fallen to the ground and hardened. What he felt now was the same sadness he had felt back then. They are creatures. I am a human being. We are human beings. This distinction is still alive in me.

It's hard to fathom twenty million white people dying—no white man can—he reassured himself. Why had his mind not conjured up such a comparison? A comparison that had cropped up spontaneously in this young man's mind at the very start. To feel the pain of another as thine own—that, they say, is the beginning of spirituality. A Christian ought to think like that. But how many among the tens of thousands of whites in India would have felt so, if only for a fleeting instant?

A young man who possesses an innate spiritual latitude, Aiden reasoned. No, he simply hasn't begun to see the world yet. He hasn't seen wars, or the terrible famines that follow them, or the deadly diseases. His mind was yet to marinate in the tenets of administration. Neither was it hardened by its daily monotony. Had I arrived at the present moment, a freshly minted youth, I, too, would have had the same notion.

But as soon as he thought that, his heart recognised it to be untrue. Whatever else a young white man might know, he knows, without fail, that he is a cut above the rest. That feeling cements in his heart even before he turns five. His is a blessed race. A mighty race. And he, a man from a nation that's ordained to assume responsibility for the world. Every single youth sees through those very same eyes. All the young men who journeyed with this youth and landed on these shores will be filled, at once, with mercy and disgust at the sight of these simple people. Even as they think of saving their lives, they will also deem it most natural that they should perish. With time, their mercy will dry up, leaving behind nothing but disgust. Disgust is a valuable emotion. A necessity to live in this place. About the same as a mosquito net. It keeps malaria and other diseases at bay. It secures a safe habitat.

This young man is about to face a grand demolition not too far in the future, Aiden concluded. His Cross has been forged somewhere, already. He is Christ's companion. Aiden smiled. Outside sat another companion. Christ is never alone.

Aiden had not realised that they had crossed the city's limits. Since the path had hardened considerably, the horses drew the carriage with ease. The scrape of the wheels and the sound of the hooves were all that could be heard. Noticing a variation in the sounds, Aiden parted the drapes and looked through the small window of his carriage. Densely thicketed hillocks were keeping them company on both sides. Trees whose verdure did not dull even in the summer. Thorny shrubs, like giant green mushrooms. Great beast-like hills stood in line, chafing against one another. Stunted trees dotted the hills, like pores on their backs. A gust of wind rolled down the slopes, through the trees, and swept across the road, flooding it like a wave. The smell of baked red earth.

The afternoon sun had begun to dip. Shadows slanted southeast. A sleeping jungle at the feet of an upright wilderness. Concluding their period of rest, the crows took flight. They swam the sunlight with their black wings and waded away. Aiden felt weary. Should I head back? he ruminated. Perhaps the sweet languor and nostalgia this moment evokes in me may never return. I may change into a different person, forever and ever.

The carriage screeched to a halt. The horses protested. "Serrr," Joseph whistled.

"What's wrong?"

"Here's your first sight of the famine," he said, with the air of one making a routine introduction.

"What do you mean?"

"Look towards your right, under the banyan tree."

Aiden opened the door just a fraction and squinted into the distance. In a second, like a worm touched by a drop of acid, his mind jerked and struggled; then, with unbearable, life-ending agony, writhed and twisted; shaking itself, it snapped and shuddered. Under the huge banyan, corpses lay as if shovelled in a heap. More than half of them children. A clutch of dogs, having torn into the bodies and ripped out their guts, were now feasting on them. Their growls, and grunts as they dug in, chewed, and strained at the innards, could be heard distinctly. From the boughs above, the crows and a miscellany of other birds rent the air with their bazaar-like raucous cries. When the crows dared to descend from the branches, the dogs set out after them with loud snarls. The birds took wing, only to settle down again.

A couple of dogs lifted their heads, pricked their ears

forward, and glanced up at the carriage. As soon as Aiden opened the door, they constricted their bodies, lifted a foreleg, dropped it behind, and, moving backward, lowered their noses warily. Hearing the sounds raised by the two alert dogs, the others turned to look. Weak in the knees, Aiden held on to the frame of the carriage. Having appraised him, the dogs went back to straining and tearing at the bodies with their ears still perked up in vigilance. The feet of the infant corpses they had sunk their teeth into shook from side to side, creating the illusion that they were still alive.

Infant arms. Infant legs. Though withered and emaciated, a child-like quality still lingered in them. Their big toes had twisted away from the other digits, as when children sleep in their cradles. An infant face, its lips peeled off, rocked in an open-mouthed laugh. Another one, as though making a dire attempt to grab the intestines snaking out of its own belly, overturned and fidgeted. The dog that had dragged out the entrails held it down with its foreleg and, sinking its haunches to the ground, began to chew on it. The entire place reeked of wasting flesh. Gripped by nausea, Aiden shook his body.

"Get in, sir," said Joseph, tugging at the reins. Aiden grabbed hold of the carriage door. His eyes fell on Andrew, who was seated inside, his face buried in a white handkerchief, sobbing silently. In the moment that Aiden placed a foot on the carriage step, a faint moan fell on his ears. Parsed from the sounds of the dogs and the crows, he heard it distinctly.

"Wait," said Aiden, and looked over his shoulder. Those distressed moans sounded as though they were beseeching him. Was it a hallucination? Some of the bodies, their lips ripped out of their faces, lay laughing. Was it their call? Suddenly, Brennen's words came back to him. Was it the call of death? Of Satan? His teeth clenched. His every limb, as though turned to stone, felt detached and distant from him. That call of distress, again. Yes, it was a human voice.

"Don't! Don't, Captain," Andrew's broken voice echoed behind him. Aiden stepped over the bushes; the tips of his fingers rested on his gun. *Rrrr*, a dog growled, baring its thorn-like porcelain fangs from within its blood-stained maws. Aiden threw his arms about, shooed loudly, and proceeded forward. But the dog did not seem the least bit afraid. As he walked farther ahead, the canine rose to its feet, sunk its belly to the ground, and let out a low-pitched growl in Aiden's direction.

"Captain, careful!" Andrew hollered from behind. Aiden looked around. From among the bushes, the heads of a great number of dogs, their ears perked, rose up. A hundred, at the very least. They would need no more than a few seconds to attack, Aiden realised. Losing no time, he whipped his gun out and shot the dog in front. *Heeek*: a sound escaped the animal as it collapsed to the ground even as the bang of the gun ricocheted back from the hills. The dogs howled and bolted away in all directions like a swell of ripples eddying out from where stone had struck water.

Aiden collected himself and moved forward. Mauled and mangled corpses. Men and women of all ages. Their spilled guts and tattered rags had twisted together and lay spread out in the dirt in a tangled mess. Severed limbs were strewn here and there. Innumerable corpses lay scattered among the bushes. Some facedown, as though hugging the earth; some holding one another, as though in a tight embrace; some as though in a deep and soothing slumber. White bones crumbled underfoot. Skulls like old china. Hip bones with stubborn remnants of flesh. Bones caked with the mud, as though made of mud. How many people!

As Aiden took another step forward, that movement caught his eye. From the hollow of a banyan tree, a hand stirred. The moan, too, had come from there. Yes, it is the stirring of life. No, it is an illusion. Satan's illusion. An illusion of my own making. That voice, again. Yes, it was indeed calling out to him. Beyond a shadow of doubt.

Aiden became aware of a violent tremble in his thighs. He half expected to fall. Slowly, he inched towards the hollow. A voice, such as would sound at the hour of death.

"Dora."

"Dora."

Lord. Master. The refrain with which the natives addressed the whites. *Dho-ra. Dho-ra.* The *d* landed thick and heavy, the *o* short and urgent; the clipped *a* stabbed like a knife. A haunting call. He saw the face. A boy. Perhaps eight years of age. A form, as though all the flesh and fluid in its body had been sucked out by a gigantic syringe. The veins crisscrossing the bones were visibly pronounced. The bone joints had become heavy, so heavy the body could no longer support their weight, or so it seemed. Crazed eyes as if in a fever's grip. Teeth like mud pebbles, in a mouth dry as a rut of mud. A withered tongue dangled out, like a worm.

It was not one single body, Aiden realised. There were four children. A girl child, maybe two years of age. Taken together, the four were barely the size of one body. They had clung to one another, like a knot of worms. In their eyes, which were no longer bound by time and space, only an ominous stare remained. It seemed as if their eyes were smiling at him. They moved what limbs in their bodies were capable of movement. "Dora. Dora."

"We cannot do anything," Joseph called out from behind. "There is no chance of them surviving. The final delirium is in their eyes."

Devoid of all thought, Aiden stood rooted to the spot, his eyes fixed on them.

Hands extended from the children's bodies and spread their imploring fingers apart.

"Sir, please turn back. We cannot save them. These children were forsaken many days ago."

"I have food with me," Aiden said, turning on his heel.

"Father must have warned you. It is pointless to give way to emotion. Look at their hands and legs. The dogs have devoured them already. Their bodies will not have the strength to heal those wounds. Nothing can save them now."

"So what do you propose we do? Abandon them and leave?"

"That is the only thing we can do. There are thousands of people who need our help, even more than they do. People who may actually survive with our help. To waste our aid on the ones here and abandon the others—that is sin. Please come."

Aiden remained where he was, gazing into those eyes. A little girl child wiggled like a worm out of the sea of limbs around it. Extending its hand, thin, crinkled, and veined like a century-old crone's, it said: "Dora. Dora." The moan of a worm.

"It will live for one more day at the most. Rescuing it is beyond you. Get back," Joseph urged.

Aiden felt as though his feet had melted and fused with the ground. The emptiness that had occupied those children's eyes until that moment was there no longer. Their eyes beseeched. They looked at him with hope, with expectation. As soon as the hint of a retreating movement arose in his body, they were gripped by a heightened anxiety. The moment his eyes met theirs again, they acquired new hope. Within that sliver of time, they had uttered every plea one soul was capable of making to another.

"Satan." Aiden recalled Brennen's words. "The most sublime emotions are his weapons. Christ's robe is his dearest raiment. And yet he never fails to drag Christ's servants down into his dark abyss." Aiden's body was trembling all over. Who now inhabits these eyes, vacant until only seconds ago? Satan? The great power that drowns humanity in hunger and disease? Was it Satan's contrivance that was speaking to him so—this last moan of existence, this climactic wail of the desire to live? Yes, it was calling out to him. It was out to swallow him whole into the infinite and gleaming depths of its gaping maw.

"Sir, keep your thoughts on Christ. Get back, please," Joseph pleaded.

Aiden had read many a tale of sailors in the icy Arctic peaks chopping their leg off with an ice axe to extricate themselves from a rock fall. That is precisely what I'm about to do, it occurred to him, right that instant. He was hacking his own blood-gushing, pain-throbbing body to pieces. Raising his legs with great effort, he moved one scant step at a time. His carriage stood someplace far away, as if a journey of several days lay in between. The air was still. The sky and the earth, frozen.

Behind him, the faint voice of the worm entreated. Over and over. The call of a fellow human life. The hope that still lingers in it. That is the great force that has hitherto sustained the human race. The elemental relationship between man and man. The expectation that stems in the heart when a hand extends towards its own kind in hunger, when one seeks refuge in a total stranger. How many thousands of centuries would it have taken humankind to develop this emotion, bit by bit? What multitude of adversities would mankind have shielded and nurtured it through!

From where? From where did this lowly troop of apes receive such loftiness? Just as fire fell to the earth from lightning, did this, too, come from the sky? Is that why, at times of great tribulation, it looks up towards the sky? It knows: that there is something magnificent, something unfathomable and yet infinitely tender, within itself. A thing by virtue of which Man has crossed the gravest dangers, every single time. It is God's teardrop. Here I am, trampling over it, and walking away. I march on, stamping my heavy boots on God's face, his heart, his underbelly, quashing them underfoot.

Aiden's vision grew dim. Imagining that the ground was rising up towards him, he stretched his hand out reflexively; losing balance, he was on the verge of falling when Joseph grabbed him by the shoulder. "Thank you," Aiden whispered, and stood still for a time. The ground swam beneath his feet.

Then, extricating himself, he walked, deliberately lifting and setting down his legs. Step after step, he stamped the ground with force. A bone crumbled like earthenware. Behind him, those moans grew louder now. "Dora. Dora."

It was a sound he was familiar with. The sound of the people who served him, bowing in obeisance. The sound that escapes a flogged black man when he supplicates at the feet of his assailant. Every child in this country is born with this plea on its lips. A plea that settles on its tongue, and in its breath, for eternity. Yes, an entire nation, with tens of millions of hands cupped around the corners of its mouth, a deathly fever blazing in its eyes, a burning on its parched lips, clamours thus.

Before Aiden could reach the carriage, Andrew rushed out with the box in hand. Joseph moved swiftly and caught hold of him. "Stop. What are you doing? Stop," he yelled.

"There's food in here. Food," Andrew agitated.

"They cannot eat it. They will not be able to push it down their throats. They will suffocate and die right in front of our eyes," Joseph screamed.

"We have fire. Let's boil the food in water and give it to them."

"Their guts will not be capable of digesting food. We can give them only powdered sugar. Even then, they will not survive. They have been bitten and torn by dogs with mouths that have tasted flesh."

"Let them die. Let them die right here. But, now that I've seen them, it's impossible for me to leave with this food. I won't be able to stomach even a single morsel of it. God's curse is upon it now." Andrew tried to shake Joseph off and move forward. When Joseph stopped him, he lunged at him with the box and knocked him down. Huffing and heaving, his hair out of place, he strode forward like a madman.

"Stop!" Aiden cried, flinging his hand out.

"No . . . I . . ." Even as Andrew began, Aiden struck a resounding slap across his cheek. Stunned, Andrew froze in place; with misty eyes open wide and mouth agape, he stood transfixed. Aiden took the box from him. Andrew's grip loosened on its own; his palms were drenched in sweat. The wet and warm handle of the box slid into Aiden's hand.

"You are not human, the both of you. You're beasts. That food is soaked in sin. Partake of one crumb and its curse will be upon your ten generations," Andrew screamed, his voice turning shrill in a fit of passion.

"Get into the carriage," Aiden commanded. "I must get to Chingleput. Not for myself, for those like them."

Andrew's voice broke. "I won't come. Leave me to die right here. I won't come," he shrieked. Beating his own face with fury, "Jesus. Christ, I'm dying. Dying. Jesus, my Saviour," he wept.

"Come!" said Aiden in a firm voice. Joseph climbed on to the carriage. They waited without moving the vehicle an inch.

Whimpering, Andrew sank down to his haunches. After a moment or two had passed, he opened his eyes and looked all around him. Suddenly, like a man pursued, he made a dash for the carriage. Grabbing hold of the handle with all his might, he hoisted himself in, collapsed into his seat, and, doubling over, cupped his face with both his hands, and began to tremble visibly.

When the carriage started, Aiden looked back. The distance the child had managed to cover startled him. The movements in the bushes betrayed the pack of dogs closing in. The child kept inching forward, as though it were following the carriage. From where does this strength spring? It is life's vital force. The animating force that permeates every living being on this earth.

Is that who Satan is? Aiden contemplated. Is that what binds man to this earth? Is that what metamorphoses into attachment, into endearment, into ego? Is that what the human soul so fears? Aiden closed his eyes and fell back in his seat. The muscles in his body ached and throbbed as if from a violent fever. With a bitterness in his mouth, a burning in his eyes, and the vaporous chill of a sweat-drenched body, he felt as though he was floating away weightlessly.

7

Aiden became aware of the sound of the carriage wheels kicking and playing his consciousness around like a ball. Hoofbeats rained on his mind like a rock shower. Somewhere, a whip came down on it in a blood-splattering lashing. Somewhere, a hammer pummelled it relentlessly. Somewhere, an overwhelming sob fell as rain. Somewhere, a great cry rattled the lower skies in a ferment of lightning and thunder. A solitary word dissolved into a raging sea that slammed its head against the boulders ashore and wore them down. Somewhere, a man burrowed into the ground, descending deeper and deeper towards the deepest depths.

When the carriage halted, Aiden roused. “Our police, sir,” Joseph called out.

Aiden opened the door. The soldier who was waiting on his horse outside leaped down and dealt him a salute. A stiff twenty-five-year-old. “Sergeant Cooper, sir. Third Division of City Police,” he announced. A twenty-man infantry waited a few feet behind him. All of them Indian. Sharp-nosed Pathanis, with thick beards, like a bouquet of thorns.

“Is there some trouble with law and order here?” Aiden enquired.

"Refugees aren't supposed to enter the city, sir. Hence, this guard. If the sick get in, disease will spread throughout town and take a heavy toll."

A marvellous explanation, Aiden noted. No one can match the English in justifying their actions to their own selves. A talent that has turned them into a global superpower.

"What are your orders?" Aiden questioned.

"Only the healthy ones who can walk steadily on their own feet may enter the city. Those being carried are not permitted beyond this point, neither are vehicles," Sergeant Cooper elaborated.

"All right," said Aiden, as he turned back and placed a foot on the carriage step.

"There are many more refugees on the Vellore road than here. We stop ninety out of a hundred who take that route as far back as Sriperumbudur. Still, we've failed to control the situation there," Cooper went on. "The Scottish missionaries who undertake burials tell us that nearly twenty thousand corpses fall each day."

"Have you set up barricades?" Aiden asked.

"No, sir. We make sure there are no sick passengers in the vehicles on the road. However, only a handful of the affected commute in wagons. Most of them travel by foot, which means they could take any route through this huge forest. Though, I should say, the forest is, in itself, a mighty fortress. Many of them make it all the way here only to be felled by it. All we do is infiltrate the city in small groups and sow the fear of the sick getting in. Fear is the real governing force here."

"And what do you suppose they should fear now?" Aiden asked, a wry smile on his face.

"Sir, the weak do not fear with reason. It is their own weakness they fear," said Sergeant Cooper, returning the smile.

Aiden got back into the carriage and closed the door behind him. "Let's go," he ordered. The carriage jolted to a start.

"Beasts. Hellish creatures," Andrew cursed. His face was red as a beet. His lips, pressed tightly together, looked like a gash.

"Talk to him and you'll see," Aiden railed. "He'll firmly believe that he's performing an indispensable service for mankind. He'll claim to be saving the townspeople from the spread of disease by keeping the sickly beggars at bay. No one can live in this place without justifying their existence."

Andrew shook his head vigorously, as if in denial. His body resembled an incandescent metal statue. It felt as though the heat from his being was radiating through the carriage.

Aiden resolved not to look to his left or right. But his eyes scanned the landscape involuntarily for the very thing he wished to avoid. At the foot of every tree hemming the road lay cadavers ripped apart by dogs and jackals. An overwhelming majority of them children. How many children do evade death in this place? "Dora. Dora." The whole forest was imploring in a child's tender voice. "Dora. Dora."

Jesus. My Lord. My Saviour. Aiden drew the window curtains shut. He pressed his index finger right between his brows. Only his lips moved as he began to recite an ancient prayer that came upon them. In a minute, a realisation jolted him. It was the very prayer he and his family would recite at mealtime. His body convulsed as though racked by nausea. Jesus, my Lord, my one true Saviour.

A caravan of bullock carts was driving in their direction from the other end of the road. At the front of the line were two Pathani soldiers, armed with rifles. Old-fashioned Ferguson rifles. The Pathanis were liveried in scarlet linen jackets and khaki shorts, mimicking the British soldiers. It was evident that they were roving, itinerant mercenaries. Big white oxen followed behind them pulling cargo-laden wagons, their thigh muscles straining, heads lowered, and thick strands of saliva dribbling from their mouths. The shrill scraping of the linchpin against the axle, and the stern rebukes issued by the cart drivers when they swirled their whips, filled the air. There were eight carts in all. All of them roofed with arched palm matting glazed with black beeswax. They were likely carrying grain sacks.

Twenty spear-bearing Maravars brought up the rear. Their blue waistcloths, doubled up to their knees, were held in place by belts of palm fibre. From their shoulders hung fibrous palm shells containing food and water. The tips of their rosewood spears were whetted to the point of an aloe thorn. Faces garlanded by beehive-like beards. Eyes like pigeon eggs buried in a bush. Hair plastered with castor oil and combed into a thick knot at the back of the head.

The caravan made way for them. When Aiden crossed, the Pathani soldier at the front slapped the rifle in a patently British manner and saluted him. *Rrrr*, the horse hissed, and shifted its weight. After that, the wagons progressed onwards without paying any heed to them.

"Who are they?" Aiden asked.

"Erstwhile soldiers of the Walajah nawab. A few of them now work in the British Army. The rest make a living by offering protection to merchants, as you just saw. The British Army regards them as allies," Joseph explained.

"Do robberies take place here?"

"When there are humans as hungry as this, there ought to be robberies. But the answer is, there are hardly any. For centuries now, these people have been disconnected from violence of any kind. They have lived off the land for the most part. They have not been introduced to weapons. Nor do they know how to work as a team. A vast majority of them are abandoning the fields and settlements that were their homes and coming out into the world, perhaps, for the first time in their entire history. They would have heard of soldiers and weapons only in their stories."

"If that were so, why would there be so much security?"

"You will see for yourself, sir," said Joseph.

Many more convoys of wagons were approaching.

"Are all of them carrying food rations?"

"Yes, mainly food. Grains, pulses, oil seeds. The supply of other items has considerably reduced now. This city survives on the food shipped from the Nagapatnam port down south. What you see here are mere trifles brought by the merchants. Once they reach the city, this stock will sell for up to eight times their cost, I hear. No matter the quantity that reaches there, the food is never enough."

Twilight had begun to spread. Sunlight seeped into the foliage and fell between the trees like a blubbery forest stream. The jungles on either side of the road had started to thin into scrubland. People walked in front of the oncoming wagons, toting earthen pots that sheltered oil lamps kindled with cloth wicks. In the dim light, the flames' tongues, like the petals of a red blossom, danced this way and that.

"Is it edible oil they're burning?"

"Punnai-seed oil, sir. Made from the nut of what you call the Indian laurel, I think. It is not edible," said Joseph. "The cattle will not walk this distance during the day. That is why they travel by night. The goods wagons will keep coming until daybreak."

The wagon lines in the distance began to blur into a string of red lights. In the woods, the darkness intensified and grew thick. The calls of the birds seemed to ring resoundingly.

There arose the vaporous haze and steamy scent of Indian evenings. The light nip in the wind blowing from the direction of the sea was discernible only when it grazed the ears.

It was not long before Aiden could tell that the faint murmur they were hearing was in fact the hum of a great mob. His heart quickened. That is when it dawned on him that his mind had effortlessly pushed the grave scenes it had witnessed a mere hour earlier to the background. The mind is more artful than a strumpet. Slicker than a stage magician. Layering thought after thought over that memory, it had forged ahead. That remembrance had become dreamlike now, or a long-ago happening. Returning now amid this cacophony, it had lost its intensity, and transformed into little more than an incident he had read in some novel.

The sounds grew strident. The path took a sharp turn around a small mound and climbed up. As the bullocks dipped their heads dangerously close to the ground and pulled their loads, the wagon wheels screeched loudly. Hearing a noise, Aiden opened the door and stepped onto the footboard. Far below was a huge throng of people befitting a village fair, or a festival. Hemming in the wagons that had pierced through them, they stuck their hands out and lamented despairingly. Bodies and limbs twisted like black worms swarming over a pair of slippers plodding through mud.

The Maravars cordoning the vehicles whirled their spears in a bid to drive the crowd away. Aiden watched as the spears cut and scraped human bodies time and again. As the wounded fell to the ground, others stepped over them and continued to pursue the vehicles. When the Pathanis lifted their rifles and took aim several times, the mob parted, yielding empty space. As soon as the vehicles moved ahead, the crowd chased after them with raucous cries. The entire path resembled a cut of red meat teeming with writhing, black maggots.

The white sergeant who was heading towards them reined his horse in and came to a hesitant stop. The Pathani soldiers following in his footsteps rode a few paces ahead before stopping.

"Sergeant Simpson, sir," he said, announcing himself.

"What are you doing?"

"It's been impossible to keep order here, sir, as I'm sure you'll appreciate from these sights. The roads are crammed with similar mobs of people all the way up to Chingleput and Tindivinam, farther south. All roads leading to Madras wear the same look. The wagon drivers seem to have flung some rice or tuber at the crowd in the hope of controlling them, at first. The news travelled thick and fast, after which they began to swarm like this. The only way to control them now is through force. Hundreds of thousands of people line the streets waiting fervently for passersby only to clamour fruitlessly to death upon seeing them. We clear and bury thousands of bodies every day. Even so, corpses rot in the scrub and spread disease. These roads have become extremely hazardous. Even those who make a normal journey through these routes catch disease and die. It will be best to shut these roads off completely for a few days, sir. We have no other choice."

"All right," said Aiden, and waved his hand. The carriage started.

"Where else will these people go?" Joseph spoke up. "Most of them are untouchables. People who have been bound to the land for centuries now. Their masters have stopped paying them their wage all of a sudden. Having starved for days, they have ventured out at the cusp of death. They know nothing. All they can see are these highways. They have not come here placing faith in these vehicles. The government they see is the liveried British soldier who travels the length of these roads. It is that government that they have come to entreat."

Suddenly, Joseph's voice rose a few decibels. "It is fitting that they die here instead of in their fields. These roads are the one true achievement of the British regime. They are the courtyards of power. It is because these people drop dead here that the government is even aware of their deaths. If not for this, the turbaned lot would have recorded that no such caste existed in India. The British officers would have affixed their seal on that and filed the papers away. The governor, for his part, would have dispatched a report to London. But now the British government has at least taken on the responsibility of laying them to rest. What an honour it is for this wretched, hungering lot of Paraiyars. What good fortune to be buried by the monarch of this world, Queen Victoria herself. And if the Cross of the Son of Man who came to redeem this world were to adorn their graves, ah!"

In that moment, Aiden felt a fatal rage froth up inside of him. He wanted to whip his pistol out and empty its bullets into Joseph. Joseph, who had intuited that at once, said, "Shoot me, by all means. I, too, will lie down among my people. I, too, will be accorded a lavish space in the hell they enter. Were I to be confined to the Christian hell you have offered, it would fall on me to serve the white-skin there, too."

"Shut up," Aiden shouted.

"You need not tell us that, sir. That is the art we have trained in for hundreds of years. That is our path to salvation." He clicked his tongue and yanked the reins.

The crowd surrounded the carriage in a great uproar. "Dora. Dora. Maharasa. Dora. Dora," they keened. They were not human voices at all. A black sea of sludge rose up from both sides and crashed into the carriage. A preponderance of naked bodies. With no way to tell if they were man or woman, old or young. Dried human-fish. The miasma of already-rotting flesh turned the stomach. Dead eyes, dead mouths. "Dora. Dora. Maraasave. Dora. Maraasaa! Dora! Dharmaraasaave. Dora. Dharmam seyyunga raasaave. Dora. Pulla saavudhu dora. Ettu pulla sethu pochu dora." The aching, fervent appeals of a mother whose children were dead, whose child was dying. The aching, fervent appeals made to a white man within whose conscience it was—she believed—to be just, to be noble, to be merciful.

Word somehow spread about the arrival of a white man's carriage; tens of thousands of people pressed against it from the left and the right. Cries of "Dora. Dora." Interred, wasting corpses dug up and dragged out by the dogs. Oh, some unfathomable rule stops this lot from devouring one another. Yes, I've dared to come to this place only because they won't eat me. "Dora. Dora." The women propped up their infants for him to see. Dehydrated, emaciated, dried-fish-like infants. Glassy-eyed, rice-teethed, witless doll-like infants.

"Dora. Dora. Pulla saavudhu dora. Pulla saavudhu dora!" The same lament over and over. My child is dying, my child is dying. She bobs up and down in a crazed fit, lifting her baby into view. A black, ghost-like woman. With dried-up, dangling breasts. Eyes like sewage puddled in two sockets. "Dora. Pulla saavudhu dora." Why, are *you* not dying? But, those eyes. Even if the whole universe were to perish, it would make no difference to her. The tiny lump of flesh in her hand alone should not die. Her hands, her face, her teeth, her eyes—all of them screamed just that. It was the sole reason they existed. "Dora. Dora."

"Oh, oh, oh." Andrew was moaning without end. Seeing

that his body was shuddering as if in a feverish fit, "Start the carriage," Aiden thundered. "Don't stop. Keep going." But the mob had grabbed hold of the carriage wheels already. In a flash, someone opened the door from the outside. As though a thick spurt of sewage had gushed into the carriage, a thorny bundle of pitch-dark hands burst in. Rotting fingers caught hold of his shoes. "Dora. Dora. Dora. Rasave. Dora." Fingers, clammy as worms, swarmed all over his legs. How many of them were dead already! Oh!

"Move! Move now!" Aiden vociferated.

"They are holding on to the wheels."

"Drive the damned carriage!"

In a flash, Andrew seized the box, threw the lid open, snatched whole handfuls of bread from within, and flung them out.

"No, no," Joseph shrieked. But Andrew looked like a madman. "For Jesus, for Jesus, for Jesus," he babbled.

When the bread hit the ground, a storm of human forms erupted around it. Caught in its eye, the carriage wobbled and keeled to one side before righting itself again. A whirlwind of bodies. The bread disintegrated into bits and disappeared into them. With bulging, ghostly eyes, they licked the fingers that had touched the bread. They thrust their fists into their mouths, as though attempting to swallow their bare hands. Very soon, that urgency mutated into unbridled ferocity. They shoved and pushed one another. Screaming hysterically, they scratched each other with their teeth and hands. There arose the smell of fresh blood. Before long, Aiden noticed crimson oozing from the black bodies. Big splotches of blood ruptured in the air and splashed on the wooden carriage frames. A drop of blood dithered on the black leather surface of Aiden's boot, then unwillingly streaked down its length.

With a deafening roar, a whole multitude of others in the vicinity rushed towards Aiden's carriage. It seemed as though a pit of infinite depth had opened its maw and was drawing the entire mass of bodies towards itself.

"Sir. We must leave this moment. Chase them away!" Joseph hollered.

Aiden drew his sword and, pointing it out the carriage, slashed this way and that. "Get off. Get off," he screamed.

"Use your gun, sir," cried Joseph. The carriage bounded over the human wave. It rocked, swayed, and tossed about.

Aiden whisked his pistol out, and shot at the sky. The bang reverberated in the air and, echoing in all directions, returned to engulf him. The turbulence that had surrounded the carriage paused for a second. The human throng split as though a tree had fallen in water. Right that instant, Joseph brought his whip down on the horses and yelled frantically. The horses hesitated and fell back. Then they kicked their forelegs in the air and brayed in protest. Joseph tore into them as if in a fit. With vehement neighs, the animals leaped forward. As the carriage moved ahead with a wild jostle, Aiden felt as though it was tumbling into a ditch. He held on to the carriage grille.

"Dora. Pulla, dora!" the woman shrieked as she hurled the infant at Aiden. With clasped hands, the child flew above his head and fell to the ground on the other side of the departing carriage. It disappeared into the swell of human bodies crowding the spot.

Aiden's head banged against the grille. It felt as though the vehicle were sinking down muddy hollows and climbing up muddy mounds while making its way forward.

"You fool, stay on the road," Aiden yelled, pressing his mouth to the window.

"Sir, I am on the road."

The carriage tossed him about like a boat caught in a storm.

"Drive carefully," Aiden shouted again.

"We are driving over human bodies, sir."

"Oh, Jesus," said Andrew, rising to his feet involuntarily.

As a cold shiver ran up his rectum as if from the touch of an ice cube, and his body turned dead and numb, Aiden sat in place.

"Jesus, Jesus." Andrew moaned and clutched the door, like a man who was about to jump out.

Aiden seized Andrew's hands. "You fool. What the hell are you doing?"

"I cannot travel in this vehicle."

"If you get out, you'll die."

"Let me die. Let me die. For the sin of seating myself in this carriage, I should burn in hellfire for a thousand years. Jesus. Jesus, my Lord."

"There is no hell greater than this. Sit down."

Andrew sank to the floor right between the seats, contracted his body, and hunched over. Burying his face in his hands, he wept. Tears pooled in the webs between his fingers and trickled over.

That was when Aiden became conscious of it: tears were streaming down his face, too. His shirt collar was soaking wet. In his jacket, in his breast, he could feel the dampness of his tears. Jesus, my Saviour, is there yet such a wealth of tears in me?

When the carriage stabilised, Aiden looked out the window. In the darkness, as though sculpted from darkness, were whole swathes of human beings. Drawing on their last reserves of strength, they had dragged their bodies to pile up by the roadside. They have a keen instinct about the highway. This road leads to Madras. From where stretches a path to

London. This road is a cord that connects them to the world. A finger from the modern world that has extended to touch the ancient realm they live in.

But they were yet to apprehend that the world abroad was far more merciless than the one they lived in. That world was not a master who would merely chop their heads off. It was one that would insert a fine tube into their bodies and suck every last drop of blood. A sorcerer who would stir and swallow even the soul. It was what had shattered the very foundation they had relied on, turning them into human landfill. They lie at its very feet now, begging for mercy. The fools.

Yes. Fools, indeed. The one who knows not how to live is a fool. He should not be given a life. Yes, they must die. Why can't this mob attack those who are ensconced in full-stomached languor atop it? Why don't they sink their teeth in and drink their blood? Rip their muscles out and devour their flesh? Begging and pleading to death. There's no people more revolting than those who beg. Oh, will a torrent of noxious rain not wash away this mob of humanity without a trace? Can it not be that such a thing as this never transpired on this earth? Oh, Jesus! Jesus! Rescue me!

Then again, all humankind on this earth pleads with outstretched arms, does it not? Looking up at the skies, it has beseeched without end, hasn't it? For centuries. It has begged without shame or dignity. It has moaned and wept. Help! Help me! If there be a God, and he happens to look down, all he will see are worm-like digits straining to reach his black boots. With revulsion frothing up inside, he will run his chariot over that great swarm. Even so, he has no choice but to look at his shod feet. He has no choice but to watch the clots of dried blood on its surface, and be stunned. Jesus! Save my mind. I have lost my bearing. Jesus!

“How much farther?” Aiden asked, agitated.

“Sir, we should reach Chingleput at midnight. But we will not be able to keep up even this pace beyond it. The pile of refugees there is several times larger. They do not so much as bother with clearing the corpses in those parts.”

“It’ll suffice to go as far as Chingleput. I need to head back as soon as I meet with the town’s officials.”

“If we leave at dawn, we should be back in Chennai by the evening, sir.”

“Hmm.” Aiden shut his eyes. The dying wail of all humanity resounded outside. He sat listening to it with eyes closed. Lights from the approaching freight wagons crossed him now and again.

“So many people. Where do they all come from?”

“Sir, during the rains, the field mice scramble out as their burrows fill up. That is when we realise how large their population is. History is only now taking note of the number of us who live in this country.”

Gradually, the sound died down. Aiden looked out. People lay on the fringes of the road. By the light of the carriage, human limbs poked out like twigs abandoned by receding floodwaters.

“Are they alive?”

“There cannot be much difference.”

Seeing that there were plenty of bodies strewn around, the throng must have moved on, Aiden reasoned. Those who were unable to leave would be lying among the dead. Aware in every passing moment that they, too, were turning into the dead. The final beating of the soul. To live. To beget the next moment from the great ether. But to live was more tortuous than death itself. For this lot, to live is to hunger. A murderous hunger! How does that feel? How do they feel when they hunger for days on end?

"Joseph, how many days have you gone hungry?"

"Up to three days, sir. As a child, I knew hunger more than I knew food."

How succinctly he speaks, Aiden marvelled.

"After the first three days, you will feel no trace of hunger. From time to time, a severe ache will grip your stomach. As if lashed by a whip or seared by a hot rod. But for that you will feel nothing. There will be no such thing as awareness. One mouthful of food—your mind will become that very thought. You saw it, did you not? The soul will be emptied of all words. Blood, tears, family, kinship—none of it will mean anything. Food, and the frantic search for food, is all that will remain. You saw for yourself . . . Did any one of them think of the other? Every single person in this throng of thousands is irretrievably alone."

Sitting up with a start, Aiden grabbed hold of the carriage bars. "Yes, many of the women were without children, too."

"It is a mother's child that accompanies her till the very end. But the child, too, is shed at some point."

Aiden closed his eyes. He was listening to the throbbing of the veins at his temples. Aloneness. A stark aloneness. *You* need not tell me that. *No one* need tell me that. God has erected it all around me. Same as the sawdust that grips a bottle of champagne in place, not letting it budge an inch within its wooden box. This darkness, too, constricts me now, like sawdust. I wait. My soul sours, curdles, festers, ferments, and waits. Jesus, my Saviour, I am your sweet wine. Your life-taking addiction.

God! Is that a mere conditioning of the mind? A conceit your parents instil in you early on. Is that all it is? Whatever it might be, people the world over believe in one god or the other. "God," they lament in pain, in hunger, in ignominy, in death. If that be so, it is humanity's compulsion. Like blinking one's eyes, or scratching oneself. A biological need. Nothing more than that. No . . . if there's no God, all of this takes on a still more ruthless meaninglessness. God is but an absurdity who occupies the other end of the balance to lower such a danger.

God. Where is he? In the skies? If he be in that hungerless, deathless infinitude, what is it that we can make him understand? Hunger hurts like a whiplash, I hear. And sears like a burning rod. Does the handle of that whip rest in his hand? Is that fiery rod his boundless mercy? The Hindus, they will agree. To create, protect, and destroy are all his acts, they'll say. One of their gods is the hero of apocalypse. A universe-destroying poison has collected in his throat. Has a drop of that poison trickled down and dripped on this cursed land? Create, Protect, Destroy. A triune of duties. A triad of faces. A triad of emptiness. A triad of meaninglessness.

Is it the Eternal Triune, is it He
Who dares arrest the wheels of destiny
And plunge me in the lowest Hell of Hells?
Will not the lightning's blast destroy my frame?

Where did that verse come from? Shelley, he who has stagnated in me as septic bitterness, it is he. Yes, indeed he. He alone could stand level with God and condemn his crooked sceptre thus. Like a colour-drained butterfly, these lines, wiped of all meaning, lie in front of me as mere babble. Quivering like mere flesh and blood. With death's final wingbeat. A hell lower than hell. A death baser than death. An abject baseness that furthers baseness. It is *this* that you've pushed humans into. You've kicked them aside like refuse, into a dust heap. The wheels shuddered. A deathly moan of pain. The outline of some human form in the dark. Its bones must have crumbled. It must have crushed like a louse, smashed and flattened. With what little strength remained, it had set its arm or leg in motion and crawled in the direction of the road. The finger of the paternal hand extending to touch that of a hungry and lonely Adam—that is this road.

By now, that life would have departed. It must have risen from the body, floated in the dark, and stayed to look below. Have the departed souls sheathed this darkened sky like a vast film? The wheels of this carriage must be dripping with blood. Nothing serves better the act of crushing than a wheel. It does not stay put after it crushes. It keeps on going. It achieves movement through the very act of crushing. Wheels of destiny. Oh, this mind is my hell. And Shelley, who stands there with his blood-soaked, barbed whip, the Lord of Hell.

"Stop the vehicle." Andrew spoke up. "Please, stop the vehicle."

Aiden rapped his hand on the windowpane. The carriage stopped.

"Are you getting down?" Aiden asked, seeing Andrew reach for his bag.

"Yes," said Andrew, pointing at something. Ahead of them, an oxcart was tunnelling into the darkness. "I'll join them."

"Why?"

"That cart is full of bodies. They're headed to bury the dead."

When Aiden peered into the darkness, he could make out arms and legs sticking out of or hanging over the rear of the cart. "They must be working for the government."

"I wish to be with them," said Andrew, as he unlatched the door and got down.

“You could die. The whole land has turned noxious.”

“All I wish for now is to die. I can tell every cadaver here that. I will look into their eyes and tell them that I, too, will die. That’s all I want to do.”

“Sir, as a matter of fact, that vehicle belongs to the members of your Scottish church. They are the ones clearing the bodies,” Joseph offered.

“This is where I’m going to be. All this way, I had but one prayer on my lips. My Lord, why this, why, Jesus, I cried, banging my head against his feet. Why did you bring me here, my Lord, I sobbed. I see a clear design from the moment I left London all the way to this moment here. But to what end, I demanded. If you don’t give me an answer, I’ll give up my life on this very soil, I cried. That’s when I spotted this vehicle. This is why I’ve come here. This is the land I must live on. This is the duty I must perform.”

“You ought to be reporting to work in Calcutta—”

“I threw those papers away a long time ago.”

Aiden reached out to close the door. “May Christ be with you,” he said.

“Yes, he will always be with me. We cannot understand his wishes. We cannot alter his designs. All we can do is be close to him. Goodbye.”

Aiden watched Andrew swing his bag over his shoulder and march off. When he submerged into the darkness and vanished from sight, it looked as though he had tumbled headlong into a gigantic pit of corpses.

8

By the time Aiden came out, Duraisamy had washed the carriage. Even as he wiped down one end of its surface, beads of water shimmered on the other side in the lamplight. In the red glow of light, Aiden, who was coming down the stairs, mistook them for drops of blood and recoiled in horror. Duraisamy stepped away momentarily to stow the cloth, before returning to the carriage. The horses sensed his arrival and exhaled loudly. The black horse arched its neck and attempted to catch his scent. It stamped the ground with its hind legs and flicked its tail.

Aiden stepped on the box Duraisamy had positioned before him, climbed into the carriage, and sat down. Duraisamy was clothed in a coachman's livery complete with a crimson-sashed khaki uniform and a red turban-shaped hat edged with a white tassel. His belt and boots were finely polished. The scabbard at his hip, too, gleamed sharply. Without a word, he climbed into the driver's perch, held the whip in his hand, and waited for Aiden's command.

Suddenly, a thought struck Aiden: Had Duraisamy washed the driver's seat because Joseph had occupied it? Yes, it must be so, he said to himself. But, the next minute, he reasoned that Duraisamy must've thought it impossible to drive to the fort in a carriage reeking of blood all over. Duraisamy waited without the faintest perturbation. When Aiden rapped twice on the door, he gave the horses a light tap and set the vehicle off with a little jolt. Soon the sea breeze began to crash into him in waves and splinter apart.

Aiden removed his hat, balanced it on his knee, and ran his hand through his hair. He opened the leather-bound file resting on his lap and looked over the papers another time. His heart quickened. He closed the file, shut his eyes, and leaned back. Everything he had witnessed in the course of a full night and day lay far behind him, as if it were a dream, or a childhood memory, or some tale he could scarcely recall.

The truth was he had begun to detach himself from those events even as he was driving back that evening. He had gathered information from the Chingleput collector's office, the tehsildars' offices, the station houses, the Scottish Mission's church, and the Catholic Marian shrine, all through the day. He collected two-page-long reports from all the minor officers engaged in fieldwork and compiled them. He instructed the scribes to provide him with copies of important documents and statistics. He made brief notes of his own observations. The material ran in excess of forty pages.

Seated in his vehicle, he carefully examined the papers one by one. When, pausing for a moment he glanced at the surrounding woods, he noticed something—his mind had begun to quieten down. The terrifying dreamscape that had unfolded right in front of his eyes had transmuted into mere facts imprinted on the pages before him. That dream was beyond his grasp. It was the upsurge of a vast ocean that could sweep him away, like straw. These statistics, on the contrary, were well within the reach of his hand, of his mind. He scrutinised them endlessly and ordered them in myriad ways. Here to there, there to here, the very act of arranging and rearranging seemed to consolidate his control over them. Outside, the land of death retreated into the yonder.

Upon his return, he promptly took his place at his desk and began to make out a report. As he wrote, he observed his mind revel in a veiled joy. Gradually, his subconscious began to delight in the bewildering limitlessness of all that he could write about, and the excitement sparked by the realisation. In time, a notion that he was crafting a historic document surfaced in him. A document that could upturn the very course of history. A document that might be read a hundred years hence. His name will be on it. Captain Aiden Byrne. Yes, him indeed.

A few more sentences in, he realised that he was rendering the scenes he had witnessed into history. His brain groped for the most felicitous word and, upon discovering it, bore it on its head with foolish delight and came running. He was committing to paper the most eloquent and passionate lines he had ever written in his life. Through vivid descriptions, he manifested the visuals in language. By methodically arranging the facts, he steered the report to a logical conclusion and ended it with a sentence as sharp as a spear's point. His lines stood out with a gleaming keenness. Like a finger stroking a sharp edge, his mind ran over the sentences time and again, and delighted in them.

When he finished, he stretched his legs and reclined in the chair contentedly. David was at the door.

"Sir?" he ventured.

"Tea," said Aiden.

David came back and set down a small plate of toasted bread along with the tea. He understands my needs, Aiden said to himself. The moment he set eyes on the bread, his hunger boiled over. He devoured the bread and drank the tea. Then he went over what he had written. As he read it, his mind shrank with discontent. Every line had a crinkle at one place or the other. The ends were twisted and refused to fit. He edited each and every sentence. Changed the words. Struck out entire paragraphs and rewrote them.

When, after the third draft, he travelled through those words once again, he could see that they had moved a great distance away from him. However, that very distance had now arranged them neatly. Even so, minute errors caught his eye. But he was unable to read those words any further. They bored him, as if penned by some unknown person from some unknown land. He gave the dip pen a good rinse and returned it to its ceramic holder. Had Marisa been here, I could've asked her to copy this out in her lovely hand. I can have her come, even now. No. Let this history be written in my own hand. The hand that people would behold a hundred years hence was his.

Closing his eyes, Aiden sat in place for some time. All his experiences up until that moment, as though they had merged together and upturned a big load on him, engulfed his mind. The spate of death he had witnessed all night had morphed into something altogether different in the morning. In the pale light of the morning, he beheld a dark-black mass of humanity, immune to any kind of order, drift aimlessly. They were proceeding swathe after swathe. Like a people who, unmindful of the sights and sounds around them, were being carried by their legs involuntarily.

All along the path, they were huddled under the trees. They lay among the underbrush. Cartloads of male and female bodies were being dumped into gaping pits dug up at various places in the forest, covered with salt sacks and quick lime, and buried under heaps of sand. Watching the scene with their dead-fish-like eyes were a concourse of humans who were versions of the very corpses in front of them.

Aiden had reached the office of the Chingleput tehsildar at the first flush of sunshine. He dispatched the Talaiyari, the village assistant, to summon the revenue officer. The tehsildar turned out to be a Brahmin whose forehead flaunted a sacred vertical mark. With his moustacheless upper lip held in a peculiar curl, he waded in and offered customary greetings in an Indianised English. "We had no information of your arrival," he said. "The Inspection Bungalow is presently occupied by another tehsildar and his wife. I will ask them to vacate immediately and make all arrangements for you to freshen up and rest there."

"That won't be necessary. I have to leave shortly," Aiden replied.

Though the tehsildar's face fell, his smile remained unchanged. "I will have everything you need brought directly to your room," he declared.

"Don't bother. I just need to see all the records and reports you have gathered on the famine."

"At once, sir," he replied, and set about retrieving the files. By then, the Talaiyari who had rushed out returned with a couple of scribes. The two scribes had washed their faces in a hurry and applied religious marks on their brows. They had thrown on grey buttonless jackets over their waistcloths. Grimy white shirts peeped out from underneath the jackets. Big turban-hats rested on their head. Each held a cloth bag in one hand. "Good morning," they greeted Aiden nervously as soon as they entered, then set about their tasks.

Before long, Aiden gathered that the British administrative machinery had learned to deal with the famine in keeping with its fundamental principles. It had altogether shunned from its attention a holistic view of the famine, its root causes, and the ways to halt it. It had defined the famine as a problem of "crowds swarming the streets and bodies lining the roadsides." After the initial bewilderment, it had begun to deal with that problem efficiently.

Most of the roads had an armed battalion of Pathans led by a sergeant standing guard at intervals of five kilometres. Erstwhile soldiers of the nawab of Wallajah had been drafted for the purpose at a salary of eight annas a month. Maravars had been brought in from Madurai. They were mobilised into paramilitary units with one British constable handed charge of a band of twenty Maravars. If the vehicles on the roads obtained a receipt from the designated officer after making a payment commensurate with the value of the goods they were plying, the British government would offer them protection.

An army of Thotis—a caste of people born into the occupation of removing human waste from dry sewers—had been put together to clear and bury the corpses. Bullock carts had been hired for the purpose. The job of the Thotis was restricted to loading the corpses onto the carts and transporting them to the pits. There were others to drive the carts, dig the pits, and so on. Every unit was assigned a Kanakkupillai who was, traditionally, an upper-caste accountant. Half an anna per corpse was the designated wage. That would be divided among the unit. The Kanakkupillais were managed by sheristadars. The toll received from the vehicles was enough to defray the entire cost of this operation.

The tally of corpses and the swarm of people piled on the streets had turned into mere numbers in the documents and, having assumed the corporeal form of black ink-nut-dye symbols, lay imprinted on the page. Seeing them, a wry smile spread on Aiden's face. Children, abandoned and starving to death in a village road in Chingleput become numbers at the hands of the Kanakkupillai at the rate of half an anna per head. In the sheristadars' overall accounts, they reduce to small numbers. In the tehsildar's aggregate, a fraction of a single head of expenditure. In Aiden's report, a passing line. For the governor, a glance of the eye. For God, would it even be a momentary thought?

Were I to return with my faith intact, I'll take it that Jesus has not abandoned me, he told himself as he boarded his carriage again. How long will Jesus be by Andrew's side and protect him? If his faith were to abandon him at some point, he would shatter to pieces that very moment. Disease should take him before that happens. Should one wish to pray for him, that ought to be the prayer.

It appeared to him, though, that faith was not external. How far I have moved away on the back of a few words. Andrew is incapable of it. People like him know not the art of veiling their soul with words. He apprehended the true meaning of the famine the moment he set eyes upon it. I, on the other hand, am kicking it around with my words. I manoeuvre it this way and that, to bring it to a place that suits me.

Was this why Man created letters and numbers? To alienate himself conveniently from the life that swells right in front of his eyes, to create a private world inside them and dwell there? Once again, he looked over the report and the documents he had appended to it. No, it isn't so. What I had seen at first was the full-blown form of the problem. I have essentialized it now. That is all I can put forth to the duke. If, perchance, he understands it, I might be able to put an end to the dance of death I witnessed back there.

Put an end? Yes, without a doubt. Stop the export of grains from Madraspatnam, Nagapatnam, and Vizagapatnam, and the famine will end within a week. There's no British officer who's unaware of that. The question is, can the duke pull it off? Those grains feed the British armies fighting in desert lands, in ice fields, in dense jungles, to conquer the world. Can he halt the British Empire that spreads like grass fire? He is only a speck floating in its current. Same as me. Same as any other officer.

A weariness enveloped him. This is a fruitless enterprise, I should turn back, he told himself. At the very least, I must refrain from turning in this report. All they will do is give it a cursory glance and say a few perfunctory words. In deference, in praise. But laughter will lurk somewhere in their eyes. A laughter only another Englishman can intuit. An Englishman's smile is like the glow of a furnace. Sometimes, a guillotine. Yes, an Irishman can never reach those depths.

The carriage neared the boundary wall of Fort St. George. Next to the cannons on the four parapets over the low-slung ramparts of the fort burned small lamps. The thin silhouettes of the sepoys stationed on top emerged into view. The entrance to the fort itself lay wide open and unguarded. It was poorly lit, too. Small, open-roofed pleasure coaches streamed in one after the other. Men wearing bicornes rode their one-horse phaetons at top speed. At the back of the slightly bigger, driver-manned phaetons, British ladies in tricorne hats sat clutching the folds of their capacious gowns lest they lift off in the wind. The candle lamps that hung from the base of the carriage dangled to and fro, making the shadows of the spokes dance on the walls and yards around. The coachmen tinkled the carriage bells, kindling the feeling of a huge herd returning home.

Inside the fort, a line of pantile-roofed, Indian-style houses passed them by on both sides. Low-ranking police officers and other white-skinned employees had made them their homes. Coal gas, whose production was a very recent addition in the fort, was distributed through copper piping to light up the lamps installed in the fort's precincts. Like glass eggs, lamps shone in a glare of yellow in every house. Aiden often felt that their sharp gleam stung the eye. The arrival of gas lamps had ruined the mystery and mellow of nighttime, or so it seemed to him.

Swiftly walk o'er the western wave, Spirit of Night! The night Shelley extolled exists no longer. They have whitewashed it, and rendered it pallid. The same light burns in the house of the junior sergeant residing in the fort, too. The gas lamp's tariff alone will swallow one fourth of his pay. Even so, he cannot give it up. It is the light of authority. The auxiliary suns of the empire upon which the sun never sets.

Turbaned chaprasis attired in white were stationed in the verandas of all the houses. Having finished the day's work, hatless, barefooted employees dressed in cotton tunics and khaki shorts lounged in the chairs laid out in the front yard, nursing their drinks. Some were with family, some with friends. A clutch of dogs barked relentlessly. Tucked away in the darkness, the horses buried their noses in the feed bags and chomped on gram.

On either side of the gateway at the entrance to the inner fort, two large paraffin oil lamps burned inside human-size, jar-like glass enclosures. A white flame rested in a tremble on the pale-blue seat that had formed over the small, rounded wicks. Four soldiers bearing Snider-Enfield rifles approached the carriage, stopped a short distance away, and fell to attention. Their sergeant proceeded forward. Aiden opened the door and stepped out. Recognising him, the sergeant saluted. Then, with a wave of his hand, he allowed the carriage entry.

Almost every building in the inner fort had at least two storeys. Sloping roofs thatched with black tiles imported from London were held up by round pillars and brick-hued walls. Light lay pooled outside the coloured glass panes of the large windows crowned with decorative arches. The hundreds of windows across Georgetown spilled light and filled the sky. The cone-shaped steeple of St. Mary's Church rose high over the buildings. Absorbing the light from below, it stood against the darkened sky, an ashen silence pointing at the firmament.

Red-stone buildings began to appear on both sides of the stone-paved road. Aiden's carriage rolled on smoothly. The horses' hooves tapped out a steady rhythm. The sweeping courtyards in front of the buildings were occupied by high-end chariots. Coachmen were seated on their haunches next to the carriages. A row of twirling horse tails poked out of a long stable a few paces away. In the verandas where the vetiver-reed screens had been rolled up, orderlies liveried in white and chaprasis sporting red turbans and white outfits fitted with golden sashes stood about. As though glued to the wall, punkah pullers, clothed in white tunics and white turbans, sat on their haunches. The passing vehicles did nothing to evoke so much as a glance from them.

The vetiver screens shielding the high windows of Clive House had been rolled up, and light poured out from within. On both extremes of the entrance shouldered by white limestone columns, big gas lanterns glowed like two moons in whose light the yard's stone floor appeared like a wet sprawl. Four chariots occupied the courtyard. The chariot that stretched out like a staggering gold ornament must be Grace Darling, the famed luxury carriage, Aiden deduced.

The carriage called to mind an ornamental, diamond-encrusted gold casket placed as a centrepiece at a royal feast. Beneath its slim, golden roof, pink Kashmir silk fluttered against the windows that opened on both sides. Exits were designed for alighting from either side of the vehicle. The front wheel was relatively small. The back wheel, big. Composed of spokes as fine as the metal wires inside a shirt collar, the wheels were slender. The carriage stood there like a British lady for whom extravagance had become both soul and being. Its coachman stood guard nearby at strict attention.

When an attendant came up to them and bowed, Aiden's carriage drew to a stop. Aiden alighted from the vehicle. He tightened his grip on the file. Sweaty hands slipped down its surface. He daubed his face and hands with a silk handkerchief. He straightened his coat and fixed his necktie. He put his hat on, set it in place, and walked towards the building. A soldier led Aiden's carriage towards a stable located far away in a corner of the premises. As Aiden closed in on the building, Clive House grew taller and taller. The breadth of the building fell out of vision until only the entrance towered in front of him.

Two of the vehicles parked in the courtyard were American-made. Concord stagecoaches from the Abbot-Downing Company. They cost a fortune even in Britain. It was astonishing to see how common they were in India. The crimson coach bodies bore curved reflections of the row of windows that spewed light from the building, calling to mind a limp string of red pearls. The coaches wore the look of the exquisitely attired owner of an American shipping company who flaunts a solitary diamond of incalculable value in his tie clip.

It was only when he drove past those coaches that Aiden noticed it. Only four of the vehicles bore the ensign of the governor of Madras. All four had been manufactured in London. A couple of them were clarences. The other two, broughams. Even though they gleamed and glistened with polish, it was evident that they were old. The duke had brought along the vehicles owned by his family and continued to travel in them, Aiden surmised. Wedged between two different kinds of ostentatious vehicles, they seemed like British gentlemen stubbornly holding on to old pride. He smiled. In that moment, he felt that he would be able to understand the duke.

As he reached the top of the stairs, four orderlies received him with a bow. One of them deftly helped him out of his long coat and took his hat. Another one extended a big white porcelain bowl in his direction. A white towel was soaking inside, in steaming hot, perfumed water. He picked up the towel and dabbed his chin and forehead. The orderlies led him to a huge waiting hall.

With pink curtains of Arabian muslin aflutter against the sea breeze, the waiting hall was open and airy. There were already eight visitors seated in the chairs upholstered in blood-red Moroccan leather. Two of them were women of rank. Four orderlies stood rock-still as though they had been painted on the wall. In the glass chandelier that descended from the ceiling like an enormous ice cluster glowed newly fitted gas lamps. On the walls below, too, gas lamps shone like bubbles of light.

After greeting the ladies and then the others, Aiden took his seat. Although they returned his greeting with the requisite cheer, it was evident that they did not care for his presence. One of the ladies was more than fifty by the looks of it. She had drawn herself arched eyebrows. The skin under her eyes and around her lips was wrinkled like white silk. The flab under her chin hung pouch-like. Her pouting lips were painted red. She wore an oversized linen wig over her hair. The lavender fragrance of the powder she had dusted on it permeated the room. She was dressed in a high-necked, grey gown. A walking cane with a stone-eyed, lacquer vulture head for a handle rested in her hand. She had positioned the cane across her knees.

The other woman was in her thirties. Clad in a pale-blue, off-the-shoulder gown bolstered by her ample bosoms she wore a big-rimmed hat pinned with ribbons and fake blossoms. Gloves embroidered with luminous blue diamonds sheathed both hands. Earrings studded with dazzling blue diamonds. A pearl necklace embellished with blue diamonds. There were diamonds even in the decorative leather belt secured around her waist. The six men were dressed identically, in grey suits and grey waistcoats. Wearing identical expressions on their faces, they sat still. Their red hair was combed similarly, to the right. Eyes like shards of black granite.

When one feels like a rank outsider somewhere, the greatest hindrance is one's own body, Aiden mused. It is possible to hide the mind, but the body remains blatantly in view. What must be done with it? That very thought consumes one's mind. Now, this body that I present to you is that of an Irishman. Of an ordinary captain. The body of a sailor, of a soldier. Of a reader of poetry who has ever abhorred authority. How ought I to carry it? What should I do with my hands? How should I place my legs? Where should I fix my eyes? How do I hold my lips still?

What is taking so long? Time was leaking away drop by drop. The massive door that was shut to them was perhaps imported from London. It, too, was cushioned with blood-red Moroccan leather. The lamps cast themselves as dots of flame on its brass handles, which gleamed like gold. Doors that did not permit even a single happening inside to get past them in the form of sound. The lemon-blossom fragrance that was all the rage in London had imbued the room. The scent that at first was pleasing to the nose gradually induced a headache.

Without warning, the doors turned slowly on their brass hinges and opened without a sound. Only the gloved hands of the black servant who had opened it could be seen. The white orderly stepped out and lowered his head respectfully. "The Honourable Duke of Buckingham, the Governor of Madras," he announced. All those who were seated got to their feet. The younger woman arched her waist a touch more than necessary, while the men lifted their chins as high as they could, stiffened their hands, and froze like men stuck inside an ice-block for a very long time.

The orderly was a gaunt-faced, middle-aged man with line-like lips and goat-like amber eyes. Soft wisps of hair, like lather, rested on his forehead. His neck was blood red. His face, powdered. From inside emerged the sound of heavy footsteps. Pushing his big frame and flabby form as though he had just disembarked after an overlong carriage ride, the duke walked out.

Richard Plantagenet Campbell Temple-Nugent-Brydges-Chandos-Grenville, third Duke of Buckingham and Chandos, was around fifty years of age. All the same, his physique and appearance suggested that he was past sixty. A thick beard rimmed his face like soft, dry grass. Tiny freckles dotted a long, pinched nose that presided over a clean-shaven upper lip. Deep lines ran across his forehead. He wore a red-hued wig. A blend of fragrances—of orris-root oil from the wig's powder and hammam bath oil—wafted forth. He must have woken up just then.

Rumbling with laughter, "My dear! How delightful it is to see you!" the duke shrilled phonily, and embraced the young woman. "Such beauty. Such charm," he said, as he kissed her on her cheeks with dreadful ceremony.

"Oh, oh," the woman blubbered in a paroxysm of feigned emotions, after which she teared up dramatically; lowering her head, she drew out a white silk handkerchief and dabbed her eyes. "Thank you, my Lord. Thank you. What a momentous day it is for me," she said.

"Most certainly, my dear, a great day," the duke repeated, and, turning to the old woman, said, "Your arrival honours me, my lady," and kissed her hand.

The old woman puckered her lips open and shrieked, "Oh, how wonderful! How fortunate we are!"

"My good fortune, entirely," said the duke, and he went on to shake hands with the others one by one. Stiff-necked, they extended their hands and greeted him with customary words of respect.

Aiden counted the seconds as he waited expectantly to catch the duke's eye. But the duke did not pay heed to him. When he returned to his room, the red-leather-embossed doors closed noiselessly after him and fell in place as though the restrained lips of a British gentleman were sealing shut.

Once again, everyone took their seats. Aiden felt as though he had grown even shorter, even squatter. He gathered that everyone else in that room felt his presence in their bodies as a great inconvenience. The duke must be having his tea inside, he told himself.

The orderly emerged again. The middle-aged man, who was first in line, got to his feet. "Charlie, I suppose my papers have been brought to the attention of His Grace," he said.

"I have placed your papers on top," the orderly answered.

The middle-ager adjusted his cravat and sat down. Everyone in the room held their bodies in readiness for being summoned. Just then, the door on the other end flung open, like a red mouth opening to admonish them. A tall, long-faced man with a Roman nose strode out with a natural swagger in his step. "Charlie, I presume the duke has taken his seat?" A black attendant came softly and stood behind him like a shadow.

"Yes, sir," Charlie replied with deference.

"Have him know that a few friends and I have come to meet him." So saying, he turned to the attendant and tilted his head gently. When the attendant opened the door and motioned with his hand, four men walked in. All of them Indians. Only one of them was dressed in a suit. The other three were clothed in pleated vaettis paired with grey coats. In keeping with Indian custom, they had unbuttoned their coats, baring their white tunics underneath.

The man dressed in a suit looked like a student. A thin, dark body. Eyes that held a deep gaze as though taking stock of everything. Hair cropped like an Englishman's. Even so, it was easy to fathom a tiny tuft of hair rolled up at the back of his head. No sign of a moustache, still. Couldn't be more than twenty-five, at the most.

Every one of them, with the exception of the suited man, wore studs in their ears and thick, gold medallion chains around their necks. One of them had fixed a finely embroidered Benares-zari cap on his head. The others sported woollen caps. They had slipped their watches into their coat pockets, and stuffed their crumpled handkerchiefs on top.

While the man in the suit stood stiffly, the other three looked directly at the seated crowd and evaluated them. A probing look, so characteristic of Indians. Even if one were to meet their eyes, they would not avert their gaze, or utter a word of greeting. It was evident that the four of them were either merchants or contractors. In which case, the man who'd brought them must be William Russell. He was the one who had received his letter, though it didn't seem as if he had sensed the presence of the sender in the audience. Aiden had seen him from a distance at one or another event in the past. Up close, he appeared even older.

Russell motioned to the Indians to sit down, seeing which, they took their seats somewhat hesitantly. "Pardon me," the young man in the suit said to Aiden, before sitting down next to him.

"Pleased to meet you," Russell said to the young woman with a nod of his head.

"It's a pleasure, a real pleasure," she said theatrically, and returned his nod.

"A good day, Russell," the elderly woman remarked.

"Yes, indeed," Russell replied. He acknowledged the others with subtle gestures, and sat down.

The Indians had applied a bouquet of fragrant substances on themselves. They were given to fixing a dot of punugu—a black waxy paste made from the secretion of civet cats—right between the brows. They would douse themselves in a range of perfumes extracted from plants, fruits, and tree barks, all at once. Their clothes would smell of a heady mix of slaked lime and screw pine. An approaching Indian personage could put one in mind of an ambulatory perfume store. The variety of scents in that room mingled and melded, making it hard to breathe.

The oldest among the Indians toted a gilt-trimmed betel-leaf case encrusted with red gemstones. He sat in a chair, clutching the box close to his body, his knees spread apart in such a way that his waistcloth had parted, revealing the inside of his thigh. A long red line ran up his brow. Bands of white powder adorned another man's forehead. The horizontal stripes lay boldly against his dark skin. He, too, was wearing an ear stud made of red gemstone. A Swiss watch was attached to his coat pocket with a gold chain. Until not too long ago, the Indians had refrained from wearing their religious marks to official meetings. Now they had the permission of Her Majesty the Queen.

The man with the betel-leaf case began to hum a kind of tune under his breath. His eyes were small and bright. His gaze flitted like a brisk rat. A small nose. Below a bare upper lip stretched a rather limp lower lip. Like the average Indian, he, too, seemed to possess the habit of endlessly chewing on betel leaves. His mouth was a bright crimson. Of the four of them, he alone was fair skinned. The red gemstone studs on his ears shone like two fire sparks.

The door opened. "Sir, your meeting," Charlie announced, facing Russell. Russell rose, straightened his coat, and extended his hand in the direction of his attendant. The attendant handed him a bulky leather document case. Russell tilted his chin at the four men and proceeded inside. They smoothened their clothes, adjusted their headgear, and, with a little bumping and shoving, filtered in.

Aiden felt the mounting tension in the waiting room in his bones. Faint, random movements passed through their bodies. The elderly white man cleared his throat softly and coughed. The old lady flapped her hand fan, made from slivers of ivory, close to her nose. The young woman inspected her lips in a handheld mirror.

Time ticked on. Slowly, Aiden relaxed. He held back the smile that budded in his heart from reaching his lips. He stretched his legs and trained his gaze on the two paintings that hung on the wall. Canvases bordered by thick brass frames. One of them held a distant view of old Madraspatnam's coastline. A view sketched from a vessel in the sea. Sailboats rested on the crest of foaming wavelets. The fort walls adjoined the sea. The buildings within its walls were bathed in slanting evening light. The pointed steeple and flagstaff of St. Mary's Church alone rose above them. Behind the fort was a row of volcanic-mound-like hills. Treeless rock caves. Did they really appear so to the eye, or was it pure imagination? St. Thomas Mount had been sketched in as though it were visible in the distance. Surely, there was no way one could see it from so far out at sea.

The second canvas was the Last Supper. An Italian original. One of the many canvases produced in the painting spree of the sixteenth century. The artist had paid great attention to the ripples on Jesus's maroon robe. He was holding up a piece of bread. In front of him was a glass of his own blood. The entire canvas was packed with faces, bowing, kneeling, drawing away in fear. It was difficult to tell who the artist was.

Catching the opening of the door reflected in the faces opposite him, Aiden turned around. "Captain Byrne," Charlie called out in a low voice, and tilted his head forward. Immediately, Aiden's mind went to all those merchants inside the room. Under no circumstance would matters concerning the British government be discussed in the presence of foreigners. He walked in with puzzlement. When he entered the room, he lowered his head in a formal greeting.

The duke had hung up his periwig on an elephant-ivory stand on his table. A few strands of hair stood up on his balding pate. The hair at the back had grown out and fell to his shoulders. While under a wig he had had the countenance of any other British nobleman. With a balding head, he had acquired the appearance of a kind, slow-witted father. His whole manner was colic. Russell and his companions were seated in the chairs in front of him.

When Aiden came in, the duke leaned forward with effort. "Captain Byrne?" he said with a smile.

"Yes," said Aiden.

"I have been to Ireland," the duke remarked, as he signalled towards a chair.

"Thank you, Your Grace," Aiden murmured, and sat down.

"I looked over the file you sent. Russell explained what happened," the duke went on.

"Yes, Your Grace," said Aiden. Should I begin, he wondered, beset with perturbation. Another opportunity will not present itself. And however this may end it would not be his fault.

"Generally speaking, Americans are honest where business is concerned," the duke continued.

Aiden realised that his moment had come. "That is true, Your Grace," he said. "But the situation in India has taken a different turn at the moment. That is what I wished to convey to Your Grace's society. It is also why I sought, and was fortunate enough to be granted, this audience with you."

The duke's eyes flitted towards Russell for a split second. Then, "Go on," he said, leaning back in his chair. He interlaced his fingers and rested his hands on his lap. It was clear to Aiden that he wouldn't have the measure of nuanced issues. But there was no doubt that he was a good man. Perhaps a magnanimous, even compassionate man. With a definite touch of self-conceit and quick temper.

"Your Grace, wherever one goes, workers and investors are perennially at odds with each other. That is what determines the wages. And the terms of employment, too. But out here, there is certainly no opportunity for such a negotiation to take place. For this Presidency of ours is wasting away in a famine. It's fair to say that Madraspatnam is a fallen apple buried in leaf litter. It may look ripe, red, and shiny on the surface, but its bottom half is decayed and infested with maggots."

Aiden untied his file and placed it on the duke's table. It was a massive desk. A small Union Jack was planted on an ivory stand. Russell rose from his chair and pushed Aiden's file in the direction of the duke. The duke took it in his hands and parted the cover.

"I've recorded the scenes I witnessed of the famine from forenoon yesterday till the morning today. It contains both firsthand field reports and memos from social workers. What I saw was a human tragedy of epic proportions. A moment of Christ's making to put the British sense of justice to test. That is how it seems to me."

In a flash, the duke's eyes met his before lowering again. Aiden's heart trembled. How had he received those words? It dawned on him that he was talking to a British aristocrat who had learned to keep his aspect and soul thousands of miles apart from himself.

The duke was reading. Aiden's eyes roved anxiously all over the room. The curtains undulated against the big teakwood windows like serene dancers. Above, an enormous punkah, as though offering its blessing to the whole room, brushed back and forth. A punkah with red silk flower tassels. It churned the air noiselessly. Behind the duke hung a giant portrait of Queen Victoria. A little diamond crown rested atop a decorative veil that covered her head. The icon that rules the world. The old woman who was wearing it looked like a dim-witted soul abandoned at a marketplace.

The duke looked up. He gently drew the file closer. Aiden felt a tinge of hesitation again. He repeated to himself that he would not let the moment slip. "Your Grace, every person in this country imagines the present moment to be theirs. They use the hapless condition of the famine-stricken to their advantage and profit from it. The affected are pouring onto the streets like rats scrambling out of a house on fire. These people, on the other hand, act like they are out to loot a house on fire."

Aiden could tell that his emotions were getting the better of him. "Your Grace, we banned the slave trade nearly a century ago. That praise goes to our Crown. But, today, scores of people rally together only to offer themselves up as slaves in this famine. They hawk and sell their own families. They're bought for pennies and taken to plantations all over the world as labourers. Even as far back as when the Portuguese engaged in slave trade, humans were eight times as valuable."

For a fleeting instant, Aiden wondered if he had crossed a line. Shunning the thought, he pressed on. "Every single business owner in town employs these people, only to work them the whole day in return for no more than one meal. Our contractors, too, deploy them in road-laying and construction and rake in obscene profits. The blood of these people is measured out for sale in the marketplace. This is the real backdrop of the Ice House issue."

The duke sat staring like a statue. "Your Grace, all of these people are the subjects of Her Majesty the Queen. They are your people. The responsibility of saving them is yours. You must go see their plight with your own eyes. The reports contain mere words, nothing more. Bodies are piling up all over our roads. At the rate of a thousand corpses for every reported word."

The chair creaked as the duke shifted faintly. His gaze touched Russell and returned to its place. Aiden sensed that his time was coming to an end. "Your Grace, I've made a recommendation at the end of my report. There is a very elementary and straightforward way to manage this famine. That is to stop the export of food grains from the ports of Nagapatnam and Vizagapatnam for six months. Followed by a decree that food grains ought not to be stockpiled anymore. Before long, all the hoarded grain will be out in the sun. The famine will end inside of a week."

Seeing the duke's lips part slowly, he hastened to add, "It's our duty, Your Grace. We ought to do this for the Christ who resides in the souls of us we call humans. To what avail is it to lose our soul and gain this world, so asked our Saviour. There's no glory in conquering the whole wide world while letting millions of people starve to a ghastly death, only ignominy. This is an opportunity to stand before Christ as humans, Your Grace."

When the duke's lips separated, Aiden stopped.

"I understand your sentiment fully, young man," the duke began. "What you say is right. Our collective sense of justice has been put to the test at this hour of history." For a split second, he glanced in Russell's direction, "Nevertheless, our realities put us to the test, too. We can only do what we can do. Our reality lies not in considering Madras or India alone. It falls on us to keep the whole world in mind in our deliberations."

That instant, a cord snapped somewhere. Aiden fell from the height he had occupied and hurtled towards a bottomless abyss.

"All the same, your words have touched my soul. I will certainly do what ought to be done at this point. Your report shall serve as the basis for my action. For which, I must thank you."

The duke rose from his chair and extended his hand. When Aiden held the hand gloved in white silk lightly, and shook it, he did not look up at the duke. There was a tightness in his throat. He realised that a gentle push was all it would take for him to dissolve into tears like a snow-shedding bough.

"Your dedication and genuine emotion have not escaped my attention, Captain Byrne," the duke said, tipping his head imperceptibly.

Aiden got to his feet, clicked his ankles together, and saluted stiffly, after which he bowed to Russell and exited the room. Like the red mouth of a rectum shrinking shut after ejecting waste, the doors sealed together noiselessly behind him. The white personages on the outside sat as they were; without looking in his direction, they observed him with their bodies. The elderly lady began to air herself with her ivory fan.

9

As Aiden approached the front entrance of Clive House, he faltered several times. His limbs felt as if they were made of cloth. The weariness of all his wanderings until that moment hung heavily in his body. It seemed to him that his body was a deep chasm into which he ought to drain barrel after barrel of liquor. Bearing that void on my legs, I trudge forward. There is nothing as weighty as a void.

His carriage arrived in the darkness. As soon as he climbed in and sat down, Duraisamy gave the vehicle a tap. The carriage set off with a soft creak. The horse hooves fell like seeds plopping on rock. The sound splintered into the dark recesses between the buildings. An ash-grey sky extended over the fort. It seemed to reflect the inner luminescence of the ocean.

That was when Aiden noticed whole flocks of birds making their way across the sky. As he gazed at them with keen eyes, their numbers multiplied further and further.

"Duraisamy, where did so many birds come from?" he asked.

"Sir?" said Duraisamy.

"Why are there so many birds in the sky?"

"It is the month of Aippasi . . ." Duraisamy paused, then restarted, "Sir, beginning October, you will see lots of birds in the sky hereabouts. They keep flying southward. Sometimes, when you look up, it will seem as if the sky has been sealed shut."

"Oh," said Aiden.

"The more the number of birds, the better the harvest, they say."

"Which means there'll be no famine next year, am I right?"

"What does the harvest have to do with the famine? Last year, too, we had good yields coming in. An abundance of pearl and finger millets."

Everyone seems to know the truth already, Aiden reflected. A heavy breath escaped him.

"Some reap their harvest only during the famine. You must have met the commanders of the famine back there?"

"Who?" Aiden responded instinctively. After a moment, "I didn't acquaint myself with them," he said.

"I was talking to the coachmen outside. They told me," Duraisamy went on. "Two of the visitors were from Ceylon. An old lady, by the name Madam Calvin. Her son-in-law, Mr. Calvin, is setting up plantations in Nuwara Eliya. The rest of them were from Malaya. The young woman was Lady Cornfield."

Aiden smiled. Lady Cornfield, a nice name indeed. His mind cast back to her diamonds. How many diamonds and how many pretences it takes for a farmer's daughter to become a lady. How much blood would've been shed in its quest.

"Her husband, Mr. Cornfield, owns plantations in Malaya. His younger brother has accompanied him as well. The other man was Mr. Jacobson. He, and two of his friends, are also setting up plantations in Malaya. They are in need of thousands of farmhands. If they take a hundred, only twenty survive in the end, I'm told. So, however many they take, it is never enough. You cannot raze a forest one step at a time. It will keep growing even as you bring it down. The only way is to clear the whole thing in one sweep and start the plantation. Which is why they need lakhs and lakhs of labourers for it."

After a moment's pause to assess if Aiden was taking kindly to his line of talk, Duraisamy plodded on. "Very few live in those places. Moreover, they keep away from forest work. Here, on the other hand, you can get as many workers as you need, thanks to the famine. But if the famine were to end next year, these workers will become hard to find. So the plantation owners want to ship off as many people as possible before that happens. But then, it seems that the British officers are not cooperating."

"I believe they need to pay a tax?" said Aiden.

"They are willing to pay any amount of tax is what I hear. However, every officer is using the planters' predicament to their advantage and demanding bribes. The more the planters pay, the more the bribe money goes up. The bribe, in itself, is not as much of an issue. It is the artificial delay caused to lay ground for it that pinches the planters the most. That is the grievance they are here to register."

"So, what is their demand?" Aiden asked. These coachmen can ink the history of the British government with more clarity than anyone else, he thought to himself.

"That they should be allowed to hire ships to transport the labourers. That they be granted permission directly at the level of the collector, and that the port officials not poke their noses into this business. Most likely, the governor will agree. The plantation owners are loaded with cash. I am scared to even touch the carriages they own," Duraisamy expounded. "The story goes that an officer stopped a shipload of labourers bound for Mr. Cornfield's plantation. The officer seems to have argued that a few of the labourers had dysentery and, if they travelled by the same ship, it would spread to the others. Well, if they die of disease, they will simply be cast overboard. In any case, it is the investor Mr. Cornfield who has to bear the loss, is it not?"

"Who were those people who came to meet Russell?" asked Aiden.

Duraisamy considered the question carefully. Was he being tested?

Aiden could see the doubt pass through his mind. "They were Indian businessmen. I've never seen them before. Nor were they introduced to me," he offered.

"The Brahmin with the vertical mark on his forehead was Murahari Iyengar. He is a lawyer by profession, but he is the one who advises most London-based banks on their local investments. His father was a dubhashi to the British government. Prior to that, the family had produced ministers who served the Thanjavur kings. The three other men who were with him are contractors. The youngest of them is Thatikonda Namberumal Chetty. His father, Thatikonda Ramachandra Chetty, is an eminent iron merchant. It is he who distributes all the iron wares that land in Madras."

"Oh," said Aiden.

"Apparently he is planning to get into construction, too, alongside his iron trade. After his time at Madras University, he seems to have studied architecture for two years, in London. He wants to take up contracts with the British government. Of the other two, the thickset man was Panuganti Narasimharao. The other, Chinnur Namachivaya Mudaliyar."

Aiden leaned back with a sigh. Unexpectedly, a smile rose to his lips. These were the people within and without the room when he was delivering his passionate and dramatic monologue to the duke. What must the duke have said after I left, he mused. He's a pure-blooded Brit; he wouldn't have said a word. Russell might have said something to him. Then again, he may not have, either. He might say a few words later, while bantering with his private circle of friends, his lips curling to one side as he nurses a glass in his hand. "Fascinating," his friends might remark, and smile. The duke might scribble a few lines in his journal with a dash of satire.

But, without a doubt, those Indians will break into laughter as soon as they get back to their vehicles. They will laugh all the way home. They will recount it to their wives and lovers, and titter. It could well become a joke they will remember for the rest of their lives. Were they to come face-to-face with him in the future, underneath all the deference and servility, a metallic barb of laughter will gleam in their eyes.

"Thatikonda is a village near Warangal. Ramachandra Chetty came here pulling a hand cart all the way from his hometown, to sell his wares. Today, he employs thousands of workers. The whole port is under his thumb. He makes an offering of cooked rice to a hundred Brahmins every day at the Parthasarathy temple," Duraisamy kept up. "With the British rule, quite a few Chettiars have become bigger than the kings themselves. There are hundreds of Chettiars who own a hundred-boat fleet."

Aiden felt sleep thicken and press down in his head. Never before had he experienced such drowsiness. I haven't slept in two whole days, he reminded himself. Why should I feel cheated? I've done my duty. Unlike the others, I haven't turned a blind eye nor have I rationalised the situation. I haven't thanked my stars and scrambled to the front to feed on corpses. I stand clean before my own conscience. I can face up to Christ in my last days.

But to whom am I speaking these words? Who am I trying to gratify, he asked himself. No one. Just me. Only me. Is that so? Did you, in all honesty, satisfy yourself? Aiden looked up. Whole bevies of people were flying across the sky. Their white outfits, like feathered wings, flapped in the wind. The women bore children on their hips. A great swarm filled the sky. Looking ahead, they pointed their fingers at something that lay beyond the firmament, and swam on.

Duraisamy rapped on the windowpane after reaching the house. Aiden opened his eyes. He had not the faintest idea where he was. After a time, he wiped his mouth and got down. David appeared by his side and took his coat and hat. He kicked his shoes off without assistance and kept on falling. His bed was inside a narrow, dark well. He fell into it with a soft thud.

When he woke up, sunlight had spilled into the room. It wasn't until he sat up in his bed and stretched his hands to rid himself of sleep that he noticed he'd fallen asleep in his uniform. The light blinded his eyes. David came in and paused by the wall. "Tea," said Aiden. David stayed where he was. "What?"

"Kathavarayan is here, sir," said David.

"Oh." A pause. "All right." He loathed having to meet Kathavarayan just then. He was consumed by only one thought, which was to walk away from it all and go back to the familiar grind of his erstwhile life.

He washed his face and settled into his chair. He drank the tea that David had brought in. After letting his mind wander aimlessly for a time, he stepped out of the room.

Kathavarayan was seated in the guest chair outside, watching the trilling sunbirds hop on and off the tree in the front yard. Hearing his footsteps, Kathavarayan turned around with a smile and said, "Good morning, sir."

"Good morning," Aiden greeted him in return, and sat down.

"I came with some urgent news, but I was told that you had fallen asleep in exhaustion. So I decided to wait."

"What is it?" Aiden asked, betraying a little flutter of anxiety.

"We have found the bodies of the two Ice House workers. They were beaten up and cast into the sea."

"Where?"

"Four miles from here. Near Ennore. The bodies have washed ashore. The two of them had clung to each other tight. So, their bodies have run aground together."

Aiden stared ahead as if tongue-tied.

"I had guessed this is what would have happened. There was no doubt in my mind that they had been killed. There was no time to bury them in the marshes by the sea. Even if they had, the dogs would have dug them out. Which meant that they could have only thrown them into the sea. Without the attachment of proper weights, bodies will float back to the shore. Clearly, they had no time for such details. Moreover, only the fisherfolk execute these things well. Knowing this, I had alerted my people who live by the sea."

"I'll leave right away," said Aiden, rising from his seat.

"Dead bodies are of little value these days. All the same, I have stationed four or five men to stand guard and make sure no one removes the bodies."

"Five minutes," Aiden said in response, and disappeared inside. He bathed in a hurry, threw on his uniform, and, without bothering to sit, helped himself to some buttered toast and juice, and set off.

The horse arrived in front. "Where's Duraisamy? I need the carriage," Aiden said to David.

"Sir, Duraisamy left last night as soon as you returned. If you need the carriage . . ." began David.

"You can come on your horse," Kathavarayan interceded. "I'll keep up with you. Running is easy enough for me."

Aiden mounted his horse, but set it in a slow trot. "Why would they commit murder? What's to be gained from it?" he asked.

"There is nothing to be gained. But their minds work differently. 'Why not finish them off, what harm can come of it,' is what they will think. These two might become a source of botheration, however small. So it is only prudent to finish them off. Even if their bodies are discovered later, no action will be taken once it is known that they are untouchables. In this country, the untouchables are considered the same as animals. In Thanjavur, they are killed for mere fun and games. They once tied an untouchable boy to the tail of a buffalo, set the animal on a run, and watched with glee as the boy was dragged to death . . . you must have heard the news."

For some inexplicable reason, Aiden wished to steer clear of the topic.

"Sir, I seek just one thing from you. I am well aware of your problems and the extent of your authority. I do not wish to cause you any trouble. I know very well that commissioning a full-blown investigation into these murders and bringing the culprits to task is beyond you—"

Brimming with indignation, Aiden opened his mouth to say something. Kathavarayan wasted no time. "Sir, I do not doubt your honesty. Is there a better witness to your conscience than I? It is because of the compassion shown by a few white people like you that we harbour a grain of hope about our future lives. What I am talking about is this government. British rule is no more than a grand robbery orchestrated by an alliance of officers, landlords, and contractors, is it not?"

The way those words settled on the image in his mind rattled Aiden. He looked away and gathered himself.

"There is only one thing for you to do, sir. Take the corpses to the Ice House and arrange for a parade so that the workers can identify the bodies. After that, you can dispatch the bodies away to the burial ground."

Aiden looked at him in puzzlement.

"We have planned for what will be the first labour strike in this country, sir," Kathavarayan declared.

"Labour strike? In India?" Aiden said, thrown off balance.

"Yes. The Ice House is the perfect target for it. The state of the workers in the port is far more dismal, but we cannot unite them. There are people of different castes and different languages among them. And they are too huge in number. Besides, the Indian owners who employ them will stop at nothing. The Americans fear bad press. Therefore, they will not dare to cause direct harm. Sir, these white people have a conscience and culture that is far superior to that of high-caste Indians. I have faith in their compassion.

"The Americans are the right targets for this exercise. For they will be frightened. They will want to put an end to the matter before it reaches too many ears. They will not want the news to get as far as America or, worse, become a subject of debate in their papers. If, somehow, a small word of this were to be printed in an American or British daily, that will suffice. We will be able to conclude everything in our favour."

"A strike would mean . . ." Aiden began, but he was unable to think clearly.

"It will be impossible to get these workers to agitate for

an increase in wages or for better working conditions at the present moment. Why, they would scarcely raise a voice against beatings and abuse. They have suffered all that for hundreds of years. But if they see one among them—man and wife no less—killed and cast off so coolly, they may just rise in protest in the heat of the moment. We can use that fervency to our advantage. We can get them to demand that the guilty be brought to task, that no harsh punishments be meted out at the workplace, that they be paid a minimum wage for survival.

"I can see what is running through your mind," Kathavarayan went on. "What is the point of this undertaking, you wonder. What will come of inciting a meagre band of three hundred workers to revolt against this small establishment, you may ask. Fair enough. It is a drop in the ocean. They capture our people as if they were cattle or goat, bundle them into ships, and haul them away. They make them toil for twenty whole hours for as little as one meal a day. But this is where we can make a beginning. Let the British government know that these people, too, are capable of registering a protest. Let a shadow of fear creep into the government—that they cannot reduce these people to slave labourers as easily as they think."

Reading Aiden's mind masterfully, Kathavarayan continued. "Yes, sir, the upper castes in this country will not be worried in the least. But the British government has to worry. For, back in England, it is the labourers who form the very foundation of their government. The government is watching every demonstration of theirs. It considers them with trepidation. Were this news from India to reach the British labour class, these forces will unite, or so the government will fear."

Swept up by his own emotions, Kathavarayan pressed on.

"Yes, sir, it is victory enough for us even if such an agitation were only to occur. It will be a great beginning. In a nation of crores and crores of rattle-boned refugees, a labour strike is not unlike a spark of fire flicked at a dry scrub. The government will not want the protest to spread. It will strive to offer at least a semblance of rights and protection to my people. Whatever it is we receive, we will have gained."

Aiden cleared his throat. "When you put it like that, it does sound logical. The Ice House is a small undertaking. The government won't accord it much importance. And the British do nurse a bitterness towards the Americans."

"The calculations add up, sir. A three-day protest, that is my plan. In that time, I will disseminate the news to all the papers. A couple of journalists in Chennai have promised to help me. In any case, the *Madras Mail* has been publishing news about the famine for a few months now. We will have their support. Even if the protest were to end in a compromise, the British government will think it over. It is sure to introduce a few rules and regulations concerning the employment of labourers and the fixing of wages. I trust the Duke of Buckingham. If a little drop of his compassion falls on my people, that will more than suffice. They have not so much as known what compassion is for centuries now."

Kathavarayan suddenly lowered his voice. "Besides, this is a crucial moment. Business owners are salivating at the sight of labourers inundating this city by the thousands. Never again will they get human labour as cheaply as they do now. With that in mind, they will soon pressure the British government into undertaking a few large construction projects. My people will build them for free. Every British officer and bureaucrat, all the way from the top to the bottom, will partake in those obscene profits. The British government, too, will profit from them. Never again will they be able to build at such a pittance hereafter. They can erect forts. Lay roads. Construct ports. Everyone will rake in a profit. They can measure out my people's blood, drink to their heart's content, and fatten up."

Kathavarayan gestured in the direction of the port in the distance. "A hundred years ago, there was a great famine, just like this one. That was when the Madras port was constructed. At least five workers would have perished for every brick in its body. A structure cemented with the raw blood of my people. By the time this famine ends, they will have erected a magnificent Madras."

"I met the governor yesterday," said Aiden.

"I know."

"Of course. There's no place without your men," said Aiden. "Russell had, in fact, brought along four contractors when I went to meet the governor yesterday. One of them had a peculiar name. Thatikonda . . ."

"Yes, Thatikonda Namberumal Chetty. It is in his father's service that thousands of my people toil to death as food slaves. The talk about town is that he, too, wants to become a contractor. For a whole month now building contractors have been swarming around the governor. There appear to be some major construction projects in the offing. Yesterday, they laid the foundation for the University Senate House. However, the approval is yet to come from London," said Kathavarayan.

"Well, there's much to be done here. One can't connect this vast country without good roads," Aiden reasoned.

"Indeed, sir. The work must go on. The British government will benefit from it. Businessmen will profit from it. I must admit that my people, too, will gain from it."

"How do you mean?"

"To get out of agriculture in whatever way they can bodes

well for my people. No matter what work they take to, it will liberate them. Our villages stagnate in darkness. Let outsiders reach our villages through these roads. Let my people apprehend that there is such a thing as an outside world. The sole purpose of my fight is to secure the food and clothing essential to their survival in this era of change. We will attend to other things later."

Aiden let out a sigh. Although it was only the morning sun, sweat streamed down his body. The sea breeze, too, did little to dry the sweat. Whole flocks of herons had settled down on the backwaters lagooned by the beach. He recalled the dream he had had the previous day. How was it that dreams alone were capable of such immensity?

By the time they reached Ennore, several spectators had gathered around the spot. A constable stood watch a good distance away, as though he had nothing to do with the goings-on. Sporting a Pathani beard, he held an old-fashioned Ferguson rifle in his hand. When he saw Aiden, he stiffened into a salute.

The two corpses had been dragged in and laid out on the sands. Fish had gnawed off their eyes and lips. Their teeth, which began from bare gums, appeared unusually long. Their stomachs, too, had been ripped apart. Both bodies were naked. They were undoubtedly the same man and woman he had seen before. In that instant, Aiden's mind recalled those children.

"Flip them over," Aiden ordered.

A man came forward and turned them face down. The backs of both their heads were deeply fractured. The aggressors had dealt a blow with some type of heavy iron implement and broken their skulls. Very likely, at the beach. They had then tossed them into the sea right there. In the throes of death, the two bodies had clutched each other tight.

Aiden sighed and turned to the policemen standing in

the distance. "Bring these corpses to the Ice House. Right away," he said.

"Sir," the policeman answered, and saluted him again. His bewildered face betrayed his incomprehension. The captain visiting on account of these corpses would in itself have surprised him. Had Aiden not arrived on the scene and instructed him thus, there was little doubt that the policeman would have ordered the corpses be taken to the burial ground directly.

"Take charge of the bodies yourself," Aiden instructed Kathavarayan. "I'll make the necessary arrangements." So saying, he launched his horse into a gallop and sped away along the seashore.

White foam lapped at the curves of the shoreline by his side. The sails of the catamarans in the middle of the sea had bulged and ballooned. What a distance. The horse, having remained idle for days, now flung its legs forward, taking great strides. Small stones sprang upwards in the wind and hurtled past. Without resting his weight on the horse's back, Aiden leaned forward and travelled through the air.

With the heat radiating in his ears, and short of breath, Aiden reached his office. As soon as Duraisamy hastened out and took the whip from him, Aiden went inside and sat down. Narayanan trailed after him and offered a salute.

"Naryanan, we need to lead a platoon to the Ice House immediately. Make arrangements at once."

Narayanan tarried.

"What?"

"Lieutenant Mackenzie told me that he would take care of the Ice House issue."

"It's my order," Aiden commanded. Narayanan's eyes contracted, then widened, very slowly. Aiden couldn't work out what he was thinking.

"Sir," acquiesced Narayanan. At that tone of obedience,

Aiden felt an intense anger surge in him. This ordinary havildar dares to advise me on the sly. I ought not to interfere in the Ice House issue, he warns. But this is not his voice alone.

Narayanan would send word to Mackenzie straight off, Aiden reckoned. That Mackenzie should oversee this matter was surely the colonel's order. Aiden leaned back in his chair, trying to work out the time it would take for the corpses to reach the Ice House by boat. Then he pulled out the minute book and made a brief entry of the information he had gathered during the day and the identification parade he was to hold as part of the criminal investigation.

Sam came in with the tea. After helping himself to a cup, Aiden picked up his hat and came out to the front porch. "Platoon ready, sir," Narayanan announced, appearing before him with a salute. Motioning to them to leave, Aiden walked up to his horse.

Duraisamy was standing beside the animal. As Aiden drew closer, the coachman's eyes paused on him for a fugitive second and turned away. In a flash, it struck Aiden. Duraisamy knew everything. In which case Narayanan knew everything, too, as did every other person in the office.

Aiden got on to the road. When the horse's hooves struck the gravel path, the crunch of the pebbles crumbling underfoot was all that he could hear. Behind him, as the iron shoes of the troop horses clanged against the cobblestones, the coming of the cavalry echoed like a ponderous procession of buffalos. Aiden looked over his shoulder. Chestnut-toned mares of the great Maratha breed. Slightly oversized ears, stubby legs, and short necks. But they feared not heat, hunger, thirst, or distance. It felt as though the clatter of their hooves was adrift in the wind like a black swarm of birds. The sound echoed back from the walls verging the road. Dapples of light reflected off the lance points and brushed past the expanse of the walls.

Even as Aiden neared the Ice House, it was plain to him that its people had been tipped off. Which meant that all its employees had been issued grave threats. Will they be able to stand up to that? Will Kathavarayan's instigation have its effect on them?

"There are millions of worms in the jungle, but each one of them crawls all alone." The golden words of Colonel Malcolm who had led his troop through the Malayan forests. That was the whole of the colonel's conception of Easterners, too. Yes, one needn't be frightened by their numbers. In reality, they possess no more than the strength of a lone worm. But still.

Yes, every society has a defining moment in history. When they break out of their conditioning, break off their shackles, break through that which they are, and rise up! Societies that recognise such moments readily ignite like gunpowder in the annals of world history. The first foes they ought to vanquish are their own selves. Should they manage to conquer themselves, the world will stretch out at their feet like a gigantic red carpet.

Can these people do it? They have to. If they do, it'll be an extraordinary beginning in India's history. The first movement after shaking off the inaction that has submerged this country for a thousand years. The first twitch of the eyelid after a great slumber. Just like that, Aiden was gripped by awe. What a historic moment. The first mass political act of this colossal nation. The first stirring of life of a soon-to-be-born democracy.

However, no one other than him would have realised it. Those such as Kathavarayan are pragmatists. They do not cast their vision beyond everyday reality. That is why they never cherish an immoderate hope. Neither do they tend towards hopelessness. But I am not a mere witness to this moment; I'm also a participant. Aiden's heart brimmed with feeling. The entry he was to make in his journal that night could well be the first major record of modern democracy in this country.

How would Shelley handle such a moment? He had written about the French Revolution—with tumult and helplessness. But Aiden was unable to recall any of the verses just then. The entire way, he felt every nook of his memory with the tongue tip of his mind. Eventually, he gave up, vexed.

When the platoon entered the Ice House, Parmer was waiting at the entrance. This time, his demeanour had changed. Standing there, with his hands in his pockets and shoulders slightly aslant, his face dripping with assurance and mild annoyance, he strode up to the platoon. "Good morning, officer. What brings you here this time?" he asked.

When Aiden raised his hand, the horses in his tow faltered and fell back. The mounts following the stagnant horses exhaled in protest. A few flapped their ears. Some stomped the ground. There arose the sound and smell of one of them emptying its bladder.

"I need to investigate your employees. I have some questions for them."

"Look here, officer, we received a large shipment just yesterday. There's a great deal of work to get through in the coming days. It's not the kind that can be postponed."

"Order them out. Every last one of them should line up in the front yard," Aiden said resolutely.

Confusion was rife on Parmer's face. It was plain to see that he hadn't expected that. "Everyone?" he repeated with trepidation in his voice.

"Yes. Right this moment," Aiden said, coiling his whip.

Parmer turned to Neelamegam, who was standing behind him, and spoke in a subdued voice. When Neelamegam nodded and left the scene, Parmer turned back to Aiden. "This isn't right," he said. "You're preying on us. You're trying to put us out of business. You can be sure that I'll raise this with my government."

"I'm only acting in accordance with the law," Aiden quipped.

Parmer shook his head in a pique and walked away. Aiden strode inside after signalling to his troops. The horses entered in twos and spread into an evenly spaced line-up adjoining the wall. The soft, copper hair on their coats—the shade of tender mango leaves—shimmered in the morning light. Their manes bristled as some of them lowered their necks and smelled the ground. They flicked their tails and stamped the ground restlessly, invoking benign chides from the soldiers on their backs, and becalmed to a stop. The horsemen stuck their lances upright. The glimmer of a turning blade flashed in Aiden's eye like a dart of white lightning.

The labourers began to trickle out in small numbers, as though half-decayed bodies were emerging from their tombs on Judgement Day. Mangy, scabrous wet skin. Like old, mould-ridden forest trees. A sudden disenchantment rose in Aiden. These people? Are these the people who are to speak up? Are these the people who are to realise that despite possessing separate bodies and minds they make up one historical entity? Never would they have so much as known the presence of an organ other than the stomach. Never would they have felt pride, or a sense of self. Maggots. Human maggots. Life-forms that crawl all alone.

At the peak of disillusionment, his body went limp and it felt as though he could no longer stay on the horse. He dismounted and stood on the ground. He inhaled and exhaled deliberate breaths. I should spare myself the disgrace and return with my pride intact. Yes, that is for the better. I should leave. Then again, what if a mound of sulphur lies beneath this riverbed of slush? What if a tremendous moment in history stands on the sidelines waiting for that one call? No. Never. You fool, look at these faces. Look at these soul-dead eyes. Hunger is a funeral pyre. The first thing that burns in it is the soul. That which is heaped in these people is merely its ash. No. Some unknown force has brought me here, unto this point. I have unwittingly made myself a reason for all that is happening here.

"Everyone's here, officer," Parmer announced.

"Hmm," Aiden acknowledged. "Where are Kathavarayan and his men?" The sounds of brief coughs and the blowing of noses arose from the mounted troops. *Prrr*, a horse exhaled, then flapped its ears. It sounded as if a seabird was launching into flight.

A noisome smell that emanates from wet skin when exposed to the sun began to fill the air. The smell of rotting animal hide. The smell of old sores. These humans won't be able to stand in the sun for long. For all one knows, sheer exhaustion might push them to apathy by the time the bodies arrive.

A bustle fell on his ear. Aiden exhaled in relief. Four men came hauling a coconut-frond bundle into the premises. Four others followed a few paces behind, with another bundle. Kathavarayan was not with them. He must've stayed back on the boat by the beach. An excellent decision.

As the men drew closer, Aiden saw two legs, seemingly made of clay, dangle over the edge of the bundle. They jerked with every step. Aiden cast a glance at the workers. There was nary a movement in their eyes. Their faces seemed to stare in a meaningless daze, as ever. Even as corpses, these people wear the same expression.

The policeman Aiden had seen earlier brought up the rear

of the corpse cavalcade, lugging a rifle. Upon seeing Aiden, he stiffened into a salute. "Untie them and lay them here," Aiden ordered.

As he repeated the command, the men set the corpses down on the ground. They untied the bundles and unravelled the coconut fronds in the manner of displaying for sale a large fish they had caught at sea. The man lay prone. They turned his body over. Ribs like the keys of a piano. Stomach collapsed and pit-like. A hollow formed by protruding hip bones. Below that, the thighs. Which, too, had not a hint of flesh.

"Do any of you know them?" Aiden demanded.

Narayanan repeated the question out loud in the local tongue.

The workers stood quietly. There was no trace of movement in their bodies. Their eyes were fixed on the corpses.

"Was this man your fellow worker? Do you recognise him?" Aiden appealed.

When they removed their gaze, their bodies, too, moved slowly in tandem with their eyes. The movements blended, and the whole group stirred like an avenue of wind-nuzzled trees. A stirring that made it seem as if one could see with the eye the shared thought that coursed through their bodies.

"The British government will offer all protection to the one who identifies this man," Aiden exhorted. As his words were being translated, Aiden observed those eyes keenly. Their gazes were lifeless and frozen, like the eyes of the fish arrayed in the local markets. In that moment, just as a mast rig snaps in a gale at full tilt, something snapped in Aiden. Like a boat changing course with a shudder, his body twisted restlessly. He tightened his grip on the reins and controlled himself. He cast a glance at the mounted troops. They were lined up like a row of freshly budded pongamia trees.

Fools. Infernal fools. It is for you that I assembled this

cavalry. Yes, the very same horses which for centuries past have lorded over you, beaten you to pulp, and killed without mercy. Here they are today, to protect you. Look, you imbeciles. They are your fortress. You have by your side the might of the illustrious British government. Open your mouths. Talk.

Beasts. Soul-decayed, living cadavers. For the sole crime of having pleaded to live, one of your kind lies murdered in front of you, family and all. A man like you. No, a man a cut above you. He had, at least, summoned the courage to plead. Cowards, human maggots, what *are* you doing! Won't one among you, just one, step forward and speak? So what if you should die for it? Is death more forbidding than living like this?

What am I thinking, Aiden marvelled. I'm trying to set fire to stone. However much I blow on it, it will not ignite. Indeed, it's for this cowardice that they've been trampled underfoot for a thousand years. It's as punishment for this crime that they've been burning at the stake of hunger for generations. That they've been humiliated. Killed en masse. And left to perish, like waste.

He studied their eyes, one by one. They were identical. Sweat dripped and collected on their eyebrows. Beneath eyelids that squinted in the harsh sun were pebble-like irises. Aiden averted his gaze. Was that a smirk in Neelamegam's eyes? Were those smiles quivering underneath the overseers' moustaches?

"If any of them come to me later, I'll bring them to you immediately, officer," Parmer said, servilely.

Aiden met his eyes. There was no trace of laughter in them. But every word he spoke was coated with merriment.

Aiden was consumed by an urge to tear into the crowd and whip them to shreds. Till their skin and flesh flew in all directions. Till their bones separated from their tendons. Becoming aware of a fatigue in his legs, he reached for his horse. The horse stepped forward and nuzzled its big head against him. He dusted the saddle with his hand, and prepared to mount the animal.

Just then, a voice rang out.

"Sir."

Aiden stopped. Startled, Parmer turned around.

It was Karuppan. He had failed to recognise him in the crowd, Aiden realised, even though he had seen him many times by then.

"I know them, sir," said Karuppan. "The man's name is Savari. He worked here. That is his wife next to him. We all know them."

Seeing that Parmer was about to say something, Aiden interceded.

"Are you threatening him?"

Parmer stayed his raised hand in midair for a split second before he lowered it.

"No. He's got them confused. No one else seems to know them, as you can see," he answered.

"Sir, everybody knows them," said Karuppan. "They are scared. The two of them worked here. They were thrashed and driven out. We saw it. We know who killed them."

Aiden felt a joy pulsate through his body. A tiny corner of that black boulder was reddening in the fire. It was on the verge of igniting. There—no, not yet. He is Kathavarayan's man. He has been coached by him. Even so, a voice has risen. One lonely voice. That, too, will do.

Karuppan said something to those around him in a loud voice. Out of the blue, he landed his right hand on his chest with a ferocious thump, and let out a fierce scream. Aiden watched the crowd tremble as though each of them had received the very same whiplash at the very same moment. Like a maestro conducting the crescendo of a symphony, Karuppan raised his hands high above his head; with the veins in his neck and their every knot bulging and throbbing, he thundered at the top of his voice. Then again, it sounded like no more than a meaningless wail. The utterly wordless moan of humanity!

In a second, the entire throng raised its voice. Like a gigantic beast, the throng roared, growled, pulled apart, pressed together, and tautened until it took a form of its own. With bodies glued together, it morphed into a being with hundreds of arms, hundreds of legs, and hundreds of heads. Many hundreds of hands waved in the air like bristles on a caterpillar. Many hundreds of feet crawled the earth. Then it inched forward as one body. Aiden saw the mob of individuals who had previously stood before him transform in the blink of an eye into an army with one spirit and one goal. But it was a tumultuous army. It advanced like a monstrous machine that marched forward even as its body melted and flowed under extreme heat. For a split second Aiden felt a great fear, like biting cold, clutch his soul.

Straining every nerve in their throats, they roared as loudly as they could. They stomped the ground with frightening force. They thumped their breasts and bosoms over and over. Swept up by emotion, many wailed and keened and wept. Some sank to the ground even as they sobbed. Each and every face was held in the highest apogee of emotion as though they were a part of a magnificent Venetian painting. Fear abandoned Aiden, and a type of bewilderment took its place. What is happening here? Is this what we call history? Is this how the French Revolution would have looked? Is this how its blood, tears, mad ecstasy, and murderous frenzy start, too?

Aiden's body trembled. Unsettled, his mind wandered

here and there, not knowing what it ought to watch or do. If not for the horse, he would have collapsed to the ground. I should not let these moments pass me by. My thoughts ought not to cloud my eyes. I must take in each and every second of this. Listen to each and every sound. Opening my senses, I must live fully in this moment. Perhaps this is what I was born for. This, here, is the pinnacle of my existence. These few hours are longer than the entirety of my life thus far.

Aiden watched as a great fear spread over the faces of the overseers. The last expression of those aboard a boat sinking in a stormy sea. Mouths agape, eyes wide open. Two of them stepped back silently and climbed onto the veranda. As he fixed his gaze on them, he no longer saw the crowd. He saw not his forces, with their gleaming swords and rifles and liveries, fall back involuntarily at the ferocity on display. Each of the soldiers' faces wore a distinct expression. Fear, disbelief, stupefaction, meaningless animation, foolish glee. Jesus, my Lord, how many faces do I take in! Which do I commit to memory!

None of them understood what was transpiring there. Aiden felt an urge to shout to his men: Look! History is happening right in front of you. The first people's uprising in Indian democracy. Each of you is an actor in a great play. Each of you is a part of history. Imbeciles. How they retract in fear. Jostle foolishly. Grin from ear to ear. Is history conducted on the back of such baseness? Is it through these people that God's plan forges ahead? Jesus, my Lord!

Parmer turned to Neelamegam. "You idiot, tell them. Tell them," he hollered, gesticulating urgently.

"Mr. Parmer, if you engage in violence when they haven't, our law will consider it a crime against the government," Aiden warned.

"They're rioting . . . they're rioting," Parmer shrieked, his face flushed with fear and anger. It was evident that he had lost all control. His arms and legs moved wildly. His body palpitated in the manner of someone who was about to set off on a run or begin to whirl. "Rogues. Criminals!"

"Not in the least. They're expressing their dissent in a democratic way. Her Majesty the Queen's crown endows them with the right to do so," said Aiden. "One half of my platoon will remain here. If they attack, our forces will protect you."

Parmer moved only his hand. No voice emerged from his throat. To hell with you, you hog. Still, you are blessed. Your foolish ruthlessness has carved you a place in history.

Karuppan kept up his sloganeering. He threw his arms about, flung them up and down, and issued word after word without respite. Almost everyone in the crowd, which was at least three hundred people strong, vociferated as loudly as they could. Even so, it did seem like they had heard Karuppan. Or else, were they all saying the same thing? A wounded black beast, driven up against the wall, had rebounded with a final frenzy for life. It appeared as though it would bring down the building and flatten its ramparts.

Sit down, Karuppan mimed to the crowd. He jumped up and down while he motioned to them with his hands. One by one, they sat down. Soon a sea of seated bodies blocked the entrance to the Ice House. Karuppan signalled to them to quieten down. But they were vocalising everything they had dammed within themselves from the moment they were born. They were emptying without residue the tears they had held in check in the face of lashings, abuse, hunger, and death.

Aiden trained his sight on one of the men. He was not there at all. Spreading his arms out to the sky, he was screaming soundlessly. With tears streaming down his face, and his lips twitching and trembling, he was pleading. Pleading? Or showering curses? At whom? God, fate, or was it history itself? Should he turn and look at me now, I have no recourse but to stand before him as a hardened criminal and wait for my sentence. I ought to slash my neck with the bayonet, drench the ground with my blood, and give up my life in his name. Jesus! A whole empire should collapse for each and every human being in front of me.

Aiden suddenly became aware of himself. A formal report must be sent to the colonel before a complaint goes from the Ice House, he decided. After instructing Narayanan to keep his troop there and dispatch the bodies for burial, he left the scene. The remainder of the platoon returned with him.

As he rode his horse, Aiden felt as if his body were burning all over. He felt an urge to whip the horse into a reckless sprint so that he could leap and pierce through the air. Shelley, Shelley, Shelley, Shelley, Shelley! I saw you. I was blessed with the boon of seeing your beautiful face ripple with youth, with dreams, with madness. Shelley, I, too, have been blessed. Shelley! Shelley! Shelley! Shelley! Here I am. Here, by the hot sands of an alien country. Utterly alone. Shelley! Shelley! Shelley!

Stand ye calm and resolute,
Like a forest close and mute,
With folded arms and looks which are
Weapons of unvanquished war.

Yes, that very moment. That is this. An army outfitted with bare hands tensed in silence. A human forest. Shelley, Shelley, I witnessed it just now. Humanity's soul—that which has conquered time and forged cultures—has revealed itself to me.

His inner being averred those lines. Accompanied by the beat of the horse's hooves, the verse transformed into his battle song. As he placed a hand on his chest and tipped his head back towards the firmament, his heart bubbled over and tears fell from his eyes. He did not care to wipe them. Letting the tears stream down his cheeks, collar, and chest, he pressed his lips together and, with taut neck muscles rippling and body drawn tight, kept on going.

10

Aiden was in his office, drafting the report, when Sam informed him of Kathavarayan's arrival. After he ordered for him to be sent in, Aiden quickened his pace. The dip pen spat ink in its haste. Applying quick dabs of the blotting paper, Aiden wrote on.

"Sir." Kathavarayan's voice made him look up. The suggestion of a smile was on his face.

"At last, the stone has caught fire," said Aiden.

"Yes, I knew it would. I have observed my people for a long time now. Though, I did not expect them to exercise such restraint. The lack of it was what I was afraid of," said Kathavarayan.

"What're they doing now?" Aiden asked.

"Sitting in the front yard. News about the protest has already spread throughout Beach Road. The *Madras Mail*'s journalist will be there soon. John Cooper, of the *London Daily News*, is on his way. I have sent one of my men to fetch him. I have also sent for Chris Porter, who relays news to *The New York Times*."

"A photograph. We need at least one photograph."

"I did tell Porter that. He has a camera. However, I am

not sure he has blank plates. The *Madras Mail* will most certainly have a photographer in their crew."

Aiden remembered there being a military camera in his platoon's stores. A collodion dry-plate camera. He could have had that readied. How had it not occurred to him? "Kathavarayan, I'll finish my report and dispatch it to the colonel shortly. I've stressed that it isn't a riot which is taking place but a labour protest. I've impressed upon him that the Ice House's management should acknowledge the workers' demands and lay grounds for a genuine negotiation. The report must reach the colonel before Parmer's complaint does."

"Once you send the letter to the colonel, you may meet with William Russell, sir," Kathavarayan proffered.

"Again? I don't have an appointment."

"This is an emergency, is it not? Moreover, there is a good chance that Russell will take a personal interest in this matter."

"Why?"

"It is an open secret that Russell has an indirect share in International Ice Company, which manufactures ice using coal power. That is the very reason he led you all the way to the duke. Artificial ice is several times costlier than Tudor's ice, at present. Furthermore, the whites prefer the ice made from the pure lakes of Boston to the ice manufactured from this city's waters. Any problem that besets Tudor and Co. will benefit both Russell and International Ice Co."

Aiden laid down his pen. "Kathavarayan, I'm a humble soldier. None of these strategies and counterstrategies make sense to me. My tiny mind is ill-equipped to fathom who manipulates this web and from where. Please save yourself the explanation."

"All right, sir," said Kathavarayan, laughing. Prominent teeth, so characteristic of Indians. "Please do meet with

Russell and apprise him of this protest. He will relish the fact that there's a problem at the Ice House. All the same, he will want it to be resolved before it escalates any further. He should intervene before the colonel does. It will augur well for us if they reach a decision by afternoon tomorrow. A small increase in wages and a guarantee of safety. That will suffice. The protest must meet with success. My people should come to believe that they, too, can fight. That is all I hope for."

"I'll think about it. Care for some tea?"

After partaking of the refreshment, Kathavarayan took his leave. Aiden placed a carbon sheet beneath his letter and swiftly traced his pencil over it to make a copy. Retaining the carbon copy in his file, he slipped the original letter into an envelope, printed the address on it, affixed his seal, and dispatched it to the colonel. "Tell the colonel that this letter is from me," he instructed the messenger.

"Yes, sir," the messenger acknowledged.

"If he asks you why I haven't come in person, tell him I've gone to the fort to meet the governor's secretary." After a second's thought, "Listen, you needn't wait for him to ask. Tell him yourself," he instructed.

"Yes, sir," said the messenger, maintaining a straight face despite his puzzlement.

Armed with his copy of the letter, Aiden started from his office. The horse failed to accelerate at his touch. It had tired in the heat. In less than a few strides, vaporous sweat cloaked the length of its coat. The horse neighed a few times and quickened its pace, only to slacken again. The sun stung Aiden's eyes. If not for the breeze, one couldn't travel that road even for a few seconds, he thought to himself.

Maintenance work of some kind was under way at the fort's outer entrance. Local masons were perched on bamboo scaffolding. Hundreds of people were hauling stone and sand. From a distance, the workers clad in no more than dirty loincloths appeared fully naked. Within the fort, pantile-roofed houses were hunched over in the manner of geriatric noblemen fitted with red linen perukes. Other than a few chaprasi attendants here and there, the place was eerily deserted. A couple of phaetons drove past him. They, too, had pulled down their blinds all the way to shield from the sun.

Would Russell be awake? A doubt crept into Aiden's mind. The fort's offices operate all through the night. They host banquets. Ordinarily, none of the high-ranking officers stay up during the day. Still, considering the emergency, Russell might wake up. If the colonel receives word of Aiden calling on Russell, he will not rush into action of any kind. One day, at the most. The workers will need to hold out until then. A protest that had ignited on its own, without any preparation. Then again, Kathavarayan and his men are there.

When he entered the inner fort, Aiden felt a sudden disconcertment. He could not savvy where to go or whom to meet first. There was little chance of finding anyone at Clive House, other than the most junior scribes or administrators. All the same, that is where he had to head. The Clive House he now beheld made him doubt if it was indeed the same place he had seen the previous evening. The sweeping granite-paved courtyard stood starkly empty. The sun beat down on it, generating a heat that assaulted his eyes and ears.

Aiden handed over his whip and horse to a servant who came forward, and he climbed tentatively up the stairs that led to a gaping entrance guarded by two thick, towering pillars. All the vetiver-reed blinds on the façade had been lowered. Workers tasked with sprinkling water on the blinds were filtering in from the opposite end of the veranda toting small bamboo ladders. Every hall and chamber within was submerged in darkness. As the sounds of hushed speech mingled and rose in a thrum, the whole building seemed like a gigantic leather drum.

When Aiden's sight adjusted to the darkness, the motion of a sea of punkahs swaying overhead was what caught his eye. A young Indian officer walked up to him and bowed in deference. "Respected captain, how may I help you?" he asked.

"I must meet Secretary Russell at once," Aiden replied.

"He's in a meeting," said the officer.

"Can you pass on a note to the effect that I wish to meet him on an urgent matter?"

"Certainly. If you would be so kind as to supply me with such a note."

Aiden hurriedly scribbled a few lines on a slip of paper the officer provided him. "Please come," said the young officer, and led the way. The boy is in training to become a British gentleman, Aiden noted. A lifted chin, movements tinged with a feminine softness.

On the way to St. Mary's Church, the officer entered a tile-roofed building annexed to it.

"Is this where the secretary sits?"

"Yes, this is the secretary's office. If he so pleases, he'll have you ushered into his chamber."

The long room was packed with scribes. Only seven or eight of them were white. The rest were all locals. They wore tall turban hats and open jackets over their waistcloths. Religious symbols adorned their brows. A few had traced a large *V* with lime paste on their foreheads. Against their black skin, those symbols looked like they were jutting out. They seemingly offered their bearers some type of identity, some kind of prestige. Those who flaunted such identities evidently ranked higher in one way or another. Those with no identity were starving to death in droves.

The officer returned. "The secretary's requested that you wait in the visitors' room," he relayed.

"I said it was urgent."

The officer drew his thin lips into a pleasing smile. "Your note has been handed to him," he said.

The visitors' room had large windows that opened out to the sea. There were no curtains on the brass-grilled window. The ripple and sweep of the Bay of Bengal that stretched into the distance caught Aiden's eye. Ships whose sails were furled and folded bobbed from side to side against a blue screen. Heavy recliners crafted from Indian rosewood furnished the room. The cushions, covered in silk fabric, were tailored to fit. Aiden sat down.

On the table were a few vases of fresh roses. Pink silk curtains quivered over the door. At the opposite end, a cone-shaped brass flower rested on a box placed on a low table. Aiden studied it closely, after which he eased into the chair.

An Indian butler came in. "What would you like to have, sir?" he asked deferentially, in velvety English.

"Nothing, thank you," Aiden answered. "What is that?"

"It's a phonautograph," said the butler. He walked up to it and gently rotated its handle. The strains of a piano filled the room. Beethoven.

"Can it play a whole symphony?" Aiden asked, awestruck.

"Up to three minutes, sir."

Aiden rose to inspect it. Music lay etched in the form of faint scratches on a brass cylinder. The thin brass needles touching the cylinder triggered vibrations in another plate, producing music. Three minutes. A preposterous music. It takes as long as twenty minutes for a song to attain its inherent form. What will they achieve in three minutes?

Then again, this music is permanent. The musical marvels performed by great artists will fade into oblivion in the grand sweep of time. This, on the other hand, will live on. For the first time, music takes the form of a stone inscription. An indelible music. If indelible, is it really music? If solidified as stone, can it be effervescence?

Man's hankering for history. His desire for permanence. Perhaps this is what Man has longed for from the very moment a consciousness birthed in him. To exist forever. To last forever. Dear God, this moment, it is an enduring moment of history. But here I am, wasting my time. If only I had paper and pen, I could be writing now. Writing everything. Every thought I have now is indeed history.

But what is history? This device in front of me can record Beethoven. It can record Mozart. It can record the orations of great queens. It can record political decrees. Will it record the moans of coal workers who collapse with broken backs, or the final cry of the Irish soldier who, fighting for the British in the deserts of Egypt for reasons yet unknown to him, is felled by a bullet, or the wail of the white infant who, born to a coal worker who arrives in Malaya to establish an Anglo-Saxon empire, dies of malaria? It is literature that records these voices. It is language. No, not language, but the soul. This machine is soulless. All technology is soulless.

How much longer? What on earth is happening? What am I waiting for? It suddenly occurred to him that he had missed his lunch. He hadn't felt it until then since his mind had been all aflutter. Now that it was idle, hunger squirmed and coiled in his stomach.

"Is the secretary still in his meeting?" Aiden asked.

"Yes, sir," the butler replied respectfully. "He will call you once he is free."

Aiden fell back in his chair and gazed at the sea. It seemed as if the ocean was cradling the ships in her lap and lulling them to sleep. Aiden watched the sway of the vessels. It was a movement he had seen before. But, where? Where? Yes! The movement of an elephant. Only elephants sway as languidly as this. The sails danced in the manner of elephant ears. The elephant turns to me. "Don't, don't," it says. Don't what? What am I thinking? Why do my thoughts scatter so? How far I've come. In just three days, I've turned into someone else altogether.

When he awoke, the light in the room had changed. "Butler!" he cried as he got up.

As soon as the butler appeared before him, "Did they call me?" he demanded.

"No, sir. Another meeting began a little while back," the butler answered.

"I have to leave urgently. The situation back there calls for swift action. Please remind the secretary of my message."

"I'm afraid he will not like that."

"Let me write him a note. Quick."

"The secretary wouldn't encourage that, sir."

"Do as I say," Aiden commanded, and fell to penning another note. "Urgent. Actions await my presence at the Ice House."

After dispatching the note, he paced about the hall restlessly. I fell asleep! Like a man falling asleep in a fiery battlefield. How?! Yes, it's impossible to hold one's nerves in a heightened tautness all the time. I'm counterbalancing the turmoil that has beset me since the morning. Everything is clear now. My thoughts have acquired further logic and order.

The smell of something burning. Something's going wrong, somewhere. This delay is premeditated. I should leave at once and head back. That is what I ought to do. Those workers need my help right now. Yet I cannot leave this place. My office and duty won't allow me to leave. What if I leave?

Yes, I should leave. I can do it, right now. I can put it down to a little misunderstanding, later. Perhaps offer the butler in sacrifice for it. If I sit on my hands here and now, I might end up sacrificing three hundred lives.

The butler opened the door. "Your turn, Captain," he said.

Aiden froze for a moment, then picked up his envelope, straightened his clothes, and set off. The butler led him through a dimly lit passage. He gave the door a gentle push and ushered Aiden in with a dutiful sweep of his hand.

As he walked in, Aiden was somewhat thrown off-kilter. A white man of forty was seated in conversation with Russell. It was an ordinarily decorated room, but massive in size. It had a high ceiling, limestone walls, and windows that were decorated with arches in the style of a fort's entrance. At one end of the room stood a file cabinet and a writing table. At the other end, behind a desk overflowing with papers and registers, sat Russell.

When Aiden greeted him, Russell smiled and motioned to him to have a seat. He turned to the white man. "Captain Byrne of the Imperial Police," he said, introducing him.

The man rose to his feet and extended his hand. "Robert Fellowes Chisholm. I'm an architect," he said. "The one who designed the Madras Senate House."

"My compliments," said Aiden, taking his seat. He glanced at Russell. Was the secretary going to speak in this man's presence? he brooded.

"We plan to construct some fine buildings here," Russell carried on. "Several important ones. Some are long overdue, for we didn't have the necessary allocation from London all these days. They had said that the funds were insufficient even to defray the cost of wars. It is only now that the time has ripened. You must take a look at Mr. Chisholm's drawing, Captain. It's a masterpiece. There's no doubt in my mind that when it takes shape it'll be one of the most magnificent buildings of southern India."

Russell extended a roll of blue paper in his direction. Aiden received it and spread it open.

"I believe you're trained to read these drawings. You've designed several bridges in Malaya yourself," said Russell.

Aiden could make no sense of the sketches in front of him. He stared at it blankly.

"We require a few good buildings in Tinnevelly and Tenkasi, too. In particular, we can use a summer retreat in Tenkasi. That, in point of fact, is why I introduced Chisholm to you. You might find yourself in need of his architectural hand."

"Of course. Thank you," said Aiden.

"We were in receipt of a report from the captain, yesterday," Russell said to Chisholm. "That was what finally thawed the ice. The duke had been hesitant to make this decision. He was afraid he'd be accused of burdening the country's exchequer. Naturally, the mere fact of being a duke makes him fear the House of Commons even in his dreams. Whatever he does, they will accuse him of squander and extravagance. Under the circumstances, the captain's report yesterday offered a compelling rationale. Thousands of people are dying of hunger in this country right now. A vast majority of them are able workers. The need of the hour, as it were, is to provide them the opportunity for labour. And what better way than by means of construction work. The government, too, will profit tremendously from it. Never again will labourers be available at the present wage rate. These people will be gainfully employed as well. There can't be a more impactful way to manage the famine."

"Yes. This is the time to commence our work," Chisholm chimed in.

"What's more, there's no private construction happening anywhere else on account of the famine. The contractors tell me that lime is cheaper than sand at the moment."

"That's true. The government has begun major construction projects in Calcutta, too."

Russell turned to Aiden. "Thank you for your report, Captain. It's done its job exceedingly well. It's about to offer a life to these poor folk," he said. "You may meet with Chisholm in private later and have a conversation."

"Certainly, it'll be my pleasure," said Aiden, with a flushed face. He instinctively smoothened his hair with his hand.

"We'll meet again," said Chisholm, rising to his feet. "For now, I take your leave." He shook both their hands. "Much obliged for this lovely meeting. I pray to God for its continuance." So saying, he left the room.

"Sir," Aiden began without losing a moment. "I've come on an important matter. A strike has begun at the Ice House."

"A strike?" said Russell, his eyebrows knitting almost imperceptibly.

"Yes," said Aiden. "I've brought my report," he said, extending the envelope over the table.

Russell accepted the envelope, but showed no inclination to open it. "There've been no strikes in this country thus far." His fingers were tightly interlaced. Like wrestlers wrapped in a group tackle.

"Yes, it is the first labour strike. And therefore, of immense importance. You must oversee it personally. The strike should not devolve into violence. Which is why I stationed a platoon at the site before I left to inform you."

"Do you foresee any prospect of violence?" His fingers loosened. The index finger started to tap out a beat.

"On their side, next to none. They're simple labourers who belong to the untouchable castes of this country. They're incapable of violence. On the other hand, the management may take up arms in order to curb the protest. Perhaps . . ." Aiden hesitated for a moment. "Perhaps our forces, too, might lose patience and mount an attack. If we happen to initiate violence, it'll set a terrible precedent. It'll be akin to hurling a flame at a depot of explosives. At a time when this country is in the white heat of a famine."

"Yes, that's true," Russell conceded. Even so, he did not open the envelope.

"The colonel must receive the benefit of your estimable counsel. With your permission, I'll see to it that there's no violence at this protest," Aiden pressed on. Was he employing the right words, he agonised.

"Yes, there should be no violence," said Russell. "I shall tell Mackenzie that in no uncertain terms." He pulled out a different envelope. "Per the order issued by the governor last night, you've been promoted to the position of commander of the Tinnevelly Cantonment. You'll be elevated to the rank of major very soon. The governor has sent his recommendation to the army on that account."

Bereft of words, Aiden sat as he was. Then, stirring as if he was about to rise, "Sir," he murmured.

"Congratulations," said Russell, as he handed over the envelope. "A reward for your outstanding report."

Aiden felt as though the last word, too, had withered from his mind.

"You've been relieved of your duties, effective the moment you received this order. Mackenzie has been promoted to the rank of captain and entrusted with full charge. The letter of commission was dispatched to him a little while ago. You may hand over your documents to him. Now that an administerial issue is before us, you must do so forthwith."

Aiden sat stock-still, with the envelope in his hands.

Russell rose from his chair. "Excellent. We'll meet again soon. There's a chance I might be spending the summer in Tenkasi. Maggie fancies it," he said, offering his hand.

Aiden got up, shook Russell's hand, and made his way to the exit. The door opened, releasing him into the world outside. Aiden lumbered out as if he were walking in a dream. His consciousness registered only the tolling of the bells of St. Mary's Church for the evening mass.

It was not until he mounted his ride that his mind jerked awake like a branded horse. None of it was a coincidence. His being made to wait, his transfer, all of it. He whipped the horse relentlessly, until it charged through the road as if in a mad rage. Pebbles scattered in its wake and struck Aiden's back. Two chaprasis heading in his direction leaped out of the way in panic.

Sweat was streaking down his body, like steaming water, when he reached his office. Long after he went in and sat down, his mind was still racing as fast as before. He filed the letter away and sat quietly for a time. In the gale force of stormy thoughts, it seemed as if his inner being had been stripped of its layers and rendered naked. In time, like fish rising from the waters' depths, thoughts began to bubble to the surface.

His very first thought was to go to the Ice House. He stepped out. Sam hastened after him. "Sir, tea?" he asked.

"No. Was Mac here?"

"Yes, Lieutenant saab was here, but he left just now."

"If he returns, tell him to come to the Ice House."

Aiden stepped out and walked towards his horse. Duraisamy was painstakingly rubbing the sweat off its back. Although its breathing had returned to normal, foam hung from its jaw.

Seeing Aiden, Duraisamy called out, "We have Rosie, sir. This one won't go much further anymore."

When Aiden nodded, Duraisamy led Rosie out. A mare with long legs, and black patches on a white neck. A black circle around one eye. An aspect that always made Aiden perceive a kind of foreignness in her vision. He had rarely pressed her into service. When Aiden patted her neck, she paced forward a little as if in protest, and tugged at the reins. Horses, somehow, sense the inner state of their rider.

Aiden mounted the mare. Gently pressing his legs against her flanks, he set her in motion. Rosie made her dislike of him known in the movements of her body. She staved off a few seconds before imbibing the instructions relayed by his legs. Driven to irritation, Aiden dug into her with his heel spike. When she leaped forward with a sudden jolt, Aiden lost balance and almost fell off the horse. He brought the whip down on her. The mare hurtled down the path in a crazed fit as though shattering to pieces.

As the Ice House drew closer and closer, Aiden regained his calm. He reined in the horse. The long shadow of the animal which had raced with him now lay on the sand like a wet patch. The molten silver of early evening rippled on the sea.

A crowd of more than a hundred had gathered on the beach sands in front of the Ice House. It was apparent that they were not fisherfolk. Two of them were dressed in white. As he closed in, Aiden saw that one of them was Kathavarayan. Attired in a khaki jacket and turban, Kathavarayan walked towards him.

Aiden brought the horse to a halt. "Why's there a crowd here? Who are these people?" he enquired.

"Workers who haul ice," Kathavarayan answered.

"No. They . . ."

"They have been employed at various points in time. Their names find no mention in the registers here, still, they are Ice House workers," said Kathavarayan.

"I will not stand for any violence."

"I know. That will spell danger to us, more than to anyone else. But our presence here will embolden our comrades."

"What's going on inside?"

"Our comrades are seated as before. Your army did not permit us to see them."

"Seated for this long? In the sun?"

Kathavarayan smiled.

"All right. I'll have a look," said Aiden. Should I tell him, he wondered, hanging back. The horse, which had taken a step forward, drew a full circle. "Kathavarayan."

"Sir."

"There's some bad news. I have been transferred. To Tenkasi."

Kathavarayan's eyes narrowed. "What?" he said.

"Your calculations were wrong. Russell's mind didn't work as you had imagined. He only wishes to quell this protest. If Mac takes over, you know what he'll do, don't you?"

"Yes." Kathavarayan sighed. "Sir, there's no point in continuing the protest now," he said. "Please go ahead and try talking to the management. A basic concession, even something small, will do. A promise of a wage increase, too, will suffice. We will end this."

"Fine. Let me see," said Aiden, starting his horse. Two guards armed with rifles were stationed at the gate. Seeing him, they saluted. Farther from him, the twenty horses in his platoon were lined up by the building. Coconut fronds had been roofed over them for shade. A few of the horses tore off a tiny clump of straw from the spread on the ground and chewed determinedly even as thin tubes of saliva dribbled down their jaws. The horsemen had settled into various parts of the building's verandas and stable. Many of them had kicked off their boots and sat cross-legged. When they caught sight of him, they sprang to their feet. Four or five horses turned their necks; recognising Aiden, they exhaled vehemently. A tall horse whisked its head from side to side and stamped on the stone ground.

Narayanan was seated in a chair at the building's entrance. He got to his feet and waved a salute. The horsemen urgently crammed their feet into their boots and tucked in their tunics, even as they hopped and limped to their horses.

The entire gathering of workers had occupied the ground in front. Since the sun was behind them, they looked like silhouettes. When his vision adjusted to the light, Aiden passed an attentive eye over them. The rush of passion that had imbued those faces earlier that morning was not to be seen anymore. All of them wore the self-same expression, as if they were replicas of one single face.

"Did anyone speak to them?"

"Yes, sir. They were told that they no longer have jobs here. That if they don't disperse they can stay in the sun for as long as they want. But it had no effect on them. That short young man seems to be their leader. He is unyielding," said Narayanan.

"Arrange to provide them water," Aiden instructed.

"There are no servants around."

Suppressing his anger, he said, "You'll find their friends outside. Tell them. They will serve the water."

Just then, Parmer emerged from a room at the back. "Given the circumstances, I can't let an outsider enter these premises," he interceded.

"I believe this land is under the rule of Her Majesty the Queen," said Aiden. Parmer averted his gaze.

"Go," Aiden barked at Narayanan. Then, turning back to Parmer, said, "I wish to have a word with you."

"Very well. Let's go inside."

The inner chamber was dark. Parmer pulled up a couple of chairs, after which he walked to the windows, retracted the ropes, and rolled up the thick blinds. "Have a seat, officer," he said.

Aiden sat down.

Parmer sat down opposite him.

"That this issue has arisen under Her Majesty's rule has given the administration occasion to worry," Aiden began. "I've just returned from a discussion with the governor's secretary. He expects this problem to be resolved without delay. As you can see, we're in the midst of a famine. Her Majesty's government leaves no stone unturned to alleviate the crisis. We have large-scale construction projects on the anvil. Under the circumstances, this protest will trigger decidedly adverse repercussions. Were this news to find its way into the papers, it'll inconvenience the government. The matter must be laid to rest at once."

Aiden looked into Parmer's eyes. "The *Madras Mail* is scheduled to publish the news the day after tomorrow. The paper has already carried many grim accounts of the famine. Within a month, the news will be published in Britain and America," he said.

"I'm just a manager," Parmer spoke up. "I'm not empowered to make any decision."

"You're headquartered in Boston. It'll take all of six months to receive an order from there. You can make a decision. You can put forth a constructive resolution that is within your ambit, presently."

"Sorry. I've no local authority at all. Most of the shares of Tudor and Co.'s Indian division have been purchased by residents of Madras. They're the ones who can decide."

"In that case, leave the decision to them," Aiden said, unfazed. "All you need do is propose a solution; they won't turn it down."

"What're you recommending?"

"Look, Mr. Parmer. You're an American. What's more, you belong to Boston, the seat of the War of Independence. The last thing I need to do is enlighten you about human rights. Do you, in all conscience, believe your company's methods to be just?"

Parmer fell silent for a time. "No," he said, eventually. "I'm seeing these people anew. Look, those sitting here . . . They're not the bodies I've known so far. It seems to me that their souls alone have gathered together and congregated in my front yard. I'm unable to look them in the eye. They're not the same people I ridiculed all these days." Parmer shook his head, as if to say no over and over. "What am I doing? What am I doing here? Officer, all of this makes the civilised man in me squirm in shame every day."

Tossing his head as though he were shaking something off, Parmer went on. "I don't subscribe to the Christian faith. Freedom and equality are what I believe in. It feels as if buckets of mud are being upturned on those beliefs, every passing day. The most dreadful days in my life have been these two years I've spent in this place. In this hell. In this soulless existence." His voice caught in his throat. He ran his hand through his hair. Unable to get another word out, he fell quiet.

The turmoil in his face astonished Aiden. "In that case . . ." he began.

"Officer. You should know one thing. I can't forge a new

social order here. We're businessmen. All we have here is a small factory and an office. I've no choice but to make use of the existing social structure." Parmer's lips twisted at the speed of thought; waving his arms about, he began to speak at fever pitch. "Officer, in the early days of Tudor and Co. they did try to re-create the American work culture in this country. I can name many who devoted themselves to that ideal. But the realities of this land were not conducive. We simply couldn't wrap our heads around this thing called caste. What we need are people capable of physical labour, and a managerial force that knows English. The people who come to us as labourers are, invariably, untouchables. But it's equally true that the upper castes are indispensable to administration. They're the ones who have full access to the town. They're the ones who know the rules and ways of this city.

"Frankly, it took me a whole year to grasp these realities," said Parmer. "There's a social group, or a caste as I understand it now, assigned for every kind of job in this place, and only they are allowed to engage in it. The Paradavars pilot boats, but they can't transport cargo inland. One needs Komutti Chettis for that. Without the Komuttis, there's no way for us to distribute the ice cubes inland. Why, there's even a particular caste group to supply us with the sawdust we need. Ergo, we need Brahmins to organise the various caste groups. And Reddys to back the Brahmins with arms. Yes, we have to adopt the social structure of this land without question if we are to do business here. Left with no choice, my predecessors did just that."

"What you say is true. The British, too, had to follow suit."

"Precisely my argument. It's the same slavery and merciless exploitation you witness out in this country that exists in my company as well. All the managers and overseers in our employ belong to either the Reddy or Naidu caste. They aren't brutes or bullies like you imagine them to be. They are very, very shrewd. If Tudor and Co. has turned a profit in this country, when it's teetering along in the red all across the world, it is thanks to their managerial abilities. I've been observing them closely. They are fundamentally good people. Simple. And of a hospitable nature. The faith they follow upholds one of the local deities as its god. They claim that their god is the very form of mercy, and that when the balance on earth tips in favour of evil, he will take human form. They don't break bread in the morning without offering their prayers to him. Their devotional music is truly moving. But then . . ."

Parmer's face contorted with loathing. "The disgust and hatred they harbour toward the untouchables is impossible to fathom. The most devout man among them can bring death to a thousand untouchable children without the slightest compunction. Tudor and Co. is ever-ready to offer its labourers better facilities and increased wages. But they won't allow it. They argue that the wage we're offering now is already more than necessary. We shouldn't increase it at any cost, they insist. Any type of concession we make is sure to disturb the equilibrium. In the present environment, there's no way we can function without the upper castes."

Not knowing what to say, Aiden sat mutely.

"I'm an American. Should the affairs of my factory find their way to the press back in Boston, I might as well turn the gun on myself. There can't be a greater disgrace to the education I received than what I'm doing here. My brothers will be repulsed by the very thought of me." As blood rushed to Parmer's face, he stuttered. "Sorry," he said, and burying his face in his handkerchief proceeded to wipe it. Tears streaked down in spite of himself. He kept his face down as he dabbed his eyes and nose over and over.

"Mr. Parmer," Aiden called to him in a soft voice. "Be that as it may, don't you think this is a golden opportunity? You can give these people a nominal raise at this time. You can better their working conditions, if only a little. Tell the upper castes that the strike leaves you no alternative but to do so."

"Yes, that's one possibility." After giving his nose a good wipe, Parmer looked up.

"You may submit a letter to me soliciting an investigation into the murders. I'll tell them to end the protest myself. The very occurrence of this protest will make the supervisors think twice before they attack the workers openly."

"Yes, but . . ."

"You must decide," Aiden urged. "Perhaps history has sent you here for this very reason, Mr. Parmer. It may well be the purpose of all the education you received. You've come face to face with the first labour protest in India. Bring it to an amicable close. Let it make for a promising beginning. If such a thing were to happen in your tenure, you could look upon it with pride for the rest of your days."

"I can't tell how far my authority extends."

"Mr. Parmer, do you really believe a decision of yours can be disregarded?"

"If I pass a decision in writing, they can do nothing about it, legally speaking. But . . ."

"Do it. If, after making this decision, you land up in any kind of trouble, your conscience will be by your side."

"What should I do?"

"Write a letter as though you're making a direct announcement to the workers on strike. Declare the benefits you're prepared to offer and tell them to return to work. Publish it here as an official letter from the company. The strike will end. Whatever happens afterwards, we'll talk about it."

Parmer looked on for a few seconds, his eyes filled with thought. Then he rose to his feet and said, "Yes, that is for the best." His face brightened momentarily. "Thank you. This appears to be a new beginning. When I leave this place, I'll have something to regard with satisfaction."

"Go on," said Aiden, getting to his feet.

Parmer made to go back in.

"Mr. Parmer," Aiden called out. When Parmer paused, "I'm leaving you with a debt of one kick. You may return it whenever you please," he said.

"Oh!" said Parmer, and laughed heartily.

"Forgive me. I hadn't understood you as I do now."

"It's all right. Honestly, I hadn't understood myself as I do now, either."

As Aiden made his way out, he felt a fatigue engulf his whole body. A sweet, edifying fatigue. To recline in a chair right there and close his eyes was all that occurred to him in that moment.

11

When Aiden came out to the front porch of the Ice House, Narayanan dragged up a chair for him. Aiden settled into it and stretched his legs. He watched Kathavarayan and his companions serve water to the assembled workers. Some of the soldiers who were standing by their horses with reins in hand and lances resting across the backs of their mounts also partook of the water. Only when the liquid was being emptied from a big pot did Aiden notice that it wasn't water but a thin, fermented gruel—something the locals called pulithakaadi. He had seen that to swill the kaadi in a few uninterrupted gulps was an Indian habit. Such watery gruels were preferred to liquor in tropical lands all across the world. Liquor, come to think of it, was a type of pulithakaadi, too.

The evening was tending towards the scarlet of dusk. Like a blood-soaked brook, the orange-red light swelled and flooded the entire yard. The shadows of the mounts were upon the walls. It seemed as though they, too, were tinged with red. In the light of the courtyard, the shadows of the birds returning landwards from the sea crossed over like the faint tremble of a wave. The roar of the sea seemed to have grown louder. Cool droplets of moisture were palpable in the breeze that stirred the horses' tails, the soldiers' liveries, and the leafage of the trees.

Aiden's gaze was fixed on the black people in front of him. On what faith are they seated there? Their foundation has shattered. Narayanan has no inkling that I'm no longer the captain. Nor does Mackenzie. They will, though, in a matter of a few hours. All of this should conclude before that. If not, these events will take a wholly different turn. The minute Parmer's letter is pinned up, I must order these people to disperse. They should vacate White Town altogether, to be sure.

"Call him," Aiden ordered, pointing to Kathavarayan. When Narayanan sent for him, Kathavarayan wiped his hands clean, walked up to Aiden, and stopped in the yard in front of the porch. Aiden dismissed Narayanan with a wave of his hand. Then, in a hushed tone, he said, "By the look of it, all will be well."

"Thank you, sir," said Kathavarayan.

"Parmer will offer a small wage increase. He'll arrange to support the treatment of the sick. He will acknowledge that the two people in question were identified as his employees and make me a plea to conduct an investigation."

"That will do, sir. It is far more than I expected."

"You've Parmer's conscience to thank for it. My assumptions about him were all wrong."

"I am someone who has eternal faith in the white conscience, sir."

Aiden sighed. As he beheld Kathavarayan's beatific face, an inarticulate sadness permeated him. Even at the depths of their depravity, the caste fanatics in this country wouldn't dare inflict the great devastation the white race had wrought on Australia and South America. Was it at all possible to make him see that? In the current century alone, the white race has eliminated one quarter of the world's population in wars and famines. But that is how history unfolds. I, the member of a race oppressed for centuries, am seated now in the guise of an oppressor.

Kathavarayan intuited the course of Aiden's thoughts from the look in his eyes. "Sir, without a doubt, the white man's rule is just as brutal as any other power structure. However, the average white person has begun to apprehend what humanity is. They have begun to grapple with the idea of human equality. On the other hand, the people of this land carry on with their lives wholly oblivious to the very emergence of such ideas."

Aiden was in no mood for a debate. "When Parmer's ready with the letter, I'll instruct him to display it on the noticeboard. Once that's done, everyone should disperse immediately. It may come to light any moment now that my tenure is over. Before that happens, all of this should end peaceably. Let your men know."

"Certainly, sir," said Kathavarayan. He bowed his head and walked back.

Aiden watched the crowd as a renewed vitality and hope sparked in every one of them. There is a certain kind of virility that arises in man only at the moment of battle. In that moment the immense and everlasting aloneness that otherwise envelops him gives way. He conjoins others such as him. His arms and legs multiply without end. His body assumes gigantic form. He becomes equal to God. That is the great ecstasy of a battlefield. It is this extraordinary self-discovery which unravels in the theatre of war that forges the personality of the warrior. It is why, despite knowing that death is ahead of him, man takes to the battlefield. Once man gets a taste of it, he can never forget it. There is no stopping him after that. Right this moment, a mighty river has started to flow from its wellspring. Yes.

A carriage bell rang out. A phaeton hung back at the gate sounding its bell, hearing which the soldiers moved aside. The carriage entered and made a slight turn. As the horse changed step and paced backward, the phaeton backed up a whole foot. Without letting go of the reins, the coachman leaped down and patted the horse quiet. Then, leaving the reins on a hook, he hastened to open the carriage door. He took out a tiny ladder from the front of the vehicle and positioned it against the carriage.

Aiden recognised the personage who emerged from the carriage instantly. It was Murahari Iyengar, the man who had come to meet Russell. The moment he saw Aiden, he walked up to him with an extended hand. "I didn't expect to see you here, Captain. It's my good fortune. Delighted to meet you," he intoned, in a classic English accent. The same attire he had worn to Russell's office, the same diamond-encrusted, gold betel-leaf box, the same red line on his brow. With a captivating smile, he said, "I had intended to visit you in your office."

"Glad that we've had the occasion to meet," Aiden replied, though he was unable to fathom what had brought the man there.

"Shall we sit," said Iyengar, sweeping his hand in the direction of the chair. "In a way, it's good that we met here."

Aiden sat down. He looked intently at Murahari Iyengar, expecting him to go on.

"I own shares in Tudor and Co. I'm lawyer, auditor, and everything else to my eight fellow shareholders. I'm also the one who manages Tudor and Co.'s books," Murahari Iyengar began. "To tell you the truth, this company's chapter is over. I'm not sure how much longer it'll stay afloat. Tudor and Co.

has shut down its ice trade in several countries. A new technology has emerged. If the business still stands here, it's on account of the false belief that the waters of New England possess a singular flavour." With a chuckle, he caressed the betel-leaf box. "I've tasted all the ice there is. I can guarantee there's no such uniqueness."

Bit by bit, Aiden pieced together what was going on. All he wanted to know was whether Russell was one of the shareholders.

"So far, Tudor and Co. has sold ice only to collectors and maharajas. We're considering if we should retail from this year on, in Madras. The British soldiers and the Anglo-Indians among the locals are sure to buy. We'll be able to defer our financial troubles a little." He looked at the workers as though he was registering their presence just then. "What's this?"

Aiden gave no reply. In that time, Parmer emerged tentatively from inside.

"Good evening, Mr. Parmer. You seem tired," Iyengar remarked.

"That I am. Good evening," said Parmer.

"What's all this? I didn't know it had gone this far."

"The workers are on a strike," Parmer replied.

"On a strike? What do you mean?" His thick eyebrows joined in the middle.

"They're refusing to work," Parmer elaborated.

"Okay, start the work with whoever's willing to work, then? Let the rest go."

Parmer held his silence. With a sliver of irritation, "Mr. Iyengar," said Aiden, "a labour strike isn't as elementary as a stoppage of work. They've brought this factory to a standstill on account of their demands."

"Let them stop work. What right do they have to stop the factory? That's wanton. And illegal."

To Aiden's surprise, Iyengar's outrage made him smile inwardly. He had not imagined that the man would lose his temper. With even more composure, Aiden said, "Mr. Iyengar, what you're talking about isn't your personal property. It's a place of business. Others, too, enjoy certain rights here. You're duty-bound to regard them with respect."

Iyengar trained his gaze on Aiden for a few seconds. "What's your interest in this?" he asked.

"A peaceful resolution, nothing more," Aiden said evenly.

"Your concern is laudable. I will discuss it with my manager," said Iyengar.

Right then, Aiden resolved not to let Parmer out of his sight. "Mr. Iyengar, your manager has already made a decision which he has duly conveyed to me. The letter recording the decision has been readied, too. We were just about to make an announcement. In a few minutes, the protest will come to an end."

Murahari Iyengar's eyes narrowed. "What's this I hear, Mr. Parmer?"

Parmer paled somewhat. He was unable to bring words to his lips.

Aiden interceded. "Mr. Parmer has announced a few concessions. He has accepted the workers' demands. Mr. Parmer, please hand your shareholder a copy of the letter."

"Under the circumstances, this is the best solution. That's why I came to this decision," Parmer explained.

"I welcome it. All the same, you ought to take your shareholders' views into consideration, too," said Murahari Iyengar.

"It's a question of everyday management. The shareholders don't typically intervene in such matters." Parmer's voice echoed thinly.

"No, Mr. Parmer, no. I'm sorry to say that this is a financial decision," Murahari Iyengar countered. "I believe you're yet to publish that letter?"

"I . . . Now—"

"Even if you do publish it, I can have it revoked."

Aiden felt an agitation in his body. "Mr. Iyengar, the concessions listed in there are woefully basic. It'll hardly cause a dent in your finances." He detested the plea in his own voice.

"Isn't that for me to decide after I scrutinise the numbers?" The same beguiling smile.

"These benefits were already in the offing. To be honest . . . ," Parmer chipped in.

"They lost the right to receive those benefits the moment they held us hostage. If we succumb to such threats we won't be able to live here. If we fear such lowborn we'll no longer be our fathers' children."

Aiden felt his temper invoke a twitching in his fingers. "This is not a sum of any note, Mr. Iyengar," he repeated.

"Captain, this is business. Business is an ocean that swells one drop at a time, they say. You won't care for a lonely copper coin. You'll walk over it with your shod feet. I, on the other hand, will stop to retrieve it and touch it to my eyes before I take another step. I spare not a single coin for those who won't earn it. That's why I'm in business." Murahari Iyengar smiled. "I offer you an argument that soldiers such as you will understand. Every copper coin is a horseshoe that can bring a battle to its knees. Now, if you will excuse me," he said, and rose to his feet.

As he strode into the building, Parmer trailed behind him. Kathavarayan, who had been watching them from the distance, came up. "What is he saying?" he asked.

"It's a most unfortunate situation," said Aiden. "A very hard-nosed man. I'll have to try intimidating him a little."

"He knows you are no longer captain," said Kathavarayan. "He has come armed with that knowledge."

"So what do you propose I do?"

"We will make do with any one of the concessions. Even a promise will do. Please make an announcement in the presence of those two gentlemen that the necessary action will be taken. We will disperse."

"I'll try. It should be possible. We mustn't let this reach a point where you're left to face Mac and our army."

Kathavarayan nodded. Worry and anxiety were writ large on his face.

Aiden tapped his boots on the floor restlessly. As he brooded over what to do, like piglets that bump and squeeze through a narrow door only to freeze up, several thoughts jostled in him and came to a standstill. Time, python-like, snaked on lazily.

From the inside arose the sound of chairs being moved, of throats being cleared, of conversation. Eventually, Parmer came out. One glance at his face, and Aiden knew it.

"What is it, Mr. Parmer?" he asked in a subdued voice.

"For all intents and purposes this building, too, is his now," Parmer replied without mincing words.

Aiden stared blankly at him, not knowing what to say. His eyes turned to Murahari Iyengar as he emerged from within, bearing a large file in his hands. Wearing a monocle on his left eye, he was studying the papers even as he walked out.

Coming to a stop on the porch, he raised his hand and summoned his coachman. He said something to him in Tamil, the meaning of which became clear to Aiden when the coachman returned from inside the building bearing a big stack of files on his head and proceeded to load them into the phaeton.

Murahari Iyengar settled into a chair opposite Aiden. Placing his files on the tripod by his side, he flashed a smile at him, displaying a uniform row of teeth.

"I've conveyed my decision to Mr. Parmer. This building is in my control. These people have occupied my personal property, without my consent."

Seeing that Aiden was about to respond, he raised his hand and stopped him. "They are not my workers. I've declared so, already. I'm herewith filing an official complaint with you to evacuate them from my property at once."

"Mr. Iyengar."

"It's the responsibility of Her Majesty the Queen's government to protect my assets and my belongings. You can decide the matter. If not you, your superiors." Smiling, Murahari Iyengar handed him a sheet of paper. "Mr. Parmer has written this letter on my behalf. I need a note acknowledging your receipt of it."

"Mr. Iyengar, I will accept it, and provide you with the acknowledgement you ask. But there's really no need for it. I'll ask the workers to disperse right away. There's just one thing to be done. A fellow worker of theirs is dead. Please place a request, in writing, soliciting the British government to investigate the killing. I will, in turn, record my promise to do so on the same letter and have it displayed here. They will leave."

"The ones who were killed were not my workers."

"Mr. Iyengar, this is sheer mulishness. All right. *I* will declare that the guilty will be punished. Just stand by me and second it with your silence."

"Captain, legally speaking, the dead are not my employees. Practically speaking, an investigation over the killing of an untouchable worker will demoralise my managers. They'll lose their self-confidence and motivation, after which, they can never control this mob. My present position requires me to execute large projects that necessitate a huge workforce. In the event, I would prefer not to have my managers' control weaken."

Stopping Aiden with a raise of his hand, Murahari Iyengar carried on. "Listen to me, Captain. It is fear alone we wield to rule over this great mob. Were that fear to vanish, we will lose our perch over them. This protest is no ordinary matter. They've learned—for the very first time—that it's possible to oppose the government and the upper castes. It's the same as offering a wild animal its first taste of blood. If we leave this matter be, no one can rein it in later. It must be crushed right away."

Aiden watched as Iyengar's face turned red as a brass vessel reflecting fire. He could not speak a word.

Just then, Kathavarayan stepped forward with folded hands. A faint discharge of tears stained his face. He uttered something, in Tamil, pleadingly. Only then did Murahari Iyengar notice him. "Who're you?" he demanded.

"Their leader," Aiden answered.

"Oh, that is you?" Iyengar instinctively backed up in revulsion. Avoiding Kathavarayan's face, he looked in the direction of the wall and screamed: "How dare you step on the veranda? How dare you talk to my face? You may dress in white and forget your own caste, but I won't. Down! Get down!"

"Please, I beg you. Please see us as human beings. We are at death's door."

Was that indeed Kathavarayan's voice, Aiden wondered, dumbstruck. Never before had he seen a human being stand so small and meek before another.

"Narayana! What're you doing there? Was it you who allowed such scum to pollute me with his looks and words?

How did he enter these grounds with his turban intact?" Murahari Iyengar shrieked, quaking all over, his voice atremble. Stealing a glance at Aiden, Narayanan dithered.

"It was I who allowed him in, Mr. Iyengar," Aiden declared. "He is his people's representative. They, too, are Her Majesty the Queen's subjects."

"So it is you who encouraged these lowlifes, you who picked these worms from the mud and set them on the road. Then again, God has his own measure of justice. That is why he squashes these worms to death. By the end of this summer, these lowlifes will have reduced to the bare minimum this land requires. God is mightier than the British queen. And God's decree mightier than the state's. Want to see it for yourself? Go, take a look. Look around Chengalpattu and Kanchipuram. You'll see these lowlifes heaped dead, like garbage. You'll know then who God is."

With crazed eyes gleaming like a madman's he bored into Aiden. "They died at war, every one of them. A war they waged against God. They violated God's laws. This man who stands before us now, for the mere act of his wearing white, God will slay this mob. For daring to stand before the Brahmin that I am with a turban on his head, God will stamp a hundred thousand of them to dust. He who determined the boundaries of the sea knows the boundaries of men, too. Yes."

Kathavarayan trained his moist eyes on Murahari Iyengar. His lips curled ever so slightly in derision as he spoke in a soft yet firm voice. "Sir, I, too, believe that there is a God. Otherwise, you would not have begotten beef eaters for masters. Nor would you have given your women to them and stood fawning in worship outside their rooms."

As though a great avalanche had rained on him, Murahari Iyengar froze; the colour drained from his face as he stood transfixed. The betel-leaf box in his hand alone began to tremble suddenly as if it had been placed in a running carriage. Slowly, Iyengar rested a hand on the arm of the chair. One side of his face twitched. Was he having some kind of stroke—a momentary fear gripped Aiden. Iyengar sank into the chair and clutched the betel-leaf box to his bosom.

Kathavarayan strode away, marching through the yard, purposefully, and exited the front gate. Even as he walked out he signalled and shouted to his men to leave.

"Arrest that man, arrest him," Murahari Iyengar rasped. He could barely speak.

Narayanan stood silently, looking at Aiden. Aiden's eyes flitted back and forth between the two men. Narayanan's gaze made him feel as though a spear's point was resting on him.

"Isn't that an offence? Is his insulting me not an offence?" Murahari Iyengar exhorted. He was struggling to regain his composure. His voice hoarsened. He cleared his throat and, breathing heavily, spoke in a broken voice. "He insulted me. The lowlife." Suddenly, a whimper broke from him.

"Well, you insulted him first," said Aiden.

Murahari Iyengar ground his teeth and, with jaws clenched, glared at the crowd. His head alone trembled as if it were shivering in the cold. After a time, he slowly slackened. He relaxed his grip from the chair's arm and felt his face. He fingered it as though something repulsive had settled on his skin. He rubbed it hard.

Then, with a sigh, he gathered himself. He relaxed his legs and stretched them. When he spoke afterwards, his voice was lucid. "Captain. You're yet to provide me an acknowledgement of the letter I submitted," he said.

"Give the letter to Narayanan. Nar, furnish an acknowledgement," Aiden instructed.

Narayanan's eyes instantly moved to Aiden's evasive gaze and held sway until they met for a split second. A cold realisation washed over Aiden. Narayanan had worked out that he was no longer in office.

Wasting no time, Narayanan scribbled a few lines on paper and handed it to Murahari Iyengar. Iyengar received the note and placed it in his file. "Excellent, Captain. I now need to know what you propose to do next."

"I'll have a word with them and order them to disperse." So saying, Aiden rose from his chair. Fatigue weighed heavily in his body. He wished to bring this drama to an end as swiftly as possible.

A quasi-darkness had settled over the courtyard. Even as all the faces presented as silhouettes, the white walls alone had acquired such definition that their every fault and undulation was clear as day. The deep-red brushstrokes in the sky appeared like a dying fire. The red of the yard's brickscape had intensified further. Glimmering eyes gazed at him through the darkness. Clothes flapped in the sea breeze, here and there. The sound of the sea crashed into the silence and saturated it.

Aiden clapped his hands together. The sound seemed to set off the mass of bodies in a faint tremble, like a stone striking a tranquil pond. The next instant, in the manner of big fish erupting out of water, the soldiers sprang up in a flash and ascended their horses. They positioned their two-man-tall lances upright. The thorn-like metal tips of the weapons bore red motes of evening light. Each of those movements found reflection in the forms of the seated workers. It seemed as though their bodies were pulsating. As though their bodies were a marshscape beneath which a monstrous creature lay submerged, biding its time.

Standing near the gate, Kathavarayan was repeating something over and over through clenched teeth. It looked as if he was summoning them. Was he calling for Karuppan?

"Attention, everyone!" Aiden called out loud. "I plan to initiate a formal investigation into this case. The guilty will be identified within a week and brought to task. All of you, disperse immediately." Narayanan repeated the announcement in Tamil.

Aiden watched as the crowd, offering no response, remained seated like three hundred statues of black stone. A shudder arose in the depths of his being. "I've spoken to your leader, and he has accepted the offer. You may ask him yourself. We'll take care of everything. You must disperse at once," he urged.

Then, too, there was no movement. Every pair of those eyes, like white seashells, were fixed on him. His words dissipated in the dusk-darkened breeze and withered away.

Aiden's voice fell. "Listen here. Your leader and I have had a talk. He commands you to disperse."

Kathavarayan gesticulated wildly, all the while vociferating in the local tongue. Him, too, the crowd beheld as though beholding an outsider, and sat motionless.

Aiden's voice lost the pretence of authority. "I'm someone who speaks for you. You know that yourself. The situation is not in our control at present. You can't go on with this protest. Enough. *I* promise you that action will be taken. We will find the guilty and punish them."

Kathavarayan shouted something in Tamil, in the manner of an order. Karuppan considered him for a brief moment. Then, without rising from his position on the ground, he thundered, demanding Kathavarayan stop. With eyes enlarged in shock, Kathavarayan froze in place.

Karuppan turned to Aiden. "Sir, there is no need to search for the guilty. There they are, standing to your right. Neelamegam and Varadharaju. They are the murderers. Arrest them."

Aiden floundered. A sound, like the growl of a gigantic wild beast, rose from the crowd. Aiden raised his hand. "I will investigate them. As soon as the evidence is found, I'll take them into custody."

"Evidence? Will two people who saw those men bring the axe down on the back of the victims' heads be enough?" So saying, Karuppan rose to his feet. "Here, these are the two witnesses who saw it with their own eyes." He pointed to a couple of men. "Sudalai and Kannuchaami. Enough?"

Aiden stood silently for a few seconds. Then, as a flash of anger rushed to his head, "There's no point talking to you anymore. Disperse right now. Right now," he screamed in a broken voice.

"We will not, sir. We want justice," said Karuppan. "Our leader himself has told us to leave, but we won't leave till we receive justice."

"Disperse. Disperse," Aiden shrieked.

Karuppan shook his head in refusal and sat down. The whole throng boomed like the prolonged resonance of a mighty drum. That wordless note spoke to everyone unequivocally.

"I will order the use of force. I will tell them to attack. Disperse!" Aiden raved, gesticulating wildly. The fervour in his voice was astonishing even to him. Nevertheless, the crowd sat tight, watching Aiden's eyes intently.

His body pulsating all over with impotent anger, Aiden took in the stone-bodied mob. Yes, it is something else. A domestic creature that will do my bidding is what I had imagined it to be. But it's a great potency we don't have the measure of just yet. A force that will surge like an irrepressible colossus at the sundering of its first tether. Murahari Iyengar knows this far better than I do. That is the root of his fear and panic. Yes, his soul knows that which is before us. Why, my soul, too, knows it. His fear and my pleading spring from the very same source. For goodness' sake, what kind of thoughts are these! I'm not afraid. I'm one who loves a turbulent storm, an erupting volcano. I'm Shelley. Fool, you use Shelley to bury your conscience deep within the sand. Shelley is no more than a foaming, souring drink to you. What thoughts are these! What am I doing here? God, what am I to do with this immense agglomeration of life that is before me? How do I remove it from here? It does not comprehend my words. It seems as if it has suddenly turned into a black boulder. What do I do? How do I deal with its dark and menacing silence! Should I bang my head against it until it shatters? God, what am I thinking!

Like the grazing of a fiery rod, a thought passed through him and made him writhe. This old Brahmin and I are no different in the eyes of this mob. The Indian caste structure and British authority, no different. When this murderous beast sinks its teeth in and gorges on us, all our flesh and blood will carry the same taste. His body agitated in a fit of rage and irritation. He felt an urge to plunge into the mob with sword in hand and cut down the lumps of flesh in front of him with a vengeance. Jesus, my Saviour. What am I thinking? Is this me?

Unable to withstand the force of the thoughts surging in a boisterous swell inside him, Aiden faltered. Under its velocity, time stretched and protracted. The multitude of faces before him blinked slowly; their lips, emitting strange noises, pursed and parted very slowly. Their heads turned ever so slowly. The windswept leaves on the trees at the far end rustled slowly, as if in a dream. The equines' ears and manes stirred slowly as if wading in water. What's this? Jesus, what is this? It's something I know not. A great potency that has struck the whole world with terror. A demon that opens its eyes only in the innermost nightmares of kings. A black shadow that spreads quietly over sleeping armies and enshrouds them. A vicious poison that, oozing from an unknown fissure in some deep abyss of the world, has begun to seep all over. And here I am, standing like a mahout who attempts to speak to an elephant in the throes of musth. In its small eyes I see something else take the place of the familiar beast I know so intimately. Even as its ears, feet, trunk, and all else remain the same, I watch its soul alone alter into that of a different beast. Still, I talk to it with hope.

"Please disperse. I will present your case. I will look out for your welfare. Please." Aiden heard his voice resound somewhere far away. He was observing his own self from afar as it pleaded with the crowd that stood before him as firm and cool as a mysterious, unknown metal. "Please. Your leader and I will have a talk. Please disperse." From beyond the gate, Kathavarayan was gesticulating with both hands and keeping up his orders in Tamil. A scatter of muffled voices was all that emerged from the throng.

Feeling like a petty creature squashed beyond hope, Aiden stood motionless for a time. The rush that overtook him afterwards he would come to examine moment by moment and word by word for the rest of his life. Never once did he understand it. It was his moment of knowing. Or else, a momentous tryst with the unknowable. Is knowing that you can never know the highest knowledge? A type of arrogance, is what it is. An uncontrollable frenzy. Why? Why had it reared its head in that particular moment? Was it the effect of wounded pride? Like that of a trodden snake, or a horse that had taken a bullet. Was it merely the ego of the white man who lay ossified in him? In that moment, when he stood humbled in front of those black people, had the souls of all his ancestors, steeped in colour's pride for thousands of years, congregated inside of him?

No. That was not it. What had awoken in him that instant was the innate vanity that dwells in every warrior. What had flared up in the face of opposition was his conditioned military mind. It was a weapon. The weaponry his hands wielded were mere external manifestations of that inner weapon. My mind has been shaped and whetted by the drill of the army. I am an effective firearm. When the finger touches the trigger, I am ordained to explode. Yes, that is what I am. If any other soldier from anywhere in the world had been stationed there, he would have done as I did. Yes.

No, it was not I who did that. It was my body. My inner self was watching my body's doing with bewilderment. No. Not my body. My hand. My hand was the culprit. My hand alone was taken over by some dark angels. It was not my own hand. It was the hand of the ruthless forces of destiny that churn humanity. The hand of God, or Satan, or an even greater will that holds the two of them in everlasting conflict. No. What did my hand do? I did nothing at all. What I did was one thing. What transpired, something else altogether. *I* was not there. That which transpired has nothing to do with me. No. That's not it. Oh! Christ, my Saviour, can Man ever know what abides in him?

What had happened? Aiden questioned himself with a shiver from the very next moment. Propelled by a violent force that surged deep inside him, he took a step forward and raised his hand. The same instant, Narayanan's voice boomed as though it was erupting from his own throat. "Company charge!"

I? Was it I who screamed? Jesus. That wasn't my voice. Jesus! No. No. Stop. No! That wasn't me. In that instant, he split and cleaved into two. One of him flailed about, straining to gather the thoughts running inside him with his two hands. The other one stood wordlessly, his gaze transfixed on the scenes unfolding like a nightmare in front of his eyes.

The horses whose reins were yanked kicked their forelegs in the air. They leaped forward with loud neighs while their hooves rained like rocks over the black heads of the throng. They vaulted and cavorted over human flesh, over human bones, over human wails, human tears. Soldiers, rotating their spear shafts between their fingers, whirled about, and struck out with fierce cries. Suddenly, Aiden caught a whiff of that scent. The raw smell of blood. He could feel the globules of blood spattering in half-darkness. Launched from the horse hooves and spear shafts, they flew through the air, slammed into the walls, and, lingering for just a second, oozed down the surface.

With a loud cry, Aiden sprang to his feet and grabbed Narayanan by the collar. "No. Tell them to stop. No. You fool!" Throwing his arm towards the growing tumult of the half-bestial, half-human bodies in front of his eyes, he agitated. With neck veins bulging, and mouth widened to the point of tearing, he screamed. "No! No. Stop. No." Narayanan picked up the bugle and blew on it. The bugle issued a sharp refrain as though a blind bird, utterly alien to that place, was singing in response to some other sight, to some other thought. Reined in, the horses came to an abrupt stop. Their momentum unabated, they struggled and paced back and forth. One or two of them neighed in protest.

Black bodies, like trampled mud, lay beneath the horse hooves. Trampled bodies. Bodies created by God only to be trampled. They were piled in front of that Tyrant's eyes—he who was staging and spectating a most vulgar and macabre drama on this earth—as arms and legs and writhing. As flesh, blood, urine, and excrement. Happy? Here it lies before you. Laugh at it, you wretched scoundrel. Gorge on it, you vile sinner. For the reason that I, too, am your creation, I vow to slit my throat. Aiden unsheathed his blade. It was unbearably heavy. The force with which he tugged at it made him keel over. A gluey darkness. A giant gossamer of darkness. Embedded in the viscosity, Aiden slashed the web and, sinking ever deeper, swam forth.

12

When Aiden opened his eyes all he could see for a moment or two was darkness. From afar, a chariot's light kept advancing towards him, though the rattle of its wheels and the tinkle of its bell had stopped in the distance. In a second, a whole burden of memories cascaded over him, and Aiden sat up with a start. He became aware of a trembling in his body. Have I caught a fever? No. Still, his body shuddered of its own volition. He stuck his hands in his trouser pockets. I fell asleep in my uniform. Did I sleep? That isn't the light from a chariot. It's a lamp hanging from the ceiling. I hear the sound of the troops outside. The sound of carriage wheels. This is my office.

Aiden rose to his feet. Unable to stand on his enfeebled legs, he teetered and reached for the wall. He shut his eyes for a few moments, composed himself, then opened his eyes again. The fragrance of melting paraffin. It was an intimate smell. The smell of words, of books, of poetry. Now the location and surroundings emerged clearly in his mind's eye. The flow of thoughts regained order. What was that pain? His forehead was swollen. When he touched it, he felt a dull ache. He tucked his shirt, which had slipped out of his trousers, back in and walked cautiously.

An egg-shaped paraffin lamp burned on the desk in his office. A large paraffin lamp hung from the ceiling. The shadow of the lamp's bottom lay on the floor like a big tank of water; in its red glow, the bent shadows of the pillars were cast on the wall. Aiden sank into his chair and closed his eyes for a second. Colours tumbled down a yellow expanse. Red and blue. Bubbles exploded. What is it that overflows soundlessly? My blood? My self?

He sensed a movement next to him and opened his eyes. It was Sam.

"Tea, sir?"

"Whisky," he replied instinctively. After a moment's thought, "Tea will do," he said.

Sam returned with the tea.

"What time is it?" asked Aiden.

"More than an hour past midnight, sir."

"Oh." As though he had remembered its presence just then, he pulled a watch out of his pocket and read the time. Half past one. *What had happened?* Another wave of remembrance crashed into him and shattered his being. He sprang to his feet. "Sam. Where's Narayanan? Where is he?"

"The new captain was here. He asked us to send word once you wake up," Sam responded.

"Where's my hat?" A belch rose to his lips. Only then did it dawn on him that whisky had been forced down his throat. "Where's my hat? Where is it?" he shouted, pushing his chair away.

Sam fetched the hat and placed it on the table. As Aiden reached for it and made to leave, he caught sight of Mac coming up the stairs. When he stood up, the whole building rocked like a boat.

"Good morning, Captain," Mac said, greeting him with a wide smile. "I'd been to see the lieutenant colonel.

He was the one who gave me the news of your promotion. Congratulations."

Feeling faint, Aiden grasped the edge of the table and staggered back to his chair. Mac settled down opposite him. "How're you feeling? Jemadar Madasamy's a good physician. He confirmed it was nothing."

"What happened, Mac? What happened back there? They . . ."

"No one died," said Mac. "Many sustained injuries, but all of them survived."

"That's a lie. A lie! I saw it with my own eyes," Aiden cried, as he tried to get up.

"If there were any casualties, won't you be the one responsible for them, Captain? Why are you making matters worse for yourself?"

"It wasn't me. I didn't order the attack." Aiden sat down again.

"I examined Narayanan at length. And interrogated four cavalrymen, too. You signalled to attack."

"No. I raised my hand . . ." Aiden's skin crawled at the sound of his own voice.

"That is the signal to attack."

"No! I made no signal. I did no such thing," Aiden shrieked.

"Captain, that's a gesture designed for when a leader's injured so badly he's unable to vocalise a command. You employed it quite explicitly. There're as many as twenty or thirty witnesses," said Mac. He took his hat off and placed it on the desk. "The law cares only about witnesses, Captain," he said.

Aiden sat stupefied.

"One more thing. Even if it were true that you hadn't ordered the attack, we can't prove it. Our army is nothing but an agglomeration of this country's upper castes. They will say only one thing."

Aiden slumped in his chair wearily. In a weak voice he entreated, "Mac, I ask you only this. Tell me truthfully, how many died?"

"No one died. That's the truth." Mac smiled. "What is truth, Captain? There are many truths. This is my truth. Not a single person died. You've no choice but to believe it wholeheartedly." He rested his thick arms on the table and leaned forward. "If you don't, it can only mean that many died. Then you'll have to assume responsibility for it. British officers will gladly sacrifice an Irishman to give proof of their sense of justice and humanity."

"What happened, Mac?" Aiden held his head in his hands. "Oh, Jesus!"

"The official truth is this: nothing happened there. Neither did a protest take place nor was it suppressed. The Ice House is functioning as per usual. You'll see nothing if you go there now. Down to the last drop of blood, it's all dried up in the sea breeze. The Ice House will rise and shine tomorrow as usual. It'll operate as usual."

Emptied of all thought, Aiden sat motionless, staring ahead.

"Just forget it, Captain. Isn't that how we forget the battlefield? Why do you care about death? The instant we set out for this land of dust and disease, death accompanied us. Ergo, no death is of consequence to us. Our own death. Our children's death. All around us there is only death." Mac smiled. "From the time I left London, I've seen nothing but war and pestilence. Everyone who came with me is dead. I invented a convenient phrase for myself. 'Luckily, I didn't die.' That's it. Whenever I witness any kind of death I remind myself of that line. A pleasant breeze will sweep through my heart. I didn't die. He died, she died, but *I* am here. What a marvellous truth that is. This earth and this sky are still here for me. Many more dawns will break for me. Isn't that a great feeling?"

Chuckling, Mac picked up his hat from the table. "Your departure order will be issued the day after tomorrow. A new town, a new people. The collector of Tenkasi is known to be a great host. There are some delightful hunting grounds in the control of the local zamindars as well. The planters' wives and daughters are real beauties. Get well soon, and start a new life."

"Thanks for the advice."

"I'll be off now. I've sanctioned a small incentive and four days of leave to all the soldiers who worked for us today. I need to check if the cash disbursement is complete." Pinning his hat back on his head, Mac departed.

Aiden stared at him as he walked out. A pistol strap ran across his mildly drooping left shoulder. A belt hung loosely around his lean stomach. Long, sinewy arms with protuberant veins and dried-grass-like stubble of red hair. Mac was a quintessential British soldier. One devoid of all questions and confusions. One who never lost faith in British justice or administration. One who brooked no doubt that the British race was fit to rule the world. Nor had he any qualms about the means to such an end. Yes, he was the perfectly forged firearm. Were war and disease to spare him, he would retire from the heights this service affords and board ship to England with personal effects and savings certificates worth several millions. His children will be educated in the elite institutions of London. They will enter the next century as cultured people. The bronze figurines, peacock plumes, and ivories their father brought with him will decorate their halls. Shakespeare and Goethe will adorn their reading rooms. Their daughters will play Mozart and Beethoven with bud-like fingers. Their curtains will light up in the morning sun.

There will waft the fragrance of flowers and the scent of sun-kissed grass. The play of morning light on their red hair will conjure up a tangle of gilded wires. The golden pinnacle of civilisation. The beau ideal of life mankind has pursued for tens of thousands of years. Yes.

The quiet of an utterly defeated man. How full and complete it is. There's no God nor Satan to talk to him. No aloneness quite like his. Nothing else settles to the bottom as mere waves bereft of sound or meaning as his words do.

After a long while, Aiden came around. When, sighing, he stirred, he realised that it was Sam's warm brew that had revived him. As he sipped the tea, his thoughts settled down like a film of mud, and his mind grew more and more clear. What should I do? What can I do? There's only one thing left to do: report these events. Yes, to disclose everything that has happened. To the government, to the newspapers, to the outside world. It is only I who can do it. I will be the first to face the consequences for it, too. Nonetheless, it is my duty. If I be imprisoned for it, I shall have atoned. If I be led blindfolded before a firing squad, I shall be fulfilled.

He urgently pulled out a few sheets of paper. Cracking his knuckles, he reached for the ink pot, dropped a blob of ink in, and mixed it with water. He shook the pot twice, dipped the pen in the liquid, and gave it a couple of taps. The words loomed many miles away from his instrument. Nevertheless, they stood there as though set down by someone a long time ago. They waited like stone symbols arrayed in an open ground—black, heavy, and motionless.

Seized by a sudden thought, Aiden retrieved his files. When he picked up a large file, bound with slender wooden boards and jacketed in bran-hued leather, he felt a faint agitation in him. The moment he opened the file, he knew it—it no longer contained any of his reports on the Ice House.

Even so, he looked frantically for them, over and over. Yes, it was true. Every report and letter on the Ice House had vanished.

How does the subconscious know these things already? Aiden felt a momentary weariness in him. In that instant, how did I intuit what had happened? Am I not the I who is engaged in the present act? Am I playing a part in this drama in other guises, too? No, I'm searching in the wrong place. I must have inadvertently placed those papers in a different file.

He ransacked all the folders, spread them out, and scoured through them page by page. All the other documents were untouched. To contain the sudden rush of anger that nearly knocked the wind out of him, Aiden held his head in his hands for a time. "Sam! Sam!" Later, when he rose to his feet, he saw Sam standing in front of him. It seemed as though Sam was behind a curtain of steam. Were his eyes clouding?

"Sir?"

"Did Mac remove any papers from here?"

Sam stood silently, though he did not avert his gaze even a whit.

"Leave," said Aiden. Once Sam left, drained of his last reserve of strength, Aiden slumped back in his chair. His thoughts scattered, lifted off, then, like rain-soaked paper, descended sluggishly and settled down. Random, desultory thoughts. Of his father, mother, Ireland's lakes, Africa's dirt city, Malaya's mosquitoes, the leaf-scented breasts of yellow-skinned women, gaunt shoulders with bones shifting beneath pale skin, cheeks marred by ripe-red acne, their feline moans, cannons, gunpowder, the odour of horse dung, the odour of warm blood. What fragrance fresh blood possesses. Fire, too, possesses a similar fragrance. A stubborn scent. A scent that never leaves.

"Sam! Sam, you fool! Sam!"

"Sir," said Sam appearing again.

"Whisky."

Like a man guzzling water after having wandered the desert sands, Aiden kept drinking. Mac will return soon. I ought not to become a laughingstock in his eyes. Enough. No . . . just one more. Yes, the hymn of the drink: One more glass. One more. What am I trying to fill with this? What am I trying to dissolve in cup after cup of this?

What is Freedom?—ye can tell
That which Slavery is, too well—
For its very name has grown
To an echo of your own

Shelley. When did I read these lines? I don't remember committing them to memory. When did I read this poem first? "The Masque of Anarchy." On a cold December's night. It had snowed heavily in London that day. Powdery snow lay heaped by the roadsides. The path—forged by the grind of the carriage wheels—stretched forward like a blood-crusted, pus-filled whiplash wound. Snow hung pregnant from barren branches and roof eaves. Ice beaded the sharp spires of the buildings. The tolling of the distant church-house bell echoed from somewhere beyond that field of snow. The sky—a colourless, lightless, plate of grey—had descended within reach of the town and overlaid it.

That afternoon, I had helped myself to dried bread buttered with fat. The lard tasted like wood. It refused to melt even when exposed to fire, uncongealed reluctantly, and gave off a stench. The stench of a pig's mouth. I pressed the lard to the bread tightly, bit through the whole of it, and chewed hard. The stinking hog melted in my mouth. I set water to boil over the same fire, tossed in the last leaves of Chinese tea, and prepared a drink. I sat close to the hearth. The fire held my gaze. For how many millennia has this snow fallen? Yet the fire is still here. Right here, before my eyes. Someday, a long time ago, Man acquired it from a bolt of lightning. He passed it from twig to twig. Shielded it from rain and storm. He has carried it to this day, undestroyed. And so it shall endure. Forever. Were someone to look down at this city from atop a tower, they may think it cold and frozen beneath the snow. They may suppose it contains no such thing as heat. But red tongues of fire blaze in many thousands of hearths in this city. This snow is a reality. The fire raging within it a greater reality.

Byron's "Prometheus" rested in his hands. He set it down, rose to his feet, and searched for Shelley in his trunk of books. *Triumphant where it dares defy*—he caught himself reciting Byron's line at the velocity of a chant. Funny indeed—while lamenting Byron he'd reached Shelley. He knew not, himself, which verse of Shelley's he was seeking. But the moment the book fell into his hands he knew that that was it. It was a book published in the year 1832 by Edward Moxon with a fiery preface by Leigh Hunt. Shelley had composed the poem as far back as 1819. It was his response to the massacre orchestrated by the British government when it set its army upon commoners at St. Peter's Field in Manchester. However, it was only after Shelley's death that the book went to press. Aiden had acquired it from the streets. Its yellowed, water-stained jacket bore Shelley's name in full. Aiden ran his fingers over the letters tenderly. Leaving the book unopened, he sat staring at the name.

He read the poem hundreds of times that night, like a lover who hadn't wearied of kissing his sweetheart. In the cool of night, as sleep and wakefulness mingled, as being and non-being coalesced, Aiden was adrift. *Rise like Lions after slumber!* Ah! How does one set fire to words? What be the magic that makes diamonds of pebbles? Shelley, where did you witness the rising of lions? I have seen it. In the grasslands of Saurashtra, a male lion arose upon seeing me—its mane billowing, chest muscles heaving, whiskers thrilling. Slowly. Very slowly. As if the entire world were waiting for it. As if its every movement had been determined already. The majesty of stillness, one beholds in the elephant. The majesty of a leap, in the tiger. The majesty of rising, only in the lion. Shelley, where did you see a lion? Did the one you beheld ascend the eastern sky, its flaming mane astir?

Aiden unbuttoned his shirt, pulled back the collar, and stared at the punkah swinging overhead. Warm beads of perspiration streamed down his neck and brow. The whole building swayed along with the punkah. *What is Freedom?—ye can tell that which slavery is, too well?* Yes. Shelley, you said it. The present moment is that very line. *What is Freedom?* The same refrain, over and over. Circling the air like a stubborn wasp, it stings. With every sting, my muscles ingest its venom and throb. *What is Freedom? What is Freedom? What is Freedom?* Go away, Shelley. Begone. Aiden swung his hands at the line thick and fast. He went at it with the board file. "Get out, out," he stuttered. *What is Freedom?* Suddenly, like a glacier caving under its own weight, his heart imploded and crumbled in a shower of rubble. A few whimpers gave way to sobs. Wilting in a ferment of tears, he cried himself to sleep.

After a while, he opened his eyes to the lamp glowing in the darkness. Rising in a huff, he proceeded to the wooden sink, filled it with water, and plunged his face into it. He forced his eyes open and watched the bubbles rise. When he ran out of breath, he pulled back and pressed the edge of his palm down his wet face. Waves of liquor-scented belches assaulted him. He walked back determinedly, grabbed his hat, and left the office.

It was still dark outside. The kind of darkness that intensifies at the crack of dawn. Even the sound of the night birds was absent. The ocean alone intoned the sonance of the universe. In the seaward sky, a faint light illuminated the lower rims of the clouds like a knife's edge. As he advanced through the courtyard, the birds on the neem tree scattered in a loud babel. Duraisamy, who was sleeping on the veranda on the far side, awoke; laying eyes on Aiden, he sprang up and hurried in his direction. Seeing that Aiden was walking towards the horse, he turned around and emerged thereafter with the bridle and saddle.

The horse stood naked. With its foreleg lifted lightly and its head hung low, it was fast asleep. Awoken by the clatter raised by Duraisamy, the hair on its back and flanks stood up as it shifted weight from foot to foot. Then it nosed Aiden and purred. Aiden patted its neck. The horse nuzzled its big head against his side. It had been rubbed down with lemongrass oil to stave off mosquitoes. Vaporous with oil, its hide felt warm to the touch in the cold of the early hours. It folded its ears in front, and nibbled at the margins of his shirt. As he pulled away, its blue-black tongue extended and curled like a beloved infant's finger. Aiden patted its muzzle. It tried to bite his shirt again.

Duraisamy fixed the saddle and tightened the straps. Inserting the bit in the animal's mouth, he secured it in place and fastened the hooks. As soon as the bridle was fitted, the childishness immanent in the animal until then exited, leaving it rigid. It stamped its forelegs on the ground impatiently and swirled its tail. Aiden mounted the horse. With a forceful exhalation, it raised its neck. He gently stroked its mane.

"Sir, shall I come . . ." began Duraisamy.

Refusing him with a shake of his head, Aiden spurred the horse into motion. He had no conception of where he was headed until he reached Beach Road. Instinctively, the horse took the beaten path. Aiden's eyes were fixed on the sea. It looked like a jet-black metalscape with the odd glimmer of light here and there. The rhythmic movement of the white surf on the shoreline was visible from afar, putting him in mind of a gigantic curtain aflutter in the wind. Aiden recognised where he was headed. His by-now cold house would be idling with bare rooms. The sea breeze would be sweeping through its large, unpeopled chambers—orphaned, aimless, and heavy.

Aiden pressed up against the horse and brought it to a halt. Then he tapped it again and set it off at a gallop. The horse streaked through the road, which lay still as a dead snake. Barking dogs shot out from the groves by the wayside and gave chase, coming to an abrupt stop where their territories ended. Igniting one after the other as if in a chain, hundreds of dogs broke into barks from near and far. Birds scattered from the heads of the coconut palms and, cawing in the darkness, flapped about in circles. The smell of the surroundings had heightened in the nighttime. Wet, pungent mud. Straw-rotting dung. Dung is scarcely a bad odour for these people. There's not a place in India that doesn't smell of dung.

Upon reaching Royapuram, he proceeded in the direction of St. Peter's Church. Above the church's stunted brick steeple a stone Cross rose in the manner of an upright question met by a horizontal response. For a time, he stood staring at the Cross. He knew then that it was not Father Brennen he had come to see. Men such as him were uncomplicated. They nurse no ambiguities, nor do they apprehend them. Sighing, he tapped the horse. He understood who it was he had come to meet.

At some other place, at some other time, Marisa had told him about her house. Every word of hers flooded back to his mind with great clarity together with the expression on her face. He turned a corner marked by an old-fashioned building. The street which lay beyond a thin creek of water was dotted with small, pantile-roofed residences. But the walls of the houses were whitewashed and their windows draped by curtains. The thresholds were bereft of the rice-powder motifs often drawn outside Indian households. Neither were there dogs. Most of all, there was no smell of dung. Instead, the faint smell of cheap perfume wafted in the air. Aiden wasn't fond of that smell. It was the scent of an aromatic herb the natives called marikkozhundhu. He had instructed Marisa to keep off it.

Aiden's horse lumbered along with heavy steps. The surrounding walls threw the sound back from within the darkness. Somewhere, an infant wailed sharply, hearing which, the mother hushed it back to sleep. A few scattered coughs. A dotard who was stretched out on a veranda looked up and peered in his direction. "Who is that?" The question came in slurred English. Coloured reed blinds screened many of the verandas. The breaths of the slumbering residents resounded from beyond the blinds. Four or five of the houses on the street were quite large. An upper storey carved from wood rested on lime-mortar walls, while big wooden pillars watched over the entrance like sentinels. Phaetons stood in front of the houses, their curtains dancing in the morning breeze. A short distance away, the horses were dozing on three legs with their heads downcast. The coachmen were sleeping underneath the carriages, on hemp sacks they had spread on the bare ground.

Aiden stood near her house. *This is the one.* All the houses in the vicinity looked more or less identical. Even so, he could tell her house apart. Soon, the reason for his certainty became clear to him. She had once told him about the night-flowering jasmine tree in front of her house. Its white blossoms had fallen to the ground in a circle. It looked as though a floral white fabric was outspread on the floor, as though the tree was a young woman sitting with her skirt fanned out in a swirl.

Aiden paused in front of the door. Should I knock? How can I be sure she'll be home right now? Her work is done by night. It's more likely that she's not around. Her mother might be there. Or the sister who bore the child of a white sepoy. She has two younger brothers as well. One of them might've returned from sea. At any rate, none of them would stand up to him. They were mere insects in front of his authority. He could get past them with as much ease as a red-hot knife slicing through a slab of butter. But. The look their eyes would hold. Never had he acted like a typical white soldier in front of Marisa. Marisa. Marisa. I'm alone now. And leaden with the weight of words. I need to talk to you. Marisa.

Why have I come here in search of her? Why else but to talk. I wish to keep on talking until I can prove that I'm innocent, that I'm just. She's my most pliant target. A place where my words will be accepted without scrutiny. No, that's not it. She's a life I value, deep down. A place I believe my innermost voice will reach. A sanctum where I stand naked, stripped of my ego and my pretences. No, it's none of that. I want to hold her. I want to press her bare body against mine and lie down. I want to subsume my aloneness in her person and be rid of it. I want to squeeze her, crush her, and listen to her moan of empty words. Those words, without passing her lips or my ears, will travel from her being to mine. Only then will I cease to be alone. I shall bury my face between her petite breasts and forget myself. I'll still be the man who was defeated, humiliated, left with nothing. But I will have a companion. Yes, that is the reason.

Yet he could not bring himself to knock on the door. The small, tile-roofed house, with its two tiny, wide-open windows and a tightly shut front door, watched him keenly. When the curtains fluttered in the breeze it looked as if its eyes were moving. He ventured to knock on that door in his imagination a hundred times. But he remained as he was, stuck to his horse. Why not leave? No, I won't be able to bear the disappointment that is sure to engulf me when I turn back. Under the weight of that emptiness, I'll shatter, crumble to pieces, and fall to the ground. Yes, I can't leave without meeting her. When she beckons me with open arms, I'll run to her like a frightened child. I'll lay down my all before her as oblation. Yes, that's why I'm here. God, how clear it all is! That is the reason I'm here. That intention has been in me all along. Only I had hidden it from my own self. Marisa. Marisa.

His heart keened without a sound. It let out a chest-shattering wail. Marisa. Marisa. As though she'd heard that infinitesimal sound, she quietly parted the curtains and looked out the window. "Marisa," cried Aiden. His voice caught in his throat. Had he screamed every word that had run through him until that moment over and over, his throat could not have been as hoarse. "Marisa."

Aiden dismounted from the horse and climbed up the stairs to the house. He could hear her unlatching the door from within. She stood in front of him, blocking the doorway. The unwavering flame of the candlelight in a glass bulb on the wall behind her enveloped the room in a red glow. Scattering the light off its surface, the wall sparkled like a roseate expanse. Marisa had wrapped a curtain-like length of cloth around her waist and thrown on a well-worn man's shirt over it. Copper streaks produced by the light capered in the upright frizzles of her tousled hair. The soft swell of her cheeks, the fuzz on her face, the delicate curve of her neck were all tinged with gold.

"What is it?" she asked. Her choked, heavy voice made her seem like a stranger.

"Marisa. It's me."

"I can see that. What brings you here at this hour?"

"I . . . I came looking for you, Marisa. I wanted to find your house . . ." What am I saying? A new scent came from her body. This isn't her usual perfume. It's her own fragrance. The scent of sweaty skin. It excited him just as the scent of the earth after fresh rain excites a young bull. "Marisa, I wanted to see you," he declared, holding his hand out.

"I don't receive anyone at home," she said. "My family is here." She met his eyes directly. But it was an altogether alien gaze.

"I wanted to tell you something. I—" He drew a deep breath. "I've been transferred to Tenkasi. I might have to leave as early as tomorrow. When I leave . . . I . . . What I mean is . . . Marisa, I wish to marry you."

A movement passed through her eyes like the sudden flicker of a lamp flame in a gust of wind.

"I'll speak to your mother about it. And to Father Brennen. I'll wed you lawfully and take you with me. You should come with me. I cannot go there alone. I cannot leave you. You must come with me. You're the only one who can understand. I've been alone all these days. I've never shared my heart with anyone—except you. You must come. I offer you everything that's mine. My title, my post, my station, all of it. Should I leave this wretched country someday and return to Ireland, you should come with me then, too. To see my mother, to see my father. I'll introduce you to them as the mother of my children. Ireland is a paradise on earth. The lakes, the mountains . . ." Astounded by his own speech, he stopped himself. Did I vocalise all those words or were they merely playing inside me?

"Why were you transferred to Tenkasi?" Marisa asked, as if slitting his stomach lengthwise with a sharp blade.

"They've made me major. I'm going to head the region's police force."

"A promotion, isn't it?"

At once his heart knew what she had concluded. Before he could open his mouth in denial, she pressed on. "A prize for your heroic deed last evening, I'm sure?"

"Marisa!"

"Or are they sending you away because it's dangerous for you to be here any longer?"

"Marisa, please try to understand me. I'm devastated."

"Are you here to wash away your guilt? This isn't a church. Nor do I listen to confessions." She made to close the door.

"Marisa," he cried, grabbing hold of the door.

"Chee! Remove your hand, you beast. The day I saw you step on the back of my people and climb down, I understood you. Get out."

"Stop. Please, stop!" Growling through clenched teeth, Aiden pitched forward and seized her hand. He pushed her back and forced the door open. "I'm not here to leave. I'm here to—"

"Oh," she said. The word crystallised on her copper lips, the shade of tender mango leaves. "If that's what you came for, be done with it. When you're done, don't forget to leave me my pay. I'll take that sinful money and pledge it to the church's famine relief."

Deflated, he let go of her hand. "Marisa," he said soundlessly.

"I'll scrub myself thoroughly with soap afterwards. That's it. A good bath is all it will take to end our relationship."

Aiden withdrew.

In a flash, Marisa moved back and flung the door shut with a bang. Startled by the sound, Aiden's horse retreated a couple of paces. Aiden stood rooted to the spot—in a realm devoid of time, in a realm devoid of thought.

After a time, he staggered down the stairs with limp, flaccid legs, trudged up to his horse, and held on to it. Like a solider who'd bled from a battle wound, he wrapped his arms around the animal, tried to clamber on, and, after slipping twice, eventually mounted it. He took the reins in his hand and sat hunched over in the manner of a corpse installed on a saddle with its legs secured on either side, swaying incongruously with every movement of the horse. The horse turned around even though he issued no command. Treading with great care, it crossed the stream.

He travelled endlessly through one dark street after another. It felt as though he had stumbled headlong into a giant anthill. Avenues that branched interminably. Crossroads. Alleyways. Side streets. He tugged hard at the horse's reins to redirect it. With ferocious kicks, he forced it into a run. The horse neighed loudly, whirled its tail, and, with hooves thudding, streaked through the darksome lanes. I am a sorceress on a broomstick soaring through hell. Through the black roads of hell. No. Through the gut of a mire-dwelling, malodorous beast. Gutways. Gutspirals. Gutwaste.

Gasping for air, he brought the horse to a stop. The equine's breath and his own resounded in unison. Impassioned by the flight, the horse strained, itching to take off again. Why are my ears clogged so? Indeed, his ears were clogged. As in the deepest depths of the ocean, an intense pressure pushed down on his eardrums. The wind blew noiselessly. No, not the wind. Rain. Not the rain, but some unknown liquid. A warm, slimy liquid, like horse spittle. It was falling from the sky. Am I standing under a labouring cow whose water has broken? No, it is indeed rain. The liquid smells familiar. Very familiar. Yes. But—

Without warning, a huge mob filtered onto the road from a dark avenue opposite him. It drifted towards him, like dirty bundles of cloth floating in a current of water. Soundlessly. A great mob. Humans kept streaming out of a hollow that resembled the mouth of an anthill. The mob crossed him unhurriedly. Not one of them was afoot. They were floating and gliding through the air, though the dark, through the cold. Every one of them was three-quarters naked. Not a scrap of cloth covered their bodies save the tattered rags concealing their waist. Skeleton-like bodies. Yes, they were long dead. Half-decayed, all-but-decayed corpses. It was a sacred procession of some sort. Shaking and swinging their hands identically, in some inexplicable way, they all marched in step. No one noticed him. But he saw the whiteness of their teeth. He saw their eyes which sparkled like beads of moisture. He saw the pale soles of big-eyed infants who stared from their perches on the hips of mothers and shoulders of fathers.

Yes, he knew many of them. From where? That old man over there had spoken to him before. Just one word. What had he said? Had he spoken in his language? Or in English? No. How could he have spoken? I had seen him at the foot of a banyan tree. His gut had wandered from his stomach, gotten tangled in the bushes and trailed a long way off. An already blackened, decayed gut. When a dog sank its teeth into it and jerked it, the man had stirred slowly as though he had just then felt the discomfort of lying down. Long teeth in a lipless mouth. A ripped-off nose. But his eyes were wide open. That was when he had said something. "Dorai!" No.

Not that. "Pasi!" No. Not that, either. Something else. This man here, I know him. And this one, too. How many people! How many thousands! How many millions! Do these many roam the darkness of this city every night? They must be sleeping inside these houses with their children huddled close. Sleeping with their blankets drawn over their bodies to keep out the cold. Here they are, lying down in the verandas, blanketed by hemp sacks. Unbeknownst to the world, a parade of epic proportions has taken shape here, right this moment. A parade bigger than that of Queen Victoria's coronation. A parade more imposing than that of any papal event. How long it's been! Have I been standing here for days on end? People flooded the streets and, with bodies packed together tightly, kept moving. Like a monstrous black river of sludge coursing through the darkness. They kept moving calmly and quietly, like a clutch of dark clouds. Where were they headed? To another corner of the city? For what? Does this parade take place all night long, all over the city? A meaningless ritual. Then again, what ritual has meaning?

Ah, I know this man, too. I know his face very well. The man turned and looked at Aiden. His big eyes lit up instantly. His bright white teeth flashed in a smile. Terrified by his gaze, Aiden sought to move back. But his horse, as though made of stone, stood frozen and motionless. He kicked it hard. Brought his whip down on its back. But the stone horse felt nothing. No, it was his own body that was frozen in inaction. His consciousness was all that remained. Bodiless and formless, it floated in the dark as pure being. Like a blob of oil on water. Having attained being solely on account of its capacity to distinguish itself from the other. The man drew close. Very close. So close, the spirals of his curly hair and the soft fuzz on his upper lip were visible to the eye. My Lord, my Saviour.

"It is me," said Karuppan. In a deeply resonant Oxonian

English, such as his teacher John Stuart Cooper would've spoken. Yes, it's the same voice. It's indeed him. But how can he be here? "Look, it is me!" Karuppan repeated.

"You? How're you . . . ?" Aiden began. With a smile that widened every second, Karuppan spoke, nay, recited a verse, in the manner of a patently Oxonian drama.

"Last came Anarchy: he rode
On a white horse, splashed with blood;
He was pale even to the lips,
Like Death in the Apocalypse."

"Shelley! Shelley! I'll blow your brains out!" Aiden screamed as he sprang up. Sitting up in his bed, he stared at the curtains flapping in the sea breeze. His body was trembling in the cold as though he had just risen out of water. He was still in his uniform. His belt alone was unfastened and rested on a tripod next to him. A terrible thirst. As though he had wandered hundreds of miles across desert sands. Where was the water? It sat on a stool, far away from him, in an earthen pitcher capped by an upturned glass. Why was it so far? Sam! David! But no sound emerged from his throat. Such was his thirst. An excess of liquor expresses every drop of water from the body.

He tried to get up. "Who's there? Hey, what're you doing? Who are you? Bring that jug. Fool, I told you to fetch that jug. What're you doing there?" As his hands instinctively groped the darkness searching for support, they stumbled on his belt. The revolver lay bulging in its thin leather pouch, like a bull's scrotum. The jug's all the way there. Beside the window through which the moonlight falls. Aaaah!

Aiden seized the revolver and, placing its muzzle on his forehead, pulled the trigger.

13

Aiden opened his eyes to the white walls of the hospital. It was his fourth awakening. The same room he'd seen three times already. Above him sloped a tile roof panelled with whitewashed palm-mat screens. From it hung a small punkah made of palm fronds. The room had two windows covered in rippling white drapes. A doorway whose curtain—stained at the height of a raised arm—had frayed a little, exposing a light-drenched courtyard beyond. On the wall hung a picture of Jesus. "My blood will cleanse you of all sin." In the corner of the room, over a ring fixed on a tripod, rested a big wooden sink.

Aiden was lying in a bed in the middle of the room. The numbness and nausea that had made his mouth seem like a strip of dried leather before were no longer present. Neither was the sensation of a free fall every time he closed his eyes. Instead, behind the thick bandage on his forehead, a severe pain was palpable. When he raised his brows, his head throbbed as if slit by a knife.

He moved his head a little to find that his neck, too, hurt. Perhaps the muscles had stiffened on account of holding his head still. He checked to see if he could get up. He was able to budge. Planting his hands on the mattress, he raised his head carefully. The pain extracted a soft groan from him.

Hearing the sound, a nurse hurried through the door. A slender-armed Indian girl. Small, puckered lips and big, bead-like eyes stared out of a round, wheat-toned face. The expression of a child whose toy had been snatched away was etched on it. She said something to him as she grabbed hold of his shoulder. Only when she repeated herself did he comprehend that she was speaking in English.

"No, you shouldn't move. Please, do not move."

"I have lain still for a very long time," he demurred. He had seen that girl once before, when he had opened his eyes earlier. In her white uniform, she resembled an oriental sparrow.

"Let me turn you over," she said, tightening her grip on him.

"No, it's all right," said Aiden, closing his eyes.

"Do you want something?"

"My head's swimming."

"We have given you opium."

"Oh . . . What's your name?"

"Elisa."

"Anglo-Indian?"

Her eyes lowered instinctively. "Hmm," she acceded with the aspect of a child on the verge of tears.

"Elisa. How many days have I been here?"

"Four days. Your condition was critical when you got here. You had lost a lot of blood. Dr. Fletcher said there wasn't much hope."

"Was there a bullet in my body?"

"No. The bullet skimmed your brow, shaving a patch of hair off your head. I saw it. It was scary, even for me. I could see the white of the skull. But Dr. Fletcher told us that the bullet had made no impact on it. Apparently, the skull is tougher than a bullet." She spoke one word at a time accompanied by myriad hand gestures.

Aiden smiled. "Not bad. You've witnessed a grand medical event. Hereafter, if someone turns up with their skull shaved off in a drunken fit, you can treat them yourself."

Her face crumpled. "I'm sorry," she said.

"Hey, what's this? I was joking. Elisa, you're a sweet girl."

"Thank you, sir," she said, and, blushing, lowered her face.

"How much longer do I need to be here?"

"Two more days, and you'll be discharged. The wound will heal in a couple of weeks. The injury is not deep; the doctors are only concerned about the possibility of infection. That's why I've been checking your temperature every two hours. Thankfully, you have no fever."

"How many months has it been since you started as a nurse?"

"Eight," she replied.

"Thought as much," he said. He smiled as he closed his eyes.

"Shall I bring you some tea? You're allowed to have a lot of fluids. Tea will give you energy."

"Yes, thank you."

The beverage did lift his spirits.

"Marisa," he called out.

"Sir?"

"Pardon me. Elisa. Elisa, can you place that pillow behind me?" As he sat up, she fixed the pillow behind his back.

"How's the pain?"

"Painful. Can I get up and walk around?"

"Yes, though, you may feel a bit dizzy since you're on opium."

"Right," he said, closing his eyes again.

"Would you like a Bible to read?"

"What?"

"The Bible."

"No."

"It's a small book, sir."

"I said no," he said, raising his voice.

"I'm sorry, sir."

"It's all right," he said, with a smile. Would this child have any inkling that humans do read more than the Bible, he wondered.

"If you'll excuse me now," said Elisa. "Please do call me if you need something. I'll be right outside." So saying, she left the room.

Outside, the cawing of the crows filled the air. From the sound of the sea he worked out that it had to be the barracks' hospital near the fort. When he closed his eyes, he saw waves of blood radiating under his lids.

He must have fallen asleep. Waking to the sound of Elisa stepping away from him, "What is it?" he asked.

"No . . . I didn't realise you were sleeping . . ."

"I'm awake now. Tell me, what is it?"

"There's someone who's been coming to see you the past two days. He's here, right now. He asked me to check if you were awake."

"Who is it? Father Brennen?"

"Father called on you yesterday. This man . . ." After a moment's doubt, "This man's name is Kathavarayan," she finished.

"Oh."

When Aiden screwed his eyes shut, the pain clutched his head in a pincer. Allowing himself to feel the throbbing of the pain in every passing second, he opened his eyes slowly. "Send him in," he said.

"Yes," said Elisa, and left the room. Aiden's heart raced as he waited with his eyes fixed on the curtains over the doorway. No, I refuse to explain or justify anything to anyone anymore. I am out of words now. In trying to take my own life, I've defined myself beyond doubt. *That* is me. So be it. There's really no room for me to explain myself any longer.

Moving the curtain aside, Kathavarayan walked in. The usual white waistcloth, khaki jacket, and a turban. Small eyes glistened in a clean-shaven face. "Good morning, sir." Despite the sameness of it all, his face had changed completely. Was his jaw somewhat askew? Or his turban a tad off-kilter?

"Good morning. Come in," Aiden greeted him. Why am I so nervous? Am I scared of him? Whatever it was, he could not meet Kathavarayan's eyes. He averted his gaze towards the wall with the fluttering white curtains.

Kathavarayan sat down on a stool next to Aiden and placed a small paper bundle near him. "Sweet narthangai, a variety of citron. I was not sure if you will like it, but to bring it for the sick is our custom."

Aiden's heart gladdened at that very instant. "Thank you," he said with a smile. "The lemon is considered a health-giving fruit in Ireland. Citrus flowers, citrus fragrances, all of them . . . Thank you very much."

"Sir, I will say it straight out. What you did to yourself was utterly foolish. Had you died, you would have forced me to contend with unbearable guilt for the rest of my life. Now, too, we harbour that guilt."

Aiden gazed at his clear eyes. "I . . . that day—" he began.

"You did not issue the order that day, sir. I know that for certain. You are not capable of it. You were rattled. Not knowing how to respond to the situation, you seethed with anger. I am able to understand it. For I was as livid as you were." Kathavarayan looked keenly into his eyes. "They had it all planned. There is no doubt about it. The havildar in question took advantage of your condition. So did each and every cavalryman stationed there that day."

"No. We mustn't jump to such a conclusion. It could've been a misunderstanding. That . . ."

"Sir, I know them better than you do. Even before he arrived on the scene, Murahari Iyengar had ordered for the necessary boats to be on standby so they could get away. Havildar Narayanan knew of his coming long before he arrived. The whole cavalry was waiting for it. Every one of them had the very same thought in their heads. There was a perfect meeting of minds. A glance of the eye was all it took for thoughts to be exchanged. You and Mr. Parmer were the only strangers to that setting."

"You're letting your imagination run wild. It might've been nothing more than a coincidence."

"Sir. It was no coincidence. It was the perfect opportunity. The fact that all of them recognised it instantly and acted in unison can mean only one thing—they had been biding their time. They had been waiting for it on a needle's point, their senses alert. When the attack broke out, I happened to catch a glimpse of Murahari Iyengar's face. You did not see him. Had you laid eyes on it, that face would haunt your every nightmare."

Aiden looked on with bewildered eyes.

"Sir, all the faces that carried out the attack that day looked exactly the same. Faces rippling with gruesome ferocity. Expressions frozen in the middle of a deafening scream. But his face, it was different, sir. It was suspended in a mad ecstasy. As if it were lapping up every sight in front of it with its eyes and ears, and sating its frenzy. It occurred to me later that a face that beholds an orgy of lust with hundreds of twining bodies would look just like that."

Leavened by that metaphor, Kathavarayan's lips slowly curled into a smile. An embittered smile. "I recall such a face now. Some tribes in the jungles of the Nilgiris where I spent my youth engage in communal mating after drinking heavily at their annual festival. When we heard about it, my friend and I made a secret trip and watched from amid the bushes. Having shed all sense of self under the influence of wild liquor, a man and a woman were coiling by the red glow of the fire struck up in the festive clearing. But what jolted me was the face of this old relic of a man sitting by the fire, gazing at them with a staff in hand. Something more intense than fire was blazing in his face. I have thought about it a great deal ever since. The old man's lust was greater than that of all human life that had weltered in the dirt that day. For it was the lust of the impotent."

"You never fail to scare me," said Aiden. He closed his eyes for a few seconds. His forehead throbbed. "I hope no one died," he said, breaking his silence.

"Why speak of that now?" said Kathavarayan.

"What do you mean? How many died?"

"Sir, what difference does it make? It has been discussed in the British Parliament that in the Deccan alone fifteen million people have died so far. Do you know what the government said when labour representatives raised a furor in the House of Commons?" Kathavarayan smiled. The same embittered smile. "'Indians are like rabbits. They breed and multiply effortlessly. One fifth of their population was wiped out in the great famine of the 1770s. Where did so many people come from now?' The man who said that was Paul Anderson, chancellor of the Exchequer. The chancellor went a step further and argued that famines are a necessity. In populous countries like India, nature itself employs such a method, he said, invoking Malthus and Darwin. It is only those who are infirm or incapable of labour or from the lowest strata of society who die. The food spared by their dying serves to prevent bigger famines than this. The able-bodied and the useful remain alive. Whatever else one might say, Britain's parliamentary debates are fascinating. They are able to present everything logically. Perhaps, in the future, these debates will serve as precedents for the new democratic world in the making."

"White morality," Aiden remarked, mockingly.

"Indeed, sir. At least there exists an institution like the House of Commons back there. For the sake of a few blacks who died somewhere far away, they stand up misty-eyed and raise their voices. Noblemen who have never known hunger. Some of them hold up the Bible in the House of Lords and make disconsolate pleas on our behalf. It is only there that we find at least a few tongues that can speak for us. In the days to come, it is only there that we will find hearts to repose faith in, too. Hearts sheathed in white skin."

"I see the faith that guides you. But I don't share that faith. I no longer have faith in mankind itself," said Aiden. "What happened to Karuppan? Is he alive?"

"Sir, there are millions of whom it is not known if they are dead or alive."

"You haven't answered my question."

"That is the answer to all your questions. We are in no position to count corpses. You can do that. We keep count of those who are alive. If we dwell on death, those of us who remain will perish, too. We focus only on life. Our lives, our progeny's lives. That is how we will triumph over the death that pursues us."

Aiden sighed.

"Which is why we speak only of the revolt that took place at the Ice House, not about its losses. There was no loss. Even if there was, it would be a mere fraction of the loss that is ever-happening. We have fought. We are capable of a fight. That is all that matters to us right now. We have begun. The first stirring of a great rebellion that is to unravel in this land for another hundred years has taken place. That is enough for us." His face had hardened as though disconnected from his words. "That is why I have instructed my men not to breathe a word to anyone about what happened at the Ice House yesterday morning."

"What happened?" Aiden asked, feeling short of breath.

"A completely new crew has been employed at the Ice House. The new workers have no experience. Following the strike, the bottom of the ice block had thawed, and was resting on a bed of powdery ice. One of the men began cracking open the block's wooden casing and clearing the layer of salt and sawdust in order to get to the ice. In doing so, he gave it an unthinking push, perhaps imagining it to be an incredibly heavy boulder. Instead, it skidded across in a flash as though sliding on water, and rammed into the opposite wall. It flattened four unsuspecting workers against the wall and crushed them to pulp."

Before Kathavarayan finished, Aiden had witnessed the scene in his mind's eye. A white boulder of ice slides with a deafening creak and smashes the wooden planks. Like an elephant raging in musth. The workers shriek.

Kathavarayan described the same scene. "One of the men who managed to escape told me that the block's edges had blunted, giving it the appearance of a gigantic white elephant. It advanced precisely in the manner of a trumpeting elephant that had lowered its crown on the brink of an attack. It butted the workers and squashed them against the wall. Apparently, blood splattered all over the place, and they were able to hear the crumbling of bones. The ice block stood like an elephant whose crown was drenched in gore, the workers said. It seems that they were too scared to even go near it. Shrieking in panic, they had run out leaving the bodies right where they were. It will turn around and attack the other way, they had cried. This man was trembling even as he narrated the episode to me. There is a malevolent spirit in the ice block, he insisted. They all believe so."

Aiden did not wish to hear any more of it. He closed his eyes.

"I was told that you may move to Tenkasi in a few days. It is possible that I may never see you again. That is why I came." Aiden placed a gentle hand on his. "Thank you, sir. In saying so, I speak on behalf of all my people. We will tell our children about you."

A faint shiver ran through Aiden's body. His eyes moistened. He wrapped his quavering fingers around Kathavarayan's hands.

"We move forward on the strength of the faith we place in people like you. This path stretches on like a never-ending tunnel. Only a few among you offer us the hope that there is light at the other end."

Suddenly, a realisation struck Aiden. "Kathavarayan, all this while I was puzzling over why your face looks odd. I see it now; your religious mark is missing from it."

"I have renounced it," Kathavarayan stated calmly. His eyes were unperturbed.

"Renounced what? The mark? Why?"

"The religion, the God, and all associated identities."

"Oh," said Aiden vacuously. A strange trembling had taken hold of him.

"I was a steadfast Vaishnavite. I studied Vaishnavism formally. I have not spared myself the practice of any Vaishnavite custom there is. On the other hand, the people of my caste have never been allowed entry into Vaishnavite temples. The situation will change someday—my descendants will walk into those temples bearing trayfuls of fruits and flowers, proudly wearing the mark of our religion on their brows—that is what I had hoped for. But . . ." The light in his eyes altered as if at the turn of a spear's point. "I have seen only one Vishnu temple in my life. It was when I ventured into an abandoned, dilapidated shrine in Rayalaseema. With moist eyes and folded palms, I kept circling the precincts. Stone horses towered over me, their legs reared and teeth bared. On their backs rode stone warriors with weapons raised overhead, glaring into the yonder with crazed eyes. A great assortment of glares. I touched the divine black form of Vishnu recumbent in the dark sanctum and submitted to him."

Aiden struggled to grasp the import of his words. Kathavarayan continued. "Sir, the assault that took place at the Ice House the other day conjured up a bizarre image in my head. Watching your cavalry, it seemed as if that temple had come alive and set afoot. The horses lunged at us with their heavy, stone hooves. The weapons thrashed and tore into us. In the middle of it all was that recumbent face. The tridental mark between its brows. It was watching our blood scattering all over with rabid ecstasy, its tongue pooled with saliva. I have had a glimpse of that god, sir, and know it for what it is."

Aiden was shivering like a slip of paper quavering in the sea breeze. Kathavarayan was oblivious to it. "I effaced the mark on my forehead that very moment. I hacked myself free in a mess of flesh and gore. I had no religion nor God anymore. Yes, that is indeed what I believed for three whole days. For three whole days, I lived in a godless darkness. But no manner of faith survives in a godless place. To be bereft of faith in these dark times is a dangerous thing. As dangerous as a lamplight going out in the pitch-dark of a forest that teems with poisonous serpents. Snakes began to slither all around me.

“That is when I recalled the swamp we had visited some time ago. Pudhupettai. Something unknown had dropped into the depths of my being back there. I did not know what it was then. Sensing that it was something valuable, I had stowed it away in my soul. I groped around for it and reclaimed it now. It was a word. You would remember.”

Aiden shook his head. Kathavarayan went on. “The word ‘punniyam.’ Merit is how I had explained it to you at that time. I have used it several times, but never quite grasped the whole of its meaning. I went in search of that old woman. She herself knew nothing. The soul of her centuries-old ancestor was speaking from within her, or so I imagined. I asked her, Why did you do that the other day? When you yourself were starving to death, what made you chase after a guest to offer food? She answered that with another glorious word. She told me, sir, that it was her dharma.

“Have you heard that before?” Kathavarayan asked, in a voice reduced to a whisper by his intensity of feeling.

No, Aiden mimed with a shake his head.

“It is a Buddhist word. I have read a Buddhist text that happened to be in my father’s collection. They speak of ‘compassion.’ Of ‘merit.’ They combine everything that is conveyed through hundreds of thousands of such words and call it ‘dharma.’ It is the seed of the wisdom that Tathāgata bestowed on us many thousands of years ago. Just like my people, that wisdom, too, was trounced and trampled to dust in this country. I am yet to comprehend that word. Still, I have discovered a few such words that I can hold up as lamplights at present. I see before me a path that I can tread trustingly.”

As Aiden listened to those words, his eyes remained

fixed on the window blinds. Kathavarayan sat quietly, like a man taking stock of his own emotions. The curtains alone fluttered in the wind as if a sprightly little girl was skipping and dancing through the chamber. After a time, Kathavarayan stirred. "I will take my leave, sir. We will meet again another day," he said.

Aiden watched him as he got up and left. Kathavarayan kept going for what seemed like an eternity. Aiden wanted to call out to him, to talk to him, but he held himself back every time. It was not until Kathavarayan turned around and said, "Sir," that Aiden realized that he had, in fact, called out to him.

"You called me?"

"Yes. I have to tell you something."

"Sir."

"You spoke about the loss of your faith, did you not?"

Kathavarayan looked at him without batting an eyelid.

"Do you know why I shot myself?"

An infinitesimal stir such as the distant opening of a window reflected in his dark pupils was all that appeared in Kathavarayan's eyes.

"I tried to blow open my skull and lay it at His feet."

Kathavarayan gave no sign of a response. His jaw alone clenched and relaxed. Aiden did not take his eyes off him. His jaw tightened again. A muscle in his neck tensed and slackened. Then, turning away, he lifted his hands, moved the curtain, stepped outside, and disappeared into the distance. The white drape fluttered restlessly.

14

"A white elephant?" exclaimed Mrs. Carter. "Really? There's a *white* elephant, too?"

"I've seen a white elephant in Burma," the collector piped up. Giving his portly frame a light jiggle, he belched. "At first, I assumed that a type of flour had upturned on the elephant. It struck me only later that its trunk was red."

"Oh!" Mrs. Brown cried with fake astonishment. "You can't imagine how I long to see something like that . . . Incredible!"

"You have seen a white hog, haven't you?" said the district magistrate. "Enlarge it ten-fold in your imagination." He raised a hand in the air. "No . . . twenty-fold. Maybe more."

"According to our religion," Srinivasa Iyengar began, "the white elephant is very sacred. We call it Airavatam. It is the mount of Indra, the king of the devas."

"What's the name, again?" Captain Sam interjected, opening his little leather notebook from which he whipped out a pencil. "The name?" he repeated.

"A-I-R . . . ," Iyengar spelled carefully.

"Are there white elephants here, in India?" Miss Jane posed coyly, as she brushed against the captain's shoulder and leaned on him. Her white gown had slipped elegantly down her broad shoulders. The cleavage of her breasts was visibly crimson.

"Not to my knowledge," said Srinivasa Iyengar.

"Must be there in the wild," the district magistrate argued. "The Indian forests are frightfully thick."

"I have heard from my father that the Thiruvithamkoor maharaja owned a white elephant," Theetharappa Mudali joined in. "It was my family that had acquired the contract for logging trees in the maharaja's forests. There was most definitely a white elephant. The maharaja donated it to the Anantha Padmanabhaswamy temple. Unfortunately, it did not live too long. It had some problem in the eye, too. But, so long as it was around, the maharaja worshipped it every day."

"Did they bow to its front, or to its rear?" the collector's wife wanted to know. Everyone laughed. Flashing her coffee-bean-like teeth, she added mirthfully, "They worship their cows from behind, you see."

"The elephant ought to be worshipped from behind, too. It can't grab you with its trunk then, can it," said Mrs. Carter.

Feeling suffocated, Aiden unbuttoned his coat. The punkah was moving at an agonisingly slow pace. The entire hall was thick with tobacco smoke. I should tell them to open more of the windows, Aiden thought to himself. However, he felt much too lethargic even to utter those words. His mind and every thought—wet, sodden, and heavy—lay congealed.

An old, black butler bearing a large tray of alcohol orbited around noiselessly. Aiden beckoned to him with a wave of his hand. The man came up and silently extended the tray, from which Aiden picked out a blue bottle.

"Oh," said Mrs. Carter with a chuckle. "Not once have you let the butler down, Major Byrne."

"Shouldn't he go easy on the drink until the injury to his head heals?" Miss Jane proffered.

"Not at all, it'll do no harm. Rather, it'll dull his pain and let him sleep easily," said Dr. Simpson with the long face, a shock of auburn hair swept leftward, and a left eye circumscribed by the impression of his monocle. "I've examined his wound. It's a minor injury, though it looks big in size."

"'The new major has had special training in liquoring up,' Mrs. Weikfield said to me yesterday. To say he drinks like a sailor would be a calumny, it seems. He drinks as much as a crew of seven or eight sailors," Mrs. Carter expounded.

Everybody laughed. Aiden mustered a feeble smile.

"Whatever you might say, it's been eight days since you arrived here. If you haven't been to church yet, it's plain wrong," said Mrs. Brown, her saggy chin jiggling like the sac of a green frog. "We are Christians, the lot of us. People who've tasted the flesh and blood of Jesus Christ."

"And tasted the fruit of sin before that," Dr. Simpson completed.

Mrs. Brown stared at him uncomprehendingly.

"We consume the fruits of sin. And drink the nectars of sin. Then, to even things out, we help ourselves to Christ's flesh and blood. Hallelujah."

"Hallelujah! Praise the Lord," cried Mrs. Brown.

"Ah, he's no churchgoer, either. He reads Shelley," said the district magistrate. "He paid me a visit every day in an effort to baptise me into the Shelley faith."

"And?" Miss Jane asked, unable to contain her giggles.

"I'd set a bottle of fine liquor on the table the moment he arrived. That's the holy blood that saved me! Ho ho ho . . ."

The room erupted with laughter.

"This Shelley . . ." Mrs. Brown resumed, "they say he's an Antichrist. The Antichrist is said to be a handsome man, and his words very sweet."

"Right. It is also said that he's Christ's brother," said Dr. Simpson. "And that he will look exactly like Christ, speak just like Christ, and die like Christ, too. Shelley also died at thirty, you know. When I look at his radiant, youthful face, it is Jesus I remember. Shelley's face contains that pure and infinite sorrow of the Saviour on the Cross. Should a talented artist re-create the Crucifixion imagining Shelley's face for Christ's, it is sure to be world-famous. Yes."

"Blasphemy," shrieked Mrs. Brown. "Yes. We, who are Christians . . ." A belch floated up and cut her off.

"Miss Jane, did you know that the Roman face we take to be Christ's was commissioned by the Roman emperor Constantine, more than two hundred years after Jesus's death?" Dr. Simpson continued. "Constantine assembled a panel of experts for the purpose. A council—composed of painters, theologians, and politicians. In the end, the council decided that the face of Constantine's younger self was the most suitable and expedient choice. The face we worship today is, in effect, that of a Roman emperor. A long, slender Italian face with small lips and blue eyes."

"It's our Saviour's face," Mrs. Brown squeaked, cluelessly. "He died on the Cross to save the poor. Without partaking of at least a drop of his holy blood, humankind can't hope for redemption."

"Indeed. Praise the Lord," said Captain Sam, and took a swill of his drink.

"In that case," the district magistrate chipped in, "how do you suppose Jesus would've looked?"

"Jesus was a Jew. No one can obfuscate that history. Don't look at the Jews who migrated to Europe and mixed with other ethnicities. Consider the original Jews, in Asia Minor. They're descendants of Abraham and David. A desert people who've lived under the scorching sun for generations. How do they look to this day? Curly hair, dark skin, big, black eyes, a broad, expressive mouth."

"Oh, that can't be true, oh," Mrs. Brown bleated. "Jesus, our Saviour. We see him in Michelangelo's paintings."

"Yes. The whole slew of paintings commissioned by the popes transformed Jesus into a white man. In truth, he was black." Dr. Simpson leaned forward. "You know how he must've looked? Just like the black people who drop dead like flies in this famine! Yes."

"That's ludicrous!" the district magistrate shot back. "These people are untouchables."

"Your honour, the Jews, too, were considered an untouchable race at the time of Jesus's birth. Why, it's still the case today."

"We're people who drank the blood of Christ and cleansed our souls," a white man hollered from across the room. "Praise be to Jesus."

The doctor raised his glass. "Except I was anointed with the holy blood of Shelley."

"Ho ho," the white man guffawed. Throwing him a wink, the doctor laughed along.

"Liquor makes us blaspheme," said Mrs. Brown. "Not to mention the maddening heat of this infernal country."

"Father Simon keeps a young lad by his side all through the summer. Every half hour, the boy dunks a mug in a pitcher of cool water and douses the pastor."

"So he cools his soul. Hahahaha!" Carter erupted with laughter. The others joined in, too.

"Nonetheless, Major Byrne, Father Simon's very unhappy that you don't attend church," Mrs. Brown persisted. "He complained to me about it. There's a chance the major could find a girl in these parts, I said to him, and then he'll have no choice but to seek you out."

Ed Carter raised his glass, "To the lady Major Byrne is about to find," he toasted. "Hear. Hear." "Oh." "Marvellous."

"Indeed." A chorus of exclamations broke out as they clinked their glasses, followed by drunken laughter and slurred speech.

"There's no such thing as a white elephant, really," Dr. Simpson resumed. "It's a skin disorder. A white elephant is an albino. There're albinos among peacocks, too."

"To hell with white elephants," said Ed Carter, chortling with laughter. "To the elephants that have gone to hell." He refilled his glass and raised it in the air. The crowd tittered. Dr. Simpson lit his pipe. Immediately, the collector's wife retrieved her gold cigarette case, flipped it open, and took out a cigarette rolled with golden paper. The captain set a light to it devotedly.

The night had grown long. Many of the guests were scattered in small groups all over the hall, nursing their drinks. Some were playing cards. Some chatting and laughing between puffs of smoke. The majority of the white guests were planters who had established their own estates in the hills. One of them was a missionary from Tirunelveli. The Indians in the gathering were either contractors or lawyers. The white men who had removed their coats and draped them over the arms of their chairs lounged in their sleeveless vests. The Indians, on the other hand, sat stiffly, without unbuttoning even the sleeves of their long coats. Crinkling their eyes, they paid keen attention to the words uttered by the white guests. Evidently, that was how they followed the conversation. When the others laughed, they joined a fraction of a second later. Though they smiled with their lips, their eyes darted about uneasily.

Aiden downed his drink and got to his feet. He straightened his shirt and walked cautiously. A mild stagger was apparent in his gait. "Good evening, Major Byrne," said an old white gentleman who was seated in his path. "Come, join me for a glass of champagne."

"Sure," said Aiden, as he went past him.

Outside the big, barless windows, the mountains loomed beneath a pitch-black sky, as if forged from darkness, as if a line had been scribbled across the sky and the lower half smeared with black. He noticed something white on the mountains. A giant tree? Or was it smoke? Yes, it was a cascade. A cascade of white was coursing down, falling from perch to perch. A solitary star was all that occupied the sky.

Aiden lit a cheroot. He inhaled its sharp smoke, filled his lungs, and slowly blew the smoke out. Mrs. Carter came up to him with a glass in hand. "Some people always smoke alone, don't they?" she said.

"Yes," Aiden replied, with a smile.

"I like the smell of cheroots. The ones the Portuguese merchants bring possess a distinctive smell, the smell of their earth. Have you been to South America?"

"No," said Aiden.

"It's hot there, too. But, when the sun beats down on the earth back there, you get a whiff of tobacco. All you smell here is cow dung," she said.

Aiden smiled. Is she trying to provoke me? he wondered.

"I was thinking about what you said," Mrs. Carter carried on. "What did you mean by it?"

"By what?"

"I asked you why you hadn't come to church."

"Yes."

"You replied that a white elephant had trampled your Christ to death."

"Did I?"

"Yes. I assumed it was a line from Shelley. You did say something poetic, did you not?"

"I suppose so," said Aiden. "Liquor bestows high poetry."

"Decidedly!" said Mrs. Carter, with a laugh. Two of her teeth were misaligned. "Are you fond of Shelley's poesy?" she asked.

"No," said Aiden.

"Why not? He seems to be all the rage with the youngsters these days."

"I'm not a youngster."

"Oh, you can't say that," she said, gaily. "You are youthful, I assure you. You must meet Emily, my little sister. She works at a missionary school in the area. A sweet-tempered girl."

"I'm sure."

"Why don't you join us for a meal at our place on Sunday? The piglets from the hills in this region are truly delicious."

"We'll see."

Aiden dropped the cigar stub into the ashtray and began to walk. "Emily's a Shelley devotee," Mrs. Carter persisted, staying in step with him. "Shelley was my favourite poet, too, back in the day. I despised Wordsworth. Still, after landing in this god-forsaken tropical country, his descriptions seem to me as if they are speaking of God. I choked up when I read 'The Solitary Reaper' the other day."

Aiden returned to his seat.

"It is no doubt a grand scheme," Theertharappa Mudali was saying. "Profitable for everyone involved. More so, at the present hour when plenty of human labour is available for cheap, there cannot be a more profitable venture."

"Than what?" asked Aiden.

"The governor issued an important notification the day before yesterday," said Carter. "They're going to build a massive canal in Madraspatnam. It will link the whole of the Adyar River with the Cooum. A total distance of eight kilometres, which will in turn be linked to Pulicat Lake."

"No, the lake in question is known by some other name," said Dr. Simpson.

"That lake has already been connected to other lakes farther upstream. So a waterway will be established all the way up to Vizagapatnam. It will measure nearly five hundred miles, they say."

"Five hundred miles? That sounds a bit much to me," said the doctor.

"What's to be gained from this canal?" the captain interjected. "The sea is right next to it and far wider, too. Big steamers themselves take the sea, don't they?"

"Gain? Gain, you ask?" said the district magistrate, leaning in. "The Duke of Buckingham is who will gain from it. The enormous debts his father accumulated will be squared off. He can return home with an embarrassment of riches and find himself a berth in the House of Lords. Why, he can splurge on an election campaign and make minister, too. Do you know what the outlay for the canal project is? Three million. That's right."

"Three million? You could sell all of Chennapatnam for that sum of money," Carter exclaimed.

"And so Russell will, if only there were a buyer," said the district magistrate. "The duke will be left with no less than five hundred thousand at the end of the project. That's right, five hundred thousand!"

"I'd make off to America with all that money if I were him," said the captain.

"Nonsense," the district magistrate retorted. "It is politics he will turn to. He'll make minister. No question."

"It'll take at least a hundred lavish banquets to become a minister. For the cost of hosting one banquet, we could acquire an entire province here," said Carter.

"Chisholm is to develop twenty buildings in Madraspatnam. They will cost two million rupees any which way, I hear."

"Madras Central, the train station, was also constructed only after this famine set in. A long, stable-like building. The very sight of it nauseates me," said Mrs. Carter.

With a smouldering cigar in hand, Mr. Brown peeked over the row of heads, and smiled. "The canal is nothing, my friends. They're planning to expand the Chennapatnam port. And they expect it to cost eight hundred thousand."

Silence ensued around the table for a few minutes.

"My Saviour!" Mrs. Carter said eventually, placing a hand on her bosom.

"They bestowed the duke with the governorship of Madras Presidency as a reward for his loyalty and service. The general of Burma and governor of Madras are the two most lucrative positions in the whole of the empire today. The duke was given a three-year term, right in time," said the district magistrate.

"He's always in luck," the collector's wife remarked.

"My lady, under the rule of Her Majesty the Queen, nobility is always in luck," said Brown.

"Russell! What's Russell's share in this?" Carter agitated.

"He's the man who'll feast on the heart and liver," the district magistrate scoffed. "He was the one who arranged everything. The duke was hesitant to defray such a heavy expenditure. He thought the House of Commons would put him through the wringer. Apparently, Russell dispatched some captain to prepare a poignant account of the famine. I believe he showed that to the duke and prevailed upon him. Do you know what reason they've ascribed to these grand schemes, now? That they will serve to feed the black people who are dying in the famine. Famine relief work, indeed! Russell, the man who's made famine relief so lucrative, ought to be in London—that's the talk about town now."

Aiden poured himself another glass and downed it. It felt as if the alcohol had gone all the way up his nose. A mild hiccup and a sharp bite of liquor dribbled into his nasal cavity. He wrung his nose hard with his handkerchief. The insides of his nose burned.

Wishing to refill her glass, Mrs. Carter reached for the bottle. There was nothing left in it. "Butler," she called out.

A young, black butler came in and bowed respectfully. She lifted her glass in his direction; he filled it with care. Then he opened a wool-covered ice box made of soft wood. It contained only water from the melted ice.

"Forgive me, my lady, I'll bring it at once," the butler said, and excused himself.

"They'll name the canal after the duke. 'Buckingham Canal.' Doesn't it sound imposing? The duke will scarcely be able to wipe that gleeful smile off his face when he hears it. They'll throw him the skin and bones, while they dig into the heart and liver."

Mrs. Carter turned to Aiden. "I was told that this ice comes from New England, in America. Boston, to be precise," she said.

"Yes," said Aiden. A violent belch took hold of him. Liquor drained from his nose again. His handkerchief was wet and sodden already.

"Didn't they say that Tudor and Co. is shutting down?" said Dr. Simpson.

"It has to," Srinivasa Iyengar spoke up. "Murahari Iyengar has cast his evil eye on it. He'll run it into the ground, acquire the building in the auction, and put his name on it. Slowly but surely. He is like a python. He swallows only a little at a time. Have you seen a python ingest its prey?" he asked.

"No," said Miss Jane.

"The Sokkampatti zamindar rears a great many pythons. I'll take you there sometime," said Captain Sam.

"To watch a python swallow its prey is an astonishing

sight. It will seem as though the prey is desperately trying to force its way in with all its might, while the python's eyes are about to pop out."

"I'm told that the lakes of New England are exceptionally clean," Mrs. Carter resumed. "And that their waters have a unique taste. I, for one, can't tell the difference. Nonetheless, it thrills me when I drop that ice into my glass, or think about how it has travelled from America, eight thousand miles away. The very thought of Walden Pond cools my body."

Dr. Simpson looked at Aiden. "Does Walden ring a bell, my young friend?"

"No," said Aiden.

"Ralph Waldo Emerson. Walden is Emerson's own pond. His thoughts are like its waters—so very pure and full of dreams. His words imbue my heart with the balmy warmth of springtime. David Thoreau is his friend. You may not have heard of him. Sadly, our English papers don't mention them at all. Two thousand miles from Britain, over in America, the ice thaws, bit by bit," said Dr. Simpson.

"Yes, March is their springtime," said Mrs. Carter, obtusely.

With a slight scowl on his face, Dr. Simpson cast a glace in her direction before carrying on. "A great ice age had enveloped the whole world till now. Thoughts had frozen in time. Dreams had frozen in time. Ideals had hardened and turned to stone." With a shake of his finger, and a solemn expression on his face, he said, "Have you seen the budding sun rise through a web of frost? It'll look like a drop of blood diffusing through a glass filled with ice cubes."

Aiden's eyes were riveted on him. The doctor swayed gently under the influence of alcohol. Heavy eyelids lifted only to slump. "The splendour of imminent spring. My hometown. Where, beyond the frosted, snow-sheathed woods the sun rises, growing brighter with every minute. The ice softens, melts, drips, and trickles. The jagged points of thawed ice resemble a sword's tip. White pearls that had latched on to branchlets let go one by one and fall to the ground. Then, with the crackle of glass, layers of ice crumble and slide off. The slender branchlets breathe a sigh of relief and lift upwards. The life coursing through the frozen and blackened tree barks gathers force. A trace of green, as though touched by moss, manifests on branch tips. One or two days, at most. The trees will have broken into a profusion of green buds. Fresh grass will have sprouted all over the forest floor. Tiny streams will bounce and pirouette through the gaps between the rocks, as if molten sunlight were flowing through them. Ah, spring." He threw his hands up in the air. "Spring! Spring! Ah, spring!"

Mrs. Carter giggled as though she had been tickled. Dr. Simpson glowered at her.

"Don't titter," he admonished. "It's no laughing matter, this. Spring is coming. The warmth of the sun spreads all over the world from Boston. The ice is melting. A burgeoning warmth—the warmth of humaneness, compassion, equality, and justice. The foundation of every dark edifice erected on the blood of slaves crumbles to pieces. Another world is coming. A brand new world. The world of our children. A golden world where science and philosophy will have become one."

Mrs. Carter covered her mouth as she tittered and leaned on Aiden's shoulder. Her heavy breasts pressed against him. Dr. Simpson glared at her.

The butler returned with the ice bucket wrapped in wool. "Here, quickly," Srinivasa Iyengar called out. "How long they have been waiting."

"Forgive me," said the butler as he opened the bucket, picked chunks of broken ice with wooden tongs, and dropped them into their glasses. The ice tinkled faintly as it fell in. Aiden picked up his glass. As he reached for the bottle of liquor with his other hand, something caught his eye. His body shuddered momentarily. He blinked his eyes and looked again. There were faint traces of crimson on the ice. Like minute petals of red.

"Oh no!" he cried out loud. "No! No!" He raised his trembling hands.

Everyone turned to look. There was a glass in every hand.

"What? What is it, Major?" Carter asked. By then, Aiden, racked by nausea and shivering, had slumped over the table. He pressed his handkerchief to his mouth.

"Thank God, the liquor's finally taking effect," said the district magistrate.

Aiden looked up. "Oh!" he cried. He opened his limp eyelids, which kept sliding shut, with great effort, and peered through his mist-screened eyes. Yes, the ice cubes in every single drink bore streaks of crimson blood. He could see it clearly all the way to the very last glass. This is no dream, no hallucination.

Carter mixed soda and alcohol, and lifted his glass. Gold-hued liquor swirled inside. Blood and gold. Yes.

"To the British Empire which rules the world!" Captain Sam declared, raising his glass. The crystals clinked cheerfully. The sound of gulps filled the air.

"Aye, the budding sun," said Dr. Simpson. "The red-as-blood sun!" He pointed a solitary finger towards the ceiling.

"What a lovely night it's been for you, dear," Mrs. Carter remarked, as she lifted her own drink. Aiden stared ahead. The liquor in his glass, having thrust the ice cube up a fraction, was now softening it and absorbing the melt.

"Your drink, dear," said Mrs. Carter, reaching his glass to him.

"Yes, it is," said Aiden. He took the glass in his hand, closed his eyes, and, with one mighty draught, downed the drink.

Acknowledgements

Madras, now known as Chennai, is the city of my birth. Unlike Madurai or Thanjavur, its storied cousins from the Tamil-speaking region of India, it does not have an ancient past. It is a city with a modern history that, willy-nilly, started with the arrival of the British nearly four centuries ago on its then-lonely shores.

I grew up in a neighbourhood in the southern part of the city, very close to the sprawling, densely canopied grounds of the Theosophical Society. One of its founders, the American Henry Steel Olcott, was also the moving force behind a network of free schools established for the education of Dalits, then known as Panchamas—meaning the fifth (caste). By that time, Olcott had embraced Buddhism. However, it wasn't until I read *Vellai Yaanai*, the Tamil original of this novel, that I discovered an uncanny connection. Where faith was concerned, Olcott had held great sway over Pandit Iyothee Thass, a pioneer of Dalit politics and the figure on whom Kathavarayan, a pivotal character in this novel, is modelled. Thass had even met with Olcott before formally converting to Buddhism. So much history lay so close to home, hidden from my eyes. As Jeyamohan suggests in his preface, literature is often what counters our everyday amnesia.

Yet, while literature serves to remedy our collective memory, a novel is most powerful when it dialogues with the individual self. If I travelled externally with Kathavarayan, it was with Aiden that my journey turned inward. *White Elephant* is a rare work written from the gaze of a person ensnared in the garb of an oppressor. As such, it converses with every one of us who is complicit in the performance of an injustice, whether through impotence or sheer indifference. Unlike the many Eichmanns the world has known, Aiden does not yield to what Hannah Arendt called "the banality of evil." His conscience remains alert; and yet, or perhaps inevitably, he meets a tragic end. By contrast, Kathavarayan's renunciation of faith and Andrew's renunciation of position elevate them further, making the entire novel an argument for genuine compassion and uncompromising action. In that sense, *White Elephant* is both a profoundly spiritual and profoundly political work. I am indebted to Jeyamohan for allowing me to translate it.

There are many others who have directly or indirectly contributed to this translation, to whom I express my sincerest thanks: Frank McCourt, whose deeply moving work *Angela's Ashes* brought me closer to Aiden than any account of Irish history could have; the American Literary Translators Association (ALTA) for creating a vital platform to mentor emerging translators; Kareem James Abu-Zeid, my mentor (through ALTA) who read early drafts and offered invaluable feedback and encouragement; PEN America for supporting this work through a PEN/Heim Translation Fund Grant; Rohan Kamicheril, my editor, for always responding as a sensitive reader first and editor second; Oona Holahan and the rest of the editing and proofreading team at FSG for their careful consideration of this work; Suchitra, my friend and fellow translator, for always being a call away and for being my most engaged reader; Anil Sarvepalli of *Harshaneeyam*, who was moved enough by my manuscript to translate the novel into Telugu; Kanishka Gupta, my agent and flag-bearer, who has carried my work across continents; Vijay, my partner, for the tears he shed while reading this translation—they gave me more confidence than words ever could; and finally, Maitri, my daughter, for the quiet miracle of her presence.

Priyamvada
Chennai
January 2026